~ SOLARIS CLASSICS ~

ROWENA CORY DANIELLS
THE UNCROWNED KING

THE CHRONICLES OF KING ROLEN'S KIN
BOOK TWO

D1366436

SOLARIS

This edition published 2016

First published 2010 by Solaris
an imprint of Rebellion Publishing Ltd,
Riverside House, Osney Mead,
Oxford, OX2 0ES, UK

www.solarisbooks.com

ISBN: 978 1 78108 533 2

10 9 8 7 6 5 4 3 2 1

A CIP catalogue record for this book is available from the British Library.

Designed & typeset by Rebellion Publishing
Printed in Denmark by Nørhaven

THE UNCROWNED KING

WORLD MAP

OSTRON ISLE

UTLAND ISLES

SKIRLING STONES

UTLAND ISLES

MEROFYNIA

SNOW BRIDGE

ROTHENIA

UTLAND ISLES

EQUATOR

ROLENCIA

NEARLY THREE HUNDRED YEARS AGO, WARLORD RO-
LENCE MARCHED OVER FOENIX PASS AND CONQUERED
THE RICH VALLEY, DEFEATING THE BICKERING CHIEFTAINS.
HE NAMED HIS NEW KINGDOM ROLENCIA AND DECLARED
HIMSELF KING ROLENCE THE FIRST, CLAIMING THE VALLEY
FOR HIS CHILDREN AND HIS CHILDREN'S CHILDREN.

BUT HOLDING A KINGDOM IS HARDER THAN CONQUER-
ING IT. NO SOONER HAD KING ROLENCE MADE HIS CLAIM,
THAN KING SEFON THE SECOND OF MEROFYN SET SAIL TO
PUT DOWN THIS UPSTART WARLORD, BEFORE THE WAR-
LORDS OF HIS OWN SPARS COULD GET IDEAS ABOVE THEIR
STATION.

MEANWHILE THE MERCHANTS OF OSTRON ISLE TRADED
WITH BOTH KINGDOMS, GROWING RICHER, WHILE THE
UTLAND RAIDERS PREYED ON EVERYONE, INCLUDING EACH
OTHER.

☐ SEA/LAKES

▨ ARABLE LAND

▨ FOOT HILLS

☐ MOUNTAINS

DETAIL OF ROLENCIA

DISTANCE FROM ROLENHOLD TO DOVECOTE APPROX 50 MILES AS THE CROW FLIES

CHAPTER ONE

BYREN'S EYES BURNED from the piercing cold wind, and he could no longer feel his legs. He'd been skating since late last night, since Dovecote's great hall was set alight, since Elina died in his arms. Since his twin thrust him out of the hall, barred the doors and turned to hold off the enemy, trapping himself inside the burning building.

Grief, fuelled by fury, gripped him, driving him on. Byren had no tears, only a terrible determination. But he clung to one hard kernel of satisfaction.

The old seer's prophecy had been proved wrong. He had *not* murdered his twin to gain the throne. Despite their misunderstandings, despite Lence's pig-headed conviction that Byren meant to usurp him, Byren had remained loyal to his older brother. And, in the end, Lence had chosen an honourable death. Somehow, it made his loss easier to bear.

But it also made Byren the kingsheir against his wishes. After the lies his cousin Cobalt had told, his father would never believe this.

No, the only way for him to prove his loyalty was to take word of the Merofynian invasion to the abbot. Convince the old man to give him leadership of the abbey's standing army of warrior monks and march against Rolencia's ancestral enemy, Merofynia. He had to save Rolencia, save his family.

Byren had skated through the long winter's night and the short day without rest, and now it was dusk. But the time had not been wasted, for he'd planned his battle tactics.

Having met his enemy, Byren knew that Overlord Palatyne was a ruthless man, possibly even more cunning than the Merofynian king he served.

Palatyne was sure to have escaped the burning of Dovecote's great hall. Even now the overlord would be regrouping his forces, calling for reinforcements and making plans to spear-head through Rolencia's rich, unprepared valley to take King Rolen's castle before Byren's father had time to gather his warriors.

His skates scissored over the ice, each stroke precise and powerful. His body ran on, thigh muscles propelling him over the ice, while his mind ran on how to beat the Merofynians.

The problem was timing... it was late winter. His father's lords and their men were at home on their estates, and the warlords had returned to their princedoms. Everyone was preparing for the spring planting, not war. His father would be lucky if he had two hundred experienced warriors in the castle. He might gather another five hundred eager, untrained men from the town, but even with them King Rolen wasn't ready to face Palatyne.

There was but a glimmer of hope. The Merofynian overlord's supply chain was dangerously overstretched. If Byren could retake Cockatrice Pass, then Palatyne and his warriors would be cut off from reinforcements and supplies.

It all rested on Byren reaching the abbot in time, and convincing him to place the monks under his command. The traitorous warlord who ruled Cockatrice Spar was dead and his men scattered, so Palatyne could expect no help from that quarter.

Once Cockatrice Pass was secure, all Byren had to do was lead the warrior monks down into the valley, force-march them to catch up with Palatyne's men and provoke a battle on his terms. He knew the lay of the land, the overlord didn't. He'd make sure his warriors had the high ground.

Byren believed he could defeat Palatyne. At twenty, he'd been leading warriors against upstart warlords for five years, and his father had saved Rolencia from a Merofynian invasion at eighteen. As Captain Temor, his father's friend and advisor always said, the worth of a warrior was in his head and heart, not in the years he'd lived or the strength of his arms.

Besides, he owed it to Lence. And he owed it to Elina. Her last words had not been words of love for him, but of revenge. *Burn them all, promise!*

Tears stung his eyes, blurring his vision.

As he rounded a bend, Byren hit a slippery patch and his skates slid out from under him. His body slammed down on the ice. He found himself skidding on his pack like an overturned turtle. The frozen lake had opened in front of him, but he was not headed towards it. He was headed for the bank, a solid wall of snow that hid rocks for all he knew. He had time to protect his face and curse his luck before he ploughed into it. The impact knocked the air from his chest and sent his wits spiralling away.

BYREN WOKE WITH a shiver. The brilliance of the frothing stars told him it was full dark. Shudders wracked his body, sending powdery snow slipping off his chest and face. With caution, he tested his limbs... amazingly no bones were broken.

An odd bird call sounded, soft yet imperious. It was this which had woken him. Turning his head, he saw he'd ploughed through a drift into an inlet formed by an eddy on the side of the lake. This was Viridian Lake, which meant he had another good day's skating before he reached the abbey on the side of Mount Halcyon. He would need his wits to meet the abbot, so he decided to make camp and start out fresh at sunrise.

As soon as he got to the abbey he'd ask to see Fyn. He'd have to tell his youngest brother how Lence had died. Fyn would believe Byren had not betrayed his own twin. Byren had always got on well with his younger brother, even though Fyn had been gifted to the abbey as a lad of six.

The odd bird call came again. This time it was more imperious, followed by a harsh cry that finished on a furious, rising note.

Byren rolled into a crouch to listen. A glow formed in the hollow beyond the slope at the far end of the inlet. There had to be a camp fire. Unless it was the Merofynians, and he didn't think a scouting party would be this far from the main camp, he could claim traveller's ease and share some of his provisions in exchange for a place by the fire.

As the harsh cry returned, the glow heightened.

Had the travellers captured a bird, which was objecting while they prepared to slaughter it for dinner? Even though he'd hunted the valley since he was old enough to ride a pony at his father's side, Byren did not recognise the cry.

Something wasn't right. The more he studied the glow coming from the hollow, the more it unnerved him. He went very still, his breath held. The glow did not flicker like the leaping flames of an open fire. It was too steady, like concentrated starlight.

Untying his skates, he slung them over his shoulder and crept along the bank of the inlet. After working his way up the far slope, he stretched full length in the snow to peer down into the hollow.

For a heartbeat he simply stared. Nothing could have prepared him for this. Two Affinity beasts faced each other, both were as big as dogs and both were displaying. What was that bird called, the one with the glowing crest and tail?

The name came to him... hercinia. And his bestiary studies produced the text he'd memorised with the encouragement of his tutor's switch. Hercinias were rare, only found in deep forests and greatly prized for their glowing feathers, which were worth a small fortune. This one must be a female getting ready to mate because only the females glowed like this and only when they were fertile.

Even as he watched, the hercinia opened its tail feathers in a wide arc like a fan. In the centre of each feather's tip was a glowing 'eye', an iridescent patch that pulsed bright enough to confuse and scare off a predator. Even if the bird's feathers hadn't been in their glowing state it would have been magnificent. A fine, diamond-tipped tiara of lacy feathers grew from the crown of the hercinia's head. The brilliant feather tips danced like agitated fire flies as it confronted the other bird.

For a moment Byren wondered if this was the hercinia's mate and he was witnessing a rare, exquisite dance of love. Then the other bird leapt into the air, wings flapping, long tail trailing behind it and he recognised it as a calandrius. A ripple of shimmering colour raced up its long neck collecting around its eye sockets and beak, heightening its already brilliant colouring. To call those feathers red was an insult. They were vermilion... a living, pulsing vermilion.

Calandrius were prized by healers for their ability to tell if a sick person was on the verge of death. The calandrius could inhale the breath of the diseased person, absorbing the poisonous vapours that made them ill. But the birds were used sparingly for, to overcome the disease, they had to fly towards the sun until the illness was burnt out of them. Often they did not survive. And, if they did, they would not return to the healer once set free.

Awe stole Byren's breath. He wished Orrade was with him to see this, but they'd separated after they escaped from the burning hall. With his father's murder, his best friend was now Lord Dovecote and he'd led the estate's surviving servants and villagers into the mountains. Byren hoped they had escaped Palatyne, whose cruelty had been illustrated only too graphically when he killed all the old lord's prized doves. Those beautiful birds had done nothing but bring pleasure to those who looked on them.

Unlike these birds. Oh, they were beautiful certainly, any farmer or trader who came across them would try to capture them to make their fortune, but Affinity beasts were not defenceless. The two birds were of a similar size and each probably weighed as much as a wolf hound. Sporting razor-sharp beaks and talons, they circled each other warily. Thanks to their Affinity, they were highly intelligent and attuned to threats.

Byren watched, all else forgotten as he tried to make sense of the confrontation. What were two such rare god-touched beasts doing here in Rolencia's settled farmlands?

Then the hercinia refurled its tail like closing a fan and let the display drop, so that its iridescent tail stretched behind it, twice as long as it was tall. How did it manage to fly with that weight?

At this signal, the calandrius folded its wings by its side and a ripple of shimmering colour flowed down its long neck away from its eye sockets and beak, so that the intensity of the colour eased to a deep, softly glowing magenta.

The calandrius backed up a step. The hercinia also backed up and the two birds seemed to reach an unspoken agreement. As one they fluffed their feathers and sank onto the snow to writhe about, looking for all the world like chickens giving themselves a dust bath.

The absurdity of it made Byren smile, but then his skin went cold as understanding hit him.

Only an Affinity seep would elicit this behaviour from god-touched beasts. He had no Affinity, which was why he could not sense it, but he knew the signs and he'd heard marvellous stories of this phenomena. Affinity seeps were dangerous because they attracted all god-touched beasts. The last time he'd discovered one, it had attracted a lincis. Half great cat, half wolf, the lincis were highly territorial, and Orrade had nearly died.

Cautiously, Byren checked his surroundings for signs of any further Affinity beasts. As far as he knew the ulfr pack were still on the loose. Adult ulfrs were large as a pony and more intelligent. This pack was led by a remarkable male which had shown its followers how to avoid every trap set for them.

Byren listened for their distinctive howls, but there was no sign of the ulfr pack, or other beasts. He relaxed slightly.

The discovery of another seep, the fourth since last spring, was deeply worrying. As well as attracting god-touched beasts, the untamed Affinity that seeped up from the earth goddess's heart was a source of power which could trigger latent Affinity in people. And this would mean the person had only two choices, leave Rolencia forever or serve one of the abbeys. King Rolen would not countenance renegade Power-workers in his kingdom, not after standing helplessly by while they killed his father and older brother during the last Merofynian invasion.

Byren had to report the seep to the abbot, who would send out one of his Affinity warders to contain it. They kept a store of sorbt stones for just such an event. Once the seep's power had been absorbed into the stones, the abbey became their custodian, protecting Rolencia and its people from untamed Affinity.

He should leave and make camp elsewhere.

Byren was about to go when a boy of no more than eleven broached the far rise of the hollow. He was skinny and poorly dressed for the cold, and there was something odd about his face. Having grown up with his father's generation, all of whom carried injuries from the last invasion, he recognised the injury. The child had been beaten cruelly, breaking his cheek bone. This made one eye sit slightly lower than the other.

Catching sight of the birds, a delighted smile broke across the child's strained face. He went to approach, then hesitated, his hand going to a metal collar around his neck. It was connected by a chain to the man who followed. And, as this man broached the rise, Byren recognised him for a renegade Power-worker. An Utlander, judging by the filthy symbols of power tattooed onto his forehead, and the fetishes woven into his matted hair.

'I was right, it's –' The Utland Power-worker broke off, seeing the Affinity beasts. He'd been speaking Merofynian but Byren had no trouble understanding him, thanks to his mother's patient tutoring.

With a happy, inarticulate cry the boy ran down into the hollow, only to have the keeper jerk so hard on the chain that his legs went out from under him and he sprawled in the snow, gasping, hands going to the metal collar.

Byren winced in sympathy.

Both birds gave cry and leapt into the air, just as half a dozen Merofynian warriors came over the far lip of the rise. The men stood stunned. The boy scrambled to his feet, panting.

Due to their size the birds had to work their broad wings furiously to gain height, creating great downdraughts of air, which stirred up the fine, powdery snow.

'Stop them!' the Utland Power-worker screamed. He swore, beside himself with frustration as the men fumbled to remove their gloves and string their bows. 'No. Not like that, you fools. The calandrius is worth a fortune alive –'

Thud, thud.

Two arrows struck home.

Both labouring birds cried out in distress and dropped into the seep. The boy fell to his knees in the snow with a wail of distress. The Utlander ignored the child's weeping and, after thrusting the boy's chain into the hands of the nearest man, he ploughed down the slope.

Several of the warriors made the Merofynian sign to ward off evil, though whether they were afraid of the seep or their own Power-worker's anger, Byren could not tell.

The Utlander tore off his cloak and threw it over the calandrius, which had come to its feet and was trying to creep away with a broken wing. It gave a mournful cry of protest when he swept it up in his arms.

Staggering a little with the weight, he turned to face his escort. 'You're lucky it's still alive. Come here and take it. Bring my pack, I need my sorbt stones.'

Byren tensed. He did not want to see the power of the seep fall into enemy hands.

There was some confusion as three men slithered down into the hollow, reluctantly joining the Utlander in the centre of the seep. One took the calandrius, and another went to remove the other wounded bird. The third held the boy's chain and the Power-worker's pack. The boy edged nearer the birds, eyes fixed on them. Illuminated by the bright starlight, Byren could see tear tracks glistening on the lad's grimy cheeks.

'Wait. Is the hercinia dead?' The Power-worker checked.

He must have found signs of life for he wrung the bird's neck with callous efficiency, eliciting a whimper of protest from the boy.

'Stop your moaning, brat.' He nodded to one of the warriors. 'Pluck its feathers. That's all it's good for. And don't pinch a single one. I'll know.'

'What about the body?' the man who held the hercinia asked. 'Seems a waste not to eat such a plump –'

'You're right.' The Power-worker made several signs over the bird, muttering under his breath. Byren guessed he was settling the bird's Affinity, which had been released on its death. But the signs were nothing like the ones the castle's Affinity warders used. 'There, it's safe to eat. Make camp over the rise.'

'So near the seep?' the one with the calandrius whined.

'Yes, so near. I still have to drain the seep's power. Now get going.'

The two carrying the birds retreated up the slope, while the third unslung a pack from his shoulder and opened the buckle so the Power-worker could rummage through.

'What of the brat?' he asked.

'Give her a bit of the bird's white meat as a reward. But keep an eye on her, she's just as likely to try to sneak back to roll in the seep. Little savage,' the Power-worker muttered. Byren thought this was a bit rich, coming from a renegade from the uncivilised Utland isles, and he felt sorry for the girl, who he'd taken for a boy. 'Keep an eye on her. Once I set up the active sorbt stone it will drain power from anything, including her.'

'How long will this take?'

'As long as it has to. I'm not leaving a seep for Rolencia's sanctimonious

14

monks to hoard.' He untied some cloth to reveal two stones, carved so that they slotted together like lovers. 'This isn't a large seep. Should be done by morning.' He noticed the man's expression. 'Don't worry, we'll catch up with the others tomorrow.'

The man retrieved the pack and turned to leave, but the girl was staring at the sorbt stones with a mixture of fear and fascination. The warrior casually cuffed her over the ear and walked off. She wiped her face on her sleeve and hurried after him, before the chain could jerk painfully on her collar. Her slave collar... for that's what it was.

He'd heard of such things in the tales his mother told. Parents too poor to educate a child born with Affinity might consider themselves lucky to sell the child to a Power-worker.

Merofynia was a strange place. They considered themselves more civilised than Rolencia, but the gap between the very poorest and the rich was much greater.

Byren watched as the Utland Power-worker separated the two stones. He wore gloves but, even so, he moved swiftly, touching the smaller stone that fitted into the larger very gingerly. He tucked the larger stone under his arm and placed the other in the centre of the seep. Its surface began to pulsate like the calandrius. Soon it was pulsing regularly as if it contained a beating heart, growing brighter with each throb.

'Well done, my pretty. And now for some roast bird,' the Utlander muttered, sounding like a baker who'd put his loaves in the oven and was due for a well-deserved break.

As soon as the Power-worker went over the far rise, Byren slid down the dark side of his rise and rolled to his knees. There were six warriors escorting the Utlander, too many for him to tackle, and that was without even considering the danger of confronting a Power-worker. He lacked warding talismans to protect him. Besides, the best wards the monks could build had failed to protect his grandfather and uncle all those years ago.

No, he could not release the calandrius, save that girl and take the sorbt stones for the abbot. He had a duty to Rolencia and he must not endanger himself. He should turn his back on them, bed down for the night then leave early tomorrow to see the abbot and Fyn.

Feeling sick at heart, Byren came to his feet.

But instead of heading away from their camp, he crept towards it. At least he could take a look in the dip beyond the hollow.

They were fast workers, these Merofynians. Already they had constructed three low snow-caves, just big enough for the travellers to crawl inside with their packs and a brazier. The calandrius remained rolled in the cloak but was cradled in the girl's arms. She crooned to it, feeding it slivers of something from a pack. The Power-worker ignored her.

The other bird had been plucked and now was being dismembered so that pieces would cook quickly over the braziers in the snow-caves. The men worked efficiently, retiring eagerly to the warmth of their shelters. Only one was left on sentry duty – they thought themselves safe. Few people travelled this late in the winter, when the creatures began to stir from their long slumber and those that had stayed awake were desperate for food.

The Utlander kicked the girl as he passed. 'Give me the bird and get inside.'

Without a word, she handed over the injured Affinity beast and crawled into the Power-worker's snow-cave, but not before Byren saw her cast her master a look of pure hatred.

'Is there anything I should look out for?' the sentry called as the Utlander went to follow the girl, with the bird in his arms.

'No more than usual. The seep is no longer radiating Affinity and won't attract beasts, and the Rolencians don't know we're here.'

Then he crawled into his shelter while the sentry selected a spot on the rise, where he had a good view of the undulating snow-shrouded banks of the lake, and prepared to wait out his watch, unaware of Byren.

One man was a different proposition from six, but there was still the Power-worker and Byren had no weapon that would work against him. Shuffling down the slope, he found a niche behind a rock and pulled his cloak around his body.

He would sleep and wake early, the better to get away before the Merofynians stirred. He was not worried about waking in time. Ever since he could remember, he'd had an internal sense of time.

But the moment he closed his eyes he saw Elina leap in front of him, trying to turn Lence's blade with her own. She must have known her wrists weren't strong enough. He felt her wound like it was his own, searing through his gut. With a groan he doubled up.

Elina...

Death was too good for Illien of Cobalt!

Elina would still be alive, if Lence hadn't believed Cobalt's lies, if Byren hadn't written that love poem... It had been so easy for Cobalt to twist the words to prove that Byren was Orrade's lover instead of Elina's. If Orrade hadn't confessed that he was a lover of men like Palos of legend, then Cobalt couldn't have convinced Lence and the king that the Servants of Palos had reformed to put Byren on the throne.

Frustration raged through him, for there was no secret society calling itself the Servants of Palos. Thirty years ago there had been. His father had eradicated the traitors, executing lord and commoner alike. But how could Byren prove that a secret society no longer existed, when suspicion and innuendo were enough to undermine his reputation?

Cobalt was so good at playing on people's fears. Byren cursed the day his cousin had come back to Rolencia.

Shaking with anger and exhaustion, he vowed to kill Cobalt. Elina would approve, for she was a true warrior's daughter. But first he had to expose Cobalt for the traitor he was.

Decision made, Byren welcomed sleep, letting the exhaustion that had been circling like a predator consume him. The great muscles of his weary thighs twitched from over-work and, as he welcomed the oblivion of exhaustion, in his mind's eye he saw the Affinity-slave girl cradling the wounded calandrius. Both trapped, both innocent.

How could he defeat Cobalt when he could not save them?

CHAPTER TWO·

FYN WOKE WITH the feeling that something was wrong. Then it came back to him... Rolencia was at war with Merofynia.

He rolled over, his hand going to his chest to stop the royal emblem from tangling in its chain, but he'd left the foenix pendant in Halcyon's Sacred Heart. That was when he'd planned to leave the abbey to protect his sister's secret, and needed to hide his identity.

He hadn't wanted to leave but he couldn't stay, not after Piro had revealed her Affinity to him. The mystics master would have uncovered Fyn's guilty knowledge as soon as he began training. But now that the mystics master had gone off to ambush the Merofynians, the unexpected dawning of Piro's Affinity was the least of his troubles.

He told himself his sister would be safe as long as she stayed in Rolenhold, for the castle's defences had never been breached. It did no good. Fear for his mother and Piro gnawed at his belly. Before this, he had never understood how his brothers could cheerfully lead war parties against upstart warlords, but the thought of thirteen-year-old Piro in the hands of Merofynian warriors ignited his blood.

He suspected the same feelings had kept the other acolytes awake, talking long into the night boasting how they would prove their bravery, if only they had the chance. But Halcyon's warrior monks did not send children to war, even if those acolytes were due to become monks this spring cusp with the responsibilities of men.

War with Merofynia...

Fyn didn't understand how it had come to this. His father's betrothal to

King Merofyn's daughter had heralded thirty years of peace. When Myrella's younger brother had died in suspicious circumstances, her cousin had seized the Merofynian throne. This meant Fyn's eldest brother could become betrothed to the new king's daughter, and it should have ensured another thirty years of peace. But, early yesterday, a message had arrived from King Rolen asking the abbot to send the warrior monks. So the weapons master had marched out with every able-bodied monk, leaving only the frail and the lads in Halcyon Abbey.

At nearly seventeen, Fyn and his fellow acolytes thought themselves men and had railed against being left behind.

Unable to lie still Fyn rolled over again and, once again, his hand went to settle on the absent foenix symbol. He felt its phantom presence, its shape, its weight... and the niggling sense of wrongness solidified with an uncomfortable jolt of fear. The seal on the king's message had been a fake. The foenix symbol was too small to belong to his father.

Fyn sat up in bed, nauseous with the realisation that the weapons master and nearly six hundred of Halcyon's finest warriors were skating into a trap.

He sprang out of the bunk, heart racing.

'Bad dream?' Feldspar whispered. 'Don't worry, your sister will be –'

'I'm not worried about Piro.' Fyn crouched between their bunks. For a heartbeat he considered telling Feldspar his fears, but decided against it. He'd creep upstairs to the abbot's chamber, light a candle and check the seal. If he was right, they could send someone to warn the weapons master. A single skater could travel the frozen canals faster than hundreds of warriors. If he was wrong, he'd come back to bed and put it down to a vivid imagination and no one would be any the wiser.

'Go back to sleep, Feldspar. It's probably nothing.' Fyn kept his voice low so as not to disturb Hawkwing on the other side.

Already dressed in his breeches, Fyn slipped on his indoor shoes, soft-soled slippers, and tugged his saffron robe over his shoulders. The abbey was built into the side of Mount Halcyon and warmed by her hot springs, but even so the night was cold.

Leaving the sleeping acolytes, Fyn entered the hall leading towards the spiral stairs. He was already beginning to doubt his memory of the seal and wondered if he should simply go back to bed, when an odd noise made him stop. It sounded like the distant pattering of rain. The abbey had been unnaturally quiet since the warriors set off, its empty halls and chambers magnifying every sound.

Fyn tilted his head, straining to hear. The sound made no sense. It was too cold to rain. Silent on his indoor slippers, he ran to the window which looked down into the courtyard.

Illuminated by brilliant starlight, the courtyard rippled with life. Hundreds of warriors hurried across the stone flags, their boots making a soft susurration. Fyn's mind refused to accept what he saw, even as the men crept across the courtyard, flowing into the abbey's formal ground-floor chambers.

How could the enemy have penetrated this far without sounding the alarm? The old monk on night duty must have been tricked into opening the gate. The abbey was defenceless!

Alarm made his heart race. Fyn's feet hardly felt the ground as he ran back to the acolytes' chamber, waking Feldspar. 'To arms! We are under attack!'

Feldspar threw back the covers.

Hawkwing rolled out of bed, reaching for his boots. 'Merofynians?'

'I didn't stop to ask,' Fyn admitted.

'Did you have another vision?' Feldspar asked. 'Is that why you woke?'

His last vision had been of his brother's betrothed, Isolt. What manner of king would promise his daughter in marriage then make war on his future son-in-law's kingdom?

An unscrupulous man, a cunning man. The kind of man who would send a fake message to lure Halcyon's monks away from the abbey, leaving only acolytes and old men to defend it.

The boys... they didn't stand a chance!

'What's going on?' an anxious voice asked.

'We're under attack,' Hawkwing answered. 'Get everyone up.'

Word spread like a forest fire.

Their surprised exclamations made Fyn impatient. They had no time for this. He grabbed Hawkwing's arm. 'Wake the abbot, tell him the abbey's been breached.' Fyn turned to Feldspar. The boys, aged six to twelve, were on the floor below, between them and the intruders. 'Feldspar, take the boys down to the inner sanctum and bolt the door. Do it quickly, before the Merofynians find the great stairs.'

'This would never have happened if the grucranes hadn't left us,' Feldspar muttered, putting on his slippers.

He was right. The god-touched beasts had lived in the abbey for generations. One of their flock always stood guard ready to call a warning, but...

'No time for ifs,' Fyn snapped, thinking of the day the grucrane leader had been injured, the day the old seer had foreseen this very attack. When she'd spoken of Halcyon Abbey in ruins, he'd laughed. The seer must not be proven right. 'Hurry, both of you!'

Hawkwing and Feldspar darted away.

Fyn turned to the others. They'd tugged on boots and robes and faced him. 'The rest of you, come with me.'

He snatched a lamp someone had lit and ran out the door and down the corridor. Behind him, he could hear the acolytes' boots slapping on the tiles, hear their hurried explanations as the younger acolytes poured out of their sleeping chambers. He couldn't possibly lead thirteen- and fourteen-year-olds against grown warriors. Fyn stopped in his headlong race for the armoury and spun to face them.

'You.' He pointed to a youth of fourteen, whose name escaped him. 'Take the younger ones down to the sanctum, the rest of you come with me. We must defend the abbey.'

There was muffled shouting as boys of thirteen insisted they should stay and take up arms. The thought made Fyn sick to his stomach. True, they'd been studying weapons since they were six, but experienced warriors would cut them down like chaff. Besides, the best weapons had gone with the warriors, which meant the abbey's defenders would have to make do with blunted practice swords.

Furious, he signalled for silence. The acolytes obeyed, watching him expectantly, hopefully. Who was he to decide who lived and died? Who had elected him their leader?

'I need the youngest acolytes to go down to the sanctum where they can protect the boys and Halcyon's Sacred Flame. Can you do that?'

Put that way, they nodded and ran off. He only hoped they reached the sanctum in time. 'The rest of you come with me.'

Down one flight of stairs and along the corridor, Fyn flung open the armoury, hung the lantern high on a hook and began handing out padded chest protectors, swords, long knives and pikes, whatever he could find.

'I don't understand,' a youth muttered, 'the abbeys have always been sanctuaries in time of war. Why would the Merofynians attack us?'

'Booty,' Fyn guessed. 'Both the abbeys contain great wealth, gold icons, jewelled chests –'

'Fyn?' The abbot hurried in, with half a dozen elderly monks. Hawkwing brushed past Fyn, intent on grabbing a weapon.

'Abbot.' Fyn gave an abbreviated bow. 'The message from Father was a fake. The foenix was too small to be the king's seal.'

The abbot winced. 'You're sure?'

Fyn nodded.

'The attack on the abbey is all the proof we need,' muttered Sunseed, the gardens master. Gnarled hands that had nurtured delicate seedlings strapped on a sword belt with equal efficiency. 'So, our warriors were lured into an ambush?'

'When the real target was the abbey,' Fyn agreed.

'Clever!' Old, half-blind Silverlode buckled a chest plate by feel.

'What of the boys?' the abbot whispered. 'We must protect the little ones.'

'Feldspar's taken them down to the mystics' inner sanctum,' Fyn said. 'It's big enough for all of them and the doors lock from the inside.'

'Well done, Fyn.'

'Abbot?' Hawkwing shuffled to the front of about forty lads of fifteen and sixteen. 'We're ready.'

'Good. Now listen. Their Power-workers must not steal our sorbt stones,' the abbot announced.

Fyn cursed under his breath. Of course. The stones held power drained from Affinity seeps. In the wrong hands...

'We should have destroyed the stones!'

'Power is like fire, it is only a tool. Evil is in the heart of the ones who wield it,' the abbot told him. 'They'll be heading for the great stairs –'

'To the stairs!' Hawkwing yelled and charged out the door and down the corridor, followed by eager shouting acolytes.

'There goes the element of surprise,' old Silverlode muttered, then ran after them.

Fyn was drawn along in the mad rush. He quickly outstripped the old monks.

Like the spine of a great animal, the abbey was united by the great spiral stairs, which connected the mystics' inner sanctum far below to the libraries and offices of the abbot far above. Between them lay seven floors containing the workshops, the kitchen, the bathing chambers and dormitories.

When Fyn reached the stairwell, the youths were milling on the large landing, whispering excitedly.

'Quiet!' Fyn warned. 'Quiet!'

At his order they fell silent. Far below, the rapid tattoo of running boots echoed in the stairwell, getting further and further away.

Fyn cursed just as the abbot and the old monks joined them. 'We're too late. They've sent scouts down to the inner sanctum.'

The abbot turned to the gardens master. 'Hold the stairs, Sunseed. Fyn, come with me.'

PIRO HAD BEEN in hiding since Illien of Cobalt had turned her father against her. As lord protector of the castle Cobalt had ordered her arrested, but she still had friends. And so she waited in the scullery for the cook to bring her food. For years she had been coming to the kitchens to collect the special meals prepared for her pet foenix. Now she was living on scraps and dressed in a maid's pinafore stolen from the laundry.

Rolenhold Castle was home to six hundred people. And Piro knew each one, from the lowliest stable lad to the lord protector. Tonight all those people had been fed and the last pots from the last meal of the day had been polished and hung on their hooks, gleaming in the light of the kitchen's remaining lamp. Like the kitchen boys and girls who slept under the tables, Piro was terribly tired. Soon she would slip into Halcyon's chantry and crawl behind the nave to snatch some rest. So far she had chosen a different sleeping place each night.

The spit-turners had crept off to their bed bundles and now only the cook remained awake, planning the menu for the next day. When the last of the whispers died away and it was clear the kitchen children were fast asleep under the long wooden tables, the cook put her notes away and rose, glancing to the scullery where Piro was hidden. Piro's stomach rumbled in anticipation. Just then two servants returned with laden trays.

'What's this?' the cook demanded. 'Didn't he touch his dinner? But it's his favourite.'

Piro went very still.

'The king suffers something awful. Won't eat. Can't sleep for the pain and there's nothing the healers can do for him,' the servant explained, sliding the tray onto the table. 'It's terrible to see.'

Piro's heart went out to her father. He was not the man he had been at midwinter. Back then King Rolen's deep voice had boomed across the great hall as he demanded a second serving. It was nothing for him to sit down to a meal that lasted for four hours, consuming great qualities of rich food and fine Rolencian red wine. She had always felt so safe with him but now... now he had been diminished by the renegade Power-worker Cobalt had placed in his service.

Under guise of treating her father's old war injuries, the man had been leaching the king's strength, making him dependent on a concoction of herbs that stole his will and left him a shell of the man who had saved Rolencia at eighteen. Piro and her mother had uncovered the trickery and removed the manservant, but the damage was done.

Despite her father's sudden frailty – no, *because* of it, Piro loved him fiercely.

She had to see him. She was certain she could do more than the healers. Back before these troubles began, one of the spit-turners had burnt his hand and she'd helped ease his pain, using her Affinity to draw it off, and no one had been any the wiser.

The cook glanced once in Piro's direction and dismissed the servants. Piro waited until they had gone and hurried out on soft slippers.

'I must go to Father,' she whispered, no longer hungry.

'Cobalt's sure to have told the guard to be on the look out for you,' the cook warned, plump jowls wobbling with worry.

'I know. But I must go.'

'Cobalt's offered a bag of gold for your recapture,' the cook revealed.

Piro frowned. 'Only one?'

The cook smiled briefly. 'Take care, kingsdaughter. Cobalt cannot be charmed.'

'I know,' Piro whispered. 'For he has no heart.' When she'd learnt how his bride had been murdered by Utland raiders, she had tried to ease his sorrow, and found only emptiness behind his tears.

The cook shook her head as Piro slipped away.

BYREN WOKE WITH a smile on his lips. He'd come up with a simple, elegant way to save the child and the Affinity beast. True, he could not defeat a Power-worker, but the Utlander had revealed the very tool that could kill him. Byren should have seen it right away. His only excuse was that he had no Affinity, so he wasn't used to thinking in those terms.

He mustn't fall into that trap again.

Rubbing sleep from his eyes, Byren checked the position of the wanderers against the backdrop of stars. Good, it was nearly midnight. Rising carefully, he went to find the sentry. Another man had taken the same place as the other and was dozing at his post, shrouded in a thick fur cloak. From this angle he would not see Byren enter the seep.

The hollow glowed softly, lit by the accumulated power in the sorbt stone. Byren's skin crawled as he approached the stone. It was the knowledge that this thing pulsed with untamed Affinity that made him wary, not an innate ability to sense Affinity. He'd been tested as a child and found to be blind to it, unlike his brother. Poor little Fyn.

His mother had put on a brave face when the six-year-old had to go to the abbey, but she had wept when she thought no one was looking. As a lad of barely ten summers Byren hadn't known how to console her. All he could do was hug her and bring her pretty things he'd collected especially for her.

Now Byren picked up the sorbt stone, grateful for his gloves and his lack of Affinity, and tucked it inside his vest. He needed his hands free for the sentry.

Byren did not enjoy killing a man while he slept, but it was necessary. The sentry didn't know what happened. With luck, the others would not discover his death until dawn.

Body thrumming with the heightened state of awareness that came during battle, Byren glided down into the dip and approached the Utlander's snow-cave. It had been built on a slight slope. A man does not like to sleep with his head lower than his feet, so Byren guessed that the Power-worker would be sleeping with his head at the highest point.

Feeling at his waist for the hunting knife, Byren began to cut a window in the snow-cave. This was the most dangerous part, for if the snow had not been packed tightly enough, fine powder would fall on the sleeping Power-worker and wake him. Or, when Byren tried to ease his knife under the circular window, he could lose control and it might drop into the shelter.

He was lucky. The circle of packed snow lifted out without breaking. Byren turned back to the shelter to find the girl peering out at him, head through the gap. Silently, he cursed the luck that had led him to choose the side she slept on.

Byren lifted his finger to his lips and gestured the girl aside. Her head sank back into the snow-cave and he peered inside. By the glow of the brazier, he made out the sleeping Utlander. Such was his awe of renegade Power-workers that for a heartbeat Byren doubted his plan.

The calandrius stirred, uttering a soft interrogative sound. The girl hushed it.

Too late for doubts. Byren cut away at the snow-cave, widening the window with great care. Too much and the roof would collapse. Then he pulled the sorbt stone out of his jerkin and showed the girl. Her eyes widened. Byren pointed to the Power-worker and mimed placing the sorbt stone in the Utlander's arms.

The Affinity-slave nodded.

Licking dry lips, Byren watched as she wrapped a blanket around her hands and accepted the stone. With great care, she knelt next to her sleeping master and slid the stone under the Utlander's bare hands. He slept on his side, so that he was now curled around it.

Byren knew the sorbt stone would absorb the Power-worker's latent Affinity while he slept. At best it might kill, at worst it would weaken him severely.

The girl looked to Byren, who nodded and smiled to show that she had done well, then held out his arms. He was a head taller than most men and easily big enough to lift her out of the shelter.

Without a word, the girl crawled back to the calandrius and gathered it in her arms. She passed the bird to Byren, who sat it on the snow. It seemed very docile, fed, warm and weak from injury. Even so, Byren suspected the girl had been using her Affinity to soothe it.

Then he turned back to lift the girl out. But she held up the chain and glanced resentfully at the Power-worker. Byren realised the end was fixed to the man in some way while he slept.

'I can prise open the links,' he whispered in Merofynian, drawing his knife.

The girl looked doubtful but crept over, offering her thin neck with the collar and attached chain.

Byren studied the chain. It was well made and so was the metal collar. The weakest point was where the chain had been soldered to the back of the collar. Slipping a finger inside it, he put the tip of his knife in the solder and exerted pressure at an angle. Careful not to slip and cut the girl or push too hard and cut his own finger, he increased the pressure until the solder gave way. The chain fell away but he caught it before it could make any noise. The girl placed it carefully on the blanket, so as not to wake the Utlander. Though she hated him fiercely, she obviously had a great deal of respect for his power.

Byren could do nothing about the metal collar. If he had time he could work on the joint, but, for now, he slipped his hands under the girl's arms and hoisted her out. She weighed less than he'd expected.

He set her on her feet and, with a signal for silence, led her away from the camp and the seep, towards the lake. He only had one set of skates and he was carrying out his father the king's orders. The best he could do was give her some food and send her on her way. The calandrius was almost too large for her to carry so she wouldn't be able to travel fast. But the Power-worker's escort would not be concerned with her. They'd return to report to their overlord. If the Utlander died, Byren would have dealt Palatyne a serious, though not devastating, blow. He knew the overlord was accompanied by at least two more Power-workers, rivals for their leader's trust.

'Here.' Byren paused at the lake's edge to strap on his skates, then stood up and dug into his pack, pulling out the last of his food, cold meat and two-day-old bread. The girl put the food away for later. He checked the wandering stars... midnight. He still had a long way to go.

Pointing across the lake to the mountain, which was a dark triangle against the foaming stars, he spoke in Merofynian.

'That's Mount Halcyon. Aim for it. Go around the base. On the far side is a fishing village. Tell them Byren Kingson said that they're to take you across to Sylion Abbey. The nuns will look after you, protect you.'

A shiver ran through the girl's thin frame.

Byren undid the clasp of his cloak and swung the heavy fur over her shoulders. She raised wondering eyes to him.

'We do things differently here in Rolencia,' he told her. 'For one thing we don't chain up children.'

'You're a kingson and yet you speak Merofynian?'

'My mother taught me.'

'Queen Myrella? They say her father was a good king. No one likes the new King Merofyn,' she confided, then cast a quick look at Byren to gauge his reaction. 'They also say the nuns of Sylion steal children who have Affinity and turn them into slaves.'

'It's not true. My brother has Affinity and he's been with the monks in Halcyon Abbey for ten years now. He comes to visit us every feast day. They feed him and teach him a trade. And his Affinity will be used to make Rolencia a better place for everyone.'

The girl blinked. The bird stirred.

Byren glanced at it. 'They'll care for the bird, too. I must leave. Remember, go that way.'

'Can't I stay with you?'

'I'm off to war.'

'I've been to war.'

Byren didn't doubt it. 'In Rolencia we don't send children to war. You'll be safe at the abbey.'

'I –'

'You'd slow me up. I'm on the king's business.'

The girl clutched his arm but said nothing. A light snow began to fall.

He squeezed her hand. 'The snow will cover your tracks. I've got to go now.'

She nodded, but her eyes never left his face.

There was no more he could do for her. 'What's your name?'

'Dinni.'

He realised she would be very pretty once she was fed and cleaned up, even with the lopsided eye.

'Halcyon's luck be with you, Dinni.'

'And with you, kingson.' She let him go at last.

He was wide awake now, so he set off at a good pace. If he skated all night, he should reach the abbey by mid-morning.

CHAPTER THREE

PIRO LIFTED THE key ring at her waist and unlocked the back stair to the royal wing. Before the troubles, she had done nothing but fight with her mother, but now she was grateful for Queen Myrella's quick thinking. With the queen's keys of office, Piro had access to every door. Every door, but the one that was kept locked in the top of the mourning tower, where the queen was being held prisoner.

Cobalt had convinced her once-proud father that his beloved Myrella was a spy under the influence of a Merofynian Power-worker.

Well, that was partly Piro's fault.

In front of everyone her mother had been about to slip into a seer's trance and reveal her hidden Affinity. If she had, her marriage to King Rolen would have been annulled and their four children declared illegitimate. This would have left the way open to Lord Cobalt. As the legitimate son of King Rolen's illegitimate older brother, Illien of Cobalt's claim to the throne would have been as strong as Lence's. Again Piro was grateful to her mother, this time for insisting she study Rolencian law. At best the ambiguity would have been enough for Cobalt to claim the succession and force a civil war.

To hide her mother's Affinity, Piro had darted forwards and disrupted the trance, claiming Queen Myrella had been taken over by a Merofynian Power-worker.

Everyone believed her, everyone but Cobalt. He'd seen through her because he was a master of the art of deception. He'd caught Piro on the back stairs and asked his servant to see if she had Affinity. Only an abbey warder could discern Affinity, a warder or a renegade Power-worker.

Piro had remembered Fyn's self-defence tricks and escaped. She'd run straight to her father to warn him about Cobalt, only to discover he believed his nephew over her. That was a bitter blow.

Now she crept down the hall, one hand over the keys so they would not clink. Hopefully the healers would both be asleep, but there was still one of the king's honour guard at the door to her father's chamber.

A soft snore greeted her and she bit back a relieved giggle.

It was old Sawtree, asleep on duty. She didn't know how he managed. The seats were built at an angle sloping down so that a man might rest his weight a little, but if he relied on the seat to take all his weight, he'd slide off. This wing of the castle had been built by her namesake, Queen Pirola the Fierce, in the last years of her reign and the seat's wooden surface had been polished by a hundred and thirty years of guards' bottoms to a glossy, slippery finish. Yet somehow this man, one of her father's original honour guard – which made him at least fifty – had wedged his sturdy legs at just the right angle so that his shoulders took enough of his weight against the wall for the seat to support him.

Piro smiled to herself. She was fond of old Sawtree. Like Temor, the captain of the king's honour guard, he had always been part of her life. As a small child, she used to tease him mercilessly.

Tonight, she was glad he had been chosen to guard her father. She watched and waited for his doze to deepen, trying to judge the moment before his legs relaxed and the sliding action of the seat woke him.

She didn't think any the less of old Sawtree for dozing at his post. There were rumours of a Merofynian invasion, but there'd been no confirmation. Last night they'd seen a glow to the south, possibly from the Dovecote estate. The next beacon hadn't been lit, so it was probably just a house fire. House fires were common in winter, in a land where almost every home was made of wood.

Besides, they were safe in Rolenhold. The castle had never been taken, not since King Rolence built the first tower three hundred years ago, so old Sawtree was welcome to doze at his post.

But how long before he was woken by the seat's design? Piro decided she could wait no longer.

She sidled past him. Eyes on the sleeping man, her fingers found the door latch. Silently, she slipped into the chamber. The smell of powerful herbal remedies hung on the still, hot air. Someone had built up the fire and left it to burn down, so the room was stifling.

There was no sign of the castle's two healers, though the door to the connecting chamber was a hand's breadth ajar. No doubt they were sleeping lightly, ready to spring to the king's aid. Rivalry between the nuns of Sylion and the monks of Halcyon ran too deep for one healer to let the other gain an advantage.

By the glow of the banked hearth, Piro studied her father. King Rolen was still a big man, a head taller than average. But, since they had exposed the manservant for the manipulative Power-worker he was, the king's flesh had shrunk to reveal his bones.

Now that she saw him for herself, tears stung her eyes. Even in his sleep her father looked troubled. A frown gathered between his heavy brows. He shifted, rolled over and moaned with the pain this caused him, but did not wake. The servant had said the king couldn't sleep so they must have given him something, probably dreamless-sleep, to ease his pain.

He looked so deeply under that Piro doubted if she would be able to wake him. It didn't matter. She could still ease his discomfort. In a way it was lucky he was unaware, for he would have hated her to use Affinity on him. Ever since he'd watched helplessly, while his father and older brother were murdered by renegade Merofynian Power-workers, he had hated all Affinity and only suffered those with it to remain in Rolencia if they served the abbeys.

The irony of this struck Piro as she lifted one hand, reaching for her father's forehead.

A hand closed over her mouth and an arm swung around her waist, lifting her off her feet. In desperate silence, she writhed with all her strength but she was small for thirteen summers and her captor was a full-grown man.

Remembering Fyn's lessons, she threw her head back, connecting with his chin. Her captor gave a grunt of pain but did not release her.

'For Halcyon's sake stop struggling, Piro. I'm trying to help you!'

Recognising the castle warder's voice, she stopped resisting and he set her feet back on the ground.

'Monk Autumnwind?' Turning in the circle of his wary arms she met his eyes. The Halcyon monk had served her family since the previous warders died trying to protect her grandfather and uncle thirty years ago. Piro had never been close to Autumnwind, but she believed he was an honourable man. 'Can –'

He signalled for silence and led her to the far side of the room, away from the connecting door. They stepped behind a sandalwood screen into an alcove where the healers had set up their herbals. A mortar and pestle made of white stone gleamed in the dimness.

'What are you doing here, Piro?'

'I came to see Father.'

'He's suffering.'

'I know, that's why I came.' That, and because she had hoped he would see reason and reconcile with her mother. 'When will he be better?'

Autumnwind hesitated then gave her a pitying look that made her stomach curdle with fear. She didn't want to hear what he was about to tell her.

'The healers are doing all they can, but King Rolen may not get better.' He lifted his hands, turning them palm up. 'You must realise, Piro, a man's life force is held in his body by more than health alone. The heart's gone out of the king. His queen betrayed him...' He silenced her with a gesture before she could object. 'Whether she meant to or not, the effect is the same. Lence Kingsheir refused to heed his advice and called him a coward, said he was too old to rule. And Byren is a Servant of Palos, a lover of men –'

'Lies! Byren's loyal,' Piro whispered, fiercely. 'Just as I am.'

'I believe that you believe this. But it is what the king believes that's important. And he believes his wife and children have betrayed him. I was sent to serve him after the great battle. I've seen how he strove to rebuild Rolencia these last thirty years. Now it is all falling apart around him.'

'Only Cobalt has betrayed him. Don't you see –'

'I see a frail king who trusts no one but his nephew, who he named lord protector of the castle before his health began to fail.'

'So you serve Cobalt now?' Piro eyed him narrowly.

'I serve Halcyon.'

Piro understood only too well. Kings came and went, but the abbey had survived three hundred years. She swallowed. 'Are you going to turn me over to Cobalt, Autumnwind?'

He gave her a look of exasperation. 'I should.'

'But?'

He was silent for a moment. Then he fixed on her. 'I am going to check on the king. If you are still here when I turn around I will call the guard.'

He left her behind the screen. Through the gaps in the vine-leaf carving she caught glimpses of him moving about the chamber and checking the fire.

Piro slipped out from behind the screen, heading for the door.

'What's this?' Cobalt demanded from the hall outside, his voice muffled by the thick door but easily recognisable by its distinctive Ostronite accent.

There was an uncomfortable silence as Piro imagined old Sawtree straightening up and saluting, fist to chest.

'I should have you publicly whipped for sleeping on duty!' Cobalt snarled.

'Please, Illien.' The queen's voice was barely discernible. 'This man has served my husband faithfully for over thirty years.'

There was another painful pause. Piro imagined the old warrior's proud silence. He would not plead. If it came to the worst he would take his public whipping.

'Don't let me catch you napping again,' Cobalt warned.

The door was thrust open. Piro only just had time to dart behind it as Lord Cobalt and her mother entered.

Like her brothers and father, Cobalt was tall and well made, but Piro could only see the man for the soulless manipulator he was. He nodded to Autumnwind, strode across the chamber, peered behind the screen and closed the door to the healers' chamber.

While his back was turned, Piro darted over to hide in the screened alcove. Her mother's eyes widened and she stiffened slightly but did not give Piro away.

Cobalt turned to face the queen.

Though safe behind the sandalwood screen, Piro hardly dared to breathe.

*　　*　　*

FYN RACED DOWN the spiral stairs behind the abbot with old Silverlode on his heels. Although he raced to protect the boys, it felt wrong to leave the others to face the invaders. They'd been considered either too young or too old to fight. Only the thought of Lenny and the rest of the little boys huddled defenceless in the mystics' sanctum kept him going.

Behind and above him, Fyn heard Sunseed shouting orders and Hawkwing yelling. He remembered holding Hawkwing's finger in place when it had been severed during weapons practice. Despite going white with pain, Hawkwing had joked while they waited for the healers. His friend had lost his finger and now he'd lose his life.

And Fyn was running away.

The sudden clash of steel and shouting told Fyn the main force of Merofynians had reached the central spiral stair. His heart swelled with pride because his fellow acolytes did not hesitate to defend the abbey.

Doubling over to catch his breath, the old abbot paused at the bottom of the stairs. Fyn almost collided with him, pulled up short, and peered past the two masters down a dim corridor. He could just make out the silhouettes of five lightly armed scouts, and beyond them were the double doors of the inner sanctum, securely bolted no doubt by Feldspar who was hiding inside. A pair of lamps lit the doors.

The abbot nudged Fyn, signalling for quiet, then entered the corridor. Silent in his slippers, the abbot crept up behind the last man and stabbed him under the ribs, a hand over his mouth. Shocked, Fyn froze. He could not reconcile this efficient killer with the kindly, wise old abbot.

Even as the abbot eased the body down, the man's companion turned and drew his sword. In the narrow hall, it scraped across the wall throwing an arc of sparks. This gave Silverlode time to run him through, while the abbot pulled his knife free.

Fyn hated to see an animal suffer, let alone a person. The man who'd been stabbed in the back was trying to breathe, blood bubbling on his lips. He was as good as he dead, but still he struggled.

The intruders' leader signalled the last two men to deal with the abbot and his companions, before going on.

The corridor was just wide enough for two men to stand side by side with weapons drawn. Fyn gripped his knife in his left hand, sword in the right, heart hammering.

The warriors, both seasoned veterans half the age of the masters, fell upon the old monks. Fyn knew enough swordcraft to recognise the monks' skill but their attackers were merciless. How did old Silverlode see the strokes, when he couldn't see well enough to read? Fyn felt he should help, but the pace was too furious and the space too tight to intervene. A barrage of attacks drove Silverlode back. Just a fraction too slow, the old monk failed to block. The top of his head flew off and hit the wall, followed a heartbeat later by his body.

Silverlode's attacker, a man with a scar where his right ear had been, turned to him.

Sound roared in Fyn's ears. Everything felt unreal.

He was vaguely aware of a flurry of movement behind the man as the abbot dispatched his opponent and prised his sword from the body.

The one-eared warrior's sword arced towards Fyn. Too late, his own weapon moved up to deflect it. Efficiently, the abbot caught the one-eared man from behind and cut his throat. The sword flew from the warrior's nerveless fingers.

Blood sprayed Fyn, hot and shocking.

'Are you all right?' the abbot asked.

Fyn could only nod.

The abbot stiffened and looked down as a sword point appeared from his chest.

With a savage kick, the leader of the intruders freed his sword and shouldered the abbot aside to charge Fyn.

Still reeling, Fyn side-stepped the attack, deflecting the strike with a circular motion that drove his attacker's sword hand into the wall, leaving the man's body open for a knife attack through the lacings of his chest protector. Fyn lost his grip on the knife hilt as the man slid down the wall, glaring at him even as he died.

Fyn gave him a wide berth. Stepping over the bodies, he dragged the abbot to a clear patch then knelt in the pool of blood that covered the floor. 'I'm sorry, so sorry.'

Blood covered the abbot's chin and his breath bubbled in his chest, but his eyes fluttered open and he recognised Fyn. He tried to speak. Failed. His hand felt along his waist sash for his keys. Tugging them free, he thrust the keys into Fyn's hand with painful intensity. A hiss of air left his lips. 'Take the boys and stones to Sylion Abbey.'

Fyn was so attuned, he felt it the instant the life-force left the abbot's body. Guilt lanced him. He'd frozen. That was the reason the abbot had died.

He stared at the abbot's keys. Dimly, he heard the roar of the fighting on the stairs. Why did everything sound so distant?

No time for this.

Fyn sprang to his feet. Running to the bolted doors, he thumped on the wood. 'Feldspar, it's me. Let me in.'

'Fyn?' A muffled voice came through the wood. 'Is it really you?'

'Who else?'

'A Merofynian Power-worker out to trick me.'

Fyn smiled. Trust Feldspar to be wary. But how could he convince... reveal something only he would know. 'I gave you the Fate, so you could join the mystics.'

There was the dull click of the bolt being drawn back and Feldspar flung the door open. Behind Fyn's friend huddled dozens of frightened boys.

'Are you hurt, Fyn?' Feldspar asked.

'I don't think so.'

'You're covered in blood.'

'It's not mine.' He looked down to find his saffron robe was black with blood. Disgusted, he pulled the sodden tunic over his head and let it drop. Now he wore only leggings and a knitted vest. He should be cold, but he felt nothing.

'The abbot!' Feldspar went to push past him, but Fyn stopped his friend. The sound of fighting on the stairs had suddenly ceased. Feldspar met Fyn's eyes with an unspoken question.

'The others must be dead,' Fyn said. 'We have to get the boys out of here and stop the sorbt stones from falling into Merofynian –' A shout cut him off and thundering boots echoed down the stairwell. 'They're coming.'

Fyn pushed Feldspar back into the sanctum.

A small boy tried to wriggle past them. Fyn only just managed to catch him. 'Let me go,' the boy cried. 'We'll all be killed!'

'There's no escape that way,' Fyn told him but the boy wouldn't listen. Without a word, Fyn threw the lad over his shoulder and darted through the archway. Feldspar dragged the doors shut, sliding the bolts home.

Fyn met Feldspar's eyes, and turned to find Joff surrounded by a sea of boys. Joff held a branch of candles, towering over the others. Although officially a 'boy' he was bigger at fifteen than Fyn. His Affinity had surfaced unexpectedly and he'd been faced with the choice of banishment or serving the abbey, which is what would happen to Piro if her Affinity was discovered. At least she was safe in the castle, Fyn told himself.

A stab of impatience flashed through him. He had to get the boys and the stones out of here so he could go to Rolenhold to warn his father of King Merofyn's treachery.

Did King Rolen know that Merofynians had invaded Rolencia? Had the warning beacons been lit?

The boy, who Fyn carried over his shoulder, wriggled and Fyn set him on his feet. No one spoke as Fyn surveyed the chamber. He estimated there were nearly sixty boys and young acolytes ranging in age from six to fourteen.

Booted feet pounded down the corridor and reached the sanctum's doors. Fyn heard shouting, and then the dull thump of weapon hilts striking the door, muffled by the thick wood.

'We're trapped,' a voice whispered.

'No.' Fyn rounded on the boy before the others could panic. 'Feldspar and I were chosen to serve the mystics master. We know the back way out of the inner sanctum.'

The boys' desperate eyes fixed on Fyn.

'But if they've taken the spiral stairs there is no way out of the abbey,' a skinny thirteen-year-old muttered.

Fyn held up the abbot's keys. 'Yes, there is. We're going into Halcyon's Sacred Heart.'

The boys gasped.

'It's forbidden,' the skinny one protested.

'Normally, but the abbot gave me the keys.' Fyn caught Feldspar's eye.

'He didn't want the sorbt stones falling into the hands of renegade Power-workers. Get the –'

Older boys anticipated the order, hurrying to the orderly shelves of stacked sorbt stones.

'Keep each pair together!' Feldspar shouted. 'If they're separated the active one will absorb all Affinity around it.'

The boys froze. Feldspar caught Fyn's eye. Sorbt stones were tools, but like any powerful tool they could be used to kill.

'You heard him. Take care,' Fyn prodded, then collected his thoughts. What else would they need? He didn't want to lose his way underneath the mountain. 'Bring all the candles you can find. I'll go ahead and unlock the passage.'

'What about Halcyon's Sacred Flame?' Joff asked.

Fyn glanced to the lamp which had been lit three hundred years ago when his ancestor, King Rolence the First, had gifted Mount Halcyon to the monks. It would be good to have a protected flame. 'Bring the lamp.' No one moved. 'Now!'

They scrambled, some grabbing sorbt stone pairs, some gathering candles, and others taking icons from their niches and tucking them inside their robes. Joff lifted one of the smaller boys onto his shoulders so he could unhook the lamp.

All the while, the enemy thundered on the door.

Feldspar's eyes flicked repeatedly from the busy boys to the door.

'I'll take the little ones now,' Fyn told him. 'Don't waste any time. They must have a renegade Power-worker with them. When he gets here we won't stand a chance.'

Little hands tugged on Fyn's leggings. Worried faces watched his every move. Lenny sidled up close. Like Fyn, he had been Master Wintertide's servant. Fyn had consoled Lenny as best he could when the old master died. Now he squeezed the boy's shoulder.

Feldspar glanced down to the little boys. 'Go, Fyn. We'll be right behind you.'

Fyn nodded and headed to the far side of the sanctum where a hidden passage led to a maze of private chambers known only to the mystics. Taking a lit candle from its bracket, Fyn led the way through several passages. He heard the soft shuffle of bare feet behind him and the occasional whimper of fear, followed by muttered words of assurance from the older boys.

As he recalled the route to the secret door to Halcyon's Sacred Heart, he decided it would probably be safe to use these lower passages. The abbey was huge and most of the Merofynians would be on the upper floors in the great public chambers, looting. The ones who had come down this low would be concentrating on getting into the sanctum to steal the sorbt stones.

A small hand slid into Fyn's and he looked down to see Lenny.

'I knew you'd save us,' Lenny whispered.

Fyn licked his lips. 'We're not safe yet.' He'd failed the abbot. He must not fail these boys.

CHAPTER FOUR

Fʏɴ ɢʟᴀɴᴄᴇᴅ ʙᴇʜɪɴᴅ him. All the little ones were with him and most of the bigger ones. Even as he watched, the last of the older acolytes spilled from the far door, milling in the corridor. Feldspar nodded, that was it. They were all out.

Fyn held up his candle and signalled for silence. The soft whispering stopped. In the ensuing quiet, he could just hear the deep shouts of men and the smashing of furniture and glass echoing down from far above. It sounded so wrong in a place where the clatter of busy boys and the chanting of monks were normally the predominant sounds.

'Follow me. Quickly now.' Fyn turned and hurried along the corridor, shielding the flame as he went. His slippers stirred up dust and he heard a few soft coughs behind him. Heart thudding, he led them down a flight of stairs and along another corridor. Down here the honeycomb caves had been adapted for use by the abbey. Down here it was silent, except for the rustle of their garments and the slap of their feet on the stone.

Fyn recognised the storeroom doorway where he had hidden only yesterday morning to watch as the abbot unlocked the secret entrance. It was forbidden to all but the masters. Then Fyn had been on a secret mission for the mystics master. How he wished that Master Catillum was here to advise him now. Strange, he had only come to know the youngest of the abbey's masters in the last few days but he missed him keenly. Grief tugged at him, for if he was right, and the rest of the monks had been lured into a trap, Master Catillum and the weapons master, and even Monk Galestorm who used to bully him, would all soon be dead.

'Is this it?' Feldspar asked.

Fyn realised he had come to a stop in front of the secret panel. He ran his fingers over the carvings, representations of Halcyon's bounty, the grain sheaf, the long-haired goat and more. There, that was the indentation for the key. Taller than the rest, Joff held the sacred lamp high so that Fyn could see what he was doing. The familiar scents of sandalwood and cinnamon filled the passage.

Even though the boys' frightened whispers urged him to rush, Fyn methodically tried one key after another until he heard the mechanism click and the panel slid open. A wave of relief rolled over him.

He straightened up, smiling at Feldspar and Joff, and whistled softly to get the boys' attention. 'Line up in pairs, one candle between every second pair. Remember... silence.'

They nodded, lining up as they would to march into prayer, from the youngest to the oldest.

'They're ready,' Feldspar whispered.

Fyn nodded, judging how much space the line of boys would take up. 'Lead them along the passage, turn left then left again and wait at the top of the stairs.'

Feldspar entered the passage but Lenny didn't move.

'Go on,' Fyn urged. 'I'll be right behind you.'

'Promise?'

Fyn nodded and Lenny entered the passage. The boys filed after him, jostling in their haste. Fyn glanced up and down the hall. As yet, no sign of pursuit.

When the last one had entered, Fyn checked the hall one more time and stepped inside, letting the weighted stone panel slide shut. He could hear the boys, whispering, arguing over who got to carry the lit candles.

Fyn cuffed the nearest. 'Quiet, pass it on!'

Thumps followed by silence rippled down the passage.

'You bring up the rear, Joff. I'll go ahead,' Fyn said, and pushed past the paired boys.

At the end of the passage he found Feldspar holding his candle high, peering down a flight of stairs carved from solid stone.

'I'll lead.' Fyn shielded his own candle. 'Wait here, Feldspar, and fall into line halfway along. Tell the boys to keep quiet. We're not safe yet.'

Feldspar nodded and Fyn headed down the steps, shielding the candle's flickering flame. Yesterday he had come this way in the dark, following the sounds of the masters. Now he counted and watched his step, ignoring side passages he hadn't realised were there. When the mystics master had made him memorise how to get to Halcyon's Sacred Heart, Fyn hadn't expected to be leading what was left of the abbey's boys and acolytes down here.

This second time the way felt much shorter, and it did not take long to reach Halcyon's Heart. Silent with awe, the boys fanned out as they entered the huge cavern. The boldest approached the kneeling monks, masters who had been mummified and painted with a preserving glaze, then honoured with a place in Halcyon's Heart. The mummified monks knelt on flat-topped stones, with the jars containing their organs arranged in front of them. Some had been here so long that the steady drip of Halcyon's mineral-rich water had encased them in a shimmering column of stone.

'Look,' Lenny cried in delight. 'It's Master Wintertide!'

Fyn strode over and grabbing Lenny's curious hand before he could touch the monk. 'Let him rest in peace.'

Fyn held up the candle. Several drops of the clear glaze had fallen down from the finger of stone above and trickled over Wintertide's face as if he was weeping. It would be many years before he was completely encased like the older monks. The candle, which had been left in his cupped hands, had burned down. Hidden in its wax puddle was Fyn's royal emblem. It could stay there, safe for now. It might give him away while he was trying to cross Rolencia.

'Master Wintertide looks happy. I miss him,' Lenny confided, then looked up at Fyn. 'At least we have you.'

'A poor exchange.' Fyn felt like a fraud. From across the cavern a boy spoke too loudly, his voice echoing in the vast chamber.

Feldspar joined them. He held up the Fate between them. It gleamed, an opal the size of a sparrow's egg, shaped like a spiral seashell. It hung on a silver chain. 'You might as well take this, Fyn.'

Fyn stared at the stone. During the Provings, he and Feldspar had found the Fate, ensuring their place with the mystics. Back then, he hadn't thought they would be saving it from renegade Power-workers before spring cusp.

'Halcyon's Fate?' Lenny marvelled. 'They say it can bring visions. Why didn't the mystics master take it with him?'

'Who knows?' Feldspar shrugged. 'Keep it safe, Fyn. I'm sure the mystics master would rather you had it than some Merofynian Power-worker.'

He was right but, first chance he got, Fyn intended leaving the abbey's survivors to warn his family. 'You take it, Feldspar. Your Affinity is stronger than mine.'

'But you had the vision when you found it,' Feldspar countered.

Fyn shook his head. He was going to leave them. He did not deserve the Fate. 'Keep it.'

'For now.' Feldspar slipped the chain over his neck and tucked the stone inside his robe.

'Uh, Fyn, there's only one way in and out of Halcyon's Heart,' Joff muttered. 'We're trapped down here.'

'It's worse than that,' Feldspar whispered. He glanced to the other boys and dropped his voice even further. 'There's a rich Affinity seep, here in Halcyon's Sacred Heart. It'll draw the Merofynian Power-worker. He'll find the entrance eventually. He'll force the lock.'

Lenny's fingers tightened on Fyn's hand, his fearful eyes glistening in the light of the sacred lamp.

Fyn squeezed the boy's hand. 'It's all right. There's another way out of Halcyon's Heart. Sylion's way.' Fyn prayed he was right. Yesterday, when he'd listened to the ceremony, he'd heard a woman's voice in Halcyon's Sacred Heart. Since no woman was allowed to enter the abbey and the woman had answered the abbot as his equal, he'd guessed she was the abbess of Sylion. If only the abbot had had time to tell him how to find the Sylion passage.

A boy muttered something about being trapped like rats on a sinking ship. Others took up the cry.

'Quiet!' Fyn leapt onto the back of Wintertide's dais, silently asking his old teacher's forgiveness. 'This is Halcyon's Sacred Heart. Unless we want

to remain here and end up like the monks, we must keep going. Follow me.'
He nodded to Feldspar and Joff, who herded the boys and acolytes together.

Fyn jumped down, then led them through the kneeling monks. The boys'
many candles reflected off the gleaming surfaces of the natural columns,
flickering like fiery pearls. At the far side of the chamber there was a wall
of carved stone embossed with Halcyon's symbols, the goat, the grain and
the foenix.

Fyn studied the carvings intently. The hidden entrance to Sylion's passage
had to be here. He wished the abbot had told him how to find it. He could
hear the boys whispering behind him.

'Quiet,' Feldspar ordered.

'Yeah, quiet,' Lenny ordered. 'Fyn's thinking.'

Fyn smiled grimly. Then he saw a single sylion, the embodiment of the
god. The sinuous lizard had been carved dancing on a bed of flames. The
god of winter sometimes took the form of a sylion to walk amongst them,
bringing frosts in spring and autumn, and blizzards in winter. This man-
sized lizard could quench the flames of the hottest fire with its icy breath.
Fyn stroked the carving's embossed surface, felt it give and pushed in. Lenny
gasped as a panel slid open.

Fyn hid his relief and turned to others. 'This way.'

'But I haven't got any boots and I'm tired,' the skinny boy muttered.

'We're all tired and I haven't even got a shirt,' Fyn said. 'But we have to
keep going.'

Fyn looked into the dark passage. Unlike the way down into Halcyon's
Sacred Heart, he hadn't memorised this path. Somehow, he had to lead the
boys through the mountain and out the other side. Then he had to slip past
the Merofynians to warn his father. At least Piro was safe in Rolenhold.

PIRO WENT VERY still like the trapped mouse she was.

Cobalt dismissed the warder with a wave of his hand. 'Get out and shut
the door after you. The queen needs privacy.'

Autumnwind backed out, closing the door with a final, soft click.

Cobalt gestured to the king. 'There he is, Myrella.'

She ran across the room to the bed. 'Rolen, can you hear me?'

There was no response. She lifted the king's hand and squeezed it, pressing the fingers of her other hand to his cheek. 'Rolen. I'm here.'

'He can't hear you. He's taken a double dose of dreamless-sleep.'

The queen straightened up, slowly turning to face Cobalt, her face stiff and formal. 'Then why did you tell me he wanted to see me?'

Cobalt stepped closer. Her mother was even smaller than Piro, only coming up to the middle of his chest. He lifted one hand to the queen's face, brushing away an errant curl. She did not flinch, instead she glared at him.

'So imperious, Myrella.' His voice was soft and rich with amusement and the thrill of power. 'I can remember a time when you held me in your arms.'

'As you wept over your bride's murder,' she snapped, then thrust past him, going to the fireplace, a mere body-length from where Piro hid. 'I ask again, what do you want from me?'

'Little Piro has eluded all my best efforts to catch her. Where is she?'

The queen laughed. 'What makes you think I know?'

'Because I know that you both have Affinity.'

Piro gave a little start of fear, making the keys at her waist clink ever so softly. She covered them immediately, but it was enough to make both Cobalt and her mother glance in her direction.

The queen stepped closer to Cobalt. 'Why did you come back to Rolencia, Illien? What happened to you on Ostron Isle? You are not the youth I knew and loved.'

'Better to ask me why I left. My father was born on the wrong side of the blanket. That, only that, made him unsuitable to rule. My father, the Bastard, was a man of learning and insight, a kingly man. Instead we had a buffoon for king, a brash fool who was happiest hunting and roistering. He didn't appreciate you, Myrella.'

'He's my husband.'

'And the king. I know. I grew up in this court as surety of my father's loyalty. I was fourteen when you married Rolen on your fifteenth birthday. And I watched him treat you like a convenience. It wasn't fair, not when I loved you, not when the throne should have been my father's. As the eldest son of the eldest son, I would have been betrothed to you to cement the peace. But no, my father, curse him, was loyal to the buffoon. I bore it for eight years until I could no longer stomach the way Rolen treated you. So I went to my father and demanded we make a move. He chose his half-brother over his own son, swore to reveal me as a traitor if I ever returned to Rolencia. So I spent thirteen years in exile on Ostron Isle learning the art of intrigue.

'Now I am back to take what should have been my father's, by right of birth and worth. And that is why I want Piro. She's a brat, but a pretty brat. By the time I turn back the Merofynian invasion, the people of Rolencia will only be too grateful to have the Bastard's son on the throne, especially if he's married to King Rolen's only surviving heir.'

Piro's vision faded. Were Lence, Byren and Fyn already dead, murdered by Cobalt's assassins?

'Illien, what have you done to my boys?' the queen whispered, stricken.

'Nothing.' His black eyes fixed on her face. 'Yet.'

The queen's small body grew rigid. She tried to step away from Cobalt but he caught her by the shoulders. Her slender frame made his hands look huge.

'So you see, Myrella, you must be good to me,' he said softly, as his fingers made small circles on her shoulders. 'I want you to help me find Piro. Send a message to her. Say you need to speak with her. Give me Piro. Refuse me and I will have the warder discover your Affinity. By law your marriage to Rolen will be annulled, making your children illegitimate.' He leant lower so that he could look into her eyes. 'Lure Piro out of hiding and I won't have to order your execution for hiding your Affinity.'

'I know the law, Illien,' the queen countered. 'All those who have Affinity must either serve the abbeys or leave Rolencia. The people know the law.'

'But you are their beloved queen. When it is discovered that you have been using your Affinity wiles on King Rolen all these years the people will demand your blood.' He smiled and traced the curve of her cheek. Capturing a tear on his finger tip, he lifted it to his lips to savour the taste. 'Don't weep, Myrella. Give me Piro for my wife and you can remain here, the dowager queen, loved and respected. You'll have your own wing of chambers and servants and we can be lovers at last. I've waited years for this.'

The queen drew in a shuddering breath and thrust away from him, turned and stumbled a few steps to the sandalwood screen, where she clutched the worked wood, resting her forehead on the carving.

'I will find Piro eventually, Myrella,' he warned, 'with or without your help. Be good to me and I can be very good to you.'

The queen met Piro's eyes through the screen.

Piro licked dry lips and lifted her hand to touch her mother's forehead through a gap in the screen. She felt a little surge of warmth, Affinity warmth. And for a heartbeat she did not feel so alone.

'Myrella?'

The queen fixed fierce eyes on Piro, then she shuddered and bowed her head as she turned to face her tormentor. Her whole demeanour was one of defeat. 'I would help you, Illien, but you are too late. Seela arranged for Piro to be smuggled out of the castle earlier today. She's on her way to Sylion Abbey, where the abbess will give her sanctuary. I thought it was the safest place for her.'

'Sylion Abbey?' His gaze turned inwards. 'Good. She can stay there until I am ready to fetch her.'

'Please don't expose my Affinity.'

'Expose you?' He lifted a hand, beckoning the queen.

She approached, stopping at arm's length from him.

'Why would I do that, Myrella? A sweet, compliant woman need fear nothing from me.' He closed the gap between them, lifting her hands to his lips to kiss her finger tips.

Piro saw her mother's shoulders stiffen, but Cobalt's head was bowed.

He straightened up. 'I think we understand each other at last.'

The queen nodded. 'I think we do. At last.'

The silence stretched. King Rolen moaned in his drugged sleep. Piro felt a moan of sympathy echo through her knotted stomach.

'I would like to go back to the tower now, Illien,' her mother said softly.

He slid a protective arm around her shoulders. 'Of course, my queen. Come.'

When the door closed behind them Piro sank to her knees, her legs too weak to hold her.

One thing was clear. If she remained here, someone loyal to Cobalt would recognise her despite the maidservant's smock. She must get out of the castle.

Her mother's message was clear. Sylion Abbey was a sanctuary, at least until Cobalt tried to claim her.

But it would never come to that. She refused to believe her brothers would fall victim to Cobalt's assassins. Fyn was safe in Halcyon Abbey and, like their father, Lence and Byren had always been larger than life. They would return, and when they did they would crush Cobalt.

Tomorrow she would flee the castle.

FYN KNELT ON the floor of the tunnel to study another carving.

The first time he came to a branch he had hesitated. Then he'd noticed a sylion carved into the flagstone under his feet. The head pointed the way they had come, the tail to the passage on the left. Recalling the abbot's words, Fyn turned left.

Now he followed the sylion's tail and they plodded on. Fyn was tired and sore. It felt like they had been walking all night. At one point he'd heard running water and the walls felt warm to the touch, but they did not find the hot stream.

The smaller boys grew weary and had to be carried or helped along by the bigger ones. Every time Fyn's eyes glazed with tiredness, he relived flashes of the battle in the corridor, heard the almost silent grunts as the warriors fought with vicious intensity and saw the abbot stare at the sword point through his chest.

Shame seared him. He'd frozen. He'd failed his teachers. He shut the memory away, focusing on the task the abbot had given him.

Get the boys to safety.

Another branch, another sylion pointing the way. Where did the other branches lead? He was too tired to think.

Hawkwing and Master Sunseed, they would all be dead now and the Merofynians would be pillaging the abbey. It should have outraged him, but he was too tired to care. He must not think. Must go on.

Lenny's tummy rumbled loudly. 'The others are getting hungry.'

Fyn felt a smile tug at his lips. 'We are all hungry.'

He noticed his candle had burned down to a stub so he came to a stop in a cavern and turned to face the boys. 'Time to light more candles.'

Feldspar caught his eye with a warning. They did not know how far the passage went.

'Light every second candle,' Fyn ordered.

They lit half the new candles. What if they ran out? No point in worrying. They could not go back and he knew the path led outside eventually. Fyn trudged on. Weariness dulled his mind. Hunger gnawed at him, cramping his stomach. Bruises, from blows he didn't remember, throbbed now that his muscles had stiffened up.

There was time to wonder if the weapons master and mystics master had been drawn into ambush. It shamed him to think that he was half-Merofynian. Bitterness filled Fyn, leaving a vile taste in his mouth. But even that did not last as he walked on, dragging one weary foot after another. Was the castle already under attack? First he must lead the boys to safety then warn his father.

Surely the passage would end soon.

CHAPTER FIVE

SHIVERS WOKE BYREN. He'd skated until lack of sleep made him stumble. Then he'd curled into a ball under an overhang and tried to sleep. He mustn't be stupid with weariness when he met the abbot, not if he wanted to impress the man enough for him to hand over command of the warrior monks.

Now Byren rubbed snow on his face to wake himself and stretched to get his weary muscles working. His thighs protested as he resumed skating. It had been a cold night without his cloak but he had consoled himself with the thought of the Power-worker drained by his own sorbt stone and little Dinni free.

His thigh and calf muscles soon warmed up as he headed across the lake. After a few bow shots he spotted the thin trickle of smoke from a chimney and grinned ruefully. To think he'd been so close to a farmhouse, where he might have claimed traveller's ease.

After rounding a promontory which jutted out into the lake he spotted the dwellings, their roofs so heavy with snow they were almost invisible. A sturdy defensive wall protected the farm buildings and animals from ravening winter beasts, but Byren spotted a girl of about seven wandering along the shore with nothing but a wolf hound for company, so the family can't have heard about the ulfr pack.

Behind the farmhouse, in the middle distance, Mount Halcyon rose high in the morning light. With renewed energy Byren set off, hoping the farmwife would give him breakfast. The dog barked once, a deep authoritative warning, then fell silent. The girl watched Byren approach, curious and only slightly wary.

He wanted to shake her, warn her. 'Watch out for Merofynians, take shelter in the mountains!' But that would only frighten her. He'd tell her elders.

As he glided up to the rough jetty, he smelt garlic sausages and fresh bread, and his stomach rumbled.

The dog growled softly.

'Quiet, Rusty,' the girl ordered.

'Sounds like he's a good watch dog,' Byren said, hunger cramps tying his stomach in knots. He bent to unlace his skates, his fingers trembling with haste. Shouldn't have given Dinni all his food.

He stood up, slinging the skates over his shoulder. 'How about some breakfast for a weary traveller?'

'This way.' The girl led him up the shore and through the farm yard where another wolf hound barked a warning. An old man and a boy came out of the barn to look at him. Byren realised how vulnerable his people were, going about their everyday tasks in the belief they were at peace with Merofynia.

In the kitchen, the mother and grandmother were cleaning up after breakfast. The old woman looked up from scrubbing the kitchen table, the wood almost white from cleaning. The mother wiped her hands on her apron, cheeks flushed from hovering over the hearth. No one was wary of him. This was what thirty years of peace in Rolencia's rich valley had done to his people. They were unready for war.

'What's this I hear? We have a traveller?' The father strode in with the boy and grandfather, a grin on his weathered face.

Byren pulled the royal emblem from under his vest. 'Byren Kingson. I need food and I bring bad news. The Merofynians have invaded.'

The elders sent each other worried looks, while the children watched their faces.

'We've seen no warning beacons,' the old man muttered. 'Last time the beacons were lit.'

'I'm on my way to Halcyon Abbey, to alert the abbot. I need his warrior monks,' Byren said, and his stomach rumbled loudly.

The women laughed.

'You need some food. Sit yourself down,' the mother said and the grandmother hastened to get their best plates from the shelf.

The father looked Byren up and down. 'Eh, you're a big one, too big for our cart horse, but I could loan you the draught horse.'

Byren leant back as the women ladled a spoonful of chopped sausages and beans onto his plate. 'Thanks. But I'll skate if it's all the same to you.'

They nodded, understanding his choice. Travel by frozen canal and lake was faster than going overland this time of year.

'How far are the Merofynians?' the grandfather asked.

'I saw the main army over near Dovecote two nights ago,' Byren said, talking between mouthfuls. 'And last night I ran into scouts on the lake shore, over there.' He pointed. 'They had a filthy Utland Power-worker with them. I'd get your family to the nearest town as soon as possible.'

While he gulped his meal, the elders debated the relative merits of Port Marchand's defences over Port Cobalt's. When he had done eating they walked Byren out onto the lake and saw him off, wishing him luck, insisting he take the family's prize ulfr-fur cloak.

He set off with a half-loaf of hot bread in his travel bag and a meal in his stomach, heading towards Mount Halcyon. He'd be there by midday. Once he had the warrior monks at his back, he could return to Rolenhold.

Actions spoke louder than words. When he returned to help defend the castle, his father would have to believe his loyalty.

BENEATH FYN'S FEET the flagstones gave way to unworked stone. They must have left the man-made tunnels and entered a natural cave system. Here, he slowed his pace, wondering what he would do if he came to a fork and the sylion was not carved into the floor, but he saw no more side passages.

Exhausted, the youngest boys faltered. Some sat on the ground and wept quietly, while others pleaded for food and water.

'They're only little,' Lenny told Fyn and went to help the nearest who was no bigger than him.

'Hold this.' Fyn handed Lenny his second candle, which had burnt down to a stub, and knelt next to a boy. 'Climb onto my back.'

Thin arms clasped around Fyn's neck, half-choking him. He adjusted the boy's arms then stood, his leg muscles protesting.

Feldspar pushed past the boys, joining them. 'How much longer, Fyn?'

He drew breath to confess that he did not know then stopped. Surely the air tasted fresher?

Hurrying on around the bend, he found the ground and walls illuminated by natural light. Another turn and a sliver of silver daylight greeted him. It was so bright he had to shield his eyes. He let the boy slide to the ground. Relief made him try to shout the news but his voice cracked, even so they came running.

'Stay here. I'll see if it's safe,' Fyn told the others as they rushed to join him.

He stepped cautiously out of the tunnel, blinking fiercely in the silver glow of a winter's dawn. The sun had just broken free of the Snow Bridge's highest peaks and delicate light made the snow glisten.

With the sun on his right, he faced north, into the cold. Back in Rolenhold, south would mean going into the cold. According to the monks, Halcyon Abbey sat on the equator of their world, which made sense since it was the site of the goddess Halcyon's greatest seep.

The Lesser Bay opened on his right and the Greater Bay to his left. Though he was west of Port Cobalt, where the monks took the boats across to Sylion Abbey for the autumn cusp festival, Fyn recognised the distant sheer wall and spotted the silhouette of Sylion Abbey, safe on its cliff-top eyrie.

Beyond the abbey lay Sylion Strait. Like two great arms, the cliffs formed a passage to the Stormy Sea. Fyn had never been that far. The trip across to Sylion Abbey was bad enough for him.

From where he now stood, the land fell away until it met the bay. Fyn could just make out the snow-covered roofs of a small fishing village behind its defensive palisade. Right now the village's wharves would be well above the water line. When the snow and ice melted the water levels would rise and it would become safe for the fisher folk to venture out, past the Utland Isles to the ocean fields where the great shoals of fish would be found. A fisherman's life was not an easy one, but then it was the harshness of winter that made summer all the sweeter.

Fyn knew it would take until early afternoon to reach the village, but the promise of hot food would spur the little boys on. Relief filled him. They had walked under Mount Halcyon to the mountain's far northern slope. He had done what the abbot asked of him. Soon he would be free to help his family.

'It's safe. You can come out,' Fyn called.

BYREN SHOULDERED HIS skates and strode up the rise towards the abbey. The familiar path between the pines was covered in deep snow. From this angle the pines themselves blocked out the abbey. Worry gnawed at him. Other than the royal symbol, what did he have to convince the abbot to hand over command of his warriors?

Only the conviction that he must save Rolencia.

Intent on his plan, Byren strode through the gates which traditionally stood ajar during the day to symbolise that the goddess's loving heart was always open to her children. He waved to the shadowed niche where the monks' gateman stood and strode across the fan-shaped courtyard.

Although it was midday, the acolytes hadn't swept the light carpeting of snow from the paving stones around the central fountain and its pool. Beyond the pool's stone lip, hot water steamed invitingly in the cool air.

Byren glanced to the left where the animals were housed. No sign of life. He glanced to his right. In early spring those chambers were where the monks handed out the hothouse seedlings so that the farmers could get two crops in during the intense, but brief, summer.

He skirted the fountain and headed for the central archway, directly opposite the gate. Rich, formal waiting rooms opened off this part of the courtyard. The greater part of the abbey was dug into the mountain itself, and was rumoured to extend to hidden chambers containing wealth dating from before his family ruled Rolencia, from the lost civilisation that had left those statues on Ruin Isle.

Byren grinned – treasure hunts for children. What concerned him now was convincing the abbot to hand over command of his warrior monks. And directly ahead, three levels up, were the abbot's chambers. Byren shaded his eyes and counted floors. The abbot would be behind that row of arched windows, if his memory served him right.

He heard no singing from the chantry so he must have just missed the midday prayers. A horse neighed and wandered out from the archway on his left. From inside the animal's enclosure a cow lowed with discomfort and several of the long-haired mountain goats gave voice in complaint. Byren recognised their tone. They hadn't been milked this morning.

That was odd. Was everyone down with a terrible winter fever? That might explain the silence and the neglect of the animals.

Byren went over to the horse. He let it nuzzle his hand, threaded his fingers through its mane and walked it back towards the archway that led to the animals' pens.

As he entered the arch's shadow he spotted several monks crouched in a circle as though inspecting a sick animal. Perhaps that was the problem.

Byren pulled the royal emblem from under his shirt. 'I need to see the abbot on king's business.'

The men stared at him.

Words of jest died on Byren's lips as his eyes adjusted and he realised these were not pious monks, but hard-faced warriors. They wore no surcoats to identify who they served so they were swords-for-hire.

They looked pale and bleary-eyed. None carried weapons other than their knives. As one tucked something in his pocket Byren recognised the wyvern symbol, tattooed on the man's forearm.

Merofynians. They must be escorting a wealthy merchant who had sought traveller's ease at the abbey. This made things difficult for, even though they were now the enemy, he could not confront them while they were under the protection of the abbey.

As he grappled with the ramifications, Byren caught the leader's signal to surround him. The men fanned out to cut him off. Escorts did not launch unprovoked attacks.

With a cry, Byren shouldered the closest warrior aside. The horse reared, making the two on the other side back off. A man lunged for Byren, caught the foenix symbol and tugged. With a jerk, the chain broke. Byren pulled away even as something thudded into his ribs, knocking the air from his lungs.

One man grabbed him from behind. Clenching his fist, Byren drove the point of his elbow into the man's midriff and heard a satisfying grunt of pain as he broke a rib or two. A warrior lunged forwards, slashing with a hunting knife. Byren sidestepped, caught the man's knife arm, twisted, snapped his wrist and took the knife as it fell from his fingers.

With no time to draw his own weapons and no chance of defeating so many armed attackers, Byren thrust the injured man on top of his companions and ran a few steps. He threw his arm over the horse's neck and leaped across its back.

It danced sideways, frightened by the violence and smell of blood. Byren urged the horse out into the sunshine of the courtyard, crossing the stone paving. The Merofynians followed him, shouting a warning.

Byren turned the horse towards the abbey proper. He'd ride straight up the main steps and tell the abbot the men he had given sanctuary to had raised arms at a kingson!

Merofynian warriors charged out of the abbey's central archway.

'Cut him off. It's the kingson!' a warrior from the stables cried.

Blinking in the bright winter sun, the second lot of Merofynians fumbled for absent weapons. Byren knew the signs. They'd been up all night drinking, celebrating. The only explanation was that the abbey had fallen, impossible as it seemed.

He'd been lucky. In another day, they would have set guards and organised defences.

Even as this flashed through his mind, he was turning his horse and racing for the gate, where the gate keepers finally stepped out to block him. More Merofynian warriors.

Urging his horse to a gallop, Byren kicked one man, slashed at another and charged a third, who leaped aside at the last minute.

The terrified horse galloped down the steep slope, missed the first bend and ploughed through a knee-high snow bank, venturing into the pine forest. Byren would have urged it back onto the path, but he heard shouts behind him as the invaders organised pursuit.

His head buzzed. It hurt when he breathed. Why was his side sticky and hot? He felt his ribs and his hand came away bright with blood.

Byren cursed. He could not afford an injury, not with the Merofynians after him.

How had they taken the abbey, and where was Fyn?

No time to think. He let the frightened horse have its head. The snow banks and steep slope meant his mount could go no faster than a canter. Still, he had to clench his teeth as the rhythm of its hooves made his side throb.

Soon the silence of the evergreen forest closed around him. The snow was thick, mantling the trees and meeting the ground like a trailing cloak. Only patches of the trees' deep blue-green foliage could be seen. It was impossible to tell where the deep snow drifts were. One moment his horse was fetlock-deep, next the snow came up to its belly or higher as it fought its way through. The poor beast would be winded in no time.

Speaking gently, he soothed his mount and it slowed, picking its way through the trees. Soon he was out of the pines and in open, rolling farm country.

Clenching his teeth in anticipation of the pain, Byren twisted from the waist and looked back.

What he saw made him curse. The horse had left a clear path in the snow. Worse than that, his blood was a bright marker.

Grey moths fluttered across Byren's vision. He knew the signs and panic tightened his belly. He must not pass out.

He was injured and alone. The only advantage he had was local knowledge. Wasn't there a small stream not far from here that fed into the lake?

Oddly enough, after wrestling with the Merofynians, he still had his skates.

His pursuers were searching for a man on horseback. Byren looked for a suitable spot to dismount and hide his tracks. There, a steep slope of stone stretched off to one side of the path. From the looks of it there was a ravine below. Wind had scoured the rocky slope free of snow. He guided the horse towards it.

Slipping out of the saddle, he almost fell as his legs took his weight. The icy stone was slippery, but he held onto the horse's mane with one hand and hugged his side with the other to stop the bleeding. He led the horse a little way along the scree, then sent it off with a slap on the rump. It clambered up, eager to get off the treacherous rocks, leaving the slope by a different place from where they had entered. Let his pursuers think he had thought better of travelling this way.

Byren gritted his teeth and edged crablike across the steep, exposed stone. Snow had settled in the few crevices but it was mostly iced-over rock and dangerous. If he fell into the ravine he would break his leg and lie there until he froze to death, if he was lucky. If he was unlucky the ulfr pack would find him and make a meal of him. If he was really unlucky the Merofynians would find him.

But he had always been light on his feet. Lence used to resent the way he only had to go through a dance once to get the steps. Lence... grief wound its finger through his gut and twisted sharply. He must not think of his twin.

He had to warn his father. The Merofynians had dishonoured the code of war when they took the abbey. How could they capture it? The abbey contained at least six hundred trained warrior monks. Were the monks all dead? Where was Fyn?

His head spun.

First he must save himself. The steepness of the rocky scree eased and he made better time as he picked his way down the slope into the ravine. At the base, he found he was right. There was an iced-over stream. Perched on a rock, he strapped on his skates and had to rest to catch his breath. He'd bled again. He turned the snow over to hide the signs, smoothing it with his sleeve. It would fool a man but not a tracking dog.

Then he stood. With this injury, he had no hope of reaching Rolenhold in the normal three days' skate. Frustration ate at him, for he had no warrior monks to bring to his father's aid, only bad news. He would be confirming the Merofynian invasion and bringing news of the abbey's capture. But worst of all, he had to tell his parents of Lence's death. And they had only his word for how it had happened. No doubt Cobalt would try to twist all this to his advantage.

Somehow, Byren had to avoid capture by the Merofynians and expose his cousin for the traitor he was.

He headed for Rolenhold, trying not to think of the long haul down Viridian Lake, through the connecting canals and across Sapphire Lake.

Driving his legs, he glided out onto the lake and bent forwards to get up speed. But this tugged on his wound and made him pitch onto his knees, coughing. Sparks swam in his vision. When they cleared he saw a fine spray of pink on the ice below his face. Blood.

He'd seen enough injured men to recognise the signs. The wound had pierced his lungs. He would drown in his own blood. He came to his feet, head reeling. Only one thing mattered.

He had to reach Rolenhold, had to warn his father, had to prove his loyalty before he died.

PIRO HAD NO trouble slipping into an empty covered cart in the confusion of the loading and unloading in the castle courtyard. As the cart trundled out of Rolenhold, tears stung her eyes and slid down her cheeks. Furious, she brushed them away.

Leaving the castle was the right thing to do, the only thing to do.

But it felt wrong to abandon her mother while she was locked in the tower, a prisoner of her Merofynian blood. Worse, it felt wrong to run away when her father needed her. But she could only hide for so long before someone recognised her.

Her mother was right. Sylion Abbey was the best place for her right now. An ironic smile tugged at her lips. To think how she had railed against being sent to the abbey because of her Affinity.

Now she was going there by choice. She had a small travelling pack tucked under her cloak, some food and a good gown to wear when she met the abbess of Sylion.

She would jump out of the cart before the men started loading up the townsfolk. Her father had dragged himself from his sick bed early this morning, demanding news of Byren and Lence. When he learnt none had come, but that smoke had been seen in the direction of Dovecote, he had ordered the town evacuated so that the inhabitants could not be used as hostages. Piro regretted not saying goodbye to him, but he had been told she was already on her way to Sylion Abbey so she must not look back but forwards.

Once away from the cart, she would make her way to the wharves. There were still merchant sled-ships preparing to dash back to Port Marchand before war was officially declared. She could barter for passage on one of them.

The cart went dark as it trundled through the gate into Rolenton, then rattled over the cobbles as it traversed the two blocks to Rolenton Square where the people waited. A confusion of shouting voices told her the townspeople were only too eager to take shelter in the castle. Time to slip away.

Piro pulled her hood forwards. If anyone saw her, they would think she was a servant running home before war broke out. She had her story prepared and, thanks to her mother's delight in acting out the old sagas, she had the accent right.

Hands tore the cart's rear flap open and small children and old folk were thrust in, stumbling forwards to claim a patch of floor. Piro pushed past them to the opening, where a sea of anxious faces and clamouring arms greeted her. She was surprised there were this many townsfolk still to move. The carts had been ferrying people since dawn and it was now late afternoon.

'You're going the wrong way, girlie,' a man told her, as she jumped down and thrust through the throng.

'I'm trying to get home to Marchand to see me mam,' she said, but he wasn't interested.

The sky seemed so low and oppressive it made her head hurt. It was a grey day, the air thick and still. No wind. At worst the sled-ships would have to be dragged until the wind picked up as it usually did around dusk.

Piro had to battle to cross the square, where the carts were lined up to collect people. Of course, there were the hardy souls who swore they would not leave their homes, but there were also many who thought it prudent to take shelter in the castle with their families and as much of their belongings as they could manage to bring. Piles of bedding, bed frames, chests, tables and chairs were stacked high in the square where people waited. Some families had come prepared with a packed lunch, which they shared with their servants.

'A crust of bread for my little ones,' a woman pleaded, at one of these tables. Her three small children hung on her skirts, frightened and grubby. 'We've been waiting since dawn and they're ever so hungry.'

The wealthy merchant turned his back on her.

'Jorge,' his wife pleaded.

'If we give them some, they'll all want some,' he said, but he looked uncomfortable.

'Here.' Piro reached into her pack and pulled out a loaf baked fresh that morning in the castle's kitchen. 'And I have some cheese.'

'Halcyon bless you,' the woman whispered, hastily sharing the food with her little ones.

Piro watched. If the square continued to fill with townsfolk, the children could be crushed under foot.

'Come this way.' She picked up the smallest, a toddler of two, and the mother grabbed the four-year-old while the six-year-old hung on her skirt, stuffing bread in his mouth.

With a judicious jab and an elbow in the right place, Piro pushed through to the place where Temor stood bellowing orders. Captain of the king's honour guard, he had been her father's most trusted advisor until Lord Cobalt insinuated himself into that position, earning the title of lord protector of the castle. Captain Temor had been given the task of evacuating Rolenton.

Piro slipped behind the grizzled veteran and tugged on his surcoat, which was decorated with the deep red foenix on a black background, its wings and scales picked out in gold thread.

'Eh, what?' he turned, his eyes widening. 'Piro? You're supposed to be safe in Sylion Abbey, or on your way there at least.'

She thrust the grizzling two-year-old into his arms. 'See that this woman and her children get safely to the castle.'

'What?' he protested as the woman began to thank him profusely. Piro melted into the crowd, a little smile tugging at her lips. She was pretty sure Captain Temor didn't believe that she had been passing her mother's traitorous notes to a Merofynian spy, but he had his orders to arrest her.

Luckily the crowd was so dense and the momentum towards the carts was so forceful, only the most determined could make headway.

Piro found herself on the steps of the merchants' guild hall with its great bell tower. It was from the fifth floor of this tower that her father had announced Lence's betrothal to Isolt – King Merofyn's daughter – last midwinter's day. This should have ensured the peace. Piro didn't understand what had gone wrong, but one thing was certain, from atop the bell tower she would be able to see the wharves.

Better to spot a likely sled-ship and make straight for it, than to waste time and energy struggling through the crowd. She entered through the double doors and crossed the landing heading for the tower stairs.

Further into the hall she could hear men and women arguing over strategies to protect their investments. Orders still had to be filled and ships were currently under sail, their captains unaware of the situation at home. To hear the merchants of Rolenton talk, war was an inconvenience unless they could use it to turn a profit.

Smiling to herself, Piro ran up the stairs, only puffing slightly when she reached the fifth floor. Hanging over the balcony, she peered down past the busy square, past the sloping roof tops of the terraces towards the lake and the wharves. Some of the sled-ships were already being hauled across the frozen lake. While they still could, they were heading north-east for the canal that eventually linked up with Port Marchand, or west for the canal to Port Cobalt. Watching the ships was one of her favourite pastimes and she knew many of their captains by name. She could pick the fastest and recognise which great merchant house they belonged to.

There, that three-masted sloop looked like it was making ready to depart. She only hoped she would reach it in time.

Raising her eyes, Piro looked out across Rolencia, past the chimneys of the great houses opposite, past the town to the countryside. The air was still and thick like soup. She could hardly make out the beautiful, rolling snow-covered fields of Rolencia's rich valley. How could she leave her home behind? How could she live in cold, heartless Sylion Abbey?

She blinked. What was that shadow moving on the snow?

She blinked again, her vision crawling oddly. Surely it was mist in a hollow, nothing more. Rubbing her eyes, she wished for a farseer as she strained to make sense of it.

But instead of clearing, her vision grew blurred and she slipped into Affinity-induced Unseen sight.

It was not mist. It was a mass of white cloaked men, moving like a cloud's shadow over the fields, under cover of an illusion generated by renegade Power-workers.

The Merofynian invaders were less than an hour away!

CHAPTER SIX

Piro LOOKED DOWN into the seething square. There was no time for people to wait for carts to carry their belongings. If they did not go now, they would be cut off. She flew down the stairs, boots barely touching the wood.

Instead of running out into the thronging square, she ran into the bell-ringers' little nook, deep inside the tower. Far above her the ropes stretched impossibly high and light filtered down from the great bells.

Piro only hoped she remembered the right bell sequence for the warning. It was meant to be rung by a team of three, so she would just have to do her best. Leaping off her feet, she clutched the first rope and let her weight drag it down. A thunderous stroke echoed above her. Even as the rope rode up, she was reaching for the next one. This bell was pitched higher. Prompted by the old rhyme learnt as a child when her mother used to sing her to sleep, she rang the sequence, leaping from rope to rope. She was playing it too slow, but that could not be helped. People would recognise it and realise why she was ringing the warning.

'You, girly?' A plump merchant wearing the fashions of Ostron Isle confronted her. 'What mischief are you up to –'

'Merofynians an hour away, probably less,' she shouted to be heard.

'What nonsense!' The Ostronite merchant glared at her, secure in his ermine-collared cloak.

'Send someone up to the top of the tower if you don't believe me.'

A silver-haired woman entered, with three burly male servants at her back. 'What's holding... Piro Kingsdaughter, what are you doing here?'

'Markiza,' Piro gasped, letting the bell rope go. 'Is the markiz with you?

You must get out of the town.' The Ostronite merchant stared at Piro. 'The kingsdaughter? The one that's wanted for treason?'

'The same. Servants, hold her,' the markiza ordered, ignoring Piro's warning. Three men thrust past the Ostronite.

'That was a misunderstanding,' Piro insisted. 'Today I've been sent to Sylion Abbey, ask Captain Temor. But there's no time. The Merofynians are just outside the town. Go to the top of the tower yourself, if you don't believe me.' Frustration made Piro stamp her foot. 'Would you hand everyone over to the Merofynians?'

'At least send someone to see,' the Ostronite merchant urged.

The markiza tapped one of her servants on the shoulder. 'Go to the top of the tower. Quickly now, and tell me what you see.'

As he hurried off, Piro tried to dart under the nearest man's arm and through the door.

The markiza caught her by the shoulder. 'Not so fast, kingsdaughter.'

The two servants held Piro between them.

'But I must warn Captain Temor!' Piro insisted.

'You're not going anywhere until I know what's going on,' the markiza told her.

Piro rolled her eyes.

A muffled shout echoed down the stairs.

'What was that?' the markiza called up the stairwell, thrusting the door further ajar.

'I see nothing but low-lying mist.'

'Because their Power-workers are cloaking them,' Piro snapped. 'That's why our lookouts didn't spot them.'

The markiza frowned. 'Then how could you –'

'I have Affinity. That's why I was being sent to Sylion Abbey.' Piro told the truth. It no longer mattered.

The markiza's eyes widened. 'If the Merofynians are at the gates –'

'I knew I should have left when I first heard the news,' the Ostronite merchant moaned.

Both Piro and the markiza ignored him. She nodded to her remaining servants. 'Help sound the warning bells.'

'I don't know the sequence, markiza,' the younger servant protested.

'I do. Set me down!' Piro shrugged free of the servants. 'I'll need two of your servants, markiza.'

'Take them.' She caught Piro's arm. 'Have you seen my son, Chandler? Last I heard he'd joined Byren Kingson's honour guard.'

Piro gulped. Clearly, Cobalt's accusations and her father's subsequent banishment of Byren had not reached the townsfolk and now was not the time to explain. 'Byren's honour guard set off three days ago. Chandler must be with him by now.'

'Set off for where?'

'Dovecote estate.' Right into the path of the invading Merofynians. 'I...'

'He will do what's right. He's a good boy. May Halcyon watch over him. May she watch over you, too, little Piro.' The markiza tapped the Ostronite merchant's arm. 'Now I must see to my family's investments. Come.' They hurried off.

Piro turned back to the servants. It took two sequences, but they caught on to the simple system. Soon the bells rang out their warning at the proper pace.

Piro's head pounded and her body thrummed with the effort of leaping and tugging on the great bell ropes. But she'd spent so much time hiding recently that it felt good to be active.

BYREN LIFTED HIS head as the dreaded ulfr howl echoed across the frozen lake. Snow flakes kissed his face, falling lightly from low-slung clouds. Somehow he'd kept skating. He'd stuck to the lake shore, so he hadn't made good time. Had the snow been thicker he might have risked skating directly across the lake. But the Merofynians were after him. He had heard their hunting horns. Had he been organising this search he would have separated his men into small groups. They knew he was injured and, by now, they knew he was on foot. He hoped that they would be searching on the land but he would have had his men search the lake. So he had to assume his pursuers were just as canny.

Though desperate, he had deliberately avoided the farmhouse where he'd eaten breakfast, not wanting to bring trouble down on the family there. Hopefully, they had already packed up their things and headed for the nearest fortified town. So he was injured and alone, with half a dozen Merofynian search parties tracking him. His only advantage was that he knew the area intimately and they didn't.

Since he was twelve he'd been as big as a grown man and his body had never failed him. It must not fail him now.

He'd felt certain he would reach Rolenhold before this wound stole his life force. Until now...

Now the ulfr pack was on the prowl. At least the Merofynians would be equally reluctant to meet up with the pack. But the ulfrs would smell the blood on him for sure. They'd hunt him, a single injured man. The only thing that appealed more to them was... an Affinity seep!

Without hesitation he struck out for the spot where he'd come across the Power-worker and Dinni. He hoped she was safe at Sylion Abbey by now. This was not a good time to be wandering the Rolencian valley.

Head down, powerful thighs driving him on, he winced with every breath. Grey spots ate into the corners of his vision, but he would not give in.

Lifting his head, he took note of the landmarks, shrouded in winter snow but still clear to his experienced eye. This was where he'd fallen and ploughed through a drift into a little inlet. Already the wind and snow had smoothed his passage so that others would have trouble reading the signs. He weaved through the gap in the snow drift and headed for the shore. There he unstrapped his skates and ploughed up the slope, being careful to smooth the signs of his passing.

There it was – the seep, still oozing Affinity since he had removed the sorbt stone before it could fully drain the source. Since childhood he had been trained to avoid untamed Affinity. Now he meant to hide in an Affinity seep, and every proper instinct revolted.

He hesitated on the lip of the hollow. It was empty. Had the Utland Power-worker survived the night, and what had happened to his warrior escort?

Another howl reached him, closer this time. No more delays.

He had no choice. It was the seep or death.

Praying the falling snow would finish cloaking his steps from his mortal pursuers, he plunged down into the hollow. With no Affinity to sense it, he remained blind to the power surge, but his heart raced with reluctance as he sank into the deepest part of the hollow and began to scoop out a body-length depression. The exertion made him cough. More blood, little bright red rubies scattered on the snow. He had to take shorter and shorter breaths. Time was running out.

All warriors faced death. It did not worry him.

To die dishonoured in his family's eyes, now that was a cruel fate.

There was no time to make a proper snow-cave. He intended to stretch out on his back and drag snow across his body. He hoped the ulfr-fur cloak would protect him from the cold and the seep from the Affinity beasts. Instinct screamed at him to curl into a ball, but he needed to be covered.

A strange, querulous bark alerted him. He froze in a half-crouch and stared up the slope. Silhouetted against the sullen, snow-laden clouds was an adolescent ulfr. A great ruff of silver fur sat across its broad shoulders. Its legs looked too long for its body, as it was not yet fully grown. And, from the way it tilted its head, intelligent winter sky-blue eyes studying him, it was confused by his presence.

Another ulfr joined the first. Byren recognised the clever pack leader from the night he had held them off over Orrade's unconscious body. His gut clenched, expecting the male to give one of its eerily intelligent yelps as it sent its warrior ulfrs to attack him but, like the adolescent, the pack leader hesitated.

Remembering the two birds, Byren forced all wariness and aggression from his stance. Dropping into the snow, he began to roll about as the birds had done, uttering happy crooning sounds. For a heartbeat he wondered if this was what Dinni would have done if she had been allowed to follow her instincts.

But, even as he rolled about wallowing in the seep, he watched the gathering ulfrs. Before long, they lined the rim of the hollow. It had been a tough winter with constant harassment from humans. There were only five large males left, three females and four adolescents.

His heart pounded, tugging at the wound in his side. His breath rasped in his chest as he gulped for air. Either they would tear him to shreds, or they would accept him as another Affinity beast.

With a warning growl, the pack leader trotted down the slope towards Byren. Recalling the way the castle's hunting dogs deferred to their leader, Byren rolled over onto his back and presented his vulnerable belly. The ulfr stood over him, large head and ruff almost blocking out the sky.

In that instant, Byren believed the ulfr would kill him, before the wound could. He closed his eyes and called on Halcyon herself. It was past midwinter so the goddess of the earth and growing things was in ascension. But he called on her because he loved Rolencia and she was the goddess of love.

Let me live long enough to reach my family, he pleaded. *Let me live long enough to warn them of Merofynia's treachery. Do this and I will...* what? His ancestor had dedicated Halcyon Abbey to thank the goddess for his victory. He had never been particularly religious, preferring to handle things with the strength of his body and the force of his will, rather than call on the gods. But this time...

Do this, and once Rolencia is safe, I will dedicate my life to serving you. There – he could offer no more.

All resistance left him as he gave himself up to Halcyon's care. The ulfr's hot breath fanned his face, welcome warmth, despite his instinctive reaction to the smell of death. *Run*, the primitive part of his mind screamed. *Play along*, his logical mind told him. So he did.

The ulfr sniffed him. The pack leader had to be aware that he was human and injured, but being drenched in the seep's power must have been enough to make him acceptable, because the Affinity beast, servant of the goddess, lifted its head and gave a distinctive howl.

Then it stepped back to roll in the seep, throwing up spirals of powdery snow. The other pack members padded down into the hollow and rolled about, nipping playfully if a youngster infringed on an adult's space. After a time they settled down to sleep and set up a soft whining, almost singing, that was just on the edge of Byren's hearing.

It made his head ring and seemed to fill his mind so that he had trouble remembering who he was, or even that he was lying with this winter's most notorious ulfr pack.

Warmed by the combined heat of the pack, his shivering stopped. He lost all sense of time. The heat and the sense of acceptance was so powerful that he let himself drift, taking short, quick breaths to fill what little space was left in his blood-filled lungs. All he could do was lie there as waves of weariness swept over him.

He did not know whether the goddess had heard his plea, or whether his ploy had convinced the ulfrs to accept him, but it seemed he would live long enough for the wound to kill him.

He should get up now while they were relaxed and slip away, but he knew he would not get far. Any movement would trigger coughing and one of these coughing fits would be his last. An adolescent gave a soft bark in its sleep and shifted so that its jaw rested on Byren's chest. He lifted his hand and let his fingers sink into the beast's thick shoulder ruff. So soft, so warm and silky.

He felt honoured to be accepted. Pity he would not live long enough to tell anyone about this. How Orrade would shake his head in disbelief, then his thin face would light up with wonder.

Or would he turn away?

Pain curled through Byren. He should never have compared Orrade to Lence. Despite Cobalt's threat to expose Orrade as a lover of men, his friend had remained loyal to Byren. Unlike Lence. His twin had only been too ready to believe Cobalt's half-truths. It stung to discover how easily Lence had been swayed. No wonder Orrade was furious with him. Shame filled Byren.

He wasn't in pain but it hurt to think he would die before he could apologise to Orrade. Before he could prove his loyalty to his father. The king would live on, grieving, believing his second son had betrayed Rolencia. An ache that was not physical curled through Byren, making his throat tight and his breath catch.

The ulfr at his side gave a whimper of pain as if in sympathy with him, and he felt the other pack members shift. When another whimper followed the first, Byren understood what was happening. He had watched his prized hunting bitches whelp enough times to recognise the sounds of birth.

Carefully, he lifted his hand and rested it on the female beside him. He could feel her belly tighten like a drum as her womb contracted. The power of the seep must have brought on the birth, for usually the cubs were born in the spring and spring cusp was still a little way off.

Sprawled on his back, surrounded by ulfrs, Byren watched the pack leader take up a protective stance over the whelping female. For his hunting dogs the process was usually quick and the ulfr was no exception. Byren felt the whole pack ride the contractions with her, their whining song rising in pitch with the peak of each pain. The sound triggered a vibration through the pack's chests, a vibration of attunement. It relaxed Byren's aching chest and, with this relaxation, he found his breath came more easily.

Three more contractions and the female gave a grunt of satisfaction as she expelled the pup. It rushed out in a hot, wet slither of sound. The female wriggled around to nose the newborn and lick its snout. After a moment it whimpered, and Byren heard the distinctive snuffling as it searched for its mother's nipple. The rest of the pack nuzzled closer. The pack leader drove them back and the male shared the afterbirth with the female.

As they shifted, Byren risked lifting his head to take a quick look. The mother had licked the pup clean but its fur had not dried yet. The pup had, however, settled in place attached to one of her nipples. The pack leader watched it proudly, for all the world like a human father. And, unlike his hunting hounds, there was only one pup.

Byren felt stunned and privileged as the pack settled down, still whining softly in unison, the vibration travelling through them as if they were one great animal. He lay back and concentrated on breathing, which was not so hard now. It seemed he would last out the night. If only he could live long enough to reach Rolenhold. He willed his wound to mend. There was still so much he had to do.

Finally, he slept, warm and safe in the ulfr pack. And he dreamed he was back home in Rolenhold, visiting his mother in the solarium, only he was a child and she wept because they'd just tested little Fyn and found he had Affinity. They were preparing to take him away. Byren remembered his impotent fury. How, at ten, he had volunteered to ride across Rolencia to rescue his little brother from the monks. How he had been filled with the conviction that his father's law was wrong. Strange... why had he forgotten this?

In his dream, which he now realised was really a hidden memory, his mother placed her hand on his forehead and whispered, 'Don't, Byren! Obey your father in this, or I will lose you too.' And, as she spoke, she seemed to siphon off his roiling emotions, so that he was left feeling calmer, if not happy. And he understood why he had forgotten the moment.

He was woken by a whistle that imitated a bird call, only Byren knew that this particular bird would not be out of hibernation until after spring cusp. The sound echoed across the seep. Lifting his head ever so slightly, he brought the rim of the hollow into his range of vision.

Cloaked warrior heads dotted the rim.

Would they spot him, amidst the pack, dressed in ulfr fur? No one would expect to find a human in an ulfr pack enjoying a seep.

The ulfr leader and three of the large males came to their feet, emitting a low rumbling growl from deep in their great chests. The message was clear. *Back off.*

With the newborn and the seep to defend, the pack was extremely dangerous. If Byren had come upon them like this, he would have probably had his archers climb trees and pick the animals off. Luckily there were no trees lining the seep and now that very thought seemed like sacrilege to Byren.

Would he ever be able to kill another Affinity beast?

He felt himself reach for his own knife and it startled him to realise that if the Merofynians attacked, he meant to defend the ulfr pack.

But they didn't. One of them sang a chant Byren had never heard his mother sing, though he recognised some of the phrases. He gathered the Merofynians were honouring the seep, its power and the Affinity beasts.

That's right. The Merofynian attitude towards untamed Affinity was very different. They accepted it, cultivating it. Perhaps theirs was a more realistic attitude. Fighting Affinity was like trying to turn back the tide.

Then he thought of poor little Dinni, enslaved by the Utland Power-worker. No, he didn't agree with everything the Merofynians did, but then he didn't agree with his father's laws on Affinity.

The handing-over of all children born with Affinity broke up families, and confiscating the property of those who tried to hide Affinity only encouraged greed.

All this flashed through his mind as the Merofynians honoured the seep and Affinity beasts.

And then they backed off. Leaving Byren to lie in the seep, amidst the ulfr pack, riding the resonance of the pack's subtle song.

'HERE'S PIRO KINGSDAUGHTER,' the markiza pointed.

Two of the king's honour guard frowned at Piro. One nodded to the other. 'Bring her.'

'But I'm ringing –'

'Warning's been given. Come.'

The two servants hurried off after the markiza, as Piro was bundled out and into the main hall of the guild's meeting house.

She broke free of her captors and ran towards Captain Temor, arriving in the middle of his argument with the Ostronite merchant.

'And I say you'll be safer in Rolenhold,' Temor told the man. 'Safer than heading off across the lake in a mad scramble to outrun the Merofynians. What if the wind doesn't rise at dusk? The castle's never fallen. Come, wait it out.'

'Captain Temor.' Piro tugged on his arm.

'Hush, Piro,' Temor snapped, then turned back to the Ostronite to find the man striding off. 'On his own head be it.' Dismissing the man he turned to Piro, eyes dark under heavy grey brows. 'As for you!'

One strong hand caught Piro by the upper arm and she was dragged from the guildhall to join two dozen of the king's honour guard, who waited for their captain's orders.

Out in the square, furniture and belongings lay abandoned, as people scrambled for the safety of the castle. Piro shaded her eyes, looking up at the steep road that zig-zagged several times before reaching the gates of Rolenhold. The road was packed with people, most walking, some on carts and a few on horseback.

Shouts echoed from the wharves, the weakest point of Rolenton's defences, where the Merofynians had already broken through the town's defences.

The voices held abrasive cruelty. It rubbed across Piro's nerves, making her heart thunder uncomfortably. 'Our people will never make it in time.'

'We'll have to buy them time,' Captain Temor muttered. 'Come on.'

They pounded across the square to the road leading to Southgate, then down to the gate itself, which was only just emptying of townspeople when they reached it.

Temor beckoned one of the king's honour guard. 'Sawtree, I'm entrusting you with the kingsdaughter. Make sure she reaches the safety of the castle.'

'But –' Sawtree began.

Merofynian warriors boiled out of the narrow lanes from the wharves and headed across the square, roaring a challenge.

'Get her to safety!' Temor snapped.

Sawtree caught Piro's arm, pulling her through the gate before the king's honour guard could haul it closed. She made out Temor bellowing for them to build a barrier of furniture across the road. Of course, the gate was designed to be defensible against attacks from the outside, not the inside.

'They'll be killed,' Piro panted.

'Not before they buy us time. Run!'

She turned and ran, tears blinding her. Now she knew why Sawtree had objected to taking her. He'd served beside those men for thirty years. He did not want to abandon them in their last stand.

Ahead of her, the townsfolk drove others before them, shouting and pleading with those ahead to make haste. A man cried out and fell to his knees at Piro's side, an arrow embedded in his shoulder.

'They have our range. We're packed so tight, they're aiming upwards and trusting to hit us,' Sawtree muttered. He paused and cast about them looking for something.

Piro gave a cry of surprise as an object thumped into her back, driving her to her knees.

'Piro!' Sawtree cried.

She felt over her shoulder to find an arrow shaft embedded in her travelling pack. A laugh escaped her. 'It's all right. My pack protected me.'

'Halcyon must be smiling on you.' He grabbed the arrow, pulling it out and hauling her upright. 'Here.' He snatched an abandoned bundle and held it over their heads. 'Walk in front of me, little Piro.'

His broad shoulders protected her as he manoeuvred her into position and drove her on.

The tone of the shouting at the gate changed and Piro knew Temor and his men had engaged the enemy. So did everyone around them. Dropping their belongings, they ran. But they were running uphill and the pace could not be maintained. Soon they slowed to a scrambling stagger. All around them people cried out and fell behind as they were hit. Piro stumbled over a body. Only he wasn't dead. Feeling her land on him, he groaned and clutched her, pleading for help.

Sawtree grabbed her by the back of her bodice, hauling her upright like a kitten.

'I'm sorry. So sorry,' she told the wounded man, whose eyes fixed on her in a silent plea before Sawtree dragged her off him and drove her on.

The woman in front of her stopped, looked back and uttered a sharp scream. Piro went to look over her shoulder, but Sawtree drove her on.

'Don't look back,' he warned. 'The gate's fallen.'

A moan was torn from Piro. As captain of the guard, Temor had taught her to ride. He'd given Byren and Lence their first wooden swords and taught them basic defence skills when they were six. He'd shared a place at their table and counselled her father for as long as she could remember.

She heard shouting from the walls of Rolenhold and looked up. They were within bow range of the castle defenders now. Surely their attackers would hold off, but no, even more arrows fell around them. Sawtree gave a grunt and staggered. She glanced down to see an arrow had driven right through his calf.

'Leave me.' He shoved her away.

She ducked under his arm and took some of his weight. He cursed her but kept on in an awkward, lurching stagger.

As they rounded the last bend leading to Rolenhold's gate several men ran out to help the stragglers inside, and the defenders cheered.

Two men took Sawtree from her.

Freed of his weight, Piro plunged through the gate on their heels. The long tunnel was dark and crowded, then suddenly she was in the first courtyard which was filled with townsfolk who were being urged to move on. Children cried for their parents. Old folks slumped, too exhausted to move.

Piro paused to catch her breath and check on Sawtree. The men had propped him against the wall.

'Are you –' she began.

'Go.' He thrust her away, glaring across the courtyard.

She turned to look in the direction of his gaze and her eyes met Cobalt's. He was two body lengths from her, with a dozen people between them. His eyes widened in surprise, then narrowed.

Sawtree shoved Piro. 'Get away, while you still can.'

'Out of my way, old woman.' Cobalt shoved through the crowd towards them.

Piro ducked between two merchants and took to her heels. Being small and not worried who she elbowed, she easily threaded her way through the crowd. Behind her, she heard Cobalt confront Sawtree.

'Where's Piro?'

'The kingsdaughter? In Sylion, they say –'

There was a sharp crack. Piro winced and kept running. She couldn't save Sawtree. How she wished she was big and powerful like Lence and Byren.

Blending in with the crowd of frightened townsfolk, she was carried further into the castle's maze of courtyards. None of the defenders bothered to question one more dishevelled maid, and none of the townsfolk paid her any attention as she picked through the family groups squabbling over patches of ground to call their own.

She'd entered one of the inner courtyards when the rumour spread, 'They're burning Rolenton!'

Some townsfolk moaned, others objected furiously, demanding to know what King Rolen would do about it.

Piro wondered what more they thought her father could do. At least he had ensured the people got out with their lives. She headed for Eagle Tower.

Several castle servants had thought to climb it, but they were watching Rolenton and didn't pay any attention to the grimy maid in the battered cap. From here, she could see the whole of Rolencia laid out before her. Sure enough, a plume of black smoke rose from the centre of Rolenton. As the short winter's day grew dark, she identified leaping flames centred in the square. The Merofynians were burning the goods left behind by the fleeing citizens. The tower of flames grew ever taller as more things were dragged out of the homes and burned. From the looks of it, the leader of the warriors had declared 'havoc', which meant no quarter would be given and the warriors were allowed to take anything they wanted.

Though crowded, the parapets of the castle were oddly quiet as everyone watched the fire in Rolenton.

When Piro grew tired, cold and hungry she came down from the tower. She wanted to see her mother and ask the queen's advice now that the castle was under siege, but Cobalt had seen her so he would have told his people to look for her.

Her stomach rumbled and, trusting to her maid's disguise, she made her way to the kitchen, which was chaotic. Tonight the cook was too busy to approach on the sly. It was the spit-turner who spotted her. His near-blind eyes could not be fooled by a maid's costume. He recognised her by the way she moved and his ears distinguished her familiar step amidst the confusion. He caught her hand as she tried to slip past. Drawing her aside, he led her into a dark storage room.

She ducked smoked hams hanging from the rafters. 'What is it?'

'We were told you'd gone to Sylion Abbey, but they did not call off the guard who's been watching over your foenix so I wondered.' Milky eyes fixed on her face trying to make out her expression. 'Don't worry, I've been feeding your pet.'

'Thank you.' She squeezed his hands. 'Have you seen Sawtree?'

The spit-turner hesitated.

'Cobalt spotted me with him earlier,' Piro admitted. 'I... I had to leave him and run –'

'They've got Sawtree in chains in the stable yard. You must stay away from him, kingsdaughter. Promise you will?'

She nodded, meaning to go and see if she could do anything for Sawtree later.

'Cobalt said you betrayed Rolencia, but I did not believe them,' the spit-turner admitted. 'None of us believed him.'

Tears stung Piro's eyes. 'What about my mother? She's been loyal to Rolencia since she came here as a child of eight.'

He shook his head. 'The queen is Merofynian-born and under the influence of a renegade Power-worker. Poor thing.'

Piro's heart sank. How quickly they had turned on her mother.

They'd be equally quick to turn on her, if they knew she had Affinity. She shuddered as the ramifications hit her. With the castle under siege, Cobalt would be within his rights to have her executed. She shivered.

The spit-turner rubbed her hands. 'You're cold. And hungry, I expect. Stay here. I'll find you some food.'

Again, she squeezed his fingers then let him go. He returned after several moments with a calico bag containing smelly cheese and other items.

'Promise me you'll hide?' He held the bag up between them but did not release it. 'Cobalt's looking for you.'

'I know. I'll take care.'

He did not look convinced, but he gave her the bag and she slipped away, heading for the stable courtyard.

The place was so crowded, people had camped in the passages. She picked her way over bundles and through outstretched legs. She passed two old men, both veterans of other wars by the look of them. One was without a leg from the knee down and the other's hands were crippled with the bone-ache.

'They're saying all the king's old honour guard are dead,' One-leg muttered. 'I remember Temor as a boy, remember his da. Good men, both of 'em.'

'Good men,' the other echoed. 'Young Rolen lost a lot of good men today.'

It took a moment for Piro to realise they were talking about her father.

'Eh, he can't afford to. Not with the enemy at the gates again.' One-leg shook his head. 'The Bastard's brat shouldn't have punished Sawtree.'

'Aye. Good man, Sawtree,' the other agreed.

Piro's stomach lurched and her skin went cold. So the spit-turner hadn't been entirely honest with her. She wanted to ask these old men what Cobalt had done to punish Sawtree, but she didn't dare.

'I hear the Bastard's brat's offering a reward for news of Rolen's girl,' One-leg said and spat.

Piro crept away feeling guilty. What had Cobalt done to Sawtree? She wanted to go to him and help, but that would be an insult when he had chosen to sacrifice himself for her. Tears stung her eyes. She searched for somewhere safe, somewhere that if she was found she would not endanger others.

At last she settled in a store room. Everything had gone wrong. Her two oldest brothers were missing, her mother was locked up, her father was sick and had placed his trust in a trickster and now, Rolenhold was under siege.

Unable to eat, she stared out the single high window. The stars were covered by thick cloud tonight, which meant the usual dusk breeze hadn't come in from the sea. Had the Ostronite merchant escaped?

He was probably wealthy enough to cry hostage and pay for his release but his sailors and servants would not be so lucky. The best they could hope for was to be kept as seven-year slaves. Merofynians exacted seven years' servitude in return for captives' lives. Strange to think that a kingdom which considered itself the most civilised in the known world should keep slaves and hold to such harsh laws. For all that the Merofynians looked down on Rolencians as barbarians, her father had preferred a simple beheading to the hanging, drawing and quartering of the convicted.

CHAPTER SEVEN

IT HAD TAKEN the better part of the day for Fyn to lead the boys down the slope towards the village and now he hesitated in a hollow, out of sight of the village's gate tower. Finding Merofynian invaders inside the abbey had unnerved him. Who knew where the enemy was?

He ordered the boys to wait but, with the promise of hot food only two bow shots away, the older boys muttered about the delay and the little ones cried softly.

'They're just about done, Fyn,' Feldspar protested, catching up with him. 'Can't we –'

'No, we can't!' He grimaced. 'Sorry. I don't want to lead you all into a trap.'

'Do you think the Merofynians are already there?' Joff asked.

Fyn shrugged. 'I just don't know.'

'We'll wait,' Feldspar whispered. 'Settle them down, Joff.'

He moved off and Feldspar squeezed Fyn's shoulder.

He wanted to brush off that supporting hand. Felt a fraud. No one would be following him if they knew how he'd failed the abbot.

On top of that, impatience and worry ate at Fyn. Already, he had lost a night and a day since the abbey had been taken. And he still had to cross Rolencia's ripe valley. No matter how often he told himself Piro was safe in Rolenhold, he couldn't rid himself of the worm of worry that gnawed at his belly. She was in trouble, he just knew it.

'What is it?' Feldspar asked.

Fyn glanced around the hollow while Lenny waited at his side, shivering but not complaining. This was all that remained of Halcyon's warrior monks, small boys and acolytes who were too young to go to war. A wave of loss engulfed Fyn. Tears burned his eyes as he thought of the knowledge lost with the monks' deaths. The Merofynians were probably ransacking the great library even now. On a more practical note, who would tend the hothouse seedlings? How would the farmers get two crops harvested this summer? A summer spent warring meant a winter spent starving.

Speaking of which, the boys were hungry and needed somewhere warm to sleep. It was getting dark. 'I'll approach the village, see if it's safe.'

'I'll come with you,' Feldspar decided.

Lenny shivered and his stomach rumbled loudly.

Fyn grinned. 'Wait here, Len.'

He slipped out of the hollow with Feldspar at his heels, and made for the isolated cover of stunted pines until they reached a cairn of stones about a bow-shot from the gate. This was where the traveller coming from up the path around the far side of Mount Halcyon would stop to give thanks for a safe journey before entering the village.

From behind this cairn, Fyn studied the village's single gate tower. Several youths between thirteen and seventeen were standing on the platform, hovering over a wyvern harpoon which some enterprising fisherman had mounted up there.

The business end of the harpoon was pointed at a winter-bare, gnarled tree across the field just off the path from the valley.

Feldspar shaded his eyes as he studied the village chimney pots, visible above the wall. 'No more than a dozen cottages. I think we outnumber them. I hope there's enough food to go around.'

'The abbess can replace their supplies later.' Fyn glanced to the clouds. 'More snow on the way. Good. It'll hide our trail.'

'You think the Merofynians will send warriors after us?'

'I think we have a day or so before they begin to wonder where we got to. And, if they have a Power-worker with them, which they're sure to do, they will eventually find Halcyon's Sacred Heart.' He shivered, thinking of the invaders desecrating the mummies of the old monks and tapping into Halcyon's own seep. 'The sooner you lot are safe behind Sylion's walls the better.'

'Well, something has stirred up the fisher folk.' Feldspar pointed to the tower with its cluster of defenders.

Fyn agreed. He stepped out from behind the cairn and called. 'We're from Halcyon Abbey and we claim traveller's ease.'

Several dogs barked. The youths swung the wyvern harpoon towards them. Fyn and Feldspar instinctively opened their arms to show they carried no weapons.

'Halcyon Abbey,' they yelled to be sure there were no mistakes.

The youths cheered and one of them shouted an order to the youngest. 'Fetch Lame Klimen. Tell him Halcyon Abbey has come.'

'I'll go back and get the boys,' Feldspar offered and turned around only to mutter, 'Oh, I see Joff's bringing them.'

Fyn glanced over his shoulder to find the others plodding after Joff, too eager to wait for his signal.

Another head, this one weathered by time, appeared on the gate tower. There was some confusion as the old man pushed the youths aside. Then he raised his voice to call to Fyn. 'It's just as well the abbey sent you, we have a renegade Power-worker trying to get in.' He pointed to the gnarled tree.

Secretly terrified, Fyn fixed on the tree. How he wished he'd completed his training under the mystics master. He was no match for a Power-worker.

No one spoke.

The gnarled tree continued to look innocuous.

'Come out, you heathen wyvern!' Lame Klimen yelled. Several more heads had joined him on the gate tower and they added their abuse to his.

Nothing happened.

Joff jogged over to join them. 'There must be something you can do, Fyn.'

'Neither of us are trained mystics,' Feldspar whispered.

'True.' Fyn's fear receded as he thought things through. 'But if the Power-worker is so powerful, why is he hiding behind a tree, dodging the harpoon?'

'I'd be scared of a wyvern harpoon,' Joff offered.

Feldspar grinned. 'But you have no Affinity training. You can't manipulate the Unseen world.'

Fyn reached a decision and set off across the field towards the tree. As he approached, he made out someone huddled behind it, someone young with a large bundle that they cradled like a baby.

Fyn came to a stop as frightened, slightly lopsided eyes looked up at him from a dirty, tear-stained face. Odd, the renegade Power-worker might look like a grubby street urchin but they were wrapped in a rich Rolencian travelling fur, fit for a king.

The bundle in their arms stirred and made a soft interrogative sound that reminded Fyn of his sister's foenix. At the same moment his nostrils stung with a rush of Affinity power. 'What have you got there?'

The child's arms moved protectively and they muttered something that sounded Merofynian.

Fyn switched to his mother's native tongue. 'Whatever that is, it's giving off enough Affinity to make me sneeze.' And before he could help himself he did, sneezing three times in a row.

The child smiled reluctantly and let the blanket fall away to reveal a rare, feathered Affinity beast. 'It's a calandrius but it's injured. The kingson told me to take it to the village and ask for safe passage to Sylion Abbey in his name, but no one speaks Merofynian and they won't let me in.'

'Kingson, you say?' Fyn tried not to sound too excited. 'Byren or Lence?'

The child shrugged. 'He was nice and he had a crooked smile.'

'Byren.' So Byren was somewhere in the Rolencian valley. 'Where is he?'

She shrugged. 'He was on the king's business. He sent me here, but they won't let me in.'

'Well, you're lucky I came along. What's your name?'

'Dinni.'

Fyn leant forwards and offered his hand. 'Come on, Dinni.'

She did not accept his help or let him take the bird, but struggled to her feet alone. And, as she did, Fyn noticed a thick metal collar around her neck which had left angry marks on her pale skin. He had heard of Affinity-slaves but never actually seen one before. 'You're a runaway slave.'

'Sold to a Power-worker who beat me, but the kingson freed me and saved the calandrius.'

'That sounds like Byren.' A rush of pride filled Fyn, making it hard to speak. 'When did you see him?'

'Last night.'

So they were only a day apart. If Byren had run into a Merofynian Power-worker, and Fyn could not imagine how his brother had bested the Power-worker, Byren had to be headed back to Rolenhold to warn their father.

If Fyn set out tomorrow he would be two days behind Byren, with no chance of catching up. He had to reach the castle to report the violation of the abbey and the destruction of the warrior monks. That would be a blow to his father's battle plans.

'Master monk?' Dinni whispered.

'I'm no master, not even a monk, only an acolyte,' Fyn told her. 'Come on.'

He led her down the slope back to Feldspar and the others. Their eyes widened as he approached.

'Beware, Fyn,' Feldspar called. 'I smell Affinity on her from here.'

'It's safe,' Fyn assured them. 'The Affinity's coming off the calandrius. My brother sent her.'

'Calandrius?' Feldspar approached to take a look at the bird. The rest fell into step beside Fyn, giving the girl a wide berth. Fyn blinked a snowflake from his right eye as he looked up at the wary heads on the gate tower. 'This is Dinni, an escaped Affinity-slave who wants to claim sanctuary at Sylion Abbey. She brings a prized calandrius with her as a gift to the abbey. Open up.'

In a moment the gate was winched open. Fyn watched, thinking that the village's defences would hold off the occasional brigand or small raiding party, but not a Merofynian army. What would become of these people then? His father could not protect every small village across Rolencia's rich valley.

'Apologies, master monk,' Lame Klimen greeted Fyn, giving him the title of master even though the old man would have known by his plait that he was still an acolyte. 'We did not understand the slave.'

'And you were being cautious which is understandable, grandfather.' Fyn gave him the honorific title, and slowed his pace so that the fisherman could keep up with them, despite his pronounced limp. On closer inspection, Klimen was not so old, just weathered by the sea and too injured to remain a fisherman. When the five youths had a good look at Dinni they mocked each other, shamefaced.

Inside the wall, each little house had its own vegetable plot, empty now of anything but snow. The path wound through these blanketed gardens to the village square. Not even a bow shot across, it sloped down to the wharves.

By the time most of the boys had reached the square all the villagers had gathered. Some carried fish-oil lanterns, bringing an early twilight as well as the oil's distinctive scent.

Recognising the village elders by their air of authority, and by the way they greeted Lame Klimen, Fyn bowed to honour them. After Klimen explained who Dinni was, he turned to Fyn. 'Why has the abbot sent Halcyon's boys and acolytes to us?'

'To save our lives. Last night Merofynians violated the sanctity of the abbey, killing everyone else.'

'No. Never!' an old woman objected. 'Never in all my days...'

The fisher folk muttered in dismay.

'But the warriors?' Lame Klimen asked. 'Surely they –'

'Lured away. Only the very old and the boys stayed in the abbey,' Fyn explained. 'We are all that remain of Halcyon's monks. We've walked all night and eaten nothing for a day.'

Lenny made a funny noise in his throat and pitched forwards.

'Oh, the poor bantling,' an old woman muttered, catching him before he could hit the ground. 'Enough talking. It's clear what these boys need.'

At her words the womenfolk stepped in, leading the boys off. There would not be enough beds, but at least they would be warm and fed. Fyn was grateful. He was so tired he could barely think and all the while there was the worry for Piro and the need to reach his father weighing him down. Lame Klimen stepped aside to organise the men, sending any male over the age of fourteen to the walls.

Lenny revived and protested as the woman tried to lead him away.

'I've got hot fish stew cooking on the hearth,' she told him.

'Go on, Lenny,' Fyn urged, then switched to Merofynian. 'You too, Dinni.'

She looked doubtful but, when the old woman smiled and nodded, she allowed herself to be led away even as Klimen returned. He gave Fyn a bow which felt wrong to him, especially in front of Feldspar and Joff, who knew he was nothing special.

'You're welcome to take your ease in my place, master monk,' Lame Klimen said.

'I'm no master,' Fyn insisted.

'If you've led these boys to safety, then you've done the work of a master,' the old fisherman told him. 'This way.'

'All I did was lead them here so they could take shelter in Sylion Abbey,' Fyn said.

'Only women and girls are allowed past the abbey's portals.'

'I think the abbess will put aside the old laws for now.'

Lame Klimen led them through the now-dark village to his home. A welcome light glowed in the single pane of uneven blown glass.

He thrust the door open and they hurried in before the warm air could escape. An incredibly ancient woman bustled about setting food on the scrubbed table. She smiled and bobbed her head.

'My mother,' he explained. 'She can't hear what you say but that doesn't stop her talking.'

They took folding stools off their hooks on the walls and placed them around the table. As Feldspar took the seat next to Fyn, he muttered, 'We're not safe yet.'

'No,' Fyn agreed and raised his voice. 'Tomorrow morning, Klimen, your people need to take the boys across to Sylion.'

'That we can do.'

'You're not coming with us?' Feldspar guessed.

'Not coming?' Joff placed the sacred lamp on the table. Its jewel-encrusted gold looked out of place amidst the wooden bowls and home-made bread.

'No. The abbot told me to get the boys to Sylion Abbey and then I –'

'You have to warn the king,' Feldspar finished for him.

Fyn nodded. 'You must tell the abbess how the Merofynians lured our warriors out and ignored the sanctity of the abbey. She'll see it's in Sylion's best interest to help Halcyon's monks to survive.'

Feldspar met Fyn's eyes. 'The Merofynians will kill you first chance they get. Take some of us with you.'

Fyn had already thought this through. 'One can escape detection more easily than several. I don't want anyone dying because of me.' No, the abbot had already paid that price. If his friends knew the truth they would not be looking up to him right now.

'Ah, food, at last. Thank you, grandmother.' Joff accepted a bowl of fish stew. 'Don't look so down, Feldspar. Fyn will get through to the king, who'll rout the Merofynians. You'll see. One day it will be Abbot Fyn. I'll be weapons master and you'll be mystics master.'

But Feldspar was in no mood for jesting. 'How can I become mystics master, when there is no one to train me?' He sighed. 'So much lost.'

'You can rebuild the abbey in all its glory. You have your lives,' Lame Klimen told them.

Both Feldspar and Joff looked to Fyn.

'Thanks to you,' Feldspar said.

He could not meet their eyes. Instead, he looked up at the single window, dark with snow, visualising his father's castle across the valley, directly opposite Sylion Abbey as the crow flies, but since he was not a crow Fyn would have to walk around the base of Mount Halcyon, borrow skates, cross Viridian Lake and thread his way along the canals to Sapphire Lake. 'The king must know of this treachery. If the Merofynians don't respect the sanctity of the abbey, who knows where they will stop?'

What if the unthinkable happened? What if Rolenhold fell? Would the Merofynians recognise the time-honoured right of royal captives to be held hostage, or would they simply execute Piro and his mother?

He had to get home.

CHAPTER EIGHT

PIRO LONGED TO ask her mother's advice, but Cobalt was sure to have spies watching the queen. If he had remembered a little detail like Piro's love for her foenix, he won't have left any avenue open for her to reach her mother or father.

Even so, after she had eaten, she found her feet taking her to the mourning tower, where her mother was captive. The tower's courtyard was filled with animals, which the townsfolk had penned in hastily rigged shelters. Chickens and goats had settled for the night, making the area smell like a farm yard. And there, at the top of the steps to the tower's first floor, was one of the king's honour guard.

That reminded her of Sawtree. She knew of a window where she could look down into the stable courtyard. She'd go there next and see what she could do for the old guard.

The guard in front of her was one of the young ones loyal to Cobalt, lord protector of the castle. That role should have gone to Captain Temor...

That reminded her of Temor and his stand at the last gate. A sob caught in her throat.

Furious, she pressed the pads of her fingers into her eye sockets until she saw swirling patterns of rage. No point in crying. No point in feeling sorry for herself. Feel sorry for Sawtree instead. Maybe there was something she could do for him... sneak him food, since she had saved some from her last meal. Or, if she was really lucky, she might slip him a knife and he could free himself when he had the chance. How had Cobalt punished him, by crippling him? She hoped it wasn't something permanent.

One more grubby maid amongst so many, Piro made her way to the wing that overlooked the stable courtyard. It housed the castle hospice, packed now with injured townsfolk. Many had loved ones with them, nursing them, so there was a constant coming and going, with children crying and grown-ups bickering over space.

From a narrow window in the hospice she saw a man in the centre of the courtyard with his arms tied above his head, toes off the ground, head slumped. There was an ominous dark patch in the snowy ground under his feet. It was only as he slowly swung around that she saw the arrows in his chest. Stunned, she found it hard to credit what she saw.

It appeared as though, at Cobalt's orders, Sawtree's fellow men-at-arms had used him for target practice.

Impotent anger rose up in her, threatened to choke her, and hot tears ran down her cheeks as she left the hospice. Cobalt would pay for this.

Miserable fury raged through her as she wandered her home, recalling the many dreams where she had run down the corridors chased by wyverns, the Merofynian symbol. She should have heeded those dreams instead of trying to quell them with dreamless-sleep.

Halcyon must have been watching over Piro, for she found herself near the goddess's chantry with no memory of how she got there. She had slept under the nave last night. With the wardess dead there was only the healer to serve the temple and both Halcyon and Sylion's healers had been caring for her father. So the chantry would be empty of nuns.

As Piro had suspected it was empty of church officials, but thick with the scent of burning votive candles and full of desperate townspeople, praying to the goddess to bring them to safety. Piro entered, just one more desperate penitent. She ignored her royal family's private box and found a dark corner where she prayed, then dozed.

Not the cold, not the hard stone or the crowding, nothing could not stop her from falling into the deep sleep. Tomorrow was another day. Things would be better.

She had to believe this.

* * *

FYN SHOULD HAVE been asleep on the stone hearth in front of Lame Klimen's fire but he could not rest. Every time he closed his eyes, he saw himself fleeing down the abbey's stair while the others held off the Merofynians on the landing above.

He knew it was illogical to feel guilty about leaving the old masters and his fellow acolytes to die – without him, Lenny and the rest of the boys would have been trapped and killed. But this did not stop the sick rush of emotion.

It had been the kind of critical tactical decision the weapons master had been training him for all this time and he understood it, even if he didn't like it.

What really ate away at him was the knowledge that, if he hadn't frozen, the abbot might still be alive and able to rebuild the abbey.

Why had he seized up? He'd never failed in practice.

That was practice, this was nothing like the bouts with the weapons master.

Oakstand had taught that sometimes it was necessary to kill to save an innocent life. But when Fyn had imagined enemies they were faceless warriors with bad hearts, not ordinary men like his father's loyal men-at-arms, whose misfortune it was to serve the wrong king.

He rolled over and tried to think of something pleasant. At least Piro was safe in Rolenhold. But this didn't make him feel any better. He felt a niggle of worry every time he thought of her.

Feldspar jerked awake, alert and troubled, hand pressed to his heart.

'Bad dream?' Fyn asked, lifting on one elbow.

Feldspar inhaled sharply and sat up. 'Don't you feel it? My Affinity is itching like a –' His eyes widened and he glanced down to where his hand pressed to his heart. No, not to his heart. He pulled the Fate out from under his vest.

The seashell-shaped stone glowed fiercely, bright as a captured star. Fyn swallowed.

'It's beautiful,' Joff marvelled, as he also sat up. 'Perhaps the goddess herself has seen our plight and seeks to comfort us.'

Feldspar's hand closed over the stone, trapping the light so that only a deep orange seeped through the crevices between his fingers. Fyn wondered if it felt as hot as it appeared. As he watched, his friend's beatific expression faded and a sheen of sweat covered his skin. Feldspar's breath caught in a gasp and, when another breath failed to follow, Fyn grabbed the hand that held the Fate intending to prise it free, but...

...the instant he made contact with the Fate, a vision swamped him.

Cold leached into the very marrow of his bones. As good as dead, he lay wedged between bloodied corpses. Above him on the edge of a rocky ledge, torch-wielding men tossed another body over and it plummeted down, landing on top of him, burying him alive. His heart tried to climb out of his throat.

An imperative came to him.

Run. Leave the abbey. Flee for your lives. We are betrayed!

Fyn tried to run but his body wouldn't obey. His legs felt strangely stiff and disjointed. He recognised that terrifying dream sensation, where every movement takes incredible effort and happens too slowly. Yet he knew this wasn't a dream. It was a vision, and it was imperative he escape. It felt as if his heart would burst with the effort.

'Fyn!' Joff bellowed, as something snapped his head around, making one side of his face throb. Another blow sent him off his knees onto his back, knocking the air from his chest.

His sight cleared to discover Joff hovering over him, ready to deliver a third blow.

'Stop,' he croaked, lifting arms that ached from exertion, even though he had been sitting still.

Joff scrambled aside and turned to Feldspar. Fyn struggled to his knees to find his friend collapsed on the hearth stone, bleeding from his nose.

'You didn't have to hit him so hard, Joff,' Fyn protested, his voice a mere thread.

'I didn't hit him at all. His nose started to bleed when you touched the Fate.'

Fyn crawled over, touching Feldspar's forehead, feeling for the pulse in his throat, for signs of breathing. Good. He wasn't dead. 'Feldspar, can you hear me?'

His friend's eyes flickered open, fixing on Fyn.

'Have to escape!' Urgency warred with exhaustion.

'We've already escaped. We're safe. Remember?'

Feldspar frowned, then nodded and tried to sit up. Fyn went to help him but the Fate brushed his hand and he jerked back instinctively. Joff cast him a quick glance, then helped Feldspar, who hugged his knees, trembling.

'What did you two see?' Joff whispered. 'Was it the same thing?'

Fyn glanced to Feldspar who shivered, either unable or unwilling to speak.

'A mass grave filled with bodies,' Fyn whispered. 'Men with torches were throwing more bodies in on top of me... on top of Master Catillum, I mean.' He looked to Feldspar for confirmation.

'If you say so,' Feldspar muttered. 'All I felt was cold, a terrible cold. And the need to run.'

Joff turned to Fyn for an explanation.

'Sensation without sight,' Fyn guessed. That would have been even more terrifying. But he didn't say anything. Feldspar had always been the clever, nervy one, now his friend looked fragile.

Feldspar wiped blood from his lips and chin. 'If the Merofynians are throwing bodies into a mass grave, Master Catillum amongst them, the weapons master and all the warrior monks must be dead.'

Fyn nodded. 'So we know for certain that they were ambushed and the cream of Halcyon's warrior monks defeated. The Merofynians would have travelled with Power-workers just as we had our mystics. It's a wonder Master Catillum had any strength left to use the Fate.' Fyn imagined the mystics master injured, half-frozen with the use of only one arm. 'Poor Catillum, he wasn't dead when they threw him into the mass grave, but –'

'They couldn't have dug a trench,' Joff, the farmer's son, objected. 'The ground is still frozen. They must be throwing them into a ravine.'

'Whatever it was,' Fyn conceded, 'Master Catillum was being buried alive.'

'Probably the safest place for him,' Feldspar muttered. 'Lay low until they leave, then crawl out.'

Fyn nodded slowly. 'If he can get out with that withered arm.'

No one spoke for a while. A branch crumpled in the fire, revealing glowing coals. Fyn shivered, shaken by the vision, even if the experience had been secondhand.

'You must let him know we are safe,' Feldspar whispered and removed the Fate's chain, thrusting it towards Fyn.

Fyn shook his head, eyeing the seashell stone where a residual glow still lingered in its opalescent spirals. 'I'm not touching that thing.'

'You have to. You have an Affinity with the Fate. I don't. Take it.' Feldspar forced it into Fyn's hands. 'Since I joined the abbey, all I ever wanted was to train as a mystic. But I know my limits. When the Fate had me I felt like my head was going to burst. Any more and I think it would have.' He touched his nose, which was still bleeding sluggishly, then fixed on Fyn. 'You have to concentrate on Master Catillum to make contact, then send him a picture of us escaping from the caves and looking across to Sylion Abbey. He can guess from that where we'll be hiding. We need him.'

Fyn's stomach churned. He did not want to summon the Fate's powers again. But Master Catillum had risked exposing himself to the Merofynian army's Power-worker to contact them. He deserved to know the abbey's boys were safe. If the master could get to Sylion Abbey, Catillum could begin to rebuild Halcyon Abbey.

'What...' Joff began. 'What if you contact the wrong Power-worker? The nearest one must be with the Merofynians who took the abbey.'

Feldspar met Fyn's gaze, waiting for his response.

Fyn closed his eyes. Could he reach only Master Catillum? He shivered, remembering the cold, and the way the body plummeted towards him. It was so easy to imagine himself back in that moment. 'I think I can.'

Feldspar offered Fyn his hand. Another bead of blood seeped from his nostrils. 'Do you want my help?'

'No, I'll manage.'

Fyn closed his eyes, the better to concentrate. It was not hard to recall the body spiralling down towards him, the sense of entrapment...

All around him it was quiet, the quiet waiting of the dead. He was weighed down by the dead...

He was the mystics master.

Fyn recalled the fisher folk sheltering the boys. He visualised the distant cliffs with Sylion Abbey standing silhouetted against the sky.

A sense of relief washed over him and he realised it was Master Catillum's emotion. The sensation was so unnerving, he pulled back instinctively. The world dropped out from under his feet. He fell through nothing.

He was nothing... the gorge rose in his throat.

Suddenly he was in his body again, pitching forwards as he threw up all over his knees.

The horrible wracking spasms eventually passed and Fyn wiped his mouth with the back of his hand, supporting himself with a trembling arm.

'Here.' Joff offered Fyn a beaker of water from the bucket by the fire.

'Thanks.' Fyn could only croak.

'Fish stew,' Feldspar muttered. 'Smells just as bad the second time around. Think I'm –'

As he gagged, Fyn felt another spasm take him and, together, they staggered outside to throw up in the snowdrift by the door. They both heaved until they had nothing left to bring up.

Fyn sat back on his heels and picked up a handful of fresh snow to wipe his face. He laughed, even as tears stung his eyes.

'You're crazy,' Feldspar muttered, but he also grinned.

Fyn felt weak but oddly lighter and happier. They both sucked on fresh snow to rinse their mouths.

By the time they returned to the cottage, the old woman had lit a fish-oil lamp and was already cleaning up. She took one look at them and clicked her tongue on the roof of her mouth. 'Off with those clothes.'

Both Fyn and Feldspar protested but she couldn't hear them and, anyway, she wouldn't have taken no for an answer, so they stripped down. Joff didn't bother to hide his grin. Fyn removed his abbey leggings and the borrowed shirt with a sense of finality. Feldspar removed his robe. The old woman took the clothes off to wash and they were left in nothing but their breech cloths, huddled before the fire.

Lame Klimen fetched a patchwork quilt. It smelt just like him and was still warm from his body but they accepted it gratefully.

Under cover of the quilt Fyn undid the chain that held the Fate. 'I'm not going to Sylion Abbey. You keep this, Feldspar.'

Pale and shaken, his friend shook his head. 'No. You keep it, Fyn. I can't use it.'

Fyn gave an unsteady laugh. 'What makes you think I can?'

'If it's activated again while I'm wearing it I fear my brains will come pouring out my nose,' Feldspar said, his face naked of pretence.

Fyn shuddered.

Without warning, the woman pulled the quilt off their shoulders. Thrusting an armful of clothes at them, she said, 'Might be a bit big.'

Fyn and Feldspar unrolled the leggings and fisherman smocks. They dressed hastily, cold despite the thick walls of the cottage.

After tugging the smock over his shoulders, Feldspar pulled the acolyte plait free. 'At least Catillum knows we escaped. You did well, Fyn.'

But he couldn't shake the feeling that he had failed. If only he'd realised the original message from King Rolen was a fake. Then the abbot wouldn't have sent the fighting monks out and the abbey wouldn't have fallen. If only Fyn hadn't frozen, then the abbot would still be alive.

A wave of despair washed over him.

He could not change the past but he could influence the future. He must warn his father that the abbey had fallen. King Rolen would have to rethink his battle campaign.

CHAPTER NINE

BYREN FELT A prod in his back, then another. What was Lence up to? Couldn't he see he was sleeping? Trust his twin to get pleasure out of waking him. He shouldn't have drunk so much last night. On top of that his side hurt with every breath he took. Must have been in a fight.

'Look what I found, Da,' a child's high voice pierced Byren's foggy brain. 'A dead man.'

And it all came back to Byren with horrible clarity.

Lence was dead. Rolencia had been invaded and the abbey had fallen. He'd been mortally injured. He must reach his father while he still had breath in his body. King Rolen had to know that there was no help coming from the abbey.

'Go stand with Miron.' The adult spoke sharply.

'Is he dead, Da?' a third voice asked, cracking on the last word. Byren placed him at about thirteen winters.

'Lotsa blood. Smells real gamey, been sleeping in the snow,' the father muttered. 'If he's not dead, he should be.'

Byren felt hands roll him over and managed to prise his eyes open. There was barely enough light to see in the pale, predawn grey of late winter but he did notice the man's stained fingers. A dyer by profession.

'Ulfr... 'ware the pack!' Byren croaked.

'What's he saying, Da?' the thirteen-year-old asked.

'Must've seen the same tracks we saw.' The dyer peered down into Byren's face. 'You're lucky Rodien spotted your body half-covered in snow. Rolencia's been invaded, so we're headed for the Divide. Or maybe I don't need to tell you that?'

'Merofynians,' Byren whispered.

'Should we take him with us, Da?' Miron asked.

'Can't leave him here.'

'Seep,' Byren warned. 'Pack inna seep.'

'No sign of a seep around here,' the dyer told him, making Byren wonder if it had all been a hallucination for, as far as he knew, he was in the same place where he had lain down with the pack. Or thought he had. Had he been delirious?

'Do you think you can stand? Reckon I can't lift a big fella like you.' The dyer helped haul him upright.

Byren gasped as he felt the wound tug something fierce, but made it to his feet. He was too weak. He had to face it. He couldn't get the message to his father.

The man studied Byren. 'Reckon you need a healer. Have to put you on the sled.'

No healer could save him. 'No point.'

'Can't leave a man to freeze in the snow,' the dyer muttered. 'Come along.'

Byren didn't have the energy to argue as the dyer helped him up the slope towards his sons. At a glance Byren took in Miron. He had the look of a boy who had grown fast, as if he hadn't had time to get used to the length of his arms and legs. The youth soothed the pony as Byren approached, while a boy of about four watched him with wide brown eyes. The pony pulled a sled laden with belongings which the father rearranged to make room for him.

'Wait,' Byren protested as they strapped him onto the sled. 'Have to get to Rolenhold. Merofynians –'

'I know. Marching on Rolenton,' the dyer agreed. 'My eldest, Miron, came home as soon as the king ordered the townsfolk into the castle.'

Byren blinked. 'The abbey's fallen. Can't look for help from them. Must warn m'father –'

'I know who you are!' The dyer announced, peering into his face. 'You're Byren Kingson. You have the look of King Rolen. Served a summer under him when I was seventeen, keeping the warlords in their place. My eldest was going to offer service when his time came.'

'I'm offering now,' Miron insisted. 'I only come back to warn you, Da.'

Byren nodded. Most able-bodied men served a summer or two on the high Divide. 'Send your boy to the castle. He must warn my father that the abbey's fallen.'

But how would this skinny youth convince the king that the message came from Byren, when he'd lost his royal foenix pendant? Byren reached inside his woollen vest, feeling for the two leather thongs he wore. Should he send the foenix spurs taken when he and Lence tried to capture the foenix, or the leogryf teeth? The leogryf was most recent. He hauled the leather thong with its teeth out from inside his vest and lifted his head to remove it. Even this exhausted him.

Blinking blearily, Byren fixed on the earnest Miron. 'Take this to King Rolen. Tell him the abbey has fallen, that I have been injured and that Lence...' Byren could not go on as the loss hit him. He shuddered and his stomach heaved. 'Lence died bravely.'

The dyer squeezed his shoulder. 'My boy will make sure your message gets to King Rolen.'

Byren nodded, and let himself slip into a state of numb exhaustion. Now that he wasn't bringing the abbey's warriors to help his father crush the invaders, how would he prove his loyalty?

PIRO KNEW SHE was dreaming and she knew how it would end but she couldn't escape. With her mother and old nurse locked up there was no dreamless-sleep to dull her Affinity-induced premonitions. All she could do was hold on and go along for the ride.

In the vision, she hovered just behind her father as he rode out of Rolenhold, resplendent in the manticore chestplate that was Byren's gift. Behind him rode half a dozen of his oldest and most trusted honour guard, men who had been youths and stood at his back when it seemed his kingdom would fall thirty years ago. Now they rode with him to face the Merofynians again.

A wash of frustration rolled through Piro. What was wrong with people? Why couldn't they get on with their lives, instead of making war?

With typical dream suddenness her father now confronted a warlord in Rolenton Square. The warlord rode under the banner of Merofynia but it was clear he was a spar warrior. This was different. In the previous dreams, Merofynian warriors had been in the castle, masquerading as wyverns as they hunted her family.

She knew with the omniscience of a dreamer that the warlord had demanded Rolencia's surrender and that her father had no intention of surrendering. He wanted to meet his enemy to get the man's measure. But the warlord had other ideas.

He dropped his guise, dissolving into the form of an amfina, the twin-headed, winged lizard-snake. While one head smiled and talked with her father, the other signalled assassins in the form of wyverns.

Piro tried to warn her father, but he couldn't hear her dream voice. Frustration tore at her.

Still smiling, the Amfina warlord stepped back and the wyverns plunged in, aiming straight for her father. Old Lord Steadfast tried to protect him but a wyvern shattered his head with one terrible blow. Though Piro had never liked the pompous man, tears stung her eyes. She could do nothing as the wyverns tore her father and his honour guard to pieces.

'Girlie, here girlie. Wake up,' a creaky old voice urged, breaking the paralysis that held Piro captive to the dream vision.

She rolled into a crouch like a cat, heart pounding, stomach heaving. The logical part of her mind told her she didn't have to worry about her father, safe in his sick bed.

The woman eyed Piro warily but her words were kind enough. 'Bad dream, eh? Well, that's not surprising for all that we're safe behind Rolenhold's great walls. Take heart, love. The king defeated Merofynia once before. He'll do it again.'

Piro nodded. Even if her father was crippled by Merofynian treachery, there were still her brothers. Lence and Byren were mighty warriors and canny strategists. She shuddered and pushed back dark tangled hair from her face, thinking how her old nurse would frown to see her like this.

'Feeling better?' the woman asked.

Piro nodded.

'Come share our breakfast. It's not much, but it's hot.'

Piro smelt honey-oat cakes and her stomach heaved. 'Thank you, but I don't think I can eat right now.'

The woman nodded. 'Then come sit by the brazier.'

Piro gave in and joined the family group, who'd had the forethought to bring a small travelling brazier. Oat cakes lay toasting on its griddle and cinnamon milk steamed in a pot. Several children made room for her and she started to feel a little better. It was odd to sit here in the chantry, which was usually so solemn, and see it turned into an impromptu home for so many.

'Nan, Nan.' A boy of about ten darted through the other family groups to join them. 'King Rolen's about to ride out to speak with the Merofynians.'

Piro sprang to her feet. 'But he's sick. He can't ride out.'

'He is!' the boy insisted. 'I saw him and his honour guard heading for the stables. And he's wearing a real manticore chestplate!'

Piro ran. No one tried to stop her as she dashed out of the chantry, heading through a courtyard, along a hall, down stairs and out into the stable yard.

Good, she wasn't too late. It was still packed with spectators, stable lads, old gaffers offering advice and men-at-arms. She hesitated, taking in the crowd.

No sign of Sawtree. What had they done with his body?

No sign of Cobalt. He was probably up on the gate tower.

The king and his honour guard rode out of the stables, already mounted. In his armour, helmet and cloak her father still looked magnificent, but she had seen him bedridden last night. What had the healers given him to help him get about today? Whatever it was, it was sure to take a toll on his reserves.

Piro darted between the mounted men and grabbed her father's boot.

'Eh, Piro? They told me you'd gone to Sylion Abbey.' He frowned down at her, then cupped her cheek in one hand, his face a mixture of pain and love. 'You shouldn't be here, little Piro. You should be safe at the abbey.'

'You mustn't meet the warlord.'

His expression hardened.

She recognised that look. This was the face he wore when he was dispensing justice or sending her brothers out to protect Rolencia's borders. Even so, she had to try. 'You mustn't, Father. You should be in bed. You're sick.'

He grimaced. Through the contact of his roughened hands she had a flash of Affinity-induced insight. He did not fear death, he had faced it enough times to know this old foe. What he feared was dying by degrees, a shrivelled, pitiful parody of what he had once been.

Even so, she had to try. 'You can't go out there, Father. The Merofynians will turn on you.'

'No harm will come to us under a flag of truce. I'm only going to size up the enemy, Piro. Besides, I can't sit up here and not answer Palatyne's bluster!'

'But...' Unlike her mother, who had let her own father sail to his death, Piro could not let her father ride out to his. Besides, he already knew she had Affinity so she had nothing to lose. Piro strained on tip toes, keeping her voice low. 'I had a vision. I saw them turn on you and your men.'

He drew back, shaking his head. 'This is war, Piro. We have our code. He might be a spar upstart but he is overlord of the Merofynian army now, in service to King Merofyn. As such he's bound by the code of –'

'I've seen into his heart. He's a two-headed snake, Father. He smiles with one head and spits death with the other.'

Revulsion for anything to do with Affinity travelled across King Rolen's face. His features hardened. 'Let go of my leg and not another word. You are a kingsdaughter, Piro, you should understand. I must go out to meet this overlord or be shamed before my men.'

She understood. He rode to his death for the sake of honour. With a sob she turned and fled.

FYN STOOD ON the wharf to farewell the last of the acolytes and boys, who were about to sail across the bay to Sylion Abbey.

The small fishing boats looked vulnerable as they set off under a low-slung grey sky, travelling across a sullen, dark green sea. Hardly a ripple disturbed the bay's oily surface and only the tips of ice chunks could be seen, with most of their bulk just visible below the water line. Mere minutes in that water would mean death. Fyn repressed a shudder. Although he could swim, he hated the sea.

About a bow shot from the wharf, safely on the way to Sylion Abbey, Joff waved Halcyon's Sacred Lamp, a small warm glow in the otherwise grey day. Fyn smiled as Lenny waved solemnly from Joff's side. Feldspar was already waiting on the far shore with the rest of the acolytes and Dinni.

This morning, a chapter of Fyn's life had ended, and he felt the finality of it. With a shiver, he tightened the toggles on his borrowed sheepskin jacket. The sea was Sylion's domain. He belonged to Halcyon and he was glad he was going by land.

'Ready?' Lame Klimen's granddaughter asked. She was about ten years of age, and her face almost disappeared under a too-large cap. The tips of her dark plaits were streaked gold by the summer sun. She grinned at him. 'Though I don't know why you would walk, when you could sail halfway there!'

'You feel at home on a ship's deck, I prefer solid ground,' Fyn told her. The elders had tried to convince him to sail to Port Marchand, then skate the lakes and canals to Sapphire Lake. Fyn had considered this, but decided against it. With a pair of borrowed skis and skates, he could reach the nearest canal and be in Rolenton in three days, or less if he did not stop to rest.

The girl led Fyn away from the wharves. 'Come on, Great Granna has travelling food prepared for you, master monk.'

'I am not a master, not even a monk, only a –'

'If you don't want to be known as a monk, wear this.' She tugged off her sheepskin cap, reaching up to plant it crookedly on his head. 'Cover your skull tattoo and pretend that skinny plait comes from a full head of hair.'

Fyn straightened the sheepskin cap, which covered his ears and was wonderfully warm. His plait had not been cut since he entered the abbey at the age of six, and it fell to his waist. This spring cusp it would have been shaved off, when he left the ranks of the acolytes and became a monk. Already a dark fuzz threatened to cover the tattoos because he hadn't shaved his head for two mornings. In a couple of weeks he would be able to cut off his plait and no one would guess he had been a monk. They'd think he'd been sick and had shorn his head because of the fever.

Loss tugged at him, but he did not have time to mourn.

'There's Great Granna and Granda,' the girl said, skipping towards the old woman and Lame Klimen. He waited at the gate along with the rest of the village who had come to see him off.

The old woman handed Fyn a shoulder pack, saying. 'This should last you.'

He thanked her even though he knew she couldn't hear.

'Your clothes are a bit big, but you'll be safer as a fisherman than a monk,' Lame Klimen told him.

Fyn looked around at the villagers then held the old man's eyes for a heartbeat. They needed to talk. Privately.

Taking his meaning, Lame Klimen stepped through the gate with him.

Fyn gestured to the gate and wall. 'Your defences won't hold against the Merofynians. You must go to Port Cobalt.'

The old man rubbed his chin. 'The port defends the valley from the Lesser Sea. The Merofynians are sure to attack it to bring in supplies. But our village...' He shrugged. 'Who would bother to attack us? Besides, we can run up to the cave. I'll have my people store food and blankets up there. We always kept it stocked when I was a youth, but we haven't bothered since I was a young man. That's what thirty years of peace does to you.'

Fyn bent to strap on his skis. 'I hope you are right. I appreciate your help. I don't know what's going to happen,' he straightened up, 'but if we come through this I'll –'

'Don't worry.' Lame Klimen touched his arm. 'When the nobles make war they make their names. When the people make war they make sacrifices. Remember this and you will be a good king, one day.'

'I'm not going to be king,' Fyn objected, but Lame Klimen only nodded, smiled and stepped back to wave him off.

The villagers on the gate tower waved and cheered.

Fyn returned their wave and set off. Somehow he must get across Rolencia with Merofynian warriors roaming the countryside, and reach his family.

PIRO'S SLIPPERED FEET made no sound as she raced through the busy yards and passages. When she found herself in the courtyard at the base of the mourning tower, she could only think of one thing, telling her mother. The queen had always been able to guide the king with a subtle word here or there. If anyone could convince her father not to ride out, her mother could.

She surveyed the courtyard. Between townsfolk come to check on their animals and others come to discuss the news, the courtyard was as busy as a hiring fair market. The shouts of a pugnacious, bald man attracted her attention. He was disputing the ownership of a goat with a harassed pregnant woman. His bullying manner told Piro he had every intention of winning the argument.

Determined to get past the guards, Piro snatched a red speckled bantam hen that had slipped its cage and headed across the courtyard, with the vague intention of attempting bribery.

Two of the guards stood on the bottom of the external stair to the first-floor entrance, deep in discussion. She knew them to be honourable men. They weren't part of her father's original honour guard but they both knew her by sight, so that ruled out approaching them herself.

The bald bully raised his voice again and gave the pregnant woman a shove. That decided Piro. She tapped a boy of about six on the shoulder and thrust the chicken into his arms.

'Give this to the guards. Tell them the bald man sent it.' She jerked her head towards the two who were still arguing.

The boy nodded and tucked the chicken under his arm. Piro watched as the guard received the chicken, glanced to the man and went over to settle the argument.

Piro smiled, because these were honourable men, they would not accept bribes.

She ran up the steps. Now there was just the guard at her mother's door, but when she got there she found he had left his post. Probably stepped out to relieve himself, knowing the others guarded the base of the tower.

'Mother?' Piro tapped at the door.

'Piro? What are you doing here? Where's the –'

'He's gone.' Piro gulped, her words rushing over themselves. 'Father's going to ride out to meet the Merofynian commander. Palatyne will kill him. I know he will. You've got to stop it.'

There was a moment's silence.

'Mother?'

'Listen, Piro.' It was Seela, her old nurse. 'Can you see the key?'

She glanced around. There was a tray, with what was left of the guard's breakfast right under the narrow window. 'No.'

And even as she said it, she realised it was pointless to worry her mother with Father's fate, when there was nothing the queen could do. 'I'm sorry. I –'

'Don't fret, Piro,' Seela told her. 'You can't be sure. Dream visions –'

'Piro?' her mother broke in. 'Run to the top of Eagle Tower. From there you can see Rolenton Square. And I can see the top of Eagle Tower from my window. If Rolen falls, signal me. Can you do that?'

'I can. I'll wave my smock,' Piro whispered. Perhaps there was something her mother could do. 'I'm going now.'

'Wait. Piro?'

'I'm still here.'

'If Rolenhold falls –'

'It'll never fall!'

'If the castle falls we'll need to negotiate surrender. Dress as befits a kingsdaughter.'

'If it comes to that I will,' Piro agreed, dismissing it as an impossibility. 'I'm going now.'

She turned and ran down the steps, pausing on the landing at the first-floor doorway. The altercation over the goat was still going strong, only now the bully was denying that he had tried to bribe the guards with a stolen chicken.

It was the work of only a few minutes to reach Eagle Tower. By the time Piro climbed to the top, her heart was pounding like a drum, but she wasn't hot and bothered. Instead shivers shook her body and her teeth chattered so that even clenching her jaw didn't stop them.

The castle's parapets were thick with people watching the confrontation, while a dozen castle servants had climbed Eagle Tower. Piro burrowed through them to get a viewing spot. They were all straining to see the king's party and no one paid her any attention. The family's banner, a flash of deep red on black, attracted her eye as her father and his companions rode into Rolenton's square. The large bonfire had burned down, only a thin finger of smoke rose on the air.

Overlord Palatyne waited astride his great black warhorse. The Merofynian banner stood behind him, stretched on two poles. Piro could just make out the shape of a rearing wyvern depicted in rich azure.

Her father rode out under a flag of truce. According to the code of war the overlord would threaten and bluster, while King Rolen would dare him to do his worst. They would trade insults, then the Rolencian party would ride back to the castle and wait for the warrior monks to arrive. That was how it should have gone, but Piro knew better.

Being so far away she could only read large actions. Overlord Palatyne gestured to his warriors. King Rolen gestured to the castle.

Movement drew Piro's eye to insect-like creatures which crept across the roofs of the houses that faced onto the square. Bowmen... silent assassins. Her mouth went dry.

Their presence might just be a display of strength.

But when they stood and drew their bows, notching arrows, she knew. A silent scream of warning drove the air from her lungs.

Overlord Palatyne gestured to the roof tops around the square. It was the same gesture his second amfina head had used in her vision.

She read defiance in her father's stance, defiance and contempt.

Tears stung her eyes. He would get his wish. King Rolen would die in battle. Palatyne raised his arm. The arrows flew.

The king's chitin chest plate withstood the barrage, while around him his honour guard went down. The survivors drew swords and tried to engage the Merofynians, but Palatyne's swordsmen held back, letting the bowmen soften them up before they moved in.

King Rolen's horse reared as he signalled his remaining men. They formed a defensive circle around the banner, raising their shields. At this, the swordsmen rushed them, dragging the men from their mounts.

Piro's breath caught in her throat. At this distance she could only just hear the clash of metal and roar of voices. Her father and his men were like characters in a play as they fought on, hopelessly outnumbered.

Numbly, she watched the struggle. The Rolencian banner dipped, then fell. Finally, the fighting ceased. Men pulled back, wiping their weapons, leaving a litter of bodies. One man plucked something from amidst the fallen, then strode over to Palatyne to present the foenix banner.

The overlord swung it by the pole so all could see. He cantered his mount over to the still-burning remains of the bonfire, tossing the banner into the flames. His men cheered.

Piro's vision swam. Her father was dead. Hot fury seared away her grief. King Rolen had refused to use the foreknowledge her Affinity gave her. He had chosen to die. She was so angry with him she could have hit him.

And it struck her that, although she had not made the same mistake as her mother, her father had still died.

High on Eagle Tower, all around Piro the servants exclaimed, stunned and indignant.

Piro ran to the far side of the tower. Several courtyards over, the mourning tower's top floor was visible above the intervening roofs. Two pale faces peered from a window. Piro tore off her white maid's over-smock and waved it. Someone bumped her and the smock fell like a wounded bird, fluttering all the way down to the crowded courtyard below.

'Sorry,' a young candle-trimmer muttered. His eyes widened when he recognised her.

Piro pressed a finger to her lips and he nodded. She took off down the stairs.

She had to reach her mother and make plans. Rolenhold would not be taken.

The loyal warlords would come to their aid. Byren would bring back the abbey's warrior monks, and he and Lence would crush the Merofynians. They had only to shut Rolenhold's gates and hold out until help came. The people would be dismayed by Palatyne's treachery but they must not lose heart. What the castle needed now was strong leadership.

With all the confusion, perhaps she could steal the key from the guard and free her mother. Quick as thought, her feet carried her across the first courtyard, where she heard the cries of despair and outrage as the news of the king's murder spread. Many townspeople wept openly and it struck Piro that they had loved her father.

With their reaction came understanding. The Merofynian overlord had broken the code of war and killed King Rolen, to break the will of Rolencia, but he would not succeed.

By the time Piro reached the courtyard below the mourning tower, the news was already ahead of her and the townsfolk lamented loudly. Piro's hands closed in fists, nails biting into her palms. She wanted to shake the townsfolk. All they had to do was remain resolute and wait for help. Now was the time for her mother to prove her loyalty to Rolencia and provide that strong leadership.

Even the animals responded to the mood, with their own cries of distress. There was no sign of the two guards, who had probably run to their commander. If the third man on guard outside her mother's chamber had also left, then there would be no chance to steal the keys.

Piro raced up the stairs. Her calves would be aching tomorrow from all this running up tower steps. She reached the top floor and peered around the corner. No guard.

Only slightly out of breath, she padded over to the door. 'Mother?'

'Piro? Don't let the guard see you!'

'He's gone. Even the courtyard guards have gone. I'm going to try to get you out of here. The people need their queen.'

From the courtyard below someone screamed and Piro heard the clash of steel on steel.

When she ran to the window her mind denied what she saw, as warriors in Merofynian blue poured through the far arch. This could not be happening. The castle was too strong to be taken by force.

She craned out even further and saw the curve of her mother's cheek as she did the same from her window.

'Mother.'

But the queen did not hear her. Piro snatched the remains of the guard's bread bun and threw it at her mother, who turned and caught sight of her. About a body length of slightly curved dressed stone wall separated them.

Piro gestured below. 'How could they breach our defences?'

'Guile.' Her mother pointed. 'See the direction they're coming from. A traitor must have opened the postern gate!'

CHAPTER TEN

PIRO STARED DOWN to the courtyard where the fighting was hand-to-hand, with the men in dark red falling before the azure and black-clad forces, as the townsfolk tried to grab their children and run.

But there was nowhere to run to.

'What is it?' Seela demanded from inside the cell. 'I must see.'

Piro could just make out the old woman's silver head as she peered into the courtyard. The panicked screams from below made Piro's stomach churn. Her old nurse withdrew and, after a moment, the queen reappeared at the window.

'Who would betray us, Mother?'

'Illien of Cobalt, if it suited him.' The queen spoke in a strange flat voice. 'Only in the last few days have I realised the depths of his trickery. I've been a fool.'

'No.' Piro's denial was instinctive, but no one could deny the searing clash of metal on metal. Men shouted, screaming as they died. The king was dead and Queen Myrella imprisoned, just when they needed her to rally the castle's defenders. Or was she? Piro judged the width of the small decorative ledge that connected the two window sills. 'I know. You can climb out the window and work your way along the ledge to this one.'

Her mother stared at her in disbelief.

'You can hold onto the roof to keep your balance,' Piro insisted.

'I could never –'

'I'll come out and lead you around.' Piro swung her weight onto the window sill and prepared to lift herself out.

'Stop, Piro. You'll fall.'

'I won't. I know I can do it.'

Her mother shook her head. 'Maybe you could, but I couldn't and I'm certain Seela couldn't get through the window.'

She was right. Piro slumped on the window sill.

Her mother leant sideways, hand outstretched towards Piro who craned as far as she could so that their fingers just touched.

'It is for the best, Piro. Soon they will come for me. If this is all part of Cobalt's plan I will be his prize for surrendering the castle.' Her mother tried to smile. 'Don't worry, he won't let them hurt me. The sooner we negotiate our surrender, the better. There is no need for this slaughter. Merofynians are not barbarians.'

'Surrender?' Piro baulked at the thought. Had the queen reverted to her birth allegiance?

'How else can we regroup and fight back?' her mother countered.

Pride filled Piro. How could she have doubted her mother? 'I will stand at your side. I'm not afraid.'

She was petrified.

'Of course you are afraid,' Seela snapped, out of sight but not out of the conversation.

The queen smiled. 'Go, put on your best gown. You must look every bit a kingsdaughter if we are to use you to our advantage. When the time is right, I will say your full name, then you must come out of hiding and join me. If I don't call you *Pirola* then stay hidden, for you are more use to me as a free agent. Remember how you played the goatherd when Byren was negotiating with the overlord of Unistag Spar?'

Piro nodded. 'That was fun.' When it hadn't been terrifying.

'Good. Lence is now king. If I call you *Piro* you must take this message to him. Tell him not to let fear for my safety stay his hand. He must retake the castle. Can you remember that?'

Piro nodded. 'But it doesn't feel right leaving you.'

'I'm a captured piece in the game of Duelling Kingdoms. I've been a piece since I was betrothed at the age of eight.' She grimaced. 'Sometimes you must sacrifice a piece to win, you know that.'

Piro nodded, blinking tears from her eyes. Her mother's face swam in her vision. 'But –'

'Go now, Piro, and may Halcyon watch over you.' The queen's fingers tightened on hers. 'And, Piro, promise me this?'

Piro nodded, ready to promise anything.

'I prayed my children would not inherit my Affinity, yet you have it. Do not deny it as I have done. Learn from my mistakes.'

There was so much Piro wanted to say, but her throat felt too tight to speak. She nodded and let her mother's fingers go. Her shoulder and side ached from the strain of leaning so far and the hard stone sill had cut into her thighs.

She jumped lightly to the floor, heading down the stairs. In the shadowed doorway of the first-floor landing, she hesitated. The courtyard was empty of living things, except for a boy of about eleven wearing Merofynian blue. He chased a chicken around the yard, swinging another one by its legs, both squawking indignantly.

The boy cornered the chicken at last.

'I'm going to wring your neck m'self then throw you in the pot!' he told it and promptly dispatched both birds.

Piro had been taught the court Merofynian and he spoke a rough common version, but she had no trouble understanding him.

He tucked the bird under his arm and left. Nothing remained but three dead bodies, crushed cages, trodden animal dung and assorted chicken feathers.

Piro swallowed. Where had they taken all the townsfolk? If this had been a normal battle, she would have been tending the wounded. She'd trained in basic healing at her mother's side. Many was the time she had helped stitch up Byren and Lence. Now she was at a loss.

Crossing the courtyard, she took a short cut through the menagerie where her pet foenix was housed. The bird's eager cry drew her and she hurried across, furious to discover he had been caged. She had never locked him away, letting him roam the glass-roofed courtyard freely.

'Oh, you poor thing!' she dropped to her knees, unlocking the cage. Freed, he made a soft crooning noise in his throat and rubbed his head on her face.

She stroked his soft, fur-like feathers. It pained her to see how dull his colour had grown in just a few days. She glanced inside the cage where there was water and food aplenty. That wasn't the problem. He'd missed her and her Affinity.

At the thought of it, she felt her power stir and, before she could stop it, her hands began to tingle with a build up of Affinity.

This winter she'd grown into the habit of letting the unistag lick the excess power off her fingertips but, when they'd been forced to leave the Affinity beast with the new warlord of unistag, she hadn't been able relieve her Affinity build-up. Now the foenix grew excited as it rubbed its throat and cheeks on her hands and, even as she watched, its feathers regained their usual brilliance.

'So you were absorbing Affinity from me all along and I wasn't even aware of it,' she whispered.

'Here? You!' A Merofynian warrior addressed her in badly accented Rolencian. 'Leave that... that... Is that a foenix?'

'Yes, sor.' Piro instinctively dropped into the dialect of a badly educated servant girl. 'Belonged to Piro Kingsdaughter, herself. Was my job to feed the beastie.'

He swung the cloak off his shoulders and approached, obviously intent on capturing the foenix.

Piro sprang to her feet. 'You can't eat it, sor. It's full of Affinity.'

'I know that.' He glared at her. 'That's why I'm taking it to the overlord. He collects treasures. Close your mouth and lend a hand.'

'He won't hurt it, will he?'

The warrior clipped her over the ear. 'You'll get more of that if you give me cheek. Now, catch it for me.'

The foenix had ducked behind Piro and was shaking with fright. Stomach churning, she took the cloak from the man and spoke coaxingly as she scooped it up.

She turned to face the Merofynian. 'He needs –'

'I'll take that.' He snatched the beast from her greedily as though it was pure gold. 'As for you, get inside. All servants are to gather in the great hall.'

She nodded and turned to slip away, unable to believe her good luck.

'Wait.'

*　　*　　*

IT WAS MIDSUMMER'S day and Byren walked across the shingles on the shore of Sapphire Lake, the soles of his feet burning with each step. Try as he might, he could not reach the inviting cool shallows of the lake, which remained forever just out of reach. So thirsty, so hot... He could have roared with frustration, but only a whimper escaped him. To make matters worse, someone was poking him in the side with a spear, driving him on, making every breath a sharp pain. Couldn't they see he was doing his best to reach the lake?

From a great distance he heard a voice muttering.

'...burning up with fever. Shakin' like a leaf.'

He struggled to open his eyes but they would not obey him for more than a heartbeat. Frustration made him grind his teeth.

'Kingson, hold on. I'm taking you to a healer.' The dyer spoke slowly to reach Byren through the delirium of the fever.

But no healer could save him. At least, not one you'd find in a Rolencian village. Maybe the greatest of healers could have used their Affinity... he should have gone to Sylion Abbey the moment he realised the dagger had pierced his lung, but he'd wanted to reach his father. And, if he had, he would never had met up with the ulfr pack.

Pity he'd never get the chance to tell Orrade about it. Sylion take him, Orrade was angry with him. He'd compared his best friend to Lence. He should never have done that. Orrade's heart was true. It was his preference for men that was a problem.

He missed Orrade. Missed the pack. Missed their warming presence, missed their song. He seemed to hear it in his head, feel it in his body. It soothed him.

Byren felt a small hand pat his chest in sympathy. The boy laughed. 'He's just like Puss. He's purring, Da.'

Byren felt the dyer press his hand to the same place.

'You're right, Rodien. He's not shakin', he's purring like a cat. Wonders never cease.'

'Thirsty,' Byren managed to croak.

Something cool touched his face and watered wine slipped past his lips.

His drank eagerly.

They took it away much too soon. He tried to grab them, but they'd tied his arms down. For a moment he fought panic as he imagined them handing him over to the Merofynians, then he remembered them securing him to the sled. Now they were taking him to a healer. No point.

Who would mourn him? Certainly not King Rolen.

Lence was gone and Elina... his gut clenched and a moan escaped him. He'd failed Elina. He should never have left her at Dovecote. But she'd refused to speak with him because she believed he was in love with her brother.

Orrade, Sylion take him. Orrade was angry with him because he'd let Elina die. But Byren could not have saved her, not when she'd tried to turn Lence's sword to save his life. Her wrists were not strong enough to stop the full force of the blow. Elina had known. She'd given her life for his and thought it a fair trade.

Tears stung Byren's eyes, slipping down his cheeks, trickling into his ears where they tickled. The sled gave a jerk and started moving again, making his body vibrate, making him ache in every bone.

He was sick, very sick, not thinking clearly.

That's right, he was dying. Why didn't they let him do it in peace?

Piro paused, heart thudding. As she turned back to face the warrior, she summoned a stupid expression.

'Are there any more Affinity beasts?' the Merofynian asked, eyes bright with avarice.

'No, sor. The unistag died this winter just gone.'

He looked disappointed, then grinned, patting the foenix. 'Better than nothing, and easier to transport than a unistag. Get going, girl.'

She darted away, entering the connecting passage where she saw two men-at-arms, the azure crests on their black garments stained purple with blood. They confronted several castle servants and Halcyon's healer.

'I can't go to the hall. I must tend the injured,' the healer objected. She was nearing seventy and Piro had known her all her life.

Thwack.

The nearest Merofynian backhanded her. Knocked off her feet, the healer flew into the wall, reminding Piro how Lence had unintentionally killed the old seer with one swing of his hand.

Before Lence had thrust her aside, the seer had said the queen lived a lie and because of it Rolencia would fall and those she loved would die. Piro had been certain she had been mistaken. But now she wondered what they might have learnt if they had used the seer's foresight to their advantage.

No point in *if onlys*. Her father would never have listened to a seer. He wouldn't even listen to her!

The Merofynian's blow had not killed the healer, for she moaned and clutched her shoulder. The two maidservants gasped and bit back cries of protest.

'Help her up and get moving.' The Merofynians drove their captives around the bend. Piro longed for a keen sword and the strength of her older brothers. But it was clear from today's events that strength and a good heart were no match for treachery and cruelty.

Blood rushed in Piro's ears, filling her head with a roaring sound as a waking memory superimposed itself over the now empty hall. In Piro's mind's eye she saw her recurrent nightmare given flesh. Today wyverns stalked the halls of Rolenhold. Her vision had come true and that made her wonder about the old seer's unspoken words.

The seer had been about to direct a foretelling to Piro, whose fear at the time had been that her Affinity would be exposed. She'd been grateful to Lence when he silenced the seer, then shocked when she realised he'd killed her. What would they have learnt if the seer had lived?

Had she been about to warn them that the castle would fall? Why couldn't the seer have been more specific? A hint about Cobalt's betrayal and the postern gate would have been really useful. Piro felt a bitter smile tug at her lips.

Well, no one was going to wipe out her family!

She had half a mind to slip away and find Lence and Byren right now, but her mother had told her to dress the part of a kingsdaughter, so she hurried to where she had stashed her bundle and hastily changed in the dubious privacy of a store room, amidst jars of cherry and apricot preserves. Doing the best she could with a wet cloth she cleaned her face, hands and feet, hearing her mother's voice in her head. *No daughter of mine will appear before visiting nobles grubby as an urchin!*

Tears stung her eyes as she slung an old cape over her shoulders and took the servants' stairs to the great hall. From an archway on the mezzanine floor she stood in the shadows trying to locate the queen amid the confusion. Servants scurried about, terrified by the Merofynian men-at-arms, who were swift to speed them on their way with a blow as they set the tables for a great feast. As yet, there was no sign of the victorious overlord.

Through the forest of decorated columns Piro identified her mother. The queen and most of the servants had been herded into the space to one side of the great hearth. The Rolencian royal banner had been torn down from above the fireplace, leaving a square of pale golden sandstone. The remaining servants clung to one another, terrified. In their midst Queen Myrella stood pale but resolute with old Seela at her side.

Piro's heart swelled with pride. Now all she had to do was wait and follow her mother's directions.

A ripple of excitement drew her gaze to the far end of the hall where a group of powerful men entered. Piro recognised Cobalt. He walked a step behind the leader, and a surge of pure fury made her body burn at the sight.

Had he truly been lord protector of the castle, he would be dead, not following in the overlord's footsteps like a faithful dog.

As for the overlord, if she hadn't known him by his swagger and his elaborate surcoat – emblazoned with the twin-headed golden-scaled amfina on a black background – the reaction of his men would have told Piro who he was. They sprang to attention, greeting him with a respectful and wary silence that spoke of fear.

Piro shivered.

She recognised the same indefinable aura which had surrounded her father. Like King Rolen, Palatyne was big and raw-boned, a leader of men, but her father's men had followed him out of love and admiration. Palatyne's men watched him, as though their lives hung on his reaction.

She had expected the overlord to be accompanied by mystics from the two great abbeys of Merofynia, but there were no religious Affinity workers with him. Instead, there were two advisors. The first was a stooped, iron-haired man who had once been tall and broad-shouldered. He wore the indigo robes of a noble scholar but even without calling on her Unseen sight she could see the power shimmering off his skin.

Taking two steps to every one of his was a thin little silver-haired man, an Utland Power-worker by his warding tattoos and the fetishes woven into his waist-length beard. In Rolencia, these men would have been trained to serve the abbey and the common good. But these two Power-workers were motivated by personal ambition rather than religious fervour.

The overlord took off his azure crested helmet and shook his head. His hair was worn loose down his back in the style of Merofynian nobles and, right now, it was lank with sweat. Tucking the helmet under one arm, he lifted a goblet of wine, gulped a mouthful and spat the wine with great deliberation onto the Rolencian banner which lay on the flagstones. 'Throw it in the fire!'

Hastily, three men ran forwards to lift the intricate tapestry and toss it into the fireplace. The overlord crossed the hearth stone in two long strides and tossed the rest of his wine into the fireplace. Instantly flames surged up, devouring the Rolencian banner.

Palatyne spun to face the hall, both arms raised. 'So falls Rolenhold. And they said it could not be done!' His deep voice carried, and he spoke Merofynian with the accent of the spars.

Even as his men dutifully cheered, one hurried forwards with the foenix wrapped in his cloak. 'A treasure for you, my lord.' He pulled the cloak back a little to reveal the foenix's brilliant neck and chest colours. 'A royal foenix, the pet of the kingsdaughter herself!'

The overlord stiffened, regarding the beast intently, then he smiled and his whole stance radiated satisfaction. He nodded to the noble scholar. 'See, Lord Dunstany. What was theirs, will be mine. This foenix will be a gift for my betrothed.' He pulled a ring from his finger and tossed it to the man, who caught it eagerly. 'Have the beast cared for.'

As the man hastily backed out, Palatyne raised a hand to stroke the pendant resting on his chest plate. With a start Piro recognised her father's royal emblem. And his death hit home. She bent double, her stomach cramping with pain.

Through the rushing in her ears she heard her mother's voice and straightened up to find the queen had stepped away from the servants to confront Palatyne.

'Queen Myrella greets you, overlord.' In the sudden silence her beautifully modulated voice carried through the great hall. 'On behalf of the people of Rolencia, I claim the rights of surrender, as it seems the castle's lord protector has failed in his duties.' Her royal demeanour faltered, voice growing rich with scorn. 'How could you, Illien?'

Cobalt lifted a hand as if to ward off her accusations.

Palatyne spun away from her, staggering back several steps so that he put a body length between them. 'What's this? I ordered all King Rolen's kin killed!'

Piro's heart missed a beat. Unable to breathe, she saw the warriors hesitate. From their expressions, none of them wanted to strike down an unarmed woman. A woman who was the daughter of their old king.

Cobalt glanced from the overlord to the queen.

An inarticulate sound of protest escaped old Seela's lips.

Piro clutched the door frame, faint with horror. She couldn't stand still and let them kill her mother. But what could she do?

Unarmed, alone and also marked for death, she raged against her weakness.

FYN SKIED AROUND a bend then froze, unable to believe his bad luck. He had stumbled right into the path of a band of Merofynian warriors. What were they doing on the little-travelled foothills below Mount Halcyon?

'You, fisherman,' one addressed him in poor Rolencian.

Heart thudding, Fyn shuffled closer.

'Have you seen an injured man?'

'No, I haven't seen anyone.' How would a lone fisherman react to a party of seven Merofynian warriors? Cautiously, that was certain. Better pretend that he thought they were escorting a pilgrim to Halcyon Abbey. 'Did your injured pilgrim get lost? Should I send him this way if I see him?'

They laughed.

'Yeah, tell the kingson we want to take him home to meet our mothers!'

one muttered in Merofynian.

Fyn fixed a smile on his face and nodded, as though he did not understand but his heart raced with the knowledge that Byren (it had to be Byren for, if it was Lence, they would have said kingsheir) had met up with the Merofynians. At least he had escaped, albeit injured.

'This friend of yours, how will I know him?' Fyn asked.

'He's big and bad-tempered. If you see him, keep away from him. Ski up to the abbey and let them know. Their healers can help him,' the first one told Fyn.

The others nodded, exchanging looks that said they enjoyed a private joke.

Fyn nodded. All he wanted to do was get away from them before they saw through his disguise. The tattoos of learning were still visible through his sprouting hair. If his fur cap was knocked off... he must not think like that. He must act the part of a fisherman. It was customary to offer to share food with pilgrims.

'I'm off to see my sister who's expecting her first, come spring cusp,' he said. 'Our mam sent her some fish stew. There's not much but I'm sure –'

'So that's the smell,' the rude one complained in Merofynian. 'Mulcibar's balls, send him on his way before he offers us fish stew.'

The others chuckled. Fyn managed a chuckle of his own, as though he was trying to ingratiate himself with them, despite being unable to understand their speech.

'Be off with you and watch out for our pilgrim. Remember, he's bad-tempered so don't go near him. Let us know if you see him,' the spokesman insisted.

Fyn nodded. Relief made him lightheaded as he shuffled past them and slid down the slope, weaving through the evergreens until he was well and truly out of sight. By then his knees were shaking so badly he had to stop and bend double to clear his head, so he sat for a few moments in lee of a snow-skirted tree.

After a few moments he heard the Merofynians pass on the other side of the tree, returning to the abbey.

'...all as thick as him they deserve to lose their kingdom!' the rude one was saying.

'Do you think he'll report it if he sees the kingson?' a different one asked.

'The kingson is most likely dead,' the spokesman said. 'No one could lose that much blood and keep going.'

'True,' the rude one agreed. 'And with the ulfr pack in the area, anyone travelling alone and injured doesn't stand a chance. No wonder we can't find his body. We're on a wild goose chase!'

Their voices faded, drowned by the rushing in Fyn's ears. When his vision cleared he was bent double, staring at the perfect snow in front of his nose. Wracking shivers shook him.

Byren was dead. At least, the Merofynians believed he was. Cheeky, laughing Byren. Kindest, most thoughtful of his brothers...

Fyn's heart felt as if it would break.

Determination drove him to his feet.

If Byren was dead, it was up to Fyn to carry news of the abbey's fall to their father. He set off, his resolve renewed by grief.

CHAPTER ELEVEN

PIRO SWAYED. STANDING high on the mezzanine floor, she had a perfect view of the tableau below. Like a play, the actors said their lines, but it was her mother they planned to kill.

'You cannot mean to murder the queen,' Cobalt objected. He glanced from the overlord to Piro's mother and back to the overlord. 'She can be used to unite Rolencia.'

'He's right, my lord.' Lord Dunstany proved an unexpected ally. 'She's a valuable kingdom piece, make use of her. She cannot harm you if you are back in Merofynia.'

'Oh, no?' Palatyne rounded on him. 'You're the one who foretold Rolen's kin would be my downfall!'

Dunstany went very still.

Palatyne rounded on the nearest warriors, the ones who had been so eager to burn the Rolencian emblem. He stabbed one hand in the queen's direction. 'Well?'

'Overlord?' Cobalt covered the two steps between them in one long stride, caught the man's arm and said something in an intense, low whisper. They were about the same height, but very different men. Despite his Rolencian birth, Cobalt had the bearing of an Ostronite aristocrat, from his perfumed curls to his high-heeled boots. The overlord was a barbarian from Amfina Spar, and no amount of gold or brocade could hide it.

Before Cobalt could finish, Palatyne threw off his restraining arm.

'You think to bargain with me, Illien of Cobalt, or should I call you the Bastard's son? That's why you betrayed them, your uncle and cousins, because your father was denied the crown. Prove your loyalty to me. Kill her yourself!'

Piro gasped. All along Cobalt has sworn his love for her mother, but Piro did not doubt that it was a self-serving love.

'Let me relieve you of this troublesome woman, overlord.' The little Utland Power-worker strutted closer. With each step his staff struck the ground and its carven tip flared as though eager to shed blood.

Piro's stomach cramped.

'No.' Palatyne seemed to be enjoying himself now. 'The Bastard's son can prove his worth.'

Cobalt took a step back from the overlord, which took him closer to the queen, who was right behind him. Piro noticed how her old nurse's hand rested lightly on her waist where Seela kept her dagger hidden. No one would expect death from a plump, silver-haired old woman but Piro had seen Seela use that knife to kill Cobalt's spy only a couple of days ago. Pride filled Piro, then her spirits plunged, for in a few heartbeats her mother and nurse would both be dead.

The very intensity of her gaze must have alerted Seela, for the old woman's eyes lifted as she looked through the forest of columns, up to the mezzanine floor. The nurse was not fooled by Piro's cloak. She went very still, then her hand dropped from her waist and she took a step back from the queen, abandoning Piro's mother to her fate.

'Well, lord protector of the castle?' Palatyne mocked Cobalt.

'Let me save you from this dilemma, Illien!' The queen sprang forwards, drawing Cobalt's own sword before he could react.

Piro's heart leapt. Here was a chance to run Palatyne through. Destroy the head and the body would fall, leaving the Merofynian army leaderless.

'Death to betrayers!' the queen cried, swinging the blade in an arc that was aimed to cut through the side lacings of Cobalt's chest plate, driving deep into his heart and lungs. But before it could drive home Cobalt reacted.

Though he was only half-turned towards her, he leapt, cat-light, out of her strike path. The queen let the sword's momentum carry her around in a circle, springing forwards and bringing the blade down in a diagonal blow that would have severed his head from his shoulders had he not darted sideways again.

The blow took him on the shoulder joint of his armour, slicing clean through, severing his arm. Stunned, he stood there, blood pumping from the stump. The queen continued the arc of the strike, bringing the great sword around for the killing blow.

Piro understood the problem. Her mother was a small woman. The weapon was almost too heavy for her to hold, once it had momentum she could only guide it.

This blow would have surely killed Cobalt, but one of Palatyne's warriors sprang in behind her, running the queen through. Pinned upright, she stood stunned as the sword flew from her hands. People dived out of its path. It clattered on the stone, loud in the terrible silence.

Piro whimpered.

Her mother stared at the blade which protruded between her breasts.

'Myrella?' Illien cried. He'd clamped his remaining hand over the stump of his arm, despite this, he bled copiously, swayed and dropped to his knees.

Piro's sight wavered from the Seen to the Unseen, triggered by the gathering of her mother's innate Affinity.

The queen stiffened. One hand lifted to point at Palatyne and her eyes rolled back in her head. 'You will die, knowing you have lost everything.'

Triggered by her mother's words, Piro saw Palatyne on his knees, the twin amfina heads writhing as one turned on the other.

'You will die at the hands of my children,' the queen said. 'Piro Kingsdaughter, I call on –'

'By the mother of all amfinas, she's radiating Affinity!' Palatyne came to life, springing back behind his advisors. 'Stop her before she can curse me!'

Before Dunstany could move, the Utland Power-worker swung the carved tip of his staff so that it connected with the tip of the sword that pierced the queen's chest. Unable to look away, Piro watched as the last remnants of her mother's Affinity-driven life force were drawn out of her into the staff's greedy stone tip.

The logical part of her brain told her that the carving had to be made from some kind of sorbt stone, something the mystics of Rolencia had not discovered yet, or perhaps kept a secret.

The Utlander tilted the staff upright and slammed its base into the floor.

The carved tip glowed with power and the queen dropped like an empty husk, her essence and Affinity now the Utlander's captive.

Hollowed out, fragile as glass, Piro stepped back into the safety of a darkened archway. She wanted to run down the stairs and across the hall, and smash that stone so her mother could have a clean death, but that would mean her own death. She stood poised on her toes, outrage warring with self-preservation.

Common sense won out.

Palatyne straightened, daring to step closer to the fallen queen. 'She's safe?'

'Her Affinity's settled,' the Utlander confirmed.

Yes, cannibalised by him! A surge of fury strengthened Piro's fragile limbs.

Palatyne bent down and dragged the royal emblem from around the queen's neck, dropping it over his own head to join the others.

Piro touched hers. It felt like a brand, emblazoned with her identity, condemning her to death.

Cobalt moaned, still swaying on his knees, clutching the bloody stump of his arm.

Palatyne studied him for a moment, and Piro felt Cobalt's life hang in the balance.

'Save him if you can. I can still use him.' Palatyne turned his back on the injured man and beckoned Cobalt's new servant, the one who Piro was sure was also a Merofynian spy for, the day her mother was arrested, she had seen the flash of a wyvern tail in the back of his mind when he confronted her on the stairs.

As the Utland Power-worker organised three men-at-arms to carry Cobalt away, Palatyne confronted Cobalt's servant.

'Has there been word of the kingson?' Palatyne asked, his hand going to his chest to stroke the three royal emblems that lay there.

Three?

Piro's heart faltered. Her mother and father's. Whose was the third?

Not Fyn, he was safe at the abbey. If Lence had been at Dovecote then he'd have been in Palatyne's path. If one of her twin brothers were to die, let it be Lence!

Piro experienced a surge of guilt.

'Byren Kingson has not been heard of since he was sent to bring help from Halcyon Abbey,' the man reported.

'Don't worry about him. What of Pirola?' Palatyne demanded. 'The kingsdaughter?'

'It was thought she had been sent to Sylion Abbey, but Cobalt recognised her hiding amongst the townsfolk.'

'You know her face?'

He nodded.

'Go to the gate. I've ordered the townsfolk sent back to Rolenton. If she gets past you, I'll have your head. Understand?'

The man nodded, his face growing pale.

As he scurried off, Palatyne turned to the servants. 'Is she hiding amongst you lot? Come on, give her up!'

No one spoke. They froze, staring at him like rabbits enthralled by a snake.

He threw back his head and laughed.

A voice piped up in the echo of his laugh. 'It takes a brave man to kill defenceless women and children.'

Piro winced as she recognised the blind spit-turner.

Palatyne nodded to his men, who dragged the old man over to the overlord. 'Repeat that.'

'I said, it takes a brave man to murder women and children,' he said, voice wavering only with age.

'What would you know? You can't even see!'

'I don't need eyes to see into your heart. Your men must be blind to follow –'

His words died on his lips as Palatyne thrust a hunting knife through his heart. The overlord kicked the body aside dismissively but Piro could tell the blind man's words had made the men uneasy.

'Tonight we break open barrels of the castle's best Rolencian red to celebrate in King Merofyn's name!' Palatyne roared. 'But first – a bag of gold for the man who brings me the kingsdaughter, dead or alive.'

Dozens of them scrambled to do his bidding.

As if freed from a spell, Piro turned and fled, cursing the rich embroidered gown which proclaimed her status.

She knew the castle intimately. As a child she'd played hide-and-seek with her brothers. Now, moving on soundless feet, she ran down the storage passage, heading for her usual hiding places. Then she stopped.

Hiding was pointless. Eventually she would have to come out for food. Palatyne's men would search until they found her.

What could she do?

Men yelled, their voices coming closer as they slammed doors and thundered up stairs searching room by room. This was her nightmare come true. The dreams had become reality. She should have been forewarned!

No time for regrets.

Desperate, Piro sprinted down the long corridor, darting through a stillroom into the castle laundry beyond. Here she almost tripped over a girl, whose head lay at a funny angle.

Piro turned her over. Someone must have struck her – her nose was broken. The lower half of her face was obscured by blood. Piro felt the girl's throat. No pulse. Then she noticed the overturned chair and the narrow window. The poor thing had been trying to climb out when her chair tipped and she had fallen, breaking her neck.

Biting back a sob of despair, Piro ran on, but in the storeroom beyond she caught sight of men tossing aside cured meats and smashing preserves as they searched.

Trapped.

Ducking back into the laundry, Piro stood over the slight, dark-haired girl, thinking furiously. Palatyne had sent his men to bring back King Rolen's daughter. Here was a dead girl of the right age.

Her own life hung in the balance. This was no time to be squeamish.

The poor girl's skirt and shirt weren't bloodied, but the apron was. Piro flung off her own red gown, then knelt and undid the girl's garments, begging her forgiveness for this desecration.

First, she freed the girl's hair from its bun and pinned her own cap of red velvet and gold lace in place. With no time to make a neat bun of her own hair, she twisted it up and knotted the thick length once.

As she went to pull her dress onto the girl's limp form, her emblem swung forwards. Must not forget that, and the Keys of Office. Piro tugged the emblem off and slung it over the girl's neck. Luckily the poor maid was slightly smaller than Piro so it was easy to get the costly gown laced up and belt tied with the Keys of Office in place.

She tugged on the girl's skirt and shirt, then barely had time to toss the bloodied apron onto a pile of dirty washing and pluck a clean one from the laundered clothes, dropping it over her shoulders before the overlord's men flung the door open, startling her.

Piro gave a shriek of real fear and dropped to her knees next to the body of the girl in the red velvet dress. 'Don't touch 'er, don't you touch the kingsdaughter!'

She wept and kicked, throwing herself over the body. Using the rough speech of the servants, she swore at them, repeating words she'd overheard the grooms mutter when a harness broke.

One lifted Piro by the shoulder straps of the apron, as if she was a kitten, and tucked her under his arm, while the other turned the imposter-Piro over onto her back.

At that moment Piro noticed the girl's grubby, bare feet and recalled her own hand-sewn slippers. Sick fear gripped her, but she had not come this far to be caught and killed. Quick as a thought, she slipped her toes into the slippers' heels and kicked them off. She kicked them off one after the other, weeping and writhing all the while to disguise her actions.

'The kingsdaughter is dead,' the first man muttered in Merofynian, having inspected the body. He pointed. 'Tried to climb out the window. Lost her good shoes.' He bent and scooped them up. After inspecting the beading and seeing the semi-precious stones, he pocketed the slippers.

'Dead is dead. Let's get our reward!' the other said. 'And I'll have one of them slippers, thanks.'

'Of course,' the first agreed.

Without another word, her captor threw Piro over his shoulder, while the other man scooped up the limp form of the dead serving girl in the red velvet gown. Piro prayed they would not notice the supposed kingsdaughter's dirty feet, or her own clean toes.

The men strode up the passage, talking of how they would spend their reward. Hanging over the man's shoulder, Piro felt dizzy and nauseous. When they marched into the great hall, all the rich wall hangings and men-at-arms in Merofynian colours swung past her upside-down.

Dumping her on the floor by the great fireplace with the other servants, the men marched across to their overlord with the body of the dead girl.

Palatyne rose to meet them, going around the table to inspect their trophy as they laid the body of the imposter kingsdaughter at his feet. The noble scholar joined him, kneeling to inspect the body.

'Broken neck. Her nose was broken first,' Dunstany said softly in Merofynian.

'I don't care how she died,' Palatyne announced dismissively.

Piro huddled against the edge of the fireplace, letting her hair fall over her tear-streaked face, tucking her clean toes under her skirt hem.

'Where is the emblem?' Palatyne demanded in Merofynian.

The nearest man fumbled, feeling around the dead girl's neck until he pulled off the royal pendant and presented it to his overlord. 'Here it is, my lord.'

'And here's the queen's Keys of Office.' Dunstany undid the waist sash to remove them. With a twitch of the skirt he straightened the supposed kingsdaughter's gown. Piro whispered a prayer of thanks to Halcyon, goddess of luck, for the gown was a fraction too long and covered the maidservant's grubby feet.

Dunstany tossed the keys to Palatyne, who caught and pocketed them, well satisfied. Then he hung the royal emblem around his neck, where it settled with the others on his chest. He sent the men off to collect their reward and perched on the table, swinging one leg.

The Utland Power-worker rejoined the overlord's party, pausing to inspect the supposed kingsdaughter.

'So this is Pirola Myrella Queensdaughter?' he muttered, glancing down at her. 'This one might have been useful alive. What can one little girl do?'

'You saw what the mother was capable of, and her hardly able to lift that sword.' Palatyne drained his wine. 'What of Cobalt? Will he live?'

This made Piro wonder why Palatyne suffered Cobalt to live if he believed one of King Rolen's kin would be his downfall, or did the stain of illegitimacy that had kept Cobalt's father from inheriting the throne, save Cobalt?

'I've done what I can for him,' the Utlander said. 'Only time will tell.'

'That's what I hate about you Power-workers, never a straight answer,'

Palatyne growled, but he was in too good a mood to dwell on this. 'Fill your goblet.'

Topping up his own goblet with fine Rolencian wine, he lifted it in a toast. 'To King Rolen's kin, may they all be dead by nightfall!'

The Utland Power-worker echoed the toast, as did the noble scholar and the warriors, who Palatyne had favoured with a place at the high table. Among them, Piro saw battle-hardened faces, men she guessed had been with the overlord since his days on Amfina Spar. She had expected to see the young lords of the great families of Merofynia, but there were none. Surely the great families of Merofynia had not sent Palatyne off to crush Rolencia without making sure their sons had a share of the booty and glory?

'More wine!' Palatyne called. 'If there's one thing Rolencia can do right, it's make a good red!'

His men cheered and one leapt to his feet to offer a toast to Palatyne's clever strategy. The overlord grinned and accepted the adulation as his right. All the while, he stood over the dead girl's body as though she were nothing more than a farm animal.

Piro shuddered. Not far from her, the servants huddled together, whispering and weeping. No one looked her way. There were some amongst them who, if they'd bothered to take a good look at the dead girl's bloodied face, would have realised she wasn't Piro.

She felt herself under observation and saw Halcyon's healer speaking with Seela, both turning away quickly. Piro's heart seemed to miss a beat. The healer and her old nurse would not give her away, but would the rest of the castle's servants remain loyal?

It would take only one slip to reveal her deception. Anxiously, Piro studied those who served their new masters. Perhaps they were too busy to notice one dishevelled serving girl. Perhaps they avoided looking at the body, which was just a heap of red velvet and dark hair. Or perhaps they wished to see Overlord Palatyne tricked, for no one spoke up. No one wanted to share the fate of the queen and the spit-turner.

That reminded Piro. She looked, but there was no sign of their bodies, only a stained patch on the stones.

Palatyne stood and gestured to the body at his feet. 'Get rid of this. It's putting me off my roast!'

His men laughed as if this was impossible, and Palatyne enjoyed their reaction. He didn't bother to return to his chair, but sat himself on the table and grabbed a turkey leg, tearing into it.

'There is still the other kingson, my lord,' the Utland Power-worker said, his voice carrying in a lull. Piro realised that since they did not expect anyone to speak Merofynian, they felt free to talk strategy in front of the servants.

'The abbey will have fallen by now.' Palatyne grinned wolfishly and gestured to the Utlander. 'I expect your brother to bring me Fyn Kingson's emblem by tomorrow night.'

Piro's vision blurred. Fyn, dead? Impossible. How could the abbey fall when it was protected by the warrior monks?

'What of the one that escaped?' the Utlander asked.

Lence had escaped? That meant the emblem was Byren's. Palatyne had said not to worry about him. Piro's heart sank. Remorse lanced her. How could she wish for Byren's survival when it meant Lence's death?

'He's probably hiding in the mountains with what remains of that estate's people,' Palatyne jeered. 'King of a pig pen!'

His men laughed and clapped, for in Merofynian it was not only an alliteration, but rhymed as well. Piro shivered. He was clever, this overlord, and quickwitted. And she still didn't know which twin lived, although she thought it was Lence.

'See, Dunstany, I make my own fate!' Palatyne lifted his goblet to the noble scholar.

Dunstany tipped his head in silent acknowledgement to his overlord, while the Utland Power-worker smiled, pleased to see his rival mocked.

The noise level rose as the wine flowed and the men celebrated. Piro's head began to thump with their shouting. The remaining captive servants seem to have been forgotten.

A man hurried between the gilt-edged columns, radiating self-importance as he crossed the hall. He bowed to Palatyne and waited until the overlord indicated he was to speak.

'We've found King Rolen's trophy room, my lord. Treasures that –'

'Take me there.' Palatyne swung his legs to the floor and strode off, passing within touching distance of Piro, who felt the wind of his passage on her hands as she hugged her knees. Since she had been living hand to mouth, her nails were bitten down to the quick and matched her disguise.

Half a dozen of Palatyne's warriors and the Utland Power-worker hurried past.

Lord Dunstany was the last. As he approached Piro, the healer waylaid him. On the edge of her vision Piro sensed old Seela watching them closely.

'Your pardon, Lord Dunstany,' she said in Rolencian. 'I am a healer. I should be treating the injured. May I take my servant and go?' She gestured to Piro.

The noble scholar glanced in Piro's direction.

Silently thanking the healer for her quick wits, Piro scrambled to her feet and bobbed a quick bow, head bowed. She hardly dared to breathe.

A quick glance told her Dunstany frowned, his dark eyes on her. She stared at the hem of his robe. All she could see was his muddied boots, buckled around the ankle Merofynian-style. Piro could feel waves of power exuding from him like heat from a furnace. He might be an educated noble but he was also a Power-worker, and he terrified her.

'You forget you are captives of war. Slaves. Go back to your place, healer. The overlord will assign you to serve someone.'

The healer backed off as Seela cast Piro a quick warning glance. Piro sat down again, hugging her knees. This was not so bad. As a common slave, she could escape and run away to the mountains where she could find Lence, if it was he who had survived. Tears stung her eyes. She brushed them away, furious. She had no time for weakness.

Lord Dunstany walked off but had only gone a dozen paces when he returned and stood over Piro, blocking her view of the rest of the hall. She dared one quick look.

'I have need of a slave. Stand.' He held out one hand twisted by the bone-ache.

As he pulled Piro to her feet, she felt the strength in his arm. Then she cursed, for her gesture had been that of a lady used to a servant's help. To cover her slip she sniffed and rubbed the back of her hand across her nose. 'Thankee, sor.'

She was surprised to see a light in his eyes that could have been amusement. The irises were so black his eyes seemed all pupil. So black, yet so full of light.

The revelry faded around her. Her breath caught in her throat. She was in danger of drowning.

With an effort that made her dizzy, she dragged her gaze from his and dipped her head in a servant's bow. Her tongue felt thick but she drove herself to speak. 'What can I do for you, sor?'

'You can do as you're told,' Lord Dunstany said, watching her thoughtfully.

Piro searched his face but she found it hard to meet his gaze without sliding into that other state. Now that her head was clear, she realised he had been trying to impose his will on her. Anger fired her. She was glad her father had banned all Affinity Power-working renegades, soothsayers and mages alike. Then she remembered that a slave girl wouldn't raise her eyes to a noble, especially if he was a renegade Power-worker, and she looked down quickly. 'Sorry, m'lord.'

'What can you do, girl?'

She could read and write in three languages, play the harp, paint watercolours, run a castle with six hundred inhabitants, keep the books and hand down law judgements, but none of that helped her now. The healer had said she was her apprentice so it was lucky her mother had schooled her in basic healing.

Piro bobbed her head, careful to stay in character. 'I been helping the healer. I can mix herbs and stitch a wound. An' me ma delivered babies, sor.'

His lips twitched. 'Well, I won't be needing you to deliver any babies. You can wait on me.'

'Yes, sor.'

'Lord Dunstany?' It was the man who had reported finding King Rolen's trophy room. 'Do you want to see the treasures?'

Piro could imagine them all up there with Palatyne handing out gifts to his loyal supporters.

'Treasures?' he repeated with a secretive smile. 'Those sort of treasures don't interest me. Come on, girl.'

Surprised, Piro scurried after him.

CHAPTER TWELVE

FYN REACHED VIRIDIAN Lake by mid-morning and strapped on the borrowed skates. It looked like the thaw would be late this spring, even so, Fyn kept to the edges where the ice was thickest. Twice more he had seen Merofynian search parties but managed to avoid them.

Viridian Lake, named because of the exquisite shade of its deep waters, was a long sinuous lake, connected at the far end by canal to Sapphire Lake. From there he was on the last leg of his journey to Rolenhold, where his father was probably wondering why the abbot had not sent aid.

Fyn could only hope that Byren's injury was not as bad as the Merofynians believed and that his brother had found some helpful farmers willing to risk their lives to save him.

Fyn stood on the borrowed skates. There was no wind and the sky was cloudless, which meant it would be frightfully cold when night fell, but this also meant the stars would be out in force, great swirls of effervescent colour to light his way.

And aid the Merofynian search parties.

Fear for Piro's safety and the news he had to deliver empowered him. Trusting to his disguise to fool any Merofynians who might spot him, Fyn set off. If he skated all night and all day he would reach Sapphire Lake by tomorrow evening and Rolenhold by the next day.

AS PIRO LEFT her father's hall – where she had seen him host feasts, award honours and boast of his hunting skills – she let her hair fall forwards and focused on the ground. In a matter of days she had fallen from kingsdaughter to slave, just another prize of war.

All around her the raucous warriors roistered, eating and drinking, grabbing any passing wench they fancied. A servant, who only a few days ago had filled her bath, darted past hurrying to serve new masters. Piro averted her face.

They were out of the great hall now, walking through the bloodied courtyard, heading for the main gate. All around her the people of Rolenton shuffled past, driven back to the town. Dunstany kept well away from Palatyne's men, who were tossing bodies into an open cart.

Panic spiked in Piro. There, by the gate, was Cobalt's servant, the one who had been told to look out for her. He knew her face.

Dunstany stopped suddenly, turning to her. 'What is your name, girl?'

Panic seized her. How could she hide from the servant?

'Your name?' Dunstany pressed.

She hadn't thought that far ahead and said the first thing that came to her. 'Seela, sor.' Then she remembered that was a Merofynian name and hurried to add, 'My mother's mother come from –'

'I don't want your family history,' he snapped. 'Listen, Seela. I am your master now. Walk one step behind me and do not speak unless I give you permission. Understand?'

She nodded, feeling resentful – worse, feeling trapped. How could she escape the servant's notice?

'Come.' As Dunstany strode off towards the gate, Piro considered running away but he glanced back over his shoulder impatiently and she fell into step.

'Didn't they tell you?' Dunstany asked as he approached the man. 'They've already found the kingsdaughter. Palatyne's in King Rolen's trophy room handing treasures out to his faithful servants.'

Piro hovered behind Dunstany, grateful for his broad, if stooped, back. The man thanked the noble Power-worker and hurried off, eager to get his share of the treasure.

Piro swallowed. She was safe, safe as long as the man didn't think to check her body. 'Lord Dunstany? What happened to the bodies of the queen and the others?'

He glanced swiftly to her. 'They'll have been burned by now. We don't want anyone saving a lock of hair and selling it as a relic. Come along.'

His casual attitude stung, but she was relieved to hear the bodies had already been burnt. Now Cobalt's servant would never know that another girl had taken Piro's place.

As they walked down the steep winding road to Rolenton, the townsfolk gave them a wide berth. They were silent, shuffling along, defeated. She prayed none of them took a close look at her, for she was well known in town and at any moment someone might recognise her and give her away. She wanted to get out of sight as soon as possible.

'Where are we going, Lord Dunstany?' she asked softly.

'I did not give you permission to speak. But to answer your question, I prefer my own quarters as far from the Utlander and his twin brother as possible. Mark my words, Seela, if either of them approaches you they are up to no good.'

Piro nodded. She never intended to have anything to do with the other Power-workers, and the less she had to do with Dunstany the better. At least she was safe if she stayed in his dwelling and saw only his servants, for none of them would recognise her. Once there, she would lay low until she was ready to escape to the mountains.

Focusing on Dunstany's indigo robe, she followed the tall scholar. He strode along so fast that she had to take a skipping step every now and then to keep up.

At the town gate her step faltered. There was Captain Temor's head on a spike along with others from the king's honour guard, men she had known all her life. To her right the Merofynians were throwing bodies onto a bonfire. Yet she felt nothing but relief. What was wrong with her?

The position of the sun told her that it was only mid-afternoon. It felt like days had passed since her father rode out to meet Palatyne under a flag of truce, though it had only been this morning. Not a breath of wind stirred the air. In the cold, the heads would last a long time. Her throat grew tight with unshed tears.

'Look at me, not them!' Dunstany spun her around to face him, his black eyes fierce. He gave her a little shake and a surge of anger banished her tears. 'I've called your name three times. Don't make me come after you again. Hurry up.'

Dunstany strode through the gate where Captain Temor and his men had bought enough time for Piro to retreat to the castle, a sacrifice wasted by the traitor who opened the postern gate. Fury fuelled her as she scurried after the noble Power-worker. It felt good. She nurtured the sensation.

Just inside Rolenton's gates several servants, wearing the same shade of indigo as Lord Dunstany, waited beside a heavily laden cart.

'Ahh, Soterro.' Dunstany greeted one of them in Rolencian, so he intended Piro to understand. This was confirmed when he turned to her. 'Soterro is the head of my house when I am travelling. You will obey him as you obey me.'

Piro dipped her head as a maidservant would do when greeting a higher-ranked servant. Soterro was an Ostronite name but it was not unusual to see one of the decadent Ostronites serving a great Merofynian lord.

Dunstany switched to Merofynian. 'My new slave needs warm water and fresh clothes. I won't have her take up her duties until she has been thoroughly washed.'

Piro bristled. She was not that dirty. No... but a serving girl might be and this gave her a chance to disguise the fact that her deception was not perfect.

'Give her a room that can be locked. She's from the castle and we don't want her running away.'

The servant looked her up and down and sniffed. 'If that's the pick of the castle's servants I wouldn't want to see the worst.'

Piro gave him an uneasy look, careful to give no sign that she understood anything but his tone. He spoke Merofynian with a slight Ostronite accent, which confirmed her guess.

'There's no female clothing in the chest, my lord,' Soterro said, with some satisfaction.

'Even better. Come along.' Dunstany led them along the street into the town square where the wealthiest merchant houses stood. He strode straight past the proud three and four-storey buildings, heading for the apothecary's. A man stood guard in front of the door, which hung off one hinge.

Dunstany tossed the man a coin and strode into the ground-floor room where the herbalist would have served his customers. Much had been destroyed by Palatyne's men. Cabinets with narrow drawers covered the wall on Piro's left. Some had been tipped on the floor. Symbols told her the drawers were filled with herbs both rare and common. This hadn't interested the looters. But it did interest Piro. She recognised the powdered form of hellsbane, a powerful poison. What were her chances of slipping that in the overlord's wine?

On the mahogany counter, a stack of starkiss-scented candles gave off a delicious citrus aroma even though they were unlit. On the shelves behind, glass jars containing preserved organs gathered dust.

Piro glanced to the right. There were framed illustrations of bodies, both human and Affinity beast, with detailed diagrams of their internal organs. The notes were written so small they were almost illegible.

Trust an Affinity renegade to take over an apothecary's shop.

Beyond this room there would be a hall with a chamber where the herbalist prepared his treatments and one where the family dined, then the kitchen. The family would have slept on the next floor and the servants in the attic above that. She tried not to think of the family that used to live here.

Dunstany surveyed the mess disgustedly, then pointed to the crooked door. 'Soterro, get that fixed and tidy up here.'

'Certainly, my lord.'

While Dunstany strode off, Soterro ordered the others about in Merofynian and then, seeing Piro looking lost, beckoned her impatiently.

She followed him through to the kitchen, where it seemed the looters hadn't bothered to venture, for the room was tidy. A little man who was as wide as he was tall entered from the courtyard with three chickens, their necks freshly wrung.

He tossed them to a kitchen boy. 'Don't just sit there, Grysha, get plucking. The lord will want a hot dinner and no excuses.' He paused as he eyed Piro with growing resentment. 'I supposed I'm to look after the new slave?'

'You heard the master, Cook,' Soterro said. 'He wants her washed and dressed.'

'What am I, her nursemaid?' Cook grumbled. 'There's no hot water. I've only just lit the grate.'

'Then she can use cold and be grateful for it.'

Though they spoke Merofynian, Piro suspected they would probably have been just as rude if they thought she could understand them.

Soterro turned to Piro, speaking excellent Rolencian. 'Fill a bucket with water and come this way.'

She used the pump over the stone sink to fill the bucket and the cook tossed her a rag to wash herself with. It was already filthy. Piro eyed it reluctantly, but a maidservant who had become a slave would not protest.

'Hurry up, I haven't got all day,' Soterro snapped. 'This way.'

Back in the next room he dug through one of his master's chests until he found what he was looking for, tossing her a bundle of clothes. 'Here, catch. Something will fit you. Come on.' He led her into the hall saying, 'You can call me Master Soterro. And you always call our master Lord Dunstany, or "my lord." He's a great man. He's been advisor to the kings of Merofynia for seventy years!'

Piro blinked. Except for the bone-ache that twisted his hands, Dunstany looked no older than fifty. It appeared long life was a by-product of renegade Affinity.

A youth passed them, carrying a pan of broken glass.

'Put that aside and bring your tools.'

They waited until he returned, then Soterro led them up the stairs. The head servant was puffing when he came to the second flight of much narrower stairs. At the top landing he opened door after door until he found a tiny room tucked under the ceiling. It was piercingly cold. 'What's your name, girl?'

Piro blinked. 'Seela, sor. I mean, Master Soterro.'

He gave her a sharp look. 'That's a Merofynian name.'

'I'm named after me ma's ma. She was from Merofynia. Reckon she –'

He silenced her with a wave. 'Get cleaned up.' He turned his back on her to speak with the carpenter. 'I want a bolt fixed to this door and her locked in safely before you come back downstairs.'

As the youth got out his tools, Piro sat on the single low cot to watch, while he fixed a large metal bolt to the door. He did not meet her eyes but, when he was done, he cast her a shy glance.

She turned her face away, not wanting to make friends with Dunstany's servants. The youth shut the door and she heard the bolt slide home.

As the air slowly left Piro's chest, she felt a little light-headed. The water in the bucket was cold, so she bathed quickly. Determined to keep her wits about her, she changed into the boy's leggings and the azure thigh-length pinafore of a Merofynian court page. Its heavy brocade yoke came down to her mid-chest, hiding her breasts. Dressed like this she could pass for a boy. A pretty boy. She pulled her hair into a single tight plait like the Merofynian servants wore, and sat the white rabbit-fur cap on her head. There was no mirror, but if she stood in the right spot she could just make out her reflection in the attic window.

Excellent. No one would recognise Piro Rolen Kingsdaughter now.

Her stomach rumbled. How could she be hungry after everything that had happened?

Could she climb out the window? Piro forced the catch, knocking snow off the sill. It landed on the roof of the kitchen far below. The slates of the attic roof were slick and icy. In desperation she might risk trying to cross them, but not today, not when there could be easier ways to escape.

She gazed out at the many steep, snowcapped roofs of Rolenton. Above the town Rolenhold sat on its pinnacle, with the Dividing Mountains rising high behind it, shrouded in clouds. Palatyne's azure and black flags hung from Rolenhold's two gate towers. She felt as limp as those flags.

Her home, her whole life lay in ruins. The overlord had set out to destroy King Rolen and all his kin to escape a prophecy.

I make my own fate! he'd claimed.

And so he did.

A small, grim smile tugged at Piro's lips. Overlord Palatyne might have killed her family and stolen their kingdom, but he had overlooked one small, insignificant slave girl who knew which herbs could kill. She would fulfil the prophecy!

FYN ATE WHILE skating, determined to make up time. The brilliant evening star was four fingers above the horizon when he slipped and skidded across the ice. He lay stunned for a moment, trying to catch his breath. Rolling onto his knees, he realised he'd almost dozed off. He should rest for a bit and skate later.

Grateful for the thick fisherman's coat, he built a hasty snow-cave on the shore and crawled inside. As he curled into a ball, his hand went to his chest to settle on the royal emblem that he no longer wore. Instead his fingers closed around Halcyon's Fate.

Had Master Catillum escaped the mass grave? Would he survive his injury and the dangers of Rolencia's winter? Would he reach Sylion Abbey despite all the Merofynian search parties wandering the slopes of Mount Halcyon?

Fyn knew there was a chance he could turn the Fate to his will. Logic told him not to try, when there was also a chance some Merofynian Power-worker might capture him while he was vulnerable, viewing the Unseen world, but... the Fate had shown him Isolt, daughter of King Merofyn. And it hadn't shown any visions to Piro, who had handled it before him. Unlike Feldspar and Piro, it seemed his Affinity was attuned to the Fate.

He stroked the opalised seashell's spiral surface. Like a cat stretching under a loving hand, the Fate warmed to his fingers. A flicker of light travelled through the opal, distant lightning behind stormy clouds.

Fyn was tempted...

But the memory of emptying his stomach in the snow outside Lame Klimen's cottage was still too fresh. If the Fate took that much of a toll on his Affinity he might end up as Feldspar had warned, with a brain spasm.

In the end caution won out.

Rest, then set off later tonight.

BYREN HEARD THEM whispering. He tried to move, but his limbs would not obey him. At least he was in a real bed, not being rocked to pieces on that sled. He recalled flashes of being carried inside, someone peeling off his bloodied vest. That was when he'd almost passed out.

The healer – he remembered her Sylion veil now – had given him a draught that tasted foul despite the addition of peppermint. Then, before she could finish stripping him, the dyer had interrupted her.

Now they whispered furiously in the hallway. Byren struggled to open his eyes, and saw a wall, the shadows of two people with their heads together.

'...can't stay here –'

'None of us can stay here,' the dyer said. 'My Miron's just come back with bad news. The castle's fallen. The Merofynians will rampage across the valley, taking what they want.'

Byren refused to believe it. It was the abbey that had been taken, not the castle. He had to warn his father.

That's right, he had. He'd sent word, sent it with the dyer's son, Miron who had come back because... no, the castle couldn't have fallen!

'Can we move him?' the dyer asked.

'I haven't checked the wound yet, but from the amount of blood on his vest... moving him might kill him.'

'It hasn't killed him yet. Sleeping in the snow should have killed him. He's tough as an old goat. Treat him and we'll move on. I'm guessing he's the last of King Rolen's kin. Miron says they burned the royal bodies so there would be no relics.'

'Burned who?'

'The king, his queen and the kingsdaughter.'

A moan was torn from Byren. Not Piro, not his mother.

Footsteps. Cool fingers on his forehead. Soft, female voice, calming.

Byren tried to catch her hand, but his arm was too heavy to lift. He tried to focus on the healer's face but his lids would not stay open. Not only was he useless, he'd failed his family. Another moan escaped him.

'Hush, bantling,' she whispered, speaking the kind of words mothers used to soothe small children. It amused him. He was a man, not a child of five. 'You've been very sick. You need to rest.'

How could he sleep when... 'M'mother, Piro!'

'I should have kept my voice down,' the dyer muttered.

'He should have been dead to the world. I gave him enough dreamless-sleep to knock out a horse.'

Byren lifted his head and prised his eyes open a crack, only to discover the single candle was too bright to bear. But he squinted up at the dyer, holding his eyes. 'Are you sure they're dead?'

The dyer's voice dropped as he leant closer. 'Miron met others fleeing. The overlord ordered the bodies burned.'

Byren fell back on the pillow. Hot tears seeped from his eyes, running down the side of his face. He had failed. His family were all dead but for him, and that could surely only be a matter of time.

The air escaped his chest in a long, despairing sigh. 'Don't risk your lives for me. Save yourselves and your families.' His voice was only a thread. 'Head for the mountains.'

'But Rolencia needs you,' the dyer insisted. 'You can't give up.'

Why not? He'd failed everyone who loved him, starting with Elina.

Byren turned his face to the wall as a wave of sorrow engulfed him, dragging him down.

CHAPTER THIRTEEN

PIRO WOKE WITH a start, shivering. The attic window let in a wintery twilight, so she had slept the afternoon away, burrowing under the covers for warmth. Her stomach rumbled loudly and she remembered she hadn't eaten all day. Someone rapped on the door and thrust it open without waiting.

'Lazy Rolencian slave!' the kitchen boy muttered in Merofynian and gestured for her to get up. He was about her age with a thin, mean mouth that made Piro suspect he delighted in the misfortunes of others.

She climbed out from under the bedcovers, thinking at least it would be warmer down by the kitchen fire.

When she arrived, the smell of cooking made her stomach clench with hunger. Soterro and the cook were seated at the table. It was clear these powerful members of the household shared a bond that made them a formidable team. If she wanted her time in Dunstany's household to be as painless as possible she must not antagonise these two.

Cook looked her up and down, rubbed his bristly chin, then sent her to wash the dishes.

'Lying abed while others work!' he muttered disgustedly in Rolencian, so she could understand.

She wanted to protest that she had been locked in, but thought it wiser not to.

The kitchen boy smirked as he joined the two men at the table. Piro suspected that washing the dishes had been his job, but now that she was lowest on the pecking order it had become hers.

'Why is she dressed like that?' the kitchen boy asked in Merofynian. 'That won't fool anyone.'

'Grysha's right, that outfit won't fool anyone,' Cook muttered. 'She still walks like a woman.'

Piro pretended not to understand as she scrubbed and rinsed, stacking the cooking pots and utensils on the grate to dry. She had helped her mother clean when they prepared private meals for her father, so she knew what she was doing.

Her gaze settled on a small paring knife, still grubby from preparing the vegetables. She picked it up along with several ladles and wiped them all clean, but instead of placing the knife with the other utensils, she slid it inside her sleeve. The outer sleeve was full and gathered but her inner woollen sleeve was tight, and it held the knife against her flesh, safe from detection. Ready for use.

Silently, she thanked Fyn for teaching her how to kill a man quickly, going straight for the groin, heart or throat.

Fyn... Her throat tightened and tears threatened. She must not think about him, had to be strong. Just because Palatyne had sent men to take the abbey it did not mean the abbey had fallen, and even if it had, that did not mean Fyn was dead.

She flicked her hands dry and wiped them on a cloth.

'Don't loaf about, girl,' Cook snapped in bad Rolencian. 'You can serve the master.'

Piro hurried over. Food was laid out on the table, enough for many people. She got the impression that Dunstany's servants did not go without.

Beside the cook's elbow was a dish of roasted baby potatoes, sprinkled with herbs. Melted butter glistened on their steaming skins. Piro's stomach gave a painful spasm of hunger. Without thinking, she went to take a crisp potato.

The cook slapped her hand. 'You'll eat the scraps when I say!'

Grysha giggled and Piro decided she hated him.

'Here.' The cook indicated a tray with a bottle of fine Rolencian red and a single goblet. 'Take this in. Master likes wine before his meal.'

Piro backed into the apothecary's dining room, holding a tray.

Dunstany sat before the fire, his long legs thrust towards the flames, a pensive expression on his face. Piro set the tray on the side board and poured the wine. She had served her father enough times to be a deft hand at it.

With a murmured word, she presented the goblet to the noble Power-worker. He exuded Affinity in the same way a cat might purr and knead its paws before the fireplace. His Affinity made hers stir.

The glittering black eyes lifted to Piro's face. Hastily she glanced down.

'You serve me as though I was the king himself. So many talents for a healer's assistant.' He smiled. 'Why didn't Sylion's nun have an apprentice healer from the abbey?'

The sudden change of topic startled Piro, but she recovered quickly. 'She did. The silly girl fell in love with one of the stable boys and they sailed for Ostron Isle.'

'Ah, yes. The Rolencian laws on Affinity.'

'The king would often consult my mistress about his old wounds,' Piro added, feeling she had to explain her training. 'She taught me how to serve him, so as not to shame her.'

'Did she? Well, we can be thankful you are a quick learner.' He held Piro's eyes a moment too long, making her uneasy.

There was a thunderous knocking at the apothecary's door and a voice demanded. 'Open up. Open on the overlord's business.'

For an instant Piro saw fear in Dunstany's unguarded face, but he masked it swiftly as Soterro hastily went through to answer the door.

After a quick consultation, he hurried back. In the front room they could hear several male voices all speaking Merofynian.

'It's the other Utlander. He's injured,' Soterro explained.

'Send him to the castle to his brother.' Dunstany looked up. Neither of them bothered to speak Rolencian.

Soterro hesitated. 'I think you should see this, m'lord.'

Which was odd, a servant advising his master. Before Piro could ponder this, Dunstany sprang to his feet and hurried through to the front room, snatching the lamp along the way. Piro would have slipped back into the kitchen, but Soterro caught her arm.

'So you're trained to serve royalty. Well, don't think yourself better than us. We're free men. You can make yourself useful, girl. Fetch and carry for the master.' With that he sent her after Dunstany. She heard him send Grysha, the kitchen boy, up to the castle with a message for the little Utland Power-worker.

In the front room half a dozen Merofynian warriors waited with a small bundle slung between them. Piro looked, but could not identify the Utlander's brother amongst them.

'Show me,' Dunstany said.

The men held the bundle open to reveal a shrunken, wizened old man curled into a huddled shape, no bigger than a child of six. Piro shuddered. Surely he was dead?

'On the counter,' Dunsany ordered. As they complied, he turned the lamp up. Seeing Piro, he thrust several starkiss candles into her hands. 'We'll need more light.'

She lit one from the lamp and stood the rest in a candle branch, lighting them in turn. Their flickering light dispelled the gloom, while Dunstany unwound the blankets covering the injured man and tried to straighten his limbs. But the man's body seemed to have constricted so that his limbs would not move. Piro glanced at his face. The skin was like wax parchment, sucked onto the bones. Even the man's eyes were sunken.

Dunstany managed to unwind the material around the man's stomach then pulled back with a sharp intake of breath, an Ostronite curse on his lips.

Why would he curse in Ostronite?

Piro forgot the question as she realised the Power-worker was curled around a sorbt stone. No wonder he looked like this.

She shuddered.

'What were you thinking?' Dunstany demanded of the Utlander's men. 'Why didn't you remove it? Who did this to him?'

'We couldn't get his hands off it,' their leader protested, torn between indignation and fear. 'So we brought him back.'

Dunstany massaged his temples. 'Tell me how it happened.'

'While we were on our way to Halcyon Abbey the Utlander argued with the Mulcibar mystic and we set off on our own. Then we found the seep.' The man frowned. 'Or maybe he sensed the seep, and argued so that he could hoard its power for himself.' He shrugged. 'At any rate, he set the stone in the seep to absorb its power, then we all went to bed. Next morning we found his Affinity-slave had slipped her chain, killed the sentry, placed the stone in his arms and stolen the calandrius.'

'What calandrius?'

'The one we found at the seep.'

Dunstany shook his head, as he walked around the counter, studying the contorted Power-worker from all angles. 'I doubt it was the Utlander's Affinity-slave that did this.'

'She hated him. She could've moved the stone like he did, wrapped in something. She –'

'I doubt she could kill a man. How did the sentry die?'

'Someone snapped his neck,' the man admitted. 'No signs of a fight.'

'Then she didn't do this,' Dunstany decided.

'Aren't you going to remove the stone?' the man asked.

'No point. He's dead. Was probably beyond help when you found him. If the stone was placed in contact with his skin while he was asleep, he had no mental guards in place. It would have plunged straight into where his Affinity power fed his life force and drained him at the source.'

The men shivered and muttered wards under their breath, reminding Piro how Fyn had taught her to protect herself against renegade Affinity. She must be on alert, ready to use the whispered chants and repetitive movements.

Piro glanced from the warriors to the noble Power-worker. She wasn't supposed to understand Merofynian, but anyone could tell from their stance and tone that this was serious.

'No, there was nothing you could have done,' Dunstany said slowly. 'You can go. His brother will be here soon.'

'You'll speak for us, my lord. He won't –'

'I will speak for you. You need not fear his anger.'

The men accepted this and hurried out. Piro recognised the same trust that her father's men had had in their king. While Palatyne's own men feared and fawned over him, the Merofynians respected Dunstany. More revealingly, they expected him to be fair and protect them from the Utland Power-worker.

She stared at Dunstany.

He caught her looking and spoke in Rolencian. 'This is what happens when someone with Affinity comes in contact with an unleashed sorbt stone. Never underestimate their power.'

She nodded. He seemed to expect it of her.

'You can go back to the kitchen now, Seela. Tell Cook to serve wine in the dining room and that we may have at least one more to dinner.'

Dismissed, she returned to the kitchen and delivered the message. Soterro and the cook had been helping themselves to what was left of the dismembered roast chickens and all of them had grease on their fingers and chins.

'More for dinner? That's easy for him to say,' Cook muttered in Merofynian, then asked Piro. 'So? What's going on?'

She glanced to the remains of the birds, stomach clenching and unclenching. They had almost been picked clean but...

The cook thrust the platter towards her and she began going through the bones for slivers of meat. 'It's the Utland Power-worker's brother –'

'We know that,' Cook snapped. 'Tell us something we don't know.'

'He's dead.'

They looked suitably impressed.

'Killed by an unleashed sorbt stone,' Piro supplied.

'I'll bet it was the Affinity-slave,' Soterro muttered. 'Can't keep an Affinity-touched person chained.'

The cook nodded wisely.

Piro shook her head. 'Lord Dunstany thinks not. He doesn't believe the slave could have snapped the sentry's neck without a fight.'

Their eyes widened.

'What, what? Who's dead?' the kitchen boy demanded in Merofynian, unable to follow more than the rudiments of Rolencian.

As the cook explained, Piro polished off the birds. She had only just washed her hands when the bell from the dining room rang.

Piro stood up but Soterro beat her to it, eager to hear the latest news while serving his master and guest. When he left, the cook and kitchen boy fell silent, straining to hear, but could only detect the murmur of voices. Soterro returned a few minutes later looking slightly flustered.

'How did the Utlander take it?' Cook whispered.

'He's furious. Thinks there's an enemy Power-worker wandering Rolencia,' Soterro explained with relish. 'We'll need two more goblets, Seela. Hurry, girl. The overlord's here, too. Dinner settings for three, Grysha.'

At this, Cook began to fuss over the presentation of the food while Soterro made up another tray with glasses and more wine, a Merofynian white this time. Heart thudding, Piro watched him.

Palatyne was here...

All she needed to do was slip some hellsbane into his food to avenge her family. Only she didn't have any yet.

'The door,' Soterro snapped.

Piro hastened down the short hall to hold the door open so that he could back through with the tray. She caught a quick glimpse of the room beyond.

Palatyne and the Utlander stood in front of the fireplace with Dunstany. Palatyne had discarded his battle armour for a padded black velvet vest and silk shirt of royal azure, its long sleeves pinned up with brooches. He wore a circlet of silver with a blue topaz set in the centre of his forehead. He looked like a warlord, trying to look like a Merofynian noble. Someone had broken his nose and it lay flat against his face, making him seem pugnacious, but she knew how cunning he was.

But it was the Utlander who drew her eye. He bristled as he paced the floor, radiating fury and Affinity. Grateful to escape, she let the door swing shut and returned to the kitchen, where the cook and kitchen boy exchanged looks.

'Well?' Cook demanded.

'They didn't say anything. The Utlander's furious.'

'That Utlander...' Grysha shuddered and made the sign to ward off evil. Which struck Piro as odd, because their master was a renegade Power-worker, but somehow Lord Dunstany was much more civilised.

'It's Palatyne I dread. He'll want to punish someone for sure.' The cook wiped his hands on his apron. 'We must be sure the dinner's perfect.'

Piro helped them stack more cutlery and plates on a tray while the cook freshened up the garnishes.

Soterro returned. 'Time to serve up. Come along, Seela. Give the overlord the same courtesies you'd give royalty. He might be nothing more than the most vicious of the spar warlords, but he sees himself as a suitor to Isolt Merofyn Kingsdaughter.'

So Piro had no choice, she had to serve the overlord.

She and Grysha took a tray each and trooped out after Soterro, placing the food on the sideboard. Soterro sent the boy back but kept Piro with him, giving her a severe look that promised retribution if she brought shame on Lord Dunstany's household.

'...seems a renegade Power-worker roams Rolencia,' Dunstany was saying, 'one who is our enemy but has not, so far, sought us out.'

'Could it have been a simple case of theft? He saw an opportunity, took the Affinity-slave and the calandrius? One thing is for sure, it was not the abbey's mystics master,' Palatyne remarked. 'My men tossed his body into a ditch along with the rest of the abbey's warrior monks!'

Piro paused as she placed clean cutlery on the table before each man. The abbey's warrior monks were dead? Impossible.

Soterro nudged her to keep setting the table. Fresh cutlery was a Merofynian noble custom her father had not bothered with, preferring to use his knife and fingers, but her mother had schooled her in its use.

'Then you've heard from the abbey as well?' Dunstany asked.

Close as she was to the overlord, she could not help but notice Palatyne cast the Utlander a swift look, rather like one might at a trained but vicious dog. But it was not a look of fear so much as wary, sly amusement, as if Palatyne enjoyed baiting the Utlander.

'My strategy overcame the abbey,' the overlord announced, still watching the Utlander. 'Even without your brother. Cyena and Mulcibar's mystics, along with my men, had no trouble subduing Halcyon's monks, nothing but boys and old men left to defend the abbey. They didn't stand a chance.'

Nausea roiling in Piro's belly. Fyn dead. A rushing noise filled her head.

No. She would not give up hope. He might yet have escaped. Fyn was clever and fast.

Piro stepped back, into the shadows. Dimly, she was aware that a branch of candles lit the men's faces where they sat around the table, while she stood by the sideboard in shadow. No one noticed her sudden retreat, for Soterro chose that moment to display the white meat with its fruit garnishes. Dunstany nodded his approval and Soterro returned to the sideboard to serve the food.

'This renegade Power-worker must be stopped,' the Utlander muttered, 'before he –'

'Does what?' Palatyne demanded.

Soterro nudged Piro, who took the plate from him and placed it before the overlord. He shoved it towards the noble scholar, who took a small portion from the meat and vegetables and ate them.

Piro stared stunned. She was sure this was not a Merofynian custom. Then it hit her. Palatyne feared poison. Dunstany, as host, was proving there was no poison in the food from his kitchen. Just as well she had not used the hellsbane. She didn't want to kill Dunstany.

Did she?

'Halcyon's warrior monks are all dead and the abbey is ours,' Palatyne went on. 'Sylion's sluts are trapped in their abbey where we can deal with them when we are ready. All of King Rolen's kin are either dead or soon to be recaptured. Only Cobalt remains and he's a by-blow.'

'So they found the body of the other kingson, the one gifted to the abbey?' the Utlander asked.

Piro held her breath, waiting for the answer. Soterro nudged her to take the Utlander's plate to the table. Then she returned to Soterro, who had just finished serving up Dunstany's plate.

'They sent word the moment the abbey fell. His body will be there. Then I will have one more emblem to add to my collection.' Palatyne stroked the three foenixes.

When Piro placed Dunstany's plate before him, she was close enough to the overlord to recognise the locket with Isolt Kingsdaughter's portrait, which she had last seen on Lence's chest. Her oldest brother must be dead.

Betraying tears threatened. She blinked them away fiercely, telling herself it meant no such thing. Lence might have escaped from Palatyne after losing the locket. But if Lence had been killed, then surely Byren still lived?

Not knowing which of her brothers to mourn was worse than knowing and mourning.

A finger prodded painfully in her ribs.

'You forgot the sauce. Go get it,' Soterro hissed and she hurried to obey.

Apart from one sharp glance when she returned, Dunstany paid no attention to her. The overlord and his two Power-workers ate in silence. Dunstany used the utensils with the same precise elegance as Piro had been taught. Soterro watched his master's guests eat with barely disguised disgust. Palatyne devoured his food, tearing into it with his teeth, and the Utlander ignored all but the knife, spearing his food on the end of it.

The eating done, Dunstany signalled Piro to clear the table.

'And what news of Cobalt?' Dunstany asked, as she removed the plates.

'His body's crippled now, to match his crippled claim to the throne.' Palatyne was well pleased. 'As a broken man he is even more useful. No, everything is going according to plan, but for that accursed kingson. I can't have Rolen's heir wandering Rolencia, stirring up the people against me.' He glared at his table companions.

Piro hid her dismay. He'd said 'Rolen's heir' which meant Lence was free, or did it? If Lence had been killed, Byren would be heir. She felt so frustrated she wanted to break something.

'What good are mystics and Power-workers if they can't find one troublesome warrior?' Palatyne demanded.

The Utlander and Dunstany exchanged looks, in agreement on something.

The noble scholar spoke, choosing his words carefully. 'Affinity is like fire, a tool that can be used to perform tasks. Like fire, it has its limitations. It –'

'I don't need a lecture, Dunstany. I want you to try and find him now. Let's see who is successful, the Merofynian noble or the Utlander!' Palatyne's dark eyes gleamed with cruel delight as he pulled something from inside his vest, unrolling a stained scrap of material to reveal a human finger.

Piro blinked.

'King Rolen's ring finger,' Palatyne announced.

Blood roared in Piro's ears.

'I know a little of your renegade arts.' Palatyne was very pleased with himself. 'It is easier to find someone if you have something of theirs.'

'Father's blood calls to son's!' The Utlander cackled.

She hated them, hated them all.

'Clear this, Soterro,' Lord Dunstany ordered, indicating the wine bottle and goblets.

Soterro nudged Piro and they hastily cleared the table. As Piro took the gravy dish, Dunstany said, 'Return and stand behind me, slave. I may have need of your services.'

It was only as Piro put the dish on the sideboard that she realised what the Utlander meant. They would use her father's finger to point to the missing kingson, but it would point to her since she was the nearest blood relative.

A surge of panic made her heart race. Wiping trembling fingers on her leggings, she wondered what to do. Running was hopeless. She eyed the table, clear now except for the finger which lay on the gleaming cherrywood surface. Somehow she could not see it as her father's finger. It was just a threatening object. What if she picked up the finger and flung it in the fire?

No point. It wouldn't burn quickly enough to be destroyed and her actions would betray her.

What could she do?

If the finger revealed who she was, Piro decided she would drive her hidden knife straight into Overlord Palatyne's cunning black heart. The blade felt reassuringly solid inside her sleeve.

'Soterro, bring me my Duelling Kingdoms board,' Lord Dunstany ordered. He beckoned Piro, who went to stand just behind him, slightly to his left. His formidable black eyes seemed to hold a warning that was meant only for her. 'Say nothing, slave. You will break my concentration.'

Soterro returned with the game board, which was larger than the one King Rolen used and hinged down the middle. Lord Dunstany opened it out, revealing a beautifully made Kingdoms board. A gold vineleaf border twined around the edge, salt-water wyvern scales had been set into the wood, filling the sea with gleaming blue. The two crescents of Rolencia and Merofynia were made from white mother-of-pearl while black onyx indicated the Dividing Mountains and the border of the Snow Bridge. The spars poked out from the dividing mountains like the spokes of a wheel. Like Ostron Isle and the Snow Bridge, they were made of mother-of-pearl.

Dunstany adjusted the board until he was happy with its position and, with a nod to his colleague and opponent, placed the king's finger in the Headlands, facing the valley of Rolencia. Piro noticed that the overlord's eyes gleamed and he shifted in his seat, as if he was both fascinated and fearful.

'You are dismissed, Soterro,' Lord Dunstany said, then nodded to the other Power-worker. 'You may go first, Utlander.'

Piro wondered briefly why no one used his name, then remembered hearing somewhere that Utlanders believed their names held power.

This Utlander made several passes over the finger, not touching it, but stroking the air above it. He frowned and whined a phrase under his breath, over and over. Piro felt a thickening of the atmosphere, as if a storm were imminent. Her nostrils stung as though she had inhaled repugnant fumes. They said evil renegades could be distinguished by their foul stench. Her vision wavered as she shifted to Unseen sight. The Utlander and the noble scholar both radiated Affinity. Oddly enough, a dull glow also emanated from Palatyne. So he was sensitive to Affinity. No wonder he was both fearful of it and fascinated by it. They all focused on the board and the finger. She hoped that, standing behind Dunstany, any Affinity coming off her would be mistaken for his.

Even so, she eased the knife down until its hilt rested in the palm of her hand.

All the small hairs on her body rose as the king's severed finger crawled slowly across Rolencia. Her father had been a hard worker and a fighter all his life and his hands reflected this. The work-blunted nail came to rest, pointing to Rolenton. Or to Piro who was directly in line with it, behind Dunstany.

'Ha!' Palatyne said. 'It points to Rolenton where all the king's ancestors are buried. Your focus is not refined enough, Utlander.'

Piro let her breath out slowly and eased her grip on the knife hilt, returning it to its hiding place.

'I quested for Rolen's blood kin!' the Utlander insisted. 'Rolen's children are half-Merofynian. It points to you, Lord Dunstany. You are confusing the power because you are related to the old royal line of Merofynia through their mother's great, great aunt.'

'Enough talking! I want the kingson dead,' Palatyne ground out. 'The way you Power-workers snipe and snap at each other, I swear you are more of a hindrance than a help.'

'Overlord.' Lord Dunstany gave him a smile of apology. 'Let me try.'

The Utlander sneered but watched closely, his eyes shrouded beneath bristling brows as Dunstany pressed his finger tips to his temples and closed his eyes.

This time Piro did not feel a sense of oppression. The back of her neck tingled and she felt as if she was slowly rising through the roof of her skull. She lifted higher until she hung over the table, looking down on the three men and herself.

Then she was arrowing out across Rolencia, searching.

CHAPTER FOURTEEN

WHILE ROLLING OVER in his sleep, Fyn felt something burn his chest. He sprang up, pulling the Fate from its resting place under his jerkin. The opal glowed with Affinity.

Fascinated and fearful, Fyn opened his mind to greet the mystics master. But it was a stranger, a presence which winged across Rolencia searching for something. It had to be a renegade Power-worker.

Even as he thought this, an image took form in his mind, the castle hunt-master with a bloodhound on leash, sniffing out a trail. Searching... for who or what?

The Fate? It called those with Affinity.

Fyn fought panic. He was no mystic. Without the mystics master to aid him, how could he do battle? He had to hide his presence. He concentrated on cloaking himself, and taking no action that would give him away.

The renegade Power-worker, however, did not seem to notice that Fyn had been swept along with him as he let his bloodhound follow the trail. He swooped over the starlit, snow-mantled land. The chantries and oratories in various villages glowed, but he ignored them until a Sylion oratory drew them down through the thatched roof of its residence, into the only bedroom.

A man lay there, on his side, his face turned away to the wall. With Unseen sight Fyn could see a miasma of grief and guilt radiating from him, but his actual features were blurred. Fyn's instinct was to try to help the grieving man, but he dare not do anything that might attract the Power-worker's attention, so he held back.

Beside the man knelt a veiled healer. She did not glow with power – her Affinity was only mild. She would heal with herbs, stitching and encouragement. Right now, she was bathing the blood from the man's ribs. The wound was revealed, an ugly, puckered knot of flesh.

He felt the nun's surprise. Fresh blood on an old wound. Days old.

Then where did the blood come from?

What did all this mean? Why had he been swept along in the Power-worker's search?

One thing was clear to Fyn, the nun could not heal the injury to the man's soul and, if that wasn't dealt with, he would not have the will to heal his body. Fyn could feel him relinquishing his hold on this mortal plane. It would only take a fever to carry him off. Fyn had to risk helping him.

On the Unseen plane he had no physical body, yet he reached out for the man's wounded essence. Contact stunned him. It was Byren, and his heart was broken, his sense of self destroyed.

It was too much, more than Fyn could stand.

Another presence pierced his awareness. With a heart-juddering start, Fyn realised he had betrayed himself.

For an instant the Power-worker was too startled to react, then he stretched out a questing tendril into Fyn, who wrenched himself away. Nausea coiled in his belly as he fell, spiralling down... down, down into his body.

Re-entering his corporeal form was like a kick in the stomach. It stole his breath and left him gasping. He found himself lying in the snow-cave, the Fate clutched in his hand, frozen tears on his cheeks. Fyn struggled to his knees and dry-retched. Pinpricks of light danced in his vision. It was a good eight heartbeats before his sight cleared.

He felt physically drained, but he had escaped the Power-worker and that amazed him. He studied the Fate. Its dim opal surface gave no hint of the power it contained. To think, he could be captured while he slept and dragged on a journey. Truly this Fate was a tricky tool to use. And there was no chance of training, now that he no longer served the mystics master.

Fingers trembling, he tucked the Fate inside his jerkin, wondering what to do next.

He was both relieved and worried to learn that Byren lay injured in a farmer's cottage, wounded physically and mentally. The impact of his brother's heartbreak still weighed on Fyn. Lence must be dead. Only his twin's death would be so devastating for Byren.

Lence dead... why did he feel only relief?

Unable to sit still, Fyn broke out of his snow-cave and shook himself.

Byren was not dead, but he was close to death and the Merofynian Power-worker knew where he was. That is, if he recognised him. Physical features did not hold shape on the Unseen plane, it was a person's essence that gave him form. How would someone who had never known Byren recognise him?

Fyn could only hope the Power-worker had not recognised either of them.

Wide awake now, he was ready to skate through the night. His father had to be told that an evil Power-worker roamed Rolencia using Affinity paths. If the king sent to Sylion Abbey for the mystics mistress, she would know what to do. She would be able to locate Byren and help him.

Fyn must reach Rolenhold and warn his father. Thank Halcyon Piro was safe in the castle.

PIRO PUSHED HELPING hands away and sat up, surprised to find herself lying on the floor with the noble scholar kneeling over her. She grabbed her rabbit-skin cap, which had fallen off, and pulled it down low over her ears. The last thing she wanted was to attract the overlord's attention but that was exactly what she had done.

'What's wrong with your slave?' Palatyne demanded as Dunstany helped her to her feet.

'She has not eaten since breakfast.' He gave her a push towards the door. 'Foolish child, go to the kitchen and ask Cook for a meal.'

Grateful for the reprieve, Piro headed for the door.

'What happened, Utlander?' asked Palatyne.

'Dunstany left his body for several heartbeats –'

Piro remembered the floating sensation and realised she had been carried along by the Power-worker's Affinity. She wanted to stay and learn more, but she had to obey Dunstany.

Opening the door, she found Cook, Soterro and Grysha, all listening in the short hall. They made no apology and they each held a mug brimming with Rolencian red wine. The cook shoved her aside as the door swung shut and they craned to hear what was being said in the next room. Piro stood just behind them, listening unashamedly.

'Well, Dunstany, what did you learn?' Palatyne prodded, his deep voice carrying through the closed door.

'It was hard to tell. The Unseen plane is not like ours. Things appear –'

'No excuses. What did you see?' Palatyne demanded.

'One of Sylion's oratories.'

'Who was there?' Palatyne asked. 'Byren Kingson?'

Piro bit back a gasp. Byren? They were looking for Byren, not Lence?

Could the man on the bed have been Byren? Piro tried to recall his features, but he had been turned away and it was Fyn's face that came to her. Thoughtful, kind Fyn. Sorrow carried on a wave of love swamped her. She told herself she must not give in to despair. They had not found Fyn's body. He may yet live.

'No, I did not see the kingson,' Dunstany admitted. 'It was a Sylion healer exercising her craft on an injured man. Her deep Affinity must have drawn me.'

'Another failure!' the Utlander commiserated, and there was the unmistakable edge of triumph to his voice.

'Ahh, you're useless, the pair of you. I'll have Cyena and Mulcibar's mystics try when they get here!' the overlord growled. The floor creaked as he strode to the far door.

Piro realised Palatyne must have sent the mystics from Merofynia's two great abbeys with the warriors to take Halcyon's abbey. Fight fire with fire.

The overlord spoke again. 'I'm going back to the castle to host the victory feast. You Power-workers needn't bother to attend until you have some real news of Byren Kingson.'

When the door closed after him the Utlander said, 'I'll take King Rolen's finger.'

'Be my guest.'

There was a muffled sound and the Utlander cursed. 'You dropped it!'

'Sorry. Here, let me clean it for you.'

'You keep your hands off it. I don't trust you. You'll wipe out its usefulness with a counter-spell!'

'You wrong me.'

The Utlander made a rude noise and left. There was silence from the room beyond. Soterro and Cook exchanged looks. While they were distracted the kitchen boy's hand cupped Piro's bottom suggestively. She froze in surprise, then drove her elbow into his midriff. He gave a grunt of pain.

'What?' The cook turned around and saw Grysha's pained face and Piro's anger. 'I told you if you stroked that kitten's fur the wrong way she'd scratch.'

Grysha refused to answer and Piro pretended she had not understood his Merofynian speech.

The cook waddled back to the kitchen and poured himself another goblet of wine. 'Master's got his work cut out for him, keeping one step ahead of that jumped-up barbarian overlord and the greedy little Utlander. Thanks be to Mulcibar, the twin is dead. I don't know much about Affinity, but I'm guessing losing one twin more than halves the other twin's power.' He noticed Piro and switched to Rolencian. 'Don't just stand there. Fetch the plates and do the dishes.'

At that moment, Soterro returned, beckoning Piro. 'Lord Dunstany wants you.' He added in Merofynian, 'looks like he's fed one appetite, now he wants to feed another!'

'Didn't know he had it in him.' Cook winked.

Hiding her alarm, Piro went into the apothecary's dining room. Dunstany had poured himself a wine and was swirling it around in the goblet, watching it intently. She waited, shifting from foot to foot, wondering how she was going to escape this. Surely Soterro was mistaken. The noble scholar was so old, he shouldn't want her in that way.

'You rang, sor,' she said, dipping her head in a servant's bow. 'I mean, m'lord.'

His unreadable black eyes met hers. Then he put his goblet aside. 'You make a pretty page boy, Seela.'

Piro decided she would slit his throat if he laid one hand on her, run straight up to the castle and kill Palatyne, then finish off Cobalt.

At least she'd try.

'Are you feeling better now that you've eaten? Here.' Dunstany poured a second goblet of wine and offered it to her.

She was sure slaves were not offered wine by their Merofynian masters, Rolencian servants never were. Perhaps it only happened when their masters wanted to use their bodies. Reluctantly, she approached the table and took a single sip, keeping the chair between herself and Dunstany. She put the goblet down.

'Do you know what happened tonight?' he asked, surprising her.

'No, sor.'

He studied her carefully. 'How long have you had Affinity?'

She drew breath to contradict him.

'Don't waste my time denying it. When I tried to influence you up at the castle you overcame the compulsion to serve my will. Only someone with innate Affinity could break my gaze. Then tonight, when I plunged into the Unseen plane, I unwittingly drew on your Affinity. That's why you passed out, weakened by my journey. Why didn't your family gift you to Sylion Abbey?'

Piro licked her lips. 'Me Da died years ago so I was all me Mam had. I had to support her.

'You served Halcyon's healer. Why didn't she notice your Affinity?'

Yes, why not? Piro drew breath, her mind scrambling. 'I hid it. Pretended the best I could do was stitch and mix herbals.'

'A convincing story,' Dunstany said with a half-smile. And Piro wondered just what he meant by that. 'While I was out of my body, did you sense anything? Be aware that I know when you are lying.'

'No, sor.' She was certain he was bluffing. Well, pretty certain.

'Have you ever had visions?'

Piro debated how much she should reveal. She longed for reassurance and, for a renegade Affinity Power-worker, the noble scholar seemed honourable. 'Before the overlord attacked I had bad dreams, sor. Wyverns running through the castle.' Her throat closed as she recalled her father refusing to heed her warnings. She blinked back tears.

'Most distressing,' he agreed. 'If you have any more visions let me know.

They are triggered by nexus points in the possible future paths... I see you don't understand. One day perhaps.'

'They say Affinity leaves you open to evil unless you have an abbey's protection,' Piro whispered.

'Evil cannot touch you while you are with me, Seela. I place protective wards wherever I go.' He slid her goblet towards her. 'Drink up. Did Cook give you something to eat?'

'Yes, thank you.' Piro sipped the wine, looking down into the goblet, watching the dark liquid glint in the candlelight. After everything that had happened today, she just wanted to curl up and sleep.

Piro's heart gave a little double beat of surprise, as she realised Dunstany was trying to trick her again. It was not a frontal attack like up at the castle, but a more subtle strike.

Staring into her goblet, she concentrated on resisting the dreamy sensation. The knife felt heavy in her sleeve. Could Dunstany see the outline? She let her left arm drop from the goblet so that the full over-sleeve fell down covering the inner woollen sleeve. Still the knife weighed on her thoughts.

'Is there something you wish to tell me?' Dunstany asked softly.

An answer almost tripped off her unwary tongue, but she managed to shake her head.

He stood up with a sigh, calling for Soterro. The servant hurried in, standing stiffly to hide the amount of wine he had drunk.

'Lock Seela in her room. I'm making you responsible for her. If she runs away I'll take it out on your hide. Understand?'

Soterro glowered at Piro. 'She hasn't done the washing up, yet.'

'Grysha can do it.' Lord Dunstany frowned at Piro who tried to look innocent. 'You can give it back now.'

She held out the goblet.

'No. The knife.'

Heat raced up her cheeks. Shamed at being caught out, she avoided Dunstany's eyes as she slid the knife from her sleeve and offered it hilt-first to him.

Soterro cursed.

'Just so.' Dunstany smiled as he gave Soterro the knife. 'Return this to Cook and tell him to be more careful. This slave might look as innocent as a newborn lamb, but you mustn't take your eyes off her for a moment.'

Soterro grabbed Piro's arm and dragged her into the kitchen where Cook was tipping the last of the wine into his mug.

'Here.' Soterro tossed the knife. It clattered on the table. 'She had it hidden.'

Grysha's eyes widened. Piro was tempted to hiss at him, but she wasn't supposed to have understood the cook's reference to her as a kitten.

Cook caught Piro's arm, turning her around to face him. Sweat glistened on his upper lip and bald pate, and his jowls shook with anger. 'What were you planning, girlie? Whatever it was it would do no good. Our master places protective spells wherever we go. No chance of you slipping into his bedroom and slitting his throat while he sleeps!'

'No chance of her doing it to us, either. She'll be locked up,' Soterro muttered with satisfaction.

He took a candle to light the stairs to the attic, grumbling all the way. 'Lord Dunstany's a good master, better than most. But he's a sharp one. No chance of pocketing his valuables or selling off his wine!' He unlocked the door. 'In you go.'

'Can I have another blanket? It's cold up here.'

He snorted, closed the door and locked it, leaving Piro in the dark. She dressed in all the clothes she had and climbed into the bunk, pulling the covers up. So much had happened she was sure she'd never sleep. Soterro was right, Lord Dunstany was too clever. She had to escape him before he guessed who she was. It had been close tonight.

But Byren was alive!

She hugged the knowledge to herself, letting it warm her to the core. If only Fyn was safe. Tomorrow she would escape the noble scholar and go looking for her brothers.

That reminded her. Lence must be dead, that was why they referred to Byren as kingsheir. In fact, now that their father was dead, Byren was the uncrowned king.

Tears stung Piro's eyes, and she gave in to them at last. When the sobs no longer shook her, she sang the chants to Halcyon to lay her mother, father and eldest brother to rest. The goddess would care for them in her Sacred Heart.

But it was Sylion she prayed to next, for the cruel god of winter understood revenge.

CHAPTER FIFTEEN

BYREN LIFTED HIS head, roused by someone turning his clothes on the chair before the fireplace. They left before he could gather his wits. Through the frosted panes of the small window, he heard someone in the yard outside talking gently as they eased the pony into the sled shafts.

The dyer was preparing to run for the mountains. Byren knew they should leave him behind. He'd slow them down, and they'd be executed if they were caught with him. He didn't want to fail these people as well.

He slid his legs out of the bed, careful of his bandaged ribs, and shuffled to the fire. His breeches were almost dry, so he eased them on but didn't attempt the boots. Byren unrolled his shirt. It had been washed and hastily stitched, and was warm from hanging in front of the fire. He pulled it on and lifted his vest. Someone had sponged the blood off but had not attempted to repair the leather.

As he turned for the door a wave of dizziness hit him, greyness eating into his vision. He clutched the shelf above the fireplace, feeling his legs shake and his stomach clench. A light sweat broke out on his skin. Either he was going to pass out, or his head would clear. He ground his teeth.

The dizziness cleared. He crossed the room and took a deep breath which triggered a cough. It hurt but did not tear at him inside, nor did he have that odd panicky feeling as if he could not get enough air. He checked by coughing again. No blood on his hand.

So he was not going to die. Amazing.

The healer must be blessed with great Affinity. He wondered if, by healing him, she had triggered some unpleasant side effect of Affinity, as the old seer had done when she healed Orrade. Since then his best friend had twice lapsed into visions and passed out, and had only admitted the truth to Byren the night they tackled Palatyne.

How was Orrade coping, leading the survivors of his father's estate into the mountains? Had he had any more visions? Concern for Orrade made Byren impatient with his weakness. He owed his friend an apology.

Others would turn on Orrade if they suspected he had Affinity, or if they realised he followed Palos's path. And suddenly, the fact the Orrade was a lover of men did not seem so important. Even the Affinity was a nuisance rather than a tragedy.

Had the Sylion healer triggered Affinity in him? Byren paused and searched his mind and body for some difference that he could sense. Nothing.

He was untouched by Affinity and he would live.

Yet he felt no joy.

At the door he had to pause and bend double to catch his breath. Voices came through from what smelt like the kitchen. Determined to tell them to leave him behind, he shoved the door open.

'He's awake!' the four-year-old piped up. He pushed his plate of hot oat cakes towards Byren. 'Have some. They're really good!'

Both the healer and dyer turned to Byren, startled. She had been rolling smoked meat in calico for travelling and the dyer was bent over, scraping mud off his boots by the door.

'I was hungry,' Byren said and realised it was true.

'I'll make up a plate,' the healer offered. 'Only reheated cakes I'm afraid. Not what a kingson is used to. Everyone's run off.'

'Oat cakes are my favourite,' he said, relieved there was no need to lie.

'How are you feeling?' She put a plate on the table in front of him, watching closely.

'Stiff and sore,' Byren admitted. 'But alive. You know your craft, that's for sure. I owe you my life.' This was also true, but his heart wasn't in it. He felt empty.

Still, the hot cakes smelt good and the syrup gleamed golden in the early morning light. He took a large serving, ravenously hungry.

Byren noticed the dyer catch the healer's eye.

'Come, show me where you left the harness,' the dyer said.

The healer nodded and Byren found himself alone in the kitchen with the little boy. Hadn't the man said his older son had come back? He was probably out in the yard preparing to leave with them.

Byren lifted a hot cake. 'Good as your mother makes?'

'Dunno. Ma died when I was born,' the boy answered simply.

'I'm sorry.' The loss of his own mother and sister returned to stab at Byren's composure.

'You finished, Rodien?' the dyer called. He appeared in the doorway. 'Don't want to hurry you, kingson, but we must be moving.'

Byren mopped up the last of the hot cake and washed it down with warm ale. 'That's just it. I don't want you to risk your family for me.'

He rose, meaning to tell them to leave him, but he must have stood too fast because his head swam and he nearly lost his breakfast. A strong arm with stained fingers caught him, supporting his weight.

'Come along now.'

Too weak and disorientated to argue, Byren yielded to the dyer as he helped him outside. The food felt good in his belly, now that it wasn't trying to come back up again, but his whole body ached as if he'd taken a tumble from his horse. He let himself be lowered onto the sled for now.

'But I'll walk when I can,' he insisted.

'Of course you will,' the dyer agreed.

The healer ran back into her cottage and came out slinging a travelling cloak over her shoulders. She bolted the door behind her.

'Is she coming too?' Byren asked, worried that she would also pay for helping him.

'No, I'm off to Waterford,' she nodded to the west, 'to warn them.'

Byren nodded. Someone was missing. 'Where's... what was his name, Miron? I heard you say he'd returned last night.'

The dyer lifted his little boy onto the pony's back, then turned to Byren. 'I sent him back to Rolenhold last night, kingson. I sent him to find your honour guard, give them your leogryf necklace and to tell them to join us at Cedar tradepost.' He ducked his head. 'With your leave, kingson.'

A smile tugged at Byren's lips. 'Without my leave, you mean. For a dyer you are an excellent warrior.'

The man beamed.

But his initiative would be wasted. Those honour guard who had remained loyal to Byren had come to save him at Dovecote and, if any of them survived, they would already be with Orrade in the mountains. A stab of pain hit Byren – they had lost Garzik that night. At fourteen Orrade's little brother had wanted to become a warrior and serve Byren, who had sent him to his death.

He was a failure over and over.

Because Byren hadn't returned to the castle with the warrior monks, no one at Rolenhold would believe he'd remained loyal, that is if anyone who knew him still lived. He couldn't imagine Captain Temor dropping his sword and surrendering to the Merofynians. Sorrow too deep for tears settled on him, smothering him in a blanket of despair.

He hoped Miron made it safely back to his father in the mountains. He knew only too well how rash boys on the verge of manhood could be. Poor Garzik.

They left Sylion's oratory and residence behind. At the end of the single street of empty dwellings the dyer embraced the healer, and Byren was struck by the resemblance as they parted. They were family separated by Affinity, he guessed.

The dyer had already done more than he needed to, risking his thirteen-year-old son twice for Rolencia. As soon as Byren was well enough he'd strike out on his own.

And then it hit Byren. His family were all dead and his home taken. The dyer expected Byren, King Rolen's only surviving kin, to raise an army in the mountains and retake Rolencia, but how could one man hope to achieve so much? Why would anyone follow him, when his own father had died believing him a traitor?

ELBOW-DEEP IN BREAD dough, Piro was grateful for the warmth of the kitchen. All day she had helped the cook, under Soterro's watchful eye. At first light Dunstany had been called up to the castle to treat Cobalt, who'd developed a fever. If she was lucky, Cobalt would die.

When she thought of Dunstany up there with Palatyne and the Utlander, she was surprised by a pang of concern for him.

It was evening now and they were expecting the noble scholar's return any moment. Piro planned to stay long enough to hear if there had been news of Byren, and then escape.

They shared the rear courtyard with several other fine houses, and there were four narrow lanes that led out to the main street. She was reasonably certain she could knock Grysha unconscious long enough for her to make it out into Rolenton. From there, well, she knew the town and they did not.

She twisted the bread dough into small lumps and dropped the raw buns onto the tray, careful not to look interested in what the others were saying. Grysha had been sent to buy supplies. Soterro and the cook had been helping themselves to the master's wine again and, believing she could not understand Merofynian, did not bother to guard their tongues.

'We'll be off home soon,' Soterro was saying. 'About time, too. The old king won't last long.'

The cook noticed Piro had finished. 'Brush the buns with milk and sprinkle cinnamon and sugar on the top.' He switched back to Merofynian. 'Palatyne'll be eager to get back to the king. After this victory the old man's sure to offer him a dukedom!'

'There's many a slip 'twixt cup and lip.' Soterro grimaced. 'Palatyne trusts no one, especially not our master. Dunstany's noble born and bred and the overlord can't forgive him that, not when he comes from the wrong side of the Divide.'

'Put them into the bread oven, girl. We want the buns for supper tonight, not next summer!' the cook snapped, then turned to Soterro, returning to Merofynian. 'But when Palatyne is a duke no one will remember where he was born.'

'I don't think he plans to stop at duke.' Soterro's voice was heavy with meaning.

Cook's eyes widened.

The bell rang, signalling Dunstany's return. Soterro went to answer his summons. Just then there was a knock at the kitchen door.

'Don't stand there daydreaming, girl. Wash your arms, take off that grubby apron and answer the door!' Cook told Piro.

She hurried to obey. Opening the door she faced her old nurse with a tray of hot pies. Piro stifled a gasp.

'Hot pies, lovely hot pies for sale,' old Seela sang in a fair imitation of a street-seller. 'A copper a pie!'

'Hmm. What have you got?' The cook hurried over to take a look. He sniffed. 'They smell good. But my master expects the best.'

'There's eel, steak and kidney, steak and peas, bacon and chicken –'

'We'll take one of each. And if they're not up to standard you won't be getting my lord's custom again!'

The cook went out of the room to where he hid his money, to count out his coins.

'Bless me. It's good to see you, Piro,' her old nurse whispered. 'Quick now, while he's away, out the door –'

'I can't. Lord Dunstany just came back and he may have news of Byren.'

Before they could argue, the cook returned and counted out the coins as Piro transferred the pies to the table.

'If these are good we'll take some more tomorrow. Do you have any sweet pies, apple or blueberry?'

Her old nurse nodded. 'Whatever you wish.'

Piro hid a smile. The castle pastry cook was renowned for her pies. She'd be horrified to know they were being sold for a copper each.

'I'll be back tomorrow, then,' Seela said, catching Piro's eye meaningfully, before heading off.

'Well, shut the door, girl, you're letting the cold in!' the cook snapped. Just then Soterro returned. 'What news?'

'Mulled wine for two. The overlord's with him.'

Piro's heart skipped a beat. Another missed opportunity to poison Palatyne because she hadn't stolen the hellsbane. She should steal some tomorrow and kill Palatyne first chance she got.

Yes, that's what she would do. Then she'd run away.

Relieved to have a plan, Piro put cheese and bread on a plate while Cook checked the spiced wine. She dried her hands then picked up the tray to follow Soterro down the short hall.

When Piro entered she found Dunstany stood by the fire listening to Palatyne. Soterro poured the drinks and was dismissed, which left Piro to wait by the sideboard.

Dunstany sipped his mulled wine, clearly enjoying the delicate mix of spices.

'...so it looks like Cobalt will make a full recovery,' Palatyne was saying. He gulped his steaming goblet. 'I could use some good news. The Utlander can't get a fix on Byren Kingson. He claims you cursed Rolen's finger, says it will point to Rolenton and nowhere else.'

'I'd be a fool to do something so obvious. No, the Utlander seeks to lay the blame for his incompetence on me. He hasn't the skill to differentiate between living and dead kin, as we saw last night.' Dunstany laughed softly and Piro looked down, hiding her triumph. If only they knew.

'So much for the Utlander. What about you, have you found Byren Kingson?' the overlord asked.

'I spent all day nursing your puppet king,' Lord Dunstany pointed out. 'I will seek the youth this very night.'

There was a clatter of booted feet in the front room and someone rapped on the connecting door, then marched straight in. A tall thin woman, wearing the white of a Cyena mystic, entered. She was young, but her hair was completely white and her eyes were pale pink. Piro had heard of such people, born without colouring, but never seen one. Just looking at the woman made her shiver.

'Overlord Palatyne.' The mystic afforded him a shallow bow. 'I bring word concerning the kingsons.'

Piro froze, then schooled her face to look blank, since she wasn't supposed to understand what was being said. Luckily no one had noticed her slip.

'Here is a list of what was found in the abbey.' The Cyena mystic nodded to one of her escort, who presented a written dispatch that Palatyne did not bother to open. Piro wondered if he had to sound out the words to read.

'What news of the kingson at the abbey?' the overlord demanded.

'The bodies were carefully searched. There were many youths of the right age, but none of them wore the royal emblem.'

Palatyne frowned, while Piro cheered inside. Fyn could still be alive.

'It is most curious,' the mystic said softly, 'for no small boys were found, only old men and lads nearly old enough to be monks.'

'They're hiding.'

'Obviously.'

As the mystic's odd pink eyes skimmed past Palatyne, Piro realised the mystic was blind, at least blind to the Seen world. Her Affinity would give her Unseen sight. Piro instinctively reinforced the walls she had used to hide her Affinity from the castle's nuns and monks.

'We sealed the abbey and checked every chamber, but we found no sign of them. There was not a single sorbt stone in the mystics master's inner sanctum and we did not find the way into Halcyon's Sacred Heart with its recurring seep.'

'Perhaps it is a myth?' Dunstany suggested.

Blind, pink eyes moved towards the sound of his voice. 'Our spies report otherwise. Such a treasure would be well hidden. I suspect that's where the small boys are, along with the missing sorbt stones. Someone was quick enough to warn them and I suspect this missing kingson is hidden in some deep secret chamber under Mount Halcyon.'

Palatyne smiled. 'Well, they'll have to come out sooner or later, or starve. You.' He pointed to one of the mystic's escort. 'Go back. Tell Mulcibar's mystic not to leave the abbey until he finds them.'

The man nodded and remained where he was.

'Now!' Palatyne roared and the man ran out. 'As for you,' he turned to Cyena's mystic. 'You can come up to the castle and try your luck at locating Byren Kingson.'

'I'd be happy to.' The Cyena mystic reached into the folds of her long white robe. 'Meanwhile, I do have something for you.' She held out a drawstring bag.

Palatyne snapped his fingers at Piro. 'Bring it to me.'

She swallowed. The thought of approaching the albino mystic made her uneasy. But she went over and retrieved the bag, passing it to Palatyne. At least she was braver than him!

He tugged the strings open, tipping the contents into his palm. 'A foenix emblem? I thought you said –'

'No, we couldn't find the priestly kingson's body. This one belongs to the other kingson,' the mystic said. 'About midday, on the day after we took the abbey, a man entered the courtyard and marched into the stables waving the royal emblem around and demanding to see the abbot.

'The men realised he must be the missing kingson. They tell me he went as white as me when he found Merofynian warriors inside the abbey!' The mystic allowed herself a reptilian smile. 'They tried to grab him but he fought his way out, grabbed a horse and rode off. They managed to get the emblem. And they injured him. Badly. We sent the men after him. They followed his blood trail until they lost him. That night we heard an ulfr pack on the hunt. Then his trail disappeared along with his body.'

Sickened, Piro turned away. She could not see the pastries for the tears. To think Byren had reached the abbey, as he had promised to do, only to find Merofynians had laid claim to it.

'There was just one of him and dozens of my warriors. They should have killed him!' the overlord snapped.

'He's dead. The ulfr pack finished him off.'

'You don't know that for sure. I want his body. I need proof that he's dead or the Rolencians will spread rumours about him leading an uprising,' Palatyne growled at the mystic, who looked uncomfortable.

Palatyne gestured with frustration, snapping his fingers at another of her escort. 'Chase after that other fool. Let it be known through Rolencia that I'm doubling the reward for Byren Kingson's head and that of the priestly kingson.'

Piro nursed a flicker of hope. If Palatyne feared her brothers' survival enough to double the reward they still stood a chance. She would not give up.

The man left and Palatyne dismissed Cyena's mystic. When she had gone, he turned to Dunstany. 'See, Dunstany, I help myself. A man can trust a blade to do what it's told. This Affinity of yours twists and turns so much you never give me a straight answer.' He took a step closer, glaring at the old Power-worker. 'I know where your loyalties lie, noble scholar. But you forget, King Merofyn is a sick old man. He has promised me a dukedom if I conquer Rolencia in his name.' Palatyne laughed. 'But why should I settle for a dukedom when I could have a kingdom? I'll marry his daughter and –'

'She is already betrothed.'

'Lence Kingsheir is dead.'

'The second son, Byren, is the uncrowned king of Rolencia now and honour-bound to marry Isolt.'

'If he lives. If he can escape my men. If he can raise the warlords against me. If he can retake Rolencia.' Palatyne dismissed this possibility with a sharp movement of his hand. 'No, I am here and I am the conqueror of Merofynia's ancestral enemy. In three hundred years no one has managed to crush the Rolencian royal line. No one but me.' Palatyne tossed back the last of his mulled wine. 'I'll make King Merofyn an offer for his daughter that he can't refuse.' Palatyne's eyes narrowed. 'And if you want a place in the court of Emperor Palatyne the First, ruler of Merofynia and Rolencia, then you must prove your loyalty!'

Dunstany spread his hands. 'I am at your command, overlord.'

Palatyne's eyes narrowed. 'We will see.'

He thrust his goblet aside and strode out.

Piro sagged, dizzy with relief. Dunstany met her eyes across the room. They heard the overlord's boots on the apothecary's shop floor and the slam of the front door.

'Mark my words, Seela,' Dunstany said in Rolencian. 'Palatyne is a very dangerous man. He cannot be trusted, because he trusts no one. If he wins the throne, there will be no peace for Merofynia or anyone else. So where do you think Byren Kingsheir is?'

Piro went very still as she tried to remember what she was supposed to know. They'd spoken Merofynian so she wouldn't have understood anything but the names. She decided it was best to claim ignorance. 'A serving girl like me knows nothing of kingsons.'

'No, a serving girl wouldn't,' Dunstany agreed, watching her thoughtfully.

Piro felt decidedly uncomfortable. Maybe she should forget about poisoning Palatyne and run away before the noble scholar pierced her disguise.

Dunstany seemed lost in reverie. After a moment he took a deep breath and rang the bell for Soterro, who was so quick to arrive he must have been listening at the door.

If Dunstany suspected this, he did not betray it by so much of a twist of his lips. 'Soterro, tell Cook to pack. We leave tomorrow for Port Marchand, where we sail for Merofynia. King Merofyn is going to need my advice. And before you start packing, Soterro, lock Seela in the attic.'

Piro cursed silently. No more chances to poison Palatyne. Somehow, in the rush to leave tomorrow, she must escape.

CHAPTER SIXTEEN

FYN'S SKATES SLOWED as dawn's silvery light streamed across Rolencia's valley, illuminating first the highest peaks of the Dividing Mountains then the distant pinnacle where Rolenhold stood, making the castle's towers and domes gleam as if they were coated in electrum.

His heart swelled to fill his chest. Home, seat of his family, source of three hundred years of history.

He blinked away tears, focusing on the flags that hung from the towers. The high cold air was incredibly clear but the distance was too great for detail. It would take him half the day to get across the lake. However, he did not need to see the deep red foenix on its black background. He saw it in his heart.

In the still air a pall of smoke hung low over Rolenton and the docks were almost empty of ships. The wharves were always the weakest point of any fortified port yet he could see no encroaching army laying siege to the town. That had been his secret fear, that he would be too late and find the castle and town under siege. Luckily, he'd come in time to bring his father the bad news.

He set off across the lake with a will. He'd miss breakfast but he'd be there in plenty of time for the midday meal.

WHEN SOTERRO FINALLY unlocked her door, Piro was awake and ready for breakfast, stomach rumbling. She'd been waiting for ages. It was mid-morning.

'Lord Dunstany wants to see you,' Soterro said. She stood up. 'Bring your bundle, girl. I'm not your servant!'

When they reached the ground floor, Piro found Merofynian soldiers all over the place, packing things into crates and loading them onto carts outside. So much booty stolen from Rolencia. Indignation flooded Piro, but she also rejoiced. In all this confusion, escape would be easy.

The smell of warm cinnamon buns and freshly heated hot chocolate came from the kitchen, making her mouth water, but Soterro stopped at a door and opened it to reveal a small, windowless chamber opposite the dining room, the apothecary's workroom. Starkiss candles burned, their musky citrus scent heavy on the air.

The noble scholar looked up from his notes, an array of small tools laid across the desk in front of him. Piro recognised weights and the fine metal tongs of a jeweller.

'Off you go, Soterro, and see that those buffoons don't break anything,' Dunstany ordered. The door closed and Piro was left alone with him. His intense black eyes studied her. 'Do you know why King Rolen banned Power-workers from Rolencia?' He went on to answer his own question. 'Without the protection of the gods, their Affinity leaves them open to evil. In fact some actively seek out evil. I am not one of those. But I do know something of the sinister arts, for it is necessary to be able to recognise evil, to protect yourself. My enemies find me a very dangerous man. And I don't expect my servants to murder me in my bed.'

'The knife was not for you, sor,' Piro said quickly, ready now for his questions.

'Then who was it for?'

'For my own protection, my lord.'

'My servants are under my protection. No one will harm you.'

'Tell that to Grysha!' she snapped. 'His hands wander. I had to elbow him in the ribs once already.'

He looked surprised, then glanced down to hide the laughter in his eyes. Piro felt a little thrill of power because she'd made him smile.

When he went on, however, he sounded serious. 'I will speak with him.'

'I already did and he has the bruises to prove it.'

Dunstany smiled this time.

Piro felt a surge of joy, then a tug of sadness. She wasn't going to see the noble scholar any more after this morning.

How long before they left? It looked as though they were nearly ready. It would be easy to hide in Rolenton, for she knew every lane.

Dunstany sighed and she looked a question at him. He waved a hand to the candles. 'Do you like the scent?'

She inhaled deeply and smiled. 'Starkiss. It's beautiful.'

'Did you know the monks and nuns make dreamless-sleep from the pollen of the starkiss? Dreamless-sleep brings relief from pain, but like all powerful things it can be used to harm as well as help. Combined with another drug, which I will not name, it can be used to bring on hallucinations. Knowledge is power.' His deep voice dropped to an intimate timbre. 'Have you seen one of these before? It is called amber.'

Picking up a stone with the metal tongs, he held it near the candle. The flame glowed through the stone's translucent surface, rich and alive. Piro came closer, drawn by the amber's beauty. There was an imperfection... no, something was trapped in the stone.

'This is a jewel now but long ago it was sap, dripping from a tree,' he said softly. She could almost see it happening. 'A little creature crawled into it, became trapped and was encased in the amber. That little creature was *you*.'

She blinked and the dark spot resolved its shape. She saw herself in miniature, flowing black hair, naked limbs tinted gold by the honey-coloured amber, suspended forever in a dreaming state.

Piro gasped and pulled back, heart hammering, skin clammy.

Dunstany slid a fine gold chain through the ring that was clasped to the piece of amber and hung it around his neck. 'Your untrained Affinity makes you vulnerable, Seela. I have captured a small but vital part of you now, some would call it your soul. So don't be thinking of running away, for you are mine until I release you.'

Dunstany rang the bell for Soterro.

Piro stared at him. He'd known what she was thinking, or he'd guessed. She'd been right to fear him. He was too powerful, too cunning.

Fool. She should have run when she had the chance.

Now she was trapped!

When the door opened, Dunstany told Soterro, 'Seela is ready to help with the packing and you won't need to watch her so closely. We have come to an understanding, haven't we?'

Piro nodded reluctantly, unable to banish the vision of herself trapped within amber.

Soterro led her back to the kitchen, where the cook was wrapping a leg of smoked lamb in calico.

'Grab a bun and a hot drink, then get to work, girl.'

She followed his advice, but despite her hunger the crusty bread had no taste. How could she had been so stupid as to underestimate the noble Power-worker?

Soon the soldiers had finished and ridden off in all but the last cart. The cook had cleaned out all the store of preserved food and the last of his cooking utensils were being stacked in baskets on the kitchen table when Soterro returned.

'Palatyne's commandeered a merchant's boat-sled so we'll be riding to Port Marchand in comfort. The lord's overseeing the loading of his precious cargo right now. He wants a bite to eat before we leave.'

'But everything's packed.'

Someone knocked at the back door and Piro answered it. Her old nurse held a tray of hot pies.

Seela beamed. 'Apple and blueberry just as you ordered, and some rhubarb too.'

'That was good timing.' The cook stood. 'Put the kettle on, girl.'

Piro filled the kettle and put it over the grate, while Soterro took a slice of pie to Dunstany. As soon as the cook went off to get the coins Piro slipped over to her old nurse.

'Good news!' old Seela whispered, pulling something out of her apron pocket.

Piro gasped softly. It was Byren's leogryf-tooth necklace. So he lived. Or had he sent it before the ulfr pack got him?

'Only this morning a lad brought it to the castle, looking for Byren's honour guard. Byren's in hiding in the high country. I'll wait at the end of the lane. You slip out and I'll take you to him.'

Piro's heart lifted, then sank. 'I dare not. My master is a Power-worker and he has bound me to him using my Affinity.'

'A curse on him!'

Tears stung Piro's eyes as she clasped her old nurse's arm. 'I must stay until he frees me. But I want you to go and take care of Byren. Tell him –'

'Here's your coppers,' the cook announced, counting them out as he walked over. 'Your pies will come in handy. It will be hard to cook while travelling.'

Piro backed off a step, relieved that he had failed to notice her intense exchange with the supposed pie-seller. Her old nurse accepted the coins and sent Piro a look loaded with meaning as she left.

Soterro returned. 'My lord's pleased. He says the pie is fit for a king!'

Piro hid a grim smile and finished making the hot drink. Byren was safe in the high country and Fyn... She shuddered to think of Fyn, trapped in Halcyon's Sacred Heart with the Mulcibar mystics waiting to pounce on him.

THE HUNTING HOWL of an ulfr pack made Byren's gut tighten and fear sent a pulse of energy through his aching limbs, empowering them. But the sensation of renewed vigour was illusory, for even this short journey had exhausted him.

'Kingson?' The boy looked up to him, eyes wide.

'It's all right, Rodien. I'm with you,' Byren told him.

They were alone, since the dyer had gone to check the path ahead. Byren looked up at the sky through the snow-cloaked evergreens. Nearly midday. The thaw was late this year, as though Sylion did not want to release his hold on Rolencia. That's why the ulfr pack was desperate.

The pony shifted uneasily. Byren caught the reins and put a hand on the beast's muzzle to soothe it. He carried no weapon other than a hunting knife. A flash of silvery grey moved on the edge of his vision. Rodien edged closer, arms sliding around Byren's waist.

'See that tree.' Byren nodded to a winter-bare birch. 'Climb as high as you can. Whatever happens, don't come down.'

'Don't leave me.' Rodien clung to him, desperation lending him strength.

The boy was right. He'd never survive, alone in the woods. But Byren could not defend him on the ground. He caught Rodien under the arms. As he swung the lad up onto the pony his wound protested.

The old pony shifted uneasily.

Byren would have liked a sturdy branch to use as a club, but there were none lying conveniently near. Instead he drew his knife and led the pony in the direction the dyer had taken. The silver-grey form melted back into the trees.

'Where's Da?' Rodien whispered. 'I wants my da.'

Byren kept watching the surrounding forest. 'Up a tree, most likely. Safest place to be.'

'Why don't we climb a tree?'

'If we do, Blossom here's dead.'

Rodien's eyes widened.

The tone of the pack's cries changed and Byren knew they had cornered their prey.

Rodien shuddered, responding instinctively to the sound.

A ragged cry echoed through the still, snow shrouded evergreens, a man's despairing cry.

Byren hesitated. If he hadn't been injured and hadn't had the boy to protect, he would have gone to the dyer's aid. But he couldn't lead little Rodien into danger.

Besides, he knew by the sounds it was too late. The dyer had gone ahead to draw the pack away from them. He'd known what he was doing.

Byren turned the pony in the other direction.

Rodien did not argue. Eyes very wide, the lad clutched the pony's coarse mane.

Byren increased his pace. Hopefully the pack was feeding and they would have time to get away. But they had only gone half a bowshot, down into a hollow, when a grey form detached itself from a shadow and entered the path to confront him.

Byren swallowed, recognising the leader of the ulfr pack, the one he had lain with in the seep.

The Affinity beast watched him from intelligent winter sky-blue eyes.

He froze.

Last time he had seen this creature, he had offered it his belly and it had let him live. This time he stood tall, one hand on the pony's reins, the other on his hunting knife. Now he wished he'd thought to cut the sled's tracings so that the pony could run free. But there was no time. He must not show weakness.

The pack leader padded towards them. Byren watched its approach, trying to make sense of what he saw, for there was no threat in the way the Affinity beast moved, only curiosity.

The pony shuddered and tried to pull back. Byren had to use two hands to steady it. When he focused on the ulfr again it was close enough to touch him, large head and muzzle level with his waist. On its hind legs it would be taller than him.

Delicately, the Affinity beast sniffed his chest, looked up into his face and licked his closest hand.

'He likes you,' Rodien marvelled.

The ulfr sent the boy a quick look, then turned and loped off.

Byren slowly let his breath out. What had just happened?

His head was filled with a rushing sound and sparks danced in his vision.

'Da's not coming back, is he?' Rodien whispered, after what seemed an age.

Byren swallowed. 'No.'

'You saved me from the Affinity beasts.'

'Yes.' Somehow.

'Where are we going now?'

The immensity of it hit Byren. He had an old pony and a four-year-old boy to protect, while the Merofynians searched the valley for him. This time he must not fail.

As if sensing his fears, the boy whimpered. 'I wants Miron.'

'He'll join us at Cedar tradepost.'

Rodien accepted this.

And it was decided. Byren would take Rodien to the tradepost, which was on the path coming down from the pass to Foenix Spar pass. He could leave Rodien with the family who ran it, and then...

He couldn't think further than that.

PIRO HESITATED. FOOT on the gangplank, she glanced back to her father's castle, seeing the Merofynian banners flying from Rolenhold's towers. Her stomach lurched.

Soterro clipped her across the ear, making her eyes water. 'Get moving.'

Determined not to give him the satisfaction of seeing her cry, she adjusted her bundle and turned to face the sled-boat. She used to love riding the sled-boats. Now she boarded this one knowing it was taking her away from Byren, and Fyn.

'Get a move on.' Grysha elbowed her in the ribs as he shoved past.

She adjusted her grip on the bundle and stepped onto the gangplank, vowing she would return and she would avenge her family.

FYN SKIDDED TO a halt, and bent to unstrap the skates in the shadow of a wharf. Above him the porters chanted a familiar work song as they loaded a sled-boat. From Rolenton came the equally familiar scents of cooking as people sat down to their midday meal. It felt good to be back home.

If it weren't for the churning in his stomach, Fyn would have been happy. But he dreaded telling his father the bad news.

Regaining his feet, he slung the skates over his shoulder and climbed up the wharf. A Merofynian yelled at the porters in badly accented Rolencian. If rumour of the Merofynian invasion had reached Rolenton the foreign merchants would be eager to get out before their cargoes became prizes of war.

Fyn's head came level with the wharf. A blur of azure wyverns on black surcoats met his eyes as two dozen warriors rode onto the wharf.

He blinked. The men rode like they owned Rolenton, and did not bother dismounting but milled around, their horses' shod hooves loud on the wooden planks. The porters retreated, casting them fearful glances while the Merofynian leader bellowed for the ship's captain.

Fyn ducked behind a bale to watch, as a burly sailor made his way across deck to the top of the gangplank.

'I'm the captain, what d'you want?'

'This ship has been impounded by order of Overlord Palatyne.'

'What's this?' A well-dressed man objected in Ostronite-accented Merofynian. 'Lord Dunstany has hired this sled-boat to take him to Port Marchand. We are to set off as soon as the wind rises.'

'You'll set off on Palatyne's orders or not at all!' the warrior bellowed.

Behind the bale, Fyn sank to his knees, head reeling. Overlord Palatyne had already taken the town. He was too late, much too late.

No. Just because Rolenton had fallen, it did not mean the castle had.

The clip of a single horse's hooves made Fyn rise and peer over the bale again. A man rode onto the wharf and dismounted. The warriors deferred to him. He wore a rich surcoat emblazoned with both the Merofynian azure and the twin-headed amfina. Palatyne himself, or a messenger from him.

Fyn watched the man mount the gangplank. The ship's captain deferred to him warily and they both went below.

Fyn knelt and rested his forehead on the bale. How was he going to get into a castle under siege? And what could he, one acolyte, do to aid his father?

He would not give in to despair. He had to reach the king.

PIRO NOTICED THE noble scholar's shoulders stiffen as men argued above, their words lost but their tone unmistakable. There was a pause, then heavy footsteps sounded on the gangplank. At the same moment, light footsteps ran down the narrow passage to the main cabin. Both Piro and Dunstany turned to face the door.

Grysha thrust it open without knocking. 'The overlord's here, master, and he's spitting fire.'

Dunstany cast Piro a quick look. 'Go see if Cook needs you.'

But before she could leave the cabin, heavy footsteps echoed down the passage. Grysha cast one look behind him then backed out of the way as Palatyne's broad shoulders filled the doorway.

'Overlord.' Dunstany inclined his head as much as a noble would to a powerful, unpredictable warlord. 'To what do I owe the pleasure –'

'Don't play your courtly airs on me. I know what you're up to.' Palatyne fixed black eyes on him. 'You were running back to the king to undermine me behind my back.'

'Not at all.' Dunstany spread his hands disarmingly. 'I merely saw that you no longer needed me, what with Cobalt on the mend and the mystics and Utlander to hunt down the last kingson. I simply sought to take my treasures home before the Utland raiders begin their spring ravages on the shipping routes.'

Palatyne considered this for a moment then conceded. 'We'd be safest travelling in convoy with well-manned ships and sea-hounds to fight off raiders. But you were also out to curry favour with the king, don't deny it.' He thumped his chest with one fist. 'This is my victory, Dunstany. Mine. And I will sail into Port Mero to lay it before the king.'

Dunstany bowed. 'It was never going to be any other way.'

Palatyne gave him a considering look.

Piro dared not move. Dunstany remained, head bent, waiting for a signal.

'Very well,' Palatyne muttered and the noble scholar straightened up. 'Go ahead to Port Marchand and organise a convoy of ships to carry us home. Hire sea-hounds to protect us. I know they'll charge the earth, but it's worth it. No Utland raiders will get their hands on my treasures. Arrange somewhere for me to stay when we reach Port Marchand, and see that I am treated as befits the future emperor of the Twin Kingdoms.'

Dunstany bowed. 'As you wish.'

Palatyne turned to stride out.

'Overlord?'

Palatyne waited, radiating impatience.

'Who will you leave in charge of Rolencia? Cobalt –'

Palatyne snorted. 'Cannot be trusted. I know. But I will leave the two mystics to watch over him so I rid myself of those two abbey spies. Plus I'll leave a holding force of Merofynian warriors to keep them in line.'

'I see you have planned ahead.'

'I always do, Dunstany,' he said with heavy meaning, then marched out.

Piro and Dunstany did not move until they heard Palatyne's voice on the wharf as he mounted up and rode away, and then the noble scholar sat down abruptly.

Dunstany met her eyes across the cabin. 'The overlord sees betrayal everywhere, because that is how he rose to power. I suspect the Utlander has been at work here, undermining me. Go, fetch Soterro.'

She scurried up to the deck where the Ostronite servant was deep in argument with the captain.

'...master has hired you, not the overlord, so you will obey...' Soterro broke off, seeing Piro. 'Yes, slave?'

'Lord Dunstany wishes to speak with you. We are to leave immediately on a mission for the overlord.'

Soterro allowed himself one triumphant glance to the captain and headed below. Piro had to run to keep up with him. At the base of the narrow ladder Soterro leant against the wood, looking slightly queasy. He noticed Piro watching him. 'The last time I saw the overlord in such a temper he had a man hung, drawn and quartered. How did the master divert him?'

'We are to go ahead, to prepare a convoy of ships for him and his treasure.' Soterro wiped sweat from his top lip with a trembling hand and she felt a tug of unwanted sympathy for the Ostronite servant.

'Is the Utlander Lord Dunstany's enemy?' Piro whispered. 'I thought they were just rivals.'

'No. Definitely enemies,' Soterro confirmed. 'This time last year the two Utlanders lured m'lord into a trap and almost killed him. Although we could not prove that it was they who sent the assassins.'

Piro's stomach knotted with fear for Dunstany and, oddly enough, it wasn't just because he was her protector. She liked him.

Soterro straightened. 'Don't look so worried. We'll be safe once we get home. Our lord has the king's ear.'

But the king was old and dying. Piro followed the Ostronite servant back to the cabin thinking her mother had been right. The higher you rose, the more enemies you had.

Now she was headed back to her mother's home. How she missed Queen Myrella.

CHAPTER SEVENTEEN

FYN SLIPPED THROUGH the town, just another refugee unnoticed in the bustle. There were Merofynians everywhere, drinking in the taverns, striding through the marketplace, taking whatever they wanted. In the middle of Rolenton Square, where only last midwinter his father had promised another thirty years of peace, Fyn paused to study the castle. It was invincible, built on the pinnacle with only the steep zig-zag road leading to the great gate. Deep in its cellars lay hoards of grain, wine, preserves and salted meat, plus it had its own water supply.

It was impregnable. It was... flying Merofynian banners.

Impossible.

Yet... Rolenhold's gates stood open and he could see carts making their way up to the castle. Somehow his father's castle had been taken. Despair sliced through his composure. The world as he knew it was no more – Rolenhold had fallen and Halcyon Abbey was destroyed. The old seer had been right.

What else might she have revealed, if he had only listened?

There was no point agonising over might-have-beens.

Numb, Fyn wended his way through the busy square, heading for the gate that led to the castle. Round objects on the gate's spikes made his step falter. Thirty years ago his father had made an example of the Servants of Palos – traitors who would have put King Rolen's illegitimate older brother on the throne – by leaving their heads to rot on this gate. He could only see the back of the heads from here but something told him he did not want to see their faces. Still he went on.

Merofynians stood guard at Rolenton's gate. They did not bother to stop him, for the road was thick with merchants bringing in supplies.

On the far side of the gate Fyn went ten paces then turned to stare up at the faces of the spiked heads. It had been cold and he could still recognise Captain Temor along with several men from his father's honour guard. Fyn knew them all.

He almost lost his balance, but recovered and forced himself to think.

His father would have entrusted Temor to hold the gate, so the attack must have been too swift to evacuate the city properly. Temor and his men would have been unable to hold the gate against the odds but they would have given the castle guard time to close Rolenhold's gates. Once closed, there was no way an attacker could breach the walls. Fyn turned to study the castle, which had appeared to be intact, and collided with a horse.

'Here watch it, fisherman,' a carter complained.

'Sorry.' Fyn stroked the horse's muzzle and turned to the carter, who had dismounted to adjust the traces. The cart was laden high with wine barrels. 'How did Rolenhold fall? I would have sworn it was impossible.'

The carter glanced swiftly to the heads above the gate, then to the Merofynian gate guards. When he spoke his voice was low and tight. 'All I know is this, King Rolen died when he rode out to speak with the overlord under a flag of truce. His body was burned along with the queen and kingsdaughter. They say all but one of the kingsons are dead.'

Piro, dead? Fyn staggered.

'Here.' The carter caught his arm.

Fyn had to bend double to catch his breath.

'Did you have family in the castle, lad?'

Fyn nodded.

'They may still be there. Some have been enslaved, but the majority are getting on with their jobs.'

Fyn glanced at him, shocked.

'A man's got to eat, got to feed his family.'

Prosaic but true.

The carter watched him, a sympathetic gleam in his deep-set eyes. He looked prosperous but not overly so. Fyn could tell he was a decent man, trying to provide for his family.

Fyn's head reeled. Piro and his mother dead? What was the point of going on?

'Here, I'll give you a ride. You can lend me a hand unloading,' the carter said, as he caught the rail and swung himself up into the seat, lifting the reins.

Fyn stared up at him.

'Come on, lad. Don't give up.'

There was no point. He should head off to the Dividing Mountains and join Byren. He had to hope his brother had recovered and made it to the safety of the high country.

'I don't see how the castle could have fallen!' Fyn muttered.

'As to that, I can't say. But I do know there's a bag of gold offered for news of the missing kingson's whereabouts. If he's got any brains he'll be high on the Divide by now. I don't know why they want him dead when they're keeping the cousin alive.'

'Cobalt's alive?'

The carter nodded. 'He was injured when they took the castle. Lost an arm. They say the queen attacked him but I can't imagine it. She was ever so kind. At any rate, the overlord's Power-workers saved his life. He's being held prisoner now. Are you coming, lad? I've got a job to do.'

'Yes. I'm coming.' Fyn climbed up next to him.

The carter flicked the reins and clucked to the horses, who took up the slack, bending forwards against the traces to pull the heavy load.

Fyn focused on the castle, where his cousin lay injured and captive. He'd only met Illien of Cobalt once. That was back at midwinter, when the older man returned to Rolencia after a thirteen-year absence and Fyn returned to the castle with Halcyon's monks for the Proving ceremony. But they were kin and Fyn felt it was his duty to help Cobalt.

He had failed to save Piro and warn his father. The least he could do was rescue Cobalt and take him to Byren. Together they could plan how to retake the kingdom.

Fyn helped the carter unload, thanked him and set off. He knew the castle intimately. With hundreds of servants and several hundred Merofynians, the many wings and corridors were crowded.

It was the work of a moment to grab a servant's tabard from the laundry and slip it over his shoulders. He also snatched up a basket of fresh linen. No one would question yet another servant scurrying about. Then he remembered the fisherman's cap. He needed it to cover his tattoos. Or had his hair grown back enough to hide them?

Hurrying over to the little window he peered at his reflection. Without the cap he looked like a shorn sheep. After four days his hair was still too short to hide the tattoos and the acolyte's plait was a giveaway. It was the work of a moment to remove the plait, which would have been cut off when he became a monk. No time for regrets. He tossed it into the fire that warmed the great copper where the clothes were boiling. His hair burned swiftly, smelling bad.

He needed some sort of cap. There was only one thing for it – he would have to wear a high-ranking servant's embroidered skull cap. Taking one from the drying rail, he tugged it down into place, its points covering his ears. That would do. Fyn retrieved the basket of fresh bed linen and turned for the door.

At midwinter, when Cobalt arrived, his cousin had been given a bedchamber in the family's royal wing and Fyn went straight there. Two Merofynian warriors wearing the distinctive twin-headed amfina on their surcoats stood at the doors. It seemed Palatyne trusted only his own men for crucial tasks.

Fyn simply nodded to them and stepped past. When he couldn't manage the latch one-handed, one of them opened the door for him. He thanked them and walked into the chamber.

An abbey mystic stood beside the bed, a woman wearing the pristine white robes of Cyena. This winter goddess was most often represented as an elegant swan, but she sometimes walked amongst her people as a beautiful woman, or more dangerously as a siren, who sang sailors to their death.

There was no sign of a mystic from Mulcibar abbey, which was the equivalent of Rolencia's Halcyon. Unlike Halcyon, who nurtured the land, Mulcibar took the form of a great red bull. He revelled in war, with hot breath that incinerated anything it touched. But it was Mulcibar's dung that was most dangerous. It was said the dung could fly as far as an arrow, spreading flames. Some of his father's honour guard swore they'd witnessed it on the battlefield thirty years ago.

Fyn's mother had described the rivalry between the two great abbeys of Merofynia so vividly, Fyn had no trouble recognising the Cyena mystics mistress for what she was.

She glanced his way, revealing a young face, despite her white hair and eerie, pale pink eyes.

'I come to deliver clean sheets,' he said, his throat so dry he hardly recognised his own voice.

Dismissing Fyn as unimportant, she continued to study the man on the bed.

'He hasn't touched his food,' the Cyena mystic said, indicating a tray on a side table. Fyn wondered who she was speaking to.

'As you see, the healers can do no more for him.' A man stepped out of the shadows on the far side of the bed, into the light streaming from the tall casement window.

Every nerve in Fyn's body screamed danger. Even if it hadn't been obvious from the man's Utland dress and the fetishes woven into his hair, Fyn would have recognised the Affinity in him. It exuded from his skin like a bad smell.

Fyn glanced to Cyena's mystic. She didn't radiate as much intensity, though from her stiff stance he could tell she sensed the Utlander's power and found it offensive.

Shaking knees hidden under the tabard, Fyn came to the end of the bed and placed the basket of fresh linen on the chest there. His cousin lay on the bed, covered in a light sheet. His chest and shoulder were bound, covering the stump where his arm had been. Even now it seeped and Fyn smelt the distinctive scent of rosemary which was used back at the abbey by the Halcyon healers to prevent wounds putrefying.

'Dunstany and I have done all we can to heal his body,' the Utlander said. 'It is his will that is broken. The best healer cannot restore a man's will to live.'

'Overlord Palatyne needs him alive and well,' the Cyena mystic said. She spoke in the Utlander's general direction and Fyn realised she was blind to the Seen world. It made him glad he had not been exercising his Affinity when he entered, or she would have sighted him in the Unseen world. 'You know how Palatyne hates it when anything thwarts him.'

'Then you had better pray Cobalt finds a reason to live,' the Utlander said, 'for Palatyne intends to leave him in your care and he has plans for him.'

She stiffened. 'I will speak with the overlord.'

Catching the long points of her sleeves which hung almost to the ground, she swept them over her arms as she turned towards the door, and left the room without so much as a glance at Fyn.

The moment the door closed, Fyn felt the Utlander's Affinity drop and realised he had been deliberately trying to unsettle the Cyena mystic. The display must have cost him dearly, for now he leant heavily on his staff.

'Well, get to work. Change the bedding,' the Utlander snapped at Fyn then he too headed for the door.

'Yes, master,' Fyn muttered, hardly able to believe his luck. He reached for the first bedsheet, but as soon as the door closed he let it drop, running around the side of the bed to peer into Cobalt's face.

His cousin had turned away from the window. Even so Fyn could see the heavy shadow of beard, which lay on his jaw under skin that looked so pale it was almost waxen.

Fyn was shocked. He recalled Cobalt as being a handsome man, vain about his looks, with long hair that he wore loose, curled and threaded with semi-precious stones in the Ostronite way. It was to Ostron Isle that he had been banished for thirteen years.

'Illien?' Fyn whispered. It did not feel quite right calling a man of thirty-four, whom he hardly knew, by his private name. 'Lord Cobalt?'

Dull black eyes hardly registered him. 'Leave me alone, boy. Didn't you hear him? I'm a dead man.'

'It's me, Fyn. Cousin Cobalt.' Fyn tugged off the cap to reveal the dark fuzz that didn't quite hide his tattoos.

Cobalt's eyes sprang open as his whole body stiffened. 'Little Fyn from the abbey?'

Fyn nodded.

Cobalt frowned, stunned, then amazement animated his features. 'It is you. How did you get in here?'

Fyn laughed softly, replacing the servant's skull cap. 'I've come to help you escape.'

'Oh, Fyn.' Cobalt shook his head sadly, then gritted his teeth and carefully manoeuvred himself into a seated position so that his back rested against the headboard. Even that made the sweat of pain and exhaustion break out on his skin. 'Come, let me look at you, lad. You've no idea how good it is to see your face.'

Fyn waited. While Cobalt stared at him intently he wondered how they would escape with his cousin so weak. 'Your arm...'

'You heard how this happened?' Cobalt indicated his stump.

Fyn nodded. 'I heard a rumour that Mother –'

'It wasn't Myrella's fault,' Cobalt assured him. 'She was deranged with grief for your father. Palatyne murdered him under a flag of truce. When she saw me with Palatyne she sprang to the wrong conclusion. She thought I'd betrayed Rolenhold. I don't know who opened the postern gate to the Merofynians. I was on the main gate tower telling them we'd never surrender when it happened. Dozens of men saw me there. But Myrella...' Cobalt shuddered. 'The overlord's a cruel man. He ordered me to execute your mother. Of course I couldn't.' He fixed on Fyn. 'She was a brave woman, don't let anyone tell you otherwise. She grabbed my own sword and turned it on me. Nearly killed me.'

Fyn could imagine his petite mother struggling to swing the great sword. Tears stung his eyes. 'And Piro?' His voice came out strangled.

Cobalt shook his head, unable to go on.

A sob shook Fyn's shoulders.

'I was injured, Fyn. There was nothing I could do. At least she wasn't violated. The overlord sent his men to find her and kill her. She died trying to escape, trying to climb out a window.'

'That sounds like her. She had no fear of heights.' Fyn turned away, going to the casement window. It was too high for him to see out, but he did catch a glimpse of pale, winter-blue sky far above. Piro was dead, and he felt the terrible burden of guilt because he lived.

'She couldn't have harmed the overlord. She was only thirteen.' Bitterness choked Fyn, threatening to seal off his throat. 'Why kill her?'

'There was a prophecy. The overlord's Power-worker, Lord Dunstany, told Palatyne he would be killed by one of King Rolen's kin. So he ordered them all executed. He only let me live because I don't have a legitimate claim to the throne and I'm useful to him.'

That reminded Fyn of another seer's prophecy. The filthy old woman had been proven right. Halcyon Abbey had fallen, although it had seemed impossible back before midwinter. And Piro had died because of this Lord Dunstany's prophecy.

He had failed his little sister. He would not fail his cousin.

He turned to face Cobalt. 'I'm here to help you escape. We'll go to Byren in the mountains –'

'Byren's alive and hiding in the mountains?' Cobalt held Fyn's gaze, his dark eyes intense. 'You're sure of this?'

Fyn pulled the Fate from inside his vest, to show Cobalt the seashell-shaped stone. 'I saw it in the Fate, in a vision. We can find him and –'

Cobalt shook his head, mouth grim. 'I'm useless, Fyn, too weak to ride or skate. Don't waste your time looking for Byren, who may even now be dead. No. You owe your family blood payment. Palatyne murdered them. By the Rolencian warrior code your father held so dear, you must avenge their deaths.'

Of course – Fyn's head reeled. He hadn't been thinking straight. He must avenge his murdered kin.

'You must assassinate Palatyne. But you cannot challenge him,' Cobalt warned. 'He's a hardened warrior of forty summers and you are a boy who's not yet seventeen. A duel would only see you dead and your family left unavenged. No, you must get close to him, just as you got close to me. You must slide a knife between his ribs, or cut his throat. Only then will your mother and sister rest easy.'

Fyn nodded. Assassinate Palatyne. 'And then come for you?'

Cobalt's eyes widened.

Fyn hastened to reassure him. 'Don't worry. I can wait for you to get better before we go to Byren.'

'Can you find Byren using that stone?'

'The Fate?' Fyn lifted it, staring into its opalised depths. Could he find Byren with it? Probably, but dare he risk it? 'I'll find him. I must.'

'Good.' Cobalt sat up straighter, his whole body radiating determination.

He was a different man from the one who had lain on the bed when Fyn entered the room. Fyn had given his kinsman a reason to live. 'I won't let you down, cousin.'

'I'm sure you won't. But do not throw your life away when you kill Palatyne. You must come back safely to me or I will never find Byren. You understand?'

Fyn nodded.

Cobalt caught Fyn's arm with his good hand. 'Swear it will be so.'

It seemed unnecessary but... Fyn placed his free hand over his heart. 'I swear it will be so. If I live, I will come back to you and help you find Byren.'

His cousin nodded, satisfied, and let him go. 'Palatyne trusts no one. It will be hard to get near him.'

'Where does he sleep?'

'In the king's chamber, of course.' Cobalt snorted softly.

'Then I know how to get to him.'

'A secret passage?'

Fyn laughed. 'No, that's an Ostronite custom.'

Cobalt shrugged. 'Another thing. Whatever you hear, remember that I am with you. They hold me prisoner here so I may be forced to do things that make it appear as if I support the Merofynians, but I swear on my dead father's honour, my true loyalties do not lie with them.'

Fyn flushed. 'I will hold true to you. You're my blood kin, all I have left, other than Byren.'

'Halcyon bless you, Fyn!' Cobalt held out his remaining arm and, as they embraced, Fyn was careful not to bump his wound.

They parted.

'Pass me the tray,' Cobalt said. 'I must eat if I am to regain my strength.'

Fyn brought the tray to him, knowing that he had restored his cousin's will. And Cobalt had given him direction. Now that he had a goal, he felt he could achieve anything.

A grin parted his lips. He would fulfil Lord Dunstany's prophecy by assassinating the overlord.

CHAPTER EIGHTEEN

BYREN WALKED, DRIVING himself on, senses alert for danger. Just because the ulfr pack hadn't attacked, didn't mean he and the boy were safe. There were other predators in the foothills of the Divide, especially at this time of year, when the beasts woke hungry from their winter sleep, while the ones that didn't hibernate were desperate, thanks to winter's lean pickings.

It was after dusk and the froth of stars lit the snow with a silvery-blue glow. The dyer's boy slept, draped across the pony's back. They hadn't stopped to eat.

For a while now Byren had been looking for a spot to stay the night. While he knew Rolencia's rich valley, and he had led punitive raids over the Divide, he did not know every nook and cranny of every foothill and ravine.

The pony stumbled, going down on both front knees. Rodien rolled off, waking with a startled cry. Tears of weariness made his eyes glisten.

Byren finally admitted it was time to make camp.

Scooping the boy up, he let the pony find its feet and trudged on. His wound tugged with every step, but he was no longer a dead man walking. That healer must have been skilled indeed for he had been growing steadily stronger each day. Now, though, he had to admit he needed rest.

No sign of a village or even a fortified farmhouse. Too bad. He could go no further. A huge evergreen, completely shrouded in snow, loomed ahead of them. Byren forged through its mantled lower branches to find an area near the great trunk that was sheltered from the outside. It was as large as a small cottage, with the trunk forming one central support. He put Rodien down and went back for the pony, leading it through the branches.

The pony was happy to stop at last.

Byren turned back to the little lad. 'Eh, Rodien, are you a good climber?'

The boy stirred. 'The best.'

'Then clamber up this tree and make yourself comfy.'

'What about you?'

'I'll be right up.'

He boosted the boy to the lowest broad branch and then freed the pony from its sled traces and rubbed it down, slipping its nose bag over its head. Then he unhooked a blanket from their belongings and clambered up after the boy, helping him higher.

Rodien patted the huge trunk. 'It's like the pole of a big tent.'

'Eh, the snow protects the tree and us.' Byren rested his back against the trunk. 'We'll be safe up here.'

Rodien glanced down to the dim outline of the pony below, dark against the softly glowing snow. 'What if I roll over in my sleep?'

Byren opened his arms. 'I won't let anything happen to you.'

The boy snuggled up against his chest and Byren arranged the blanket over them both.

'You won't leave me, will you?' Rodien whispered.

Byren's heart turned over and he had to swallow before he could speak. 'Not until your brother returns.' He felt the little body relax in his arms, then stiffen.

'What if the ulfr pack gets Miron, too?'

There was danger and little Rodien was no fool, so Byren chose his words carefully. 'Miron's a clever boy. And he's big and strong. He should have reached Rolenton and be on his way back by now. He'll find other travellers and stay with them. He'll be safe.'

Byren felt Rodien nod and snuggle closer. In no time at all the little boy's body went limp with sleep. Byren knew he should sleep too, but his mind wandered. Until now, he had ignored how the leader of the ulfr pack sniffed his hand and moved on.

Now he tried to make sense of the meeting with the ulfr. Although his clothes had been washed, there must have been enough residual Affinity on his skin to make him seem like part of the pack to the beast.

Satisfied with his reasoning, Byren rested his head against the trunk. He was just drifting off when he heard the pony shift uneasily. Surreptitiously, Byren eased his right arm free and felt for his knife.

Rodien stirred. Byren placed a finger on his lips.

The pony reared, pulling against the rope that tethered it to the trunk.

Something large crashed through the drooping branches, scattering snow. The pony screamed. There was an ominous crunch, then silence, then the sound of dragging.

Rodien whimpered, clinging to Byren.

He covered the boy's mouth and they remained absolutely still, listening. Nasty noises ensured as two beasts snarled over the pony's carcass.

'A lincis pair,' Byren breathed. 'Usually solitary hunters. Possibly a mother and her cub.'

'C–can they climb?' Rodien asked.

They could but... 'One pony is enough for the pair of them. We're safe.'

'Poor Blossom,' the boy muttered and dissolved into silent, wracking sobs. He hadn't cried over his father, and now he cried unrestrainedly. Byren held him until his sobs slowed and he fell asleep. The occasional dry sob still shook his little frame, making Byren realise just how young and vulnerable the lad was.

They'd have to leave the sled, carry what they could on their backs and hope to meet up with other travellers. The lincis pair would be satisfied for a day or two, maybe three.

Last time he'd met up with a lincis, Orrade had been with him, and only the old seer's arrival had saved his friend's life. To think, he'd risked his best friend's life for a few priceless lincurium stones just so he could outdo Lence's gift for his parents' Jubilee.

Now his parents were dead, as was Lence, and he would give anything to go back and warn himself. The Byren of midwinter seemed so young and thoughtless compared to the Byren who now hid up a tree, protector of a small boy.

And he had no idea where the three lincurium stones were. He'd had two set on matching rings for his parents and the largest set as a pendant for Lence to give his betrothed, but Cobalt had used them, along with a poem he'd written for Elina, to convince his father he was Orrade's lover.

Every word he'd said in his own defence had been true, but Cobalt had twisted the truth to paint him a usurper, out to steal his twin's throne.

Since then his whole life had fallen apart. Who was he to save Rolencia? He would be lucky if he could save Rodien and himself.

As Fyn stretched out along the massive oak beam, he silently thanked his father for insisting the royal family stay with tradition and live in the old wing. Below him lay his parents' chambers, only now they housed Overlord Palatyne.

The narrow, empty chamber had once been a nursery-maid's room or healer's room depending on the need, but Palatyne would have no one near him while he slept. Beyond it lay the royal bedchamber where Palatyne would sleep tonight.

Right now the overlord was down in the great hall, bestowing the title of duke on Illien of Cobalt. In return, Fyn's cousin would rule Rolencia on King Merofyn's behalf. But that didn't matter since, by dawn, Palatyne would be dead. Most of his warriors were barracked down in the town. This left those remaining in the castle vulnerable if the castle's servants rose up against them, and Fyn was sure they would, once they knew Palatyne was dead. They could retake the castle and hold off the warriors quartered in town.

Byren would hear of it and come down from the mountains with his warriors. Inspired, the townspeople would turn on the Merofynians in Rolenhold and, together with Byren's men, wipe them out. So Fyn wouldn't have to use the Fate to find him.

A snuffling whine came from just beyond the door and it swung open, bringing a shaft of lamp light. Fyn held his breath. Because of his dread of assassination, Palatyne's chambers were searched every night before he went to bed. That was why Fyn had come with the grappling hook, swung it over the beam, hauled himself up and hidden the rope and hook.

Fyn did not dare look. Instead he lay perfectly still, hardly breathing. Below, he heard the hounds snuffling as they sniffed the floor.

'Hurry up, boys,' the servant muttered. 'We're missing the feast.'

The dogs whined.

'What?' the man demanded of his hounds. 'There's nothing here. The room's empty.'

The dogs whined again, one barked. The short, sharp sound made Fyn's heart race.

'Rats,' another voice muttered from the door. 'Cook was complaining of them in the kitchen.'

'Rats? Is that it, boys?' the first voice asked. 'I've got something much tastier for you. Come on.'

He dragged them out, their nails sliding on the polished wood. Fyn relaxed gradually. The weapons master had been right. When they were indoors, people rarely looked up for threat. Outside, it was a different story, with leogryfs and cockatrices on the prowl.

Now all he had to do was wait until the overlord returned and fell asleep, then cut his throat and take the news to Cobalt. A yawn snuck up on him. He was tired. He'd hardly slept in the last four days.

BYREN WOKE, SHOULDERS cold and stiff, but he was warm from the centre out, because in his arms was a sleeping bundle of small boy. For several heartbeats he just sat there. He'd led men and youths, who were eager to be warriors. He'd taught them to hunt and kill in the defence of Rolencia, but he'd never been solely responsible for a small child before today.

Seeing Rodien's trusting face, the fan of his dark lashes on smooth cheeks, Byren was overcome with the immensity of this responsibility.

Rodien stirred and focused on him. Byren saw emotions race across his face, confusion, sorrow and fear, finally he smiled. 'I'm hungry.'

Byren laughed softly. 'You and me both. Come on.'

He climbed down, lifting Rodien to the ground. Here, a trail of blood and disturbed snow were evidence of where the pony had been dragged out from under the tree. A small gap in the branches let a ray of dawn light filter through.

'Poor Blossom,' Rodien whispered.

He seemed close to tears, so Byren began unpacking the sled. 'We'll have to leave this and take only the food we can carry.'

Rodien nodded and looked up to Byren, waiting for instructions. Everything rested on him. The fate of one small boy and the fate of a kingdom.

'Hail, fellow travellers,' a voice called.

Byren froze. The voice was male and the accent revealed he was poorly educated, possibly only one generation out from the spars.

'We offer traveller's ease,' the stranger said, giving the traditional greeting.

This didn't reassure Byren. In the mountain passes spar warriors eager for wealth preyed on travellers. End of winter, early spring was when they would come out of hiding, desperate for goods to trade for food. And, with the valley under attack, they'd know they were safe from King Rolen's justice. Many a time Lence and Byren had led punitive raids against such men.

In one swift movement Byren picked Rodien up and dropped him behind the sled. 'Stay down. Stay quiet.'

Silent, pleading eyes looked up at Byren but the boy nodded his understanding.

Byren turned to face the gap in the branches where a clump of snow fell as the man thrust his head through and peered inside.

'Sveyto, servant to Scholar Veniamyn of Rolenton.' He glanced to the sled. 'You travel alone?'

'Byren, blacksmith of Rolenton.' Letting his tongue roll the Rs, Byren adopted the speech of the peasants. The borrowed cloak hid his good quality leather vest and he had five days' growth on his chin. 'Is your master headed over the pass?'

Sveyto, if that was his name, nodded. 'Hoping to get his family through before the spring melt makes travelling dangerous and the Merofynians close the pass.'

Byren's heart sank. So it was true. Rolenton had fallen.

'Who is it? Bring them out here where I can see them,' another man called, his voice heavy with the weight of command, but Byren could detect a hint of fear, and if he could, then so could the guide.

'Step out in the open, friend.' Sveyto gestured for Byren to pass him.

Byren instinctively distrusted anyone who used 'friend' in that way.

Without looking down at Rodien, who he hoped would remain quiet, Byren stepped out from under the cover of the snow-shrouded pine into a crisp early morning. Fingers of pale sunlight streamed horizontally through the evergreens, illuminating the travellers. A well-dressed scholar stood near a serviceable horse, laden with travelling bags, and a pretty girl of about ten. On the second horse two slightly older, but equally pretty, girls rode amidst more baggage. The last horse dragged a sled covered in belongings. There were no other sell-swords.

Sveyto had called himself a servant, but Byren knew a sell-sword when he met one. The sell-sword was the kind of man a merchant hired to provide protection for his goods. Scholar Veniamyn must have hired him to guide them through the foothills and over the pass, believing his family would be safer in Foenix Spar than in the captured city.

Byren's gaze returned to the scholar. The last time they had met was at the midwinter feast in his father's castle.

Byren ducked his head in a peasant's bow. 'Byren, blacksmith of Rolenton at your service, sor.'

Veniamyn's eyes widened only slightly as recognition hit him, but he did not reveal this, keeping up Byren's pretence. 'You look like a strong young man, blacksmith. Ride with us and share the journey's dangers. We heard a Lincis's hunting cry last night. I see your horse has been taken.'

'Pony,' Byren corrected. 'But I'm only going as far as Cedar tradepost.'

'That suits us.' The scholar cast his servant an acerbic glance. 'We seem to have lost our way and have been wandering in these woods for two days now.'

Byren understood his meaning. Veniamyn had paid Sveyto to guide them, only to have him lead them astray. The sell-sword was probably leading them towards his brigand friends. Those three pretty daughters would fetch a high price on the Utlands, higher still on Ostron Isle where slavery sustained the economy.

'Cedar tradepost is about one day's travel across the ridge.' Byren pointed. 'Be glad to show you the way. But there's something you must know. I'm not travelling alone.'

He ignored Sveyto as he returned to where Rodien was hiding. 'Come on, lad. We've found some fellow travellers.'

'Then we'll be safe from the Affinity beasts?' Rodien asked.

'Aye.' Though Byren suspected they would not be safe from human predators. He finished removing the food packs and retied the sled. 'We'll have to leave it. Miron might be able to come back for it sometime.'

Rodien shouldered his bag, obviously unworried about their belongings. 'When can we eat?'

'Soon.' As Byren turned to the gap in the branches, he felt a small hand slide into his and they stepped into the open.

No one spoke for a moment. The sell-sword frowned at him and Byren guessed Scholar Veniamyn was confused, for he knew Byren had no children.

'That boy's too small, Master Veniamyn,' Sveyto protested. 'The blacksmith's son will –'

'He's not my son. I fell in with him and his da. Ulfr pack took his da yesterday.'

'Oh, the poor boy!' the eldest of Veniamyn's daughters cried. She was about Piro's age, but more rounded and traditionally pretty. 'We can't leave him behind, Father.'

'He can ride with me, Papa,' the littlest girl offered, making room for him by shuffling back. 'I'll hold him.'

Veniamyn sent Byren a silent plea. *See, these are good girls, kind girls. You are a good man, help me get them to safety.*

'I thank you, little mistress,' Byren said, swinging Rodien up onto the horse in front of the ten-year-old.

She wrapped her arms around him protectively.

'I can hold on!' he protested.

Veniamyn laughed. Sveyto turned away in thinly disguised disgust.

'We'd best set off,' Byren announced. Suiting his actions to his words, he took the horse's reins from Veniamyn and headed off down the slope, the scholar falling into step with him while Sveyto led the sled horse.

Byren dug around in his food pack, finding one of last summer's apples and passing it back to Rodien. 'Eat this.'

'Thank you, Byren Kingson, for coming to my aid,' Scholar Veniamyn whispered.

'Blacksmith for now,' Byren corrected, casting the sell-word a swift look. For all he knew there was a price on his head. At least, it seemed Veniamyn had not heard about his disgrace. Perhaps all who knew of it had been killed when the castle fell.

What a terrible thing to be grateful for!

'I assumed you are headed into the mountains to raise an army. I would stay and fight with you, but what would become of my daughters? I don't want them living wild in caves like savages. Besides,' the scholar confessed, 'I am not a fighter.'

'Each man must do what his conscience tells him,' Byren agreed. But inside he wondered how he would raise an army to retake Rolencia.

FYN WOKE WITH a lurch and the sense that time had passed, a lot of time. He lay very still, listening.

There were voices from the room beyond and the sound of furniture being moved. Light filtered through the single high window. Daylight.

He'd slept the night away.

Shame flooded him.

How could he?

His mouth went dry with anguish. It had been the perfect opportunity to kill Palatyne. Mortification ate at him. First he had failed the abbot, now this.

He waited, the voices faded.

Nothing.

He sat up and prepared to lower his weight, slinging the grappling hook and rope over his shoulder, then swinging his legs off the beam. He planned to lower himself until he hung by his arms, then drop to the floor which would be more than a body length below his feet.

The door opened without warning. Fyn froze, legs astride the beam.

'Empty,' a voice called to others in the far room.

'Good, the hold's full. If we find anything else, it can travel on the next ship. Palatyne won't miss it until he gets home.'

'Don't you bet on it,' the one in the doorway muttered. 'He'll inspect the stores, when he gets to Port Marchand. He knows every single thing he took out of the trophy room. He's as much of a pinch-purse as any merchant.' As the Merofynian closed the door Fyn heard him add, 'And I don't want him accusing me of feathering my own...'

Fyn swung his legs back up then lay full length again. He counted to a hundred, slowly, but there wasn't a sound. All the while, frustration grew – Palatyne was setting off for Port Marchand.

If the worst came to the worst he could barter a ride to the port and catch up with Palatyne there. This time he must not fail.

CHAPTER NINETEEN

MID-AFTERNOON, BYREN CALLED a halt for the third time that day. He'd been pushing the horses and they were exhausted, as were the children, but their party needed to reach Cedar tradepost before dusk, when the palisade gate was closed.

While he helped little Rodien down from the horse, he watched the surrounding trees. No birds sang, possibly because their party was large enough to scare them off. Still, he hadn't failed to note how Sveyto kept watching the pine forest. And the horses had been restive all day, spooked by something.

'Me next.' The ten year-old held out her arms trustingly.

Byren lifted her to the snow, feeling the tug of his wound. It felt weeks old, rather than days. That healer had done a fine job. He wished he could have done a better job protecting her brother, the dyer.

'Thank you, master blacksmith.' The girl beamed up at him, revealing beguiling dimples, then ran off to join her sisters.

'A few moments, that's all,' Byren called after her.

Scholar Veniamyn came over to join him, keeping his voice low as he watched his eldest daughter hand out dried fruit and nuts. Despite earlier breaks to rest and eat, it was the first chance they'd had to speak together, without the sell-sword hovering over them. 'You think Sveyto has been leading us astray?'

'Undoubtedly.' Byren glanced around the clearing. 'Speaking of which, where is he?'

'He stepped into the trees to relieve himself.'

Byren nodded. 'Think I'll follow his lead.' He raised his voice. 'Rodien, do you need to pee?'

The boy trotted over, chewing on his dried fruit, cheeks bulging. He swallowed and nodded.

Taking his hand, Byren followed Sveyto's tracks into the trees, chose a spot and unlaced his breeches. When they were done he came back and took the girls off, standing guard with his back to them.

The necessities taken care of, he returned to find there was still no sign of the sell-sword.

'Help the children mount up,' Byren told Veniamyn. 'I'm going to check on Sveyto.'

He jogged through the snow following the man's tracks. Soon he found where Sveyto had stopped to urinate, but instead of returning, the sellsword had made off through the snow and the length of his stride indicated he'd been in a hurry.

It confirmed Byren's worst fears. The man had gone looking for his companions, meaning to lead them back to cut off Byren's group before they could reach safety.

Cursing fluently, he turned around to find the ulfr pack leader only two body lengths from him, between him and the clearing.

Surprise made his heart race.

'Eh, there,' Byren whispered, deliberately making his voice low and crooning. 'Have you been following me?' Was there enough residual Affinity from the seep on his skin to fool the beast a second time? There'd been no chance for him to bathe.

Swallowing, Byren glanced around and spotted the silver-white coats of another two ulfrs, further back in the trees. No wonder the horses were skittish.

Well, they hadn't attacked him yet. Animals smelled fear. Telling himself there was no reason to be afraid – hadn't the ulfr let him pass just yesterday? – Byren gathered his courage and walked slowly up the rise towards the pack leader.

The beast watched him with eyes that held far too much intelligence for an animal. It was said, all Affinity beasts carried a little of the goddess Halcyon in them. Looking into those eyes, Byren believed it.

When he was less than a body length from the beast, Byren hesitated. It still had not moved from the path and he did not want to turn his back on it. On impulse, he dropped to his knees and raised his hand, wrist forwards, fingers down for the ulfr to sniff.

The beast's muzzle twitched delicately as it stepped forwards and accepted his offering. He felt the heat of its exhalation and then the damp of its nose as it nuzzled his skin.

'You are a beautiful beast,' Byren whispered, and he meant it. Yielding to another impulse, he edged closer, running his hand through the pack leader's thick pelt, where it grew long in a ruff behind the beast's head. The fur felt incredibly soft on his fingers and he fought the urge to apologise because he still wore the ulfr coat the farmholder had given him.

The ulfr nuzzled his ear, startling a chuckle from Byren. Strange, once he had thought the scent of ulfrs invasive and dangerous. Now it seemed as right and familiar as the scent of horses.

The dominant ulfr lifted its head, sniffed the air, uttered a soft sound like a cough and trotted off. At its signal, the others beasts melted into the snow-shrouded forest.

Not sure what had just happened, Byren came to his feet with renewed urgency. If he didn't get Veniamyn and his family safely to Cedar tradepost tonight, the girls would be gracing some fierce Utlander's piss-pot of a great hall by spring cusp.

Grim determination driving him on, Byren ran back to the others. Veniamyn blanched when he met Byren's eyes.

'Where's our guide?' the middle girl asked.

'Hush,' the eldest chided her, quick to pick up on her father's concern.

'Will we be there soon?' the youngest asked, unaware of the undercurrents.

'By dusk.' *Or not at all*, Byren thought. 'Veniamyn, you bring up the rear. I'll lead. I'm going to push the horses, so hold on. If you feel tired and grumpy, think of the lovely hot dinner and warm bed waiting for you at the journey's end.' It was what his mother used to say, when he and Lence were little and fed up with travelling.

His mother... pain twisted in his gut, but there was no time for grief.

Byren took the reins of the horse Rodien rode and set off at a jog. Each step tugged at his wound. He ignored it. The short afternoon sped by. Every time they breasted a crest, he hoped to see the tradepost, but another empty gully lay before them.

At one point he heard the cry of a lincis defending its territory. Probably one of the pair that had taken his pony. The sound came from the north, not between him and the tradepost, so he ignored it. He had enough to worry about without borrowing trouble, as his old nurse Seela would say.

Another stab of loss hit him. Did she still live? Had the Merofynians mistreated her? Surely they would respect her grey hair.

His impotence made him angry and he channelled that anger into his body, driving himself and the horses onwards.

All through that interminable afternoon, the children did not complain. Like the horses they seemed to be aware of his urgency, or they thought it was some sort of game, because they held on, ducking low branches, laughing when snow fell on them and brushing it off their shoulders with good humour.

All too soon the sun dipped, leaving a smear of brilliant salmon-pink behind the pines on Byren's right. On his left he glimpsed the first star of evening between the tree tops. No one suggested they rest or make camp.

Still, he drove himself on. How Veniamyn managed, Byren did not know. His thighs burned by the time he came to the top of a ridge and spotted the thin spiral of smoke behind the next crest.

Sucking in deep breaths, he waited for the other horses to catch up. Veniamyn had fallen a long way behind, leading the horse drawing the sled.

'Are we there?' Rodien asked.

'See the smoke?' Byren pointed.

The children nodded.

'That's Cedar tradepost.' Or he was much mistaken. 'You'll be safe inside its palisade. All we have to do is cross this gully, climb that next ridge and go down into the next gully.'

'What's taking Father so long?' the eldest girl muttered, twisting from the waist.

'Come on, Da,' the youngest called.

'Hush,' Byren warned.

All four children looked to him for an explanation.

'Sound carries. We don't want to attract attention.' It was just as well they hadn't come by the traditional route up from Rolenton, where the brigands would almost certainly be watching the trail, prepared to attack any party that looked too weak to defend itself. Sveyto's meandering meant they were coming across country.

Veniamyn joined them. He bent over double and did not lift his head for several minutes.

'I'm s–sorry,' he panted, still bent double.

'We're almost there. Catch your breath,' Byren said. 'It'll give the horses a chance to get their second wind.'

Veniamyn cast him a swift look. In that instant Byren noticed his pallor. The scholar would not last much longer. Too much time spent poring over books.

When he did straighten up, he did not look much better. Byren stepped closer and raised his arm, pointing. In the few moments that they'd been waiting the last of the colour had left the western sky, and an effervescence of stars filled the night above. By their silver-blue light, Byren could clearly make out the silhouettes of the trees on the next ridge. 'See where the stars are obscured? That's the smoke from Cedar tradepost. We're that close.'

Veniamyn nodded. 'I don't know what I would have done without you, Byren Kingson.'

'Kingson?' the eldest girl echoed. Her eyes widened with horror. 'Byren Kingson, Father? But we peed in front of him!'

Her dismay made Byren laugh softly. 'I turned m'back. Come on.'

He led the horse carrying Rodien and the youngest girl down the slope. Behind him, the two bigger girls whispered, their tone a mixture of excitement and chagrin.

They'd reached the bottom of the gully when he heard a shout and turned to his right to see a dozen dark figures break from the trees.

His party was close to the base of the next ridge but the snow was knee-deep. It would be impossible for the laden horses to make it up to the crest and over before the men reached them.

'They're not fellow travellers, are they?' the eldest girl asked grimly. She had been aware of the danger all along.

'No such luck,' Byren muttered. Tying the halter of Rodien's horse to hers, he looked up into her face. 'I'm relying on you to get the little ones up the hill, over the ridge and down to Cedar tradepost. Don't look back.' And he slapped her horse's rear.

It took off, frightened by Byren's shout.

Veniamyn came running up to Byren, the heavy sled impeding his horse's progress. 'Is it –'

'Yes. Up.' Byren caught his thigh and lifted him, almost throwing him onto the horse's back. Then he ran a couple of paces to the leather traces that connected to the sled and slashed them. 'We'll have to leave this.'

With a slap, he sent the scholar's horse after the children's horses. Then he ran along behind.

At first the horses made good time, but then they hit the slope of the next ridge. Spent horses, burdened with riders, running uphill through snow, were not much faster than determined men.

And the brigands had veered to cut them off, climbing the ridge at an angle. Faceless, menacing black silhouettes against the star-bright snow, they forged on, intent on their prey.

Byren loosened his hunting knife, wishing he had more weapons.

Halfway up the ridge, he veered towards the brigands. The nearest man huffed madly as he ran and drew his sword, intending to cut Byren down with one slash.

Byren ducked, then rose, driving his knife into the man's gut. The brigand crumpled. Byren pulled his knife free and snatched the sword.

Then he raced towards another brigand, who was trying to grab the scholar's horse by the tail with one hand, while reaching to pull Veniamyn from its back with the other. Byren slashed the brigand's back, shoved him aside and ran on as he fell.

Between the pounding in his head and the shouts of the brigands, Byren was aware of nothing but each moment, each frantic breath, each thudding step.

Amazingly, he saw the crest ahead with the children's two horses silhouetted against the stars. Veniamyn's horse snorted and struggled up the last of the incline to join them, with Byren a step behind.

Below, nestled in the valley between ridges, the welcome lights of Cedar tradepost glowed in the dark. The palisade gate was closed but they wouldn't turn away a party made up mostly of frightened children.

'There it is, go!' Byren ordered.

'What about you?' the eldest girl cried.

'Go!'

Veniamyn cast him a look of thanks, then plunged after the children.

Byren turned to face the brigands, hoping none of them carried bows. Even if they did, shooting down hill at racing targets was not easy. Their aim would be off.

He held the high ground as he confronted the first two bandits, who raced up the rise towards him. Lifting his borrowed sword, Byren waited grimly. He'd killed two but there were another ten – not good odds, as Lence would say...

His twin's loss cut deep and hard. No time for grief.

The two brigands slowed, eyeing him warily. Clearly, they weren't about to attack. As they waited for others to join them, Byren was aware of some making their way across the crest and around behind him.

He cast a look over his shoulder and spotted three horses streaking across the snow towards the palisade gate. Thank Halcyon, Rodien and the others were safe.

He, however, was about to face the brigands' anger.

There was no point running. They would cut him down the moment he turned his back. Byren preferred to die fighting. He did not regret his actions. He could not have abandoned Rodien, or Veniamyn and his girls. But he did regret failing his father, failing Rolencia.

'They're getting away!' one of the brigands panted.

'Forget them. We have a richer prize here,' Sveyto said. 'The Merofynians are offering a bag of gold for the kingson.'

For a heartbeat, Byren considered denying it, but Byren Kingson was worth more to them than Byren Blacksmith.

'What gave me away?' he asked. 'Was it something Veniamyn said?'

Sveyto laughed. 'That old fart? No. You and your twin attacked a band I was with last spring cusp. I saw you then, all high and mighty, before I ran off into the trees. Took me a while to place you, but you have the manner of a lord, not a blacksmith.'

Byren shrugged. Piro would have been disappointed in him. She was the one who loved to dress up and perform plays. He lowered his sword tip. 'So you've been after me all along, not –'

'Oh, the girls would have warmed our beds before we sold them to the Utlanders.' Sveyto spat. 'Now we'll have to sleep cold. Drop your weapon.'

There was no point resisting. They were going to capture him eventually and he would stand a better chance of escaping if he was uninjured. Byren tossed the borrowed sword and his hunting knife in the snow at Sveyto's feet and lifted his hands.

'Tie him up, good and tight,' Sveyto ordered.

Byren didn't offer resistance, but the nearest brigand stepped in and sent a punch into his belly that drove the air from his lungs. He went down on his knees in the snow. More blows followed.

'Hurry,' Sveyto warned. 'Before that nagging scholar convinces Cedar tradepost to send out warriors to rescue his precious kingson.'

Head ringing, ribs aching with each breath, Byren fought to remain conscious as two burly brigands dragged him down the hillside between them. When they reached the abandoned sled, the brigands strapped him to it, atop the belongings.

Still dazed from the blows, Byren heard their voices fade in and out along with the rhythmic thumping of his head.

'...are missing.'

Sveyto swore and suddenly his face appeared over Byren. 'That's four good men you owe me, kingson!' Another blow made his head ring.

Four men? He'd only taken down two, hadn't he?

The sled jerked as the brigands took up the shafts and dragged it over the snow through the night.

Byren knew he was in a bad way as he slipped in and out of consciousness. At one point he thought he was on Sapphire Lake in a rocking boat, fishing with Orrade. Something he said made his friend throw back his head and laugh. Wiping tears from his eyes, Orrade grew serious. 'You know I'm not like Lence. You should never have compared us. I'll always be true to you, Byren.'

He was right. And Byren wanted to ask forgiveness for ever doubting him. He grabbed Orrade, pulled him against his chest, mock-wrestling. The boat rocked alarmingly. Orrade clutched him and they froze until the boat settled.

Orrade turned his face up towards him. He wanted a kiss.

Byren woke with a jerk, his head thumping, his body wracked with shivers. And it came back to him. He was a captive, about to be handed over to the Merofynians for a bag of gold, but first they had to get him down from the foothills and back to Rolenhold.

Dark trees speared up into the starry night above him, unfolding around him as the sled was drawn along. All he needed was a chance to escape. For now he had to rest and build his strength.

Dark silhouettes plodded along behind the sled. One went down and didn't get up. Instead, the body seemed to slide silently off the track into the trees.

Byren blinked and tried to focus but they turned a bend and that part of the track was lost. What had he just seen?

Were they being followed?

He listened for the sounds of pursuit. There were none but, whoever it was, they wouldn't want to give themselves away.

Nothing happened.

Perhaps his blurred sight had misled him.

Perhaps Veniamyn had not convinced the people at Cedar tradepost to come after him. Perhaps they would set off in the morning and hope to follow tracks. Perhaps the travellers at Cedar tradepost were concentrating on getting to safety and couldn't be bothered with a kingson.

He didn't know. His head ached and he couldn't keep his eyes open.

CHAPTER TWENTY

AT SOME POINT the sled stopped moving. Byren was woken by the thump as the brigands released the shafts and it came to rest on the snow. They lit a fire, making camp for the night. The fire's heat barely reached the nearest side of him and he shivered with cold. The ulfr fur was pinned under him and gave no protection from the icy air.

His head felt a little clearer. Concentrating, he watched the brigands. There seemed to be no leader. Sveyto told them what to do and they did it... if they agreed. Right now they confronted Sveyto, shouting something about men going missing.

Byren tried to focus, counting five not eight men, so he hadn't been mistaken. He took hope.

'...all they had to do was follow the sled,' Sveyto said, voice hard and flat. 'If they lost the track that's their problem. Besides, a five-way split means all the more gold for us!'

Appeased with this cold logic, the others opened their provisions to heat food. The smell of onions and salted pork made Byren's stomach rumble and his mouth water.

'How about some food?' he called. He had to repeat it twice before they heard him.

Sveyto came over, chewing on some crackling. He took a bite, then held it under Byren's nose, moving it before Byren could get his teeth into it. 'Not so high and mighty now, eh, kingson?'

Byren studied him, as much as he could, with the fire at his back, Sveyto's face was in shadow. If they'd only let him up to pee, he might get away. He knew these foothills. 'I need to take a piss.'

'Too bad.'

'If I piss my pants my trews will freeze. Without a blanket I'll be dead of cold by morning.'

Sveyto considered this, then called over two of the brigands, the same burly ones who had manhandled him down the slope to the sled. They complained as they left the fire circle.

His eyes on the other two, Byren didn't notice what Sveyto was doing, until the sell-sword lunged in and the knife plunged into his belly. He gave a grunt of pain.

'There. You won't be running far with that.'

'It'll kill him,' one of the brigands protested.

'In a few days,' Sveyto replied, untroubled. 'By then he'll belong to the Merofynians. If they want him alive, they can set their mystic healers on him. Help him up.'

Stiff with cold and bent double with pain, Byren hung between the two brigands, weak as a day-old kitten. Blood ran down his legs as they propped him up to pee. Nothing came out.

Soon, he was back on the sled, arms tied above his head. A blanket was thrown over him, right over his face. He was as good as dead.

Yet his mind still raced, refusing to give up hope. Through the smelly, coarse weave of the blanket, he could just make out the glow of the campfire and the silhouettes of the remaining five brigands.

He hated them. Hated everything they represented, unbridled greed and cruelty. This was why King Rolence the First had taken the valley, to impose law on lawless men. This was why he and Lence had ridden the Divide, stamping out brigand nests and putting down rogue Affinity beasts.

If he had the chance, he would throttle Sveyto. Just let them free him from this sled. Even with his arms bound at the wrists, his hands were big enough to circle the sell-sword's neck and choke the life from him.

But for now, he was a captive with a belly wound that leaked his blood and body warmth into the night. What if Sveyto had miscalculated and he froze to death?

The Merofynians would probably pay up either way.

The rage evaporated, leaving him feeling light-headed and thirsty. He called for water, but they didn't hear him, or else were ignoring him.

He must have slept, or passed out, because he woke to shouts, then screams. The fire had died down. He could see nothing but a dull blur of dark bodies against the snow-shrouded pine trees.

Hope animated him.

His rescuers must have picked off Sveyto's brigands and bided their time, until the watch dozed. He would congratulate their leader and thank Veniamyn.

Someone yelped. He hoped his rescuers didn't pay too dearly for saving him. Especially if they couldn't get him to a healer in time.

The fighting ceased.

Silence stretched. He flexed his arms and legs, trying to regain circulation. His numb fingers tingled painfully. The blanket twitched, then slid down and across his body. Cold air hit his face. He blinked and sneezed. The sneeze tore at his stomach and he groaned, panting his way through the pain.

Something damp touched his temple. He inhaled, smelling...

Ulfr?

His eyes flew open. At least five silky-furred Affinity beasts stood around the sled where he lay prone.

Byren tensed, expecting to be torn to shreds before his next breath.

Nothing happened.

Something damp and warm nuzzled his face. Hot ulfr breath huffed over his cold cheeks. Byren opened his eyes to look into the silvery depths of the pack leader's own eyes.

Too stunned to speak, he could only gasp as the ulfr nudged him, as though urging him to get up.

'Can't,' Byren grunted, jerking his arms and ankles. 'Tied down.'

And, amazingly, the beast moved to where his hands were tied above his head, fixed to the frame. He felt tugs, then, as sensation returned, hot breath and soft fur on his fingers.

Once his hands were free, the beast moved to his legs, performing the same service on those leather straps. Its razor-sharp teeth chewed through the bindings in a heartbeat.

Byren tried to sit up, but couldn't. Tried to roll to one side and fell off the sled onto the snow. He huddled there, panting. So thirsty. He scooped snow into his mouth and sucked on it, knowing it was the wrong thing to do. He was already losing too much body heat.

The ulfr nuzzled him again.

With great effort, he lifted his head, coming as far as his knees. 'I don't know why you're doing this, or even how you know to do it...' His vision blurred. He'd lost too much blood. 'But I'm spent. I can't go on.'

The ulfr didn't believe him. Its solid shoulders nudged him. He fell into the snow on his hands and knees. Another beast nudged him from the other side. Like dogs herding sheep, the ulfr drove him to crawl.

When he paused to gain his breath they waited. If he took too long, they nipped him, not enough to damage, but enough to sting.

At first he was so amazed he wanted to laugh at the absurdity of it. Orrade would never believe this.

Then exhaustion made everything dull and grey. What was the point? Without a healer he'd die.

All he could do was move in the direction the ulfrs drove him. Hands numb, knees numb, blinded by pain.

When he fell over the lip of a rise, into a dip, tumbling down through the drift of deep snow, he didn't try to save himself. He went with the fall.

This was it. He could go no further. All he wanted to do was sleep.

Bleeding in the snow.

Even now, some mad part of his mind refused to give in. And he tunnelled down into the snow drift, trying to make a rudimentary snow-cave. But before he could, he felt the silky-shaggy heat of an ulfr at his back, then another at his side, then another and another, until he was surrounded by the pack.

And they started that whining vibration, with each breath, the same song they had used when the bitch whelped. He wasn't cold any more. Soon he wasn't in pain. Soon he drifted, soothed and sated.

If only he'd had time to tell Orrade how much he regretted that crack about Lence. How could he compare Orrie, who'd never done anything but protect his back and stand at his side, with his belligerent twin brother?

Byren dozed, feeling warm and safe, even as his lifeblood seeped away.

He found himself walking the corridors of New Dovecote House, looking for Elina. In the great hall, he saw the fierce Old Dove himself, feeding his prize doves. Odd, the creatures weren't caged. They flew around the hall, each bird a work of art, all frothy feathers and soft cooing.

Of course – realisation came to Byren with a surge of wonder and joy – this was Halcyon's Sacred Heart, where the righteous waited in peace for their loved ones to join them. He must be close to death, to find himself here.

'Where's Elina?' Byren asked.

Lord Dovecote indicated the far door. He seemed to have forgotten that he'd cursed Byren and banned him from setting foot on his estate. Since Byren was innocent of the crime he'd been accused of, this was only fair, and he silently thanked Halcyon.

Byren found Elina in the library, of course, legs tucked under her as she read a history of Rolencia. No, it was a book on law.

She looked up at him. 'You know, Father could have named me his heir, even though he had another son in Garzik.' She wrinkled her nose. 'Not that it matters, now I'm dead.'

He wanted to deny the harsh truth. She was just as he remembered, slightly astringent, sharp-eyed with a dash of wry humour. How could he go on living without her?

He wouldn't have to.

Dropping to his knees, Byren knelt by her chair and took the book from her. 'I left it too late. I knew Lence was flawed, but I didn't want to admit it. His boasting, his need for praise, the way he used the girls who threw themselves at us. The way he spoke of you...' He touched Elina's cheek. Her features were the female version of Orrade's, softer and riper. Illuminated by her love for him, she glowed with an inner beauty.

When he leant close to kiss her, she let him. Her lips were warm and soft on his. Inviting.

'I'm dying,' he whispered. 'We'll be together soon. Halcyon will see to that.'

'No.' She pushed him away. 'You still have things to do. You can't let Palatyne win. Think of Rolencia, think of your duty!'

Duty? He was so tired. 'How much blood do I have to shed before Rolencia lets me rest?'

But she only shook her head, fixing him with fine imperious eyes. For a moment it seemed she wasn't Elina at all, but something grander and more formidable.

And he recalled his bargain with the goddess Halcyon. He'd pleaded with her to let him reach his family in time to warn them, promising to dedicate his life to her service. But she hadn't. His family were all dead. And this...

Was nothing but the illusion of dying delirium. The revelation hit him with a certainty that went bone-deep. He'd never given much thought to the gods and goddesses, preferring to let the monks and nuns court them instead.

Now it came to him that Affinity was just a tool like fire or steel, turned to good or evil depending on the user. Suddenly, his world was a much harsher place without the buffer of Halcyon's benevolence.

He focused on Elina's face. 'There is no goddess. Life is all we have...'

'Then live it,' she told him. 'Go.'

A roaring like a great wind filled his ears as he was sucked out of the chamber, out of New Dovecote House, to hover high over the Rolencian valley.

And there he drifted, watching starlight bathe the snowy fields and frozen lakes. It was so beautiful and it was his home, even without his family.

Forget the goddess, Elina was right. He owed this land his service.

Pity he was going to bleed to death in the snow, failing Rolencia and himself.

BYREN WOKE TO find Orrade kneeling over him. Mid-morning sunlight filled the hollow, amplified by the brilliant white snow, so that they were bathed in a glare almost too bright to bear. Other than Orrade, he was alone. The ulfr pack must have moved on, as they had the last time. Either that or he was hallucinating that he'd passed over into Halcyon's Sacred Heart and it was his fate to hunt the high country until all those he loved had died and joined him.

'What, you dead too?' Byren croaked, throat so dry it felt cracked.

'Idiot,' Orrade told him fondly.

Byren frowned. 'You're here, really here? I'm not hallucinating? How did you find me?'

'Another of those damned visions. I've been travelling non-stop for three days, praying to Halcyon I wouldn't be too late.' He blinked back tears. 'Sylion's luck, Byren. When I found you, I thought you were dead, you lay so still.'

'I am dying. Stomach wound.' As he moved his hand from the wound, he heard his friend hiss in consternation.

'So much blood.'

When Byren tried to focus on Orrade's face, the glare defeated him. But Byren didn't need to see him to sense his friend's fiercely protective nature.

What would it have cost him to acknowledge Orrade's unwanted love? He'd been furious because it complicated their friendship. He'd been selfish. This was his last chance. 'I'm sorry, Orrie. I didn't deserve you. Kiss me before I go.'

'Kiss you?' His friend snorted. 'Not when you stink like a day-old ulfr carcass.' Then he denied his own words, pressing his lips to Byren's. His were hot, as were his tears and the puff of his breath on Byren's face.

It was a kiss of love that demanded nothing and gave everything. Orrade pulled back. 'Now, let's get you out of this stinking seep.'

'Seep?' Byren blinked.

But Orrade had already sprung to his feet. 'Florin, over here!'

'Florin?' A protest died on his lips. He'd thought they were alone. 'Florin's here?' The daughter of Old Man Narrows, from Narrowneck tradepost, she'd helped them kill the manticore pack. Last time he'd seen her, she'd come to Rolenhold to report the Merofynian invasion. Cobalt had denied her. Byren tried to sit up and failed.

'Wait. You'll injure yourself. Wait for Florin.' Orrade dropped to his knees again. 'She insisted on coming with me. And just as well, she knows these foothills like the back of her hand. Her nan's cottage is not far from here. We'll take you there.'

Byren wanted to ask more, but he was exhausted. He must have passed out because, when he came around, he was lying on his back, strung between two stout poles, pines passing him, their tips spearing high into the clear, ice-blue sky.

It was all a dream. He was still on the sled, being dragged by the brigands.

No, because that person carrying the end of the poles was no brigand.

'Florin?' His parched mouth hardly formed the word.

She smiled and called. 'He's awake, Orrie.'

They lowered the makeshift stretcher and knelt next to him. 'How d'you feel?'

'Thirsty.'

Orrade glanced to Florin, then back to him. 'Can't give you a drink, not with a stomach wound.'

Byren grimaced and tried to swallow. His throat scraped. 'Water.'

Eyes closed in pain, he felt something press to his lips, opened his mouth and... blessed liquid settled on his tongue. He swallowed, tasting watered wine.

'Not too much.' Florin pulled it away too soon.

'What happened? Was there a fight?' Orrade asked.

Byren licked his lips. 'Brigands. They were going to turn me over to the Merofynians for a bag of gold. Stabbed me, so I couldn't run. Said the mystic healers could save me. But the ulfr pack came and killed them. Saved me.'

'He's delirious,' Florin whispered.

Byren wanted to object, but even that required too much effort. He was vaguely aware of the sled moving again.

Next time he woke it was late and they were manoeuvring inside a hill-crofter's cottage. He smelt barley broth and goats.

An old woman, Florin's nan, fussed over him as he was lifted onto her kitchen table. Meanwhile, a boy's high-pitched voice demanded to know what was going on. Leif, Florin's little brother. He struggled to open his eyes.

'We're at Florin's nan's,' Orrade told him, unnecessarily. 'She's a herbal healer. Hold on.'

Byren nodded. They'd do their best but he needed more than a herbalist. If his blood loss was anything to go by, he needed the touch of a great mystic. 'Thirsty.'

'Soon.'

Lamps were lit, water heated, cloth torn and herbs crumbled into hot water. He smelt the astringent, piney aroma of rosemary.

'Florin, take him outside,' the old woman ordered.

Who? Oh, the boy. Leif protested. The adults ignored him.

'But I can help you, Nan,' Florin insisted.

'I won't leave him,' Orrade said with quiet certainty.

Byren forced his eyes open in time to see the old woman send Florin and her little brother off with a nod.

Then Florin's nan turned to him. Gingerly, she cut away the material covering his wound, peeling it back from his skin. Blood had made it stick. His pants felt stiff with dried, caked blood.

She made tut-tutting sounds under her breath as she worked, passing each piece of ruined clothing to Orrade. 'Burn it. He smells like a day old ulfr carcass.'

'That's what I told him.' A laugh edged Orrade's voice, but underneath it Byren could hear fear.

As the old woman worked, Byren wished he could lift his head to see the extent of the wound, but he couldn't do more than watch her and Orrade as they stood beside the table.

Once his chest was bare, her fingers fumbled with the laces on his breeches. Byren was overcome with an urge to hide himself from Orrade, something he would never have thought of. It was absurd, considering the girls they'd shared.

Luckily, the old woman peeled back his pants only enough to reveal the wound low on his belly. Then she took a warm cloth, dipped in herbal water to sponge him clean. He ached with deep pain, but there was no sharp stinging sensation. In fact, the cleansing felt soothing.

The woman gave a soft hiss of surprise as the wound became clear. 'When did you say this happened?'

'Last night,' Byren answered. 'They did it to stop me running. How... how bad is it?'

The old woman exchanged looks with Orrade, both appeared stunned, so it had to be bad. Perhaps that was why he felt no fresh pain. He was beyond help.

Wordlessly, the old woman took Byren's hand and placed it on his belly. Gingerly, he felt smooth skin and a ridge of scar tissue.

No, that wasn't right. He tried to sit up, grunting with pain. Orrade helped him, supporting his weight. Byren starred at the fresh pink scar on his belly.

'It – it –'

'Looks a week old, not a day.' The old woman washed her hands and turned to them. 'I'm no fool, boys, don't insult me with lies. Orrie, you and Florin came rushing through here late last night, in a mad hurry to reach the kingson. You described where you would find him and I told you how to get there. You'd had a vision.'

Orrade nodded slowly. 'I never had them before this midwinter, but I took a blow to the head and I've been –'

'It's my fault,' Byren revealed. 'Orrie nearly died. He would have died. There was clear fluid coming from his ears and eyes,' He reached up to clasp Orrade's hand where it supported him and met his eyes. 'I never told you, I'm sorry. I couldn't bear to let you go. An old woman came by. Even without a scrap of Affinity I could tell she reeked of it. I begged her to save your life. She said she could, but you would never be the same. I told her go ahead. I couldn't let you die and she did save you, only you were blind...'

Orrade swallowed audibly. 'The blindness passed. But the headaches, they come on me whenever I have a vision. Sylion's luck, Byren, I'll have to leave Rolencia. Your father –'

'My father's dead.' He squeezed Orrade's arm. 'And I say stay.'

'And so you should. You're the pot calling the kettle black.' The old woman's voice was sharp. 'You've healed yourself of a mortal wound, Byren Kingson. That's a mighty useful kind of Affinity.'

'I don't know anything about healing,' Byren protested. 'I couldn't –'

'I found him in a seep,' Orrade confessed. 'Could that have done it?'

'Affinity is untamed power.' The old woman shrugged. 'It has to be guided.'

'The ulfr pack,' Byren whispered.

Both turned to him.

Byren frowned as everything fell into place. 'Look on my back, up here.' He gestured and Orrade helped hold him forwards while they lifted his shirt away to study his ribs.

'A new scar,' Orrade muttered.

'Looks old,' the woman said.

'No, Orrie's right. It's new since he saw me seven days ago, yet it looks old.'

'What's this got to do with an ulfr pack?' Orrade asked.

'I was bleeding from that wound. It had pierced my lung. Thought it was only a matter of time. Plus I was being hunted by Merofynians and the ulfr pack. I took shelter in a seep. I'd no choice. My only hope was that the ulfrs would prefer the seep's Affinity to me. They did. They lay down around me... Eh, Orrie, I thought of you as I lay there, surrounded by Affinity beasts, warmed by them. One of the bitches whelped a cub. The pack did something to help her, they whined and made a strange vibrating sound, deep in their chests. It was a bit like a cat purring.'

Byren shook his head in wonder and worked his tongue in his dry mouth. The old woman offered him a sip of watered wine. He swallowed and nodded his thanks.

'And this time?' Orrade prodded.

'This time the brigands had me and the ulfrs...' Byren hesitated, not sure even now if he could believe it. 'They came after me. They took down the men. I didn't see it. They'd thrown a blanket over my face. When the blanket was pulled off me, I was surrounded by ulfrs. The leader chewed through my bonds, led me to the seep. They all stretched out with me and began that odd whining-purr again.'

'Well...' Orrade said. 'That explains the stench.'

Byren barked a laugh that ended abruptly.

Silence stretched. A log fell in the fireplace, sending spiralling ash up the chimney.

'I've never –' Orrade began.

'You would if you'd heard the old tales,' Florin's nan snapped as she dried her hands. 'After his da and brother were killed by Merofynian Power-workers, King Rolen turned his back on everything to do with Affinity. He banned Affinity unless it served the abbeys, but that's like banning sunshine, unless it falls on the king's castle. Affinity rises where it will.'

Byren caught her wiry old hand. 'You can't tell anyone. I'll be hounded out of Rolencia.'

She studied him. 'Thirty years ago your father decreed all those with Affinity had to serve the abbeys or leave. But before that, for as long as there have been people living in Halcyon's rich valley, those with Affinity served their family and friends. They healed, they had visions of raids and sent out warnings...' She gave him a gap-toothed smile. 'And when King Rolen sent out his decree, they paid him lip service, because he was their king, but they kept to their old ways, especially here in the high country. You can't change the way things really are with a royal decree. We knew it would pass. Why, your very own grandfather, King Byren the Fourth, he had Affinity.'

Byren blinked.

'Why do you think he collected Affinity beasts?' she asked. 'You take after him, I'll warrant.'

'But I was tested at six like everyone else. I'm completely normal.'

She lifted one eyebrow. 'You hid in an Affinity seep, surrounded by ulfrs –'

'Can we come in now?' Florin's plaintive voice called. 'It's awful cold out here, Nan.'

The old woman sent Byren and Orrade a wry look. 'I'll say no more. But you think on what I've said.' She raised her voice. 'Hold your horses, lass. Don't want to make you blush. We'll just get him into bed.'

Businesslike, she finished stripping Byren, bathed the blood from his body and gave him one of her dead husband's night-shirts. It only came to mid-thigh on him.

As Orrade helped him into the tiny bedroom, which was behind the chimney, Byren grimaced. 'I might be healed, but every step I take tugs on my stomach muscles.'

'You can't expect miracles,' Orrade muttered, then laughed. And Byren joined him, because it was a miracle, an Affinity-induced miracle. But even laughing hurt.

Byren stretched out carefully, letting Orrade tuck him in as if he was a child. He caught his friend's arm. 'Thank you.'

'Rest for a day or two, then we'll take you back to my camp. Remember when Dovecote fell and you headed off to the abbey? I led the servants and villagers up into the foothills of the Dividing Mountains. Well, we...'

But Orrade's voice was already fading. Byren squeezed his hand. He thought he felt lips brush his forehead as he fell asleep and annoyance flared through him. Must tell Orrade not to touch him like that. It would give people the wrong idea.

CHAPTER TWENTY-ONE

BYREN WOKE WITH the sense that something was wrong. There was no sign of the others. Last night he'd slept with Orrade on one side of him and Leif on the other, while Florin and her nan slept upstairs in the loft. At least he'd been warm and the bed was free of bugs.

Now, alone in the bed, he could tell it was late afternoon by the light that came in the single, small window.

It irked him to lie abed for so long but his stomach, although healing, was still too tender to move freely. And he knew rest was the best thing for him.

As he'd dozed he'd grown familiar with the sounds of the cottage, the bleating of the long-haired goats, the barking of the dogs and the cackle of the chickens. Speaking of which, he could smell a pot of chicken and onion broth cooking on the hearth. His stomach rumbled and he looked forward to dinner.

The thump of running boots crossed the yard outside, entered the cottage and made straight for where he lay. Byren rolled onto his side and carefully levered himself up to sitting, feet on the floor. He reached for the pants the old woman had put out for him and flinched as his muscles protested.

Orrade charged into the tiny room. 'Good, you're up. Merofynians are coming up the valley, searching the farms. We have to go.'

In the main room he heard Florin and her nan packing food, preparing travelling bundles. Their haste was evident by their clipped, concise comments.

Byren grunted with annoyance. He hated being so weak. 'Need help getting my trews and boots on.'

Orrade guided his legs into the trouser legs. The pants were a bit short and tight around the waist.

'Eh, Florin's granddad must have been a funny shape.'

'Not really.' Orrade snorted softly. 'You're wearing Florin's breeches.' Businesslike, he dragged on thick woollen socks and laced up Byren's own boots. Just as well, with the size of his feet he couldn't have worn anyone else's.

Orrade helped him stand, dragged off the night-shirt and pulled a knitted vest over his shoulders, then a thick, high-country coat of sheep hide, with the woollen side innermost. Lastly, he placed a knitted cap on Byren's head. 'Now at least you'll look the part of a hill-man, if we're caught.'

Moving with great care, Byren shuffled out to the kitchen, where Leif waited, while Nan and Florin tied the travelling bundles closed.

Florin looked up. As she took in his careful stance, her strong face grew sharp with worry and the excitement faded from her dark eyes.

'He can hardly walk. How will we get away?' Leif asked, voicing what they were all thinking.

Florin tossed her bundle to her brother. 'I'll carry him on m'back. Orrie and I can take turns.'

'Halcyon will freeze over before I let a girl carry me!' Byren drove himself to straighten further, despite the deep ache in his belly. Unfortunately, his knees gave way and he would have crumpled if Orrade hadn't caught him, sliding his shoulder under Byren's.

'Don't stand on your dignity, lad,' the old woman told him. 'If you're found here, it'll be the death of all of us.'

She was right. Byren cursed. If only he had his strength. 'I can ride, if you tie me to the saddle.'

'We have nothing but an old mountain pony. Besides, they're watching all the trails out of the valley.' The old woman shook her head. 'We must hide you for now. There are caves up in the ravines. Florin knows the way. She'll guide you. Orrie will carry you if he has to. Leif can manage your things.'

The boy slung his own bundle, as well as theirs, across his shoulders, as if to prove her point. Byren felt inadequate and hated it.

'We don't mind. You led us when we trapped the manticore pride and killed them,' Leif said, his eyes alight with excitement, fixed on Byren's face.

'You killed a leogryf with your bare hands –'

'I had a knife,' Byren corrected. 'And this is not the same.'

'All of Rolencia is talking about how you walked into Halcyon Abbey after the Merofynians took it and dared them to catch you.'

Byren shook his head. 'That wasn't how it happened.'

'No?' The old woman pinned him with her clever gaze. 'But it is how they're telling it. The people of Rolencia need Byren Leogryfslayer. So swallow your pride, lad, and get out the back door before the Merofynians arrive.'

Chastened, Byren hobbled outside, leaning heavily on Orrade. He glanced over his shoulder to see Florin hug her grandmother in the back doorway.

Meanwhile, Leif beamed as though this was a great adventure, but Byren knew better. If they were caught the Merofynians wouldn't let the boy's youth stop their swords.

Byren blinked back tears of frustration and fury. He channelled the anger into empowering his weak body. Florin strode past, her long legs and easy stride propelling her swiftly across the ground. Leif took little skipping steps to keep up with her. Byren sucked in a deep breath, feeling the wound pull.

'Concentrate on escaping and getting better,' the old woman called after him. 'You can only fight one battle at a time.'

She was right. Head down, Byren focused on putting one foot in front of the other.

Soon they were beyond the barn and workshed. Under the tall pines night was already closing in. Snow lay thick on the ground. Orrade pulled up sharply and Byren took the chance to catch his breath.

'Wait, Florin, our trail will give us away.'

She called over her shoulder. 'We thought of that. Nan's gone to bring the goats in for the night. They'll cover our tracks.'

She strode on, powerful thighs driving them upwards along the trail. Byren feared, even with Orrade's supporting shoulder under his, he would not be able to keep up with her for long.

'How far are these caves anyway?' he muttered.

'How far to the caves, Florin?' Orrade called.

She did not slow. 'We'll be there by midnight.'

He'd never make it.

'I'll carry you if I must,' Orrade whispered. He was half a head shorter than Byren and slender, but on other journeys his wiry strength had outlasted almost everyone, so Byren did not doubt him.

'What if the Merofynians follow us up to the caves?' Byren asked, between breaths.

Florin glanced over her shoulder. 'You could hide an army in the foothills of the Divide.'

They walked in silence through the deepening twilight, their breath misting with every step.

After a while, a raucous barking echoed from the farmhouse below them. They had already climbed so high that, when they paused to peer back down the hillside, they could only glimpse the snow-covered roofs and smoking chimney pot of the farmhouse between the pines.

'The dogs don't like the Merofynians,' Florin muttered.

'Nan should set the dogs on them!' her brother said. 'I would!'

'Hush, Leif. Do that and you'd get yourself killed,' Florin muttered.

'If Byren wasn't injured he'd send them to meet their gods!'

Byren shook his head. 'Not when there's a dozen of them and only one of me. Better to bide your time and attack when you know you can win.'

Florin gave him a smile. He didn't need her approval.

Driving himself to stand, he faced uphill. 'How much further?'

Orrade looked to Florin.

'Not far now.'

But Byren knew she was lying to encourage him.

They moved on. Byren's legs had seized up during the short rest and now his thigh muscles ached with each step and his injury tugged across his belly with each breath. He gritted his teeth and said nothing.

The night was clear. With the stars so bright and the white snow reflecting their light, they had no need of a lantern. The higher they went, the taller and thinner the pine trees got.

All too soon Byren's head was buzzing and his breath wheezed in his chest. He had to rest.

'We'll stop for a bit,' Florin said.

'I can keep going,' Byren lied.

'Leif needs to rest. He has to take two steps for your one,' she told him.

'I could walk all night if I had to,' Leif insisted, despite the fact that Byren could see his legs trembling. 'I don't have to rest.'

'Well, I do,' Orrade muttered. 'Byren weighs as much as a full-grown leogryf.'

As he slipped out from under Orrade's shoulder and sat on a rock, Byren noticed Florin send his friend a look of thanks.

Leif chose to sit next to Byren, who took the chance to suck in deep breaths.

'We're making good time,' Florin said. 'I only hope Nan's all right. They wouldn't hurt an old woman, would they?'

Orrade caught Byren's eye. They both knew the Merofynians would hurt the old woman, if they thought it served their purpose. He felt Leif tense at his side and lied without a qualm. 'No. Your nan will be fine.'

He only hoped he would not be proven wrong.

PIRO WATCHED OVERLORD Palatyne's food-taster eat a sliver of roast beef and thanked Halcyon she wasn't his food-taster. She would rather starve than risk poisoning to protect him.

This was their second evening in the house of a wealthy Marchand merchant, resting while their ships were being provisioned for the journey. Merofynia wasn't far as the crow flies, but it was a long journey by sea around the warlords' spars, through the scattered Utlands, and past the famous Mulcibar's Gate into Mero Bay.

'The meat is delicious, overlord,' the man said. Piro wondered what the point of a food-taster was, if someone was clever enough to use a slow-acting poison that accumulated in the body.

Palatyne tore off a chunk of meat and sank his teeth into it. His eyes closed in bliss as he chewed.

'You see,' the merchant smiled. 'My cook is the best in Port Marchand. I am a realist, Overlord Palatyne. My wealth comes from trade, I don't bother with the politics of Ostron Isle or Merofynia. A wise merchant can make a fine profit from war.'

Fury made Piro's stomach clench. Only last midsummer this man had sat at her father's high table and praised King Rolen for Rolencia's peace and prosperity. And he probably meant every word, just as he did now.

'Have you tried the sweet potatoes?' the merchant asked the Utland Power-worker. 'Or the sugared plums? They came all the way from Ostron Isle.'

'A Power-worker's body is the tool of his trade. He must not absorb impure food, and Ostronite plums are cured in wine,' the Utlander explained.

'You jest?' The merchant grinned, but then saw he didn't. 'Ah, an Utland custom.'

He caught the noble Power-worker's eyes, sending him a patronising smile which said *we are not barbarians*. Lord Dunstany did not respond.

Overlord Palatyne bristled, for he was a spar warrior and only one step up from an Utlander. 'Did you see King Rolen's royal emblems? The silver ones belonged to Queen Myrella, the kingsdaughter and Byren Kingsheir.' He stroked the pendants which lay on his chest, bright against the azure velvet. His belligerent gaze seemed to say, *you may laugh at me because I wasn't born a noble but you cannot deny I am a slayer of kings*. 'The electrum emblem belonged to Lence Kingsheir and this large golden foenix was King Rolen's.'

'Very fine,' the merchant said, looking uncomfortable for the first time.

'All I am missing is the youngest son's emblem and it looks like the religious son was not wearing his, for we searched every acolyte's body in the abbey without luck.'

'I hear you offered a reward for Byren Kingsheir, alive or dead,' an Ostronite noble said. He was young and handsome, dressed in velvet and lace Ostronite-style, yet he had a hardness about him that Piro recognised from watching her father's experienced warriors. She did not doubt he was a sea-hound captain, capable of routing Utland raiders. And he was clearly not afraid of the overlord, for now he baited him. 'Yet you have his emblem? They say he escaped from an abbey full of Merofynians.'

Palatyne glared at the Ostronite, then at his Power-workers. 'Have you any news for me on the missing kingson?'

'Nothing, overlord,' the Utlander admitted. 'He is protected by someone. I swear Halcyon's mystics master must have escaped the ambush, for I cannot pinpoint where the kingson is hiding.'

'The Utlander is right,' Lord Dunstany said, which pleased his rival. 'I have not been able to locate him either.'

'Then I must rely on my own men,' Palatyne said. 'Gold will loosen the farmers' tongues, and if that doesn't, it's hard to work a farm missing your right hand!'

Piro shuddered. The more she knew of the overlord, the more she was convinced he did not deserve to live. Pity would not stay her hand when the time came.

Lord Dunstany signalled Piro to pour him more wine. As she did, her gaze fixed on the amber pendant that hung around his neck. The tiny figure trapped in the stone was a constant reminder of her enslavement.

The merchant glanced briefly at Piro, his gaze passing right through her. He did not recognise this Merofynian page as Piro Rolen Kingsdaughter. People only saw what they expected to see.

Palatyne stood up and belched. 'Ahh, I'm for bed. We sail first thing in the morning.'

Dismay flooded Piro. She did not want to leave Rolencia. Should she steal the amber pendant, sneak into the overlord's bedroom tonight and kill him, and stow away on a sled-boat back to Rolenton?

Lord Dunstany caught her eye as he stood. His gaze held a warning. It seemed he was always one step ahead of her. The pendant never left his neck, even when he slept.

Piro fought a yawn. Freezing Sylion, she was tired. At least she didn't have to listen to Soterro's snores. He and the cook were already in bed in the servants' quarters. During the journey, Lord Dunstany had kept her with him as if she really was his page. He had even told Soterro and the cook to call her Seelon, the male version of her assumed name.

Lord Dunstany was fastidious, to the point of being prim. He wouldn't let her help dress him and had insisted she dress behind a screen. Then he had closed his bed curtains, telling her not to disturb him. In truth he had seemed exhausted. If it hadn't been for the amber pendant, Piro would have taken the chance to escape before this. Instead, she had slept on the floor at the foot of his bed like a dutiful page.

Thankfully, the noble scholar made no attempt to use her as she had first feared. She believed this was because of his weariness and ill health. His joints were swollen with the bone-ache. This morning she had seen him fumble while trying to open the stopper of a glass jar, so she had taken it from him, and rubbed healing oils on his knuckles. Her old nurse would have done as much for someone in pain.

That was the last quiet moment she'd had all day. Overlord Palatyne made everyone uneasy. He was quick to anger and slow to forgive. Accompanying the noble scholar while he served Palatyne was exhausting.

Now Piro looked forward to her warm bed, as she followed the Merofynians up a flight of stairs and along a corridor to the best chambers, which looked out from the hilltop mansion over Port Marchand. She almost trod on Lord Dunstany's long robe when Palatyne drew up suddenly.

'For all his talk of profit before politics, I still mistrust that merchant, not to mention that Ostronite sea-hound captain,' Palatyne muttered and gestured to the Power-workers. 'Take a look in my chamber, see if you can sense a threat.'

The Utlander thrust the door open and strode in, staring about violently. Lord Dunstany followed. Piro peered in. It was a large chamber, with tall windows shrouded by thick curtains to keep out the cold. A fire burned in the grate and Ostronite carpets decorated the floor. The merchant had not stinted himself on the furniture. Rich brocade curtains hung from the bed's polished brass rails and a large wardrobe stood against the far wall, its carved wooden doors gleaming. Several branches of candles burned in welcome.

Curious, Piro watched the Utlander prowl around the room, sniffing like a dog. Unbeknown to Palatyne or the Utlander, Lord Dunstany caught her eye and the corner of his mouth lifted in a wry smile, raising one side of his long thin moustache. She smiled back before she could stop herself.

'Well?' Palatyne demanded.

'You are right. I can sense a threat, overlord.' the Utlander said. 'But what form it will take –'

'What about you, Dunstany?' Palatyne demanded. Piro had noticed that he never used the scholar's title.

The noble scholar went very still. Piro felt a familiar tingle travel over her skin and her mouth watered. Dunstany had said her Affinity made her aware when he worked his and he was right. She shivered.

'You are surrounded by threats, overlord, perhaps this confuses my learned colleague,' Dunstany said smoothly. 'I sense nothing peculiar about this room. And to put your mind at rest I will take your chamber tonight.'

The Utlander cast him a furious glance. 'Overlord Palatyne, I insist you take my room. I will sleep at the foot of the bed, ready to protect you.'

'Very well. As long as I get to bed!' Palatyne marched off.

Lord Dunstany sent one of the merchant's servants for their bags, then shut the door and slipped his long indigo cloak from his shoulders, handing it to Piro. 'Hang this up.'

'You did sense something, didn't you?' Piro insisted as she unlocked the wardrobe door and reached up to find a hook. Without warning Lord Dunstany pushed her into the wardrobe, slammed the door and locked it.

A cry of protest leapt to Piro's lips.

'I'm sorry, but you were right,' he said through the keyhole. 'I did sense a threat and I want you safe.'

'Let me out!' Piro thumped the door in frustration, but the wardrobe was solidly built. Four grown men would be needed to move it. Dunstany didn't even bother to answer.

Furious, she muttered a few choice words then settled down for the night, pulling clothes off the hooks to make a little nest, grumbling to herself all the while.

She could hear the noble scholar moving around the room. The servant returned with their bags, and the candles were extinguished. No light came through the key hole. Piro drifted off to sleep, wondering why she did not hate Dunstany as much as she should.

She was still hidden in the cupboard when the attacker made his move.

Fyn had arrived in Port Marchand with the setting of the sun and asked around the market, where he learnt Overlord Palatyne was spending his last night here in a turncoat merchant's mansion, overlooking the harbour.

He fell in with a talkative delivery boy bringing fresh fish to the merchant's cook and ended up in the kitchen chatting with the servants, and by the time the meal was over he knew exactly where Overlord Palatyne slept.

The merchant's house was all abustle with extra servants hired to impress the overlord, so no one questioned Fyn when he made himself useful. Once the meal was over, he slipped away and went up the servants' steps to the bedroom wing, determined to kill Palatyne with his first strike.

Creeping along the hall, he counted down the doors. His soft boots made no noise on the polished wood. With his eyes adjusted to the dark, he did not need a light to find the door handle. The room was unlocked. It was dim but, with the bed curtains pulled back, he could see Palatyne's outline as he lay facing the wall, swathed in blankets.

Fyn slid the knife out of his boot. Moving soundlessly across the carpets, he stepped up to the high bed. Fyn's stomach churned and he hesitated. Everything Master Wintertide had taught him revolted at the thought of killing a defenceless man.

Now was not the moment to discover that he could not do this!

Surely, if anyone deserved to die it was the overlord, slayer of his mother, father, brother and Piro.

Licking dry lips, Fyn raised the knife. He had to kill this sleeping man, whether it seemed right or not. Before he could strike, someone threw a cloak over his head and tore the weapon from his fingers.

He dropped and twisted, but his attacker knew the same tricks. Disadvantaged by the enveloping cloak, struggling for breath in its heavy folds, Fyn twisted and writhed, thinking only of escape.

They careered away from the bed, onto the floor, colliding with something solid that caught him in the ribs. Fyn grunted in pain. Twisting again, he almost had the cloak off when his attacker pinned him, catching his arm so the slightest pressure would dislocate his shoulder.

Fyn groaned with pain and despair. Why had he hesitated? He should have killed Palatyne when he had the chance. Now he would die for nothing!

His attacker forced him onto one knee and pulled the cloak from his face. Fyn blinked, dragging in great gulps of air.

The banked fire's flames roared to life, illuminating them both. At the same moment Fyn felt Affinity flare and knew he faced a renegade Power-worker, everything the abbey had taught him to fear.

Still, he stared in amazement at his attacker, who was an old, iron-haired noble scholar with piercing black eyes. Despite his age, the Power-worker had fought like a young man. Fyn had been bested by a man older than Master Oakstand. Shame flooded him.

'What have we here? A vengeful monk out to kill the overlord?' his attacker muttered, studying him closely. Fyn's cap had come off in the struggle. It was seven days since the abbey had fallen and his tattoos were still visible beneath the stubble. 'I did not know Halcyon's followers were assassins as well as warriors.'

No one rose from the bed to enquire about the noise and Fyn realised he'd been fooled by the oldest trick in the book, a bundle of bedclothes. Had the servants given him away? No, he could have sworn they suspected nothing.

Affinity itself must have given him away, giving Palatyne time to set this up. Fyn's mouth went dry. This scholar must be one of the Power-workers who advised Palatyne.

'I've been wondering when you would turn up,' the noble scholar whispered, and Fyn recognised him. This was the Affinity worker who had nearly captured him twice through Halcyon's Fate. 'Let me see...' The scholar had the arm-bar firmly fixed, so he used his other hand to reach inside Fyn's jerkin and pull Halcyon's Fate out. The opal flashed, catching the fire's light. 'Just as I thought.'

'Take it and let me go. Please,' Fyn whimpered. First chance he got, he'd knock out the old man down and retrieve the Fate. 'Just let me go.'

'You can't trick me. You forget I have already tested your mettle through this tool!' The Power-worker released the Fate and it swung on the end of its chain. When Fyn said nothing, his captor laughed softly. 'Give me one good reason why I should not kill you.'

'Kill me then and be done with it,' Fyn muttered. 'Everyone I love is dead.' His captor would have to release him to kill him and the moment he did, Fyn knew at least four moves which would disable him.

'Men deal far too freely in death. I prefer to keep my weapons well honed,' the Power-worker muttered and applied his elbow to a pressure point high on Fyn's back, making him duck his head in pain.

Before he could move, the Power-worker's arms slid around his throat, cutting off his air. Fyn retaliated, trying for the first release. He was countered. He tried for the second and failed. Stars swam in his vision. Fyn went for the third, but he was too weak to complete the manoeuvre. As he went under, his chest screaming for air, he thought of Piro.

He'd failed her, failed everyone.

PIRO PRESSED HER face to the wardrobe door, trying to peer through the key hole, but there was no one in her line of vision. Frustration made her grind her teeth. She'd heard fighting, then whispering. Now nothing. Had Dunstany been killed? He might look fifty but, according to Soterro, he had to be at least ninety, and she did not see how his frail body could withstand an attacker.

If he was dead she could escape. She had to, or she would become Overlord Palatyne's property. Her stomach revolted at the thought. With a start she discovered she trusted the noble scholar to protect her from Palatyne.

'My lord, are you safe?' she whispered.

She heard a body being dragged. Then Dunstany spoke to her from just the other side of the wardrobe door.

'I am unhurt. Go back to sleep.'

There were more muffled noises, then silence, and Piro sensed the room was empty. She sank to her knees, trying to make sense of what had happened.

Dunstany must have taken his captured assassin to Palatyne to prove himself worthy of the overlord's trust. She pitied the assassin, especially since his fate would be hers if she failed to escape when she killed the overlord.

CHAPTER TWENTY-TWO

FYN WOKE, WONDERING why he wasn't dead. His head thumped, his ribs and shoulders ached, and he could not move for the ropes that bound him. He could see nothing, but he sensed he was in a confined space. Footsteps moved on the boards above his head. He smelt salt and sea. The sacking where he lay lifted and fell rhythmically. His stomach rolled with nausea.

Fyn swallowed and fought to keep his last meal down. By Halcyon's blessing he was alive, even if he was a prisoner on a ship. For some reason the Power-worker hadn't turned him over to Palatyne. His hands were tied in front of him and he felt for the Fate. Strange, it was still safe around his neck.

Now what double-game was the Power-worker playing?

Determined to free himself, Fyn lifted his hands to his mouth and tried to undo the knot with his teeth. But they were sailor's knots and there was not a thing he could do.

PIRO WOKE AS Lord Dunstany opened the wardrobe door. He was dressed for the day in his usual robes and all evidence of the struggle had been cleaned up.

Stiffly, she climbed out and looked around. 'Was the Utlander furious when you upstaged him and delivered the assassin to Overlord Palatyne?' Piro was angry – for some obscure reason, she felt as if he had let her down. 'Are we to watch his execution before we set sail?'

Dunstany went very still, his piercing eyes fixed on her. 'There was no assassin.'

She frowned.

'There was *no* assassin,' he repeated.

A buzzing filled her head and she almost forgot what she was saying but at the last moment she held onto it. 'Yes, there was. I thought you would deliver him to Palatyne to win his trust.'

Dunstany sighed. 'You might be clever, *Seelon*.' He emphasised her assumed name, watching her closely. 'But you don't know everything. The assassin was just a foolish boy, a monk from Halcyon Abbey who wanted to avenge the abbey's destruction.'

Piro's heart raced. 'So what did you do with him?'

'I slapped his wrist and sent him somewhere safe, for now. As far as the overlord is concerned nothing happened last night and that's the way we'll keep it. Right?'

Piro nodded.

Satisfied, Dunstany sent her into the bathing chamber to get dressed. Here she found rich new clothes, but they were still the clothes of a Merofynian page. She peered around the door to find the noble scholar slicing fresh bread and pouring hot chocolate for breakfast. 'Why –'

'Why? I've never had such a slave as you. On the ship you'll travel as Seelon, my page. You'll be safe in my cabin from the soldiers. Now get dressed.'

Piro nodded and dressed. It was only as she laced up her ankle boots that she realised Dunstany had unwittingly placed himself in her power. She only had to tell the Utlander about the assassin to see the Power-worker fall from Palatyne's favour. But if she did, he still had her soul encased in amber and the Utlander was sure to recognise the pendant for what it was. No, she was safer as Dunstany's slave than Palatyne or the Utlander's.

WHEN BYREN WOKE the next morning, every bone in his body ached. Across from him, Leif heated a broth over a small smokeless fire in the middle of the cave. Flatbread smelt good as it cooked on the heated stones.

'Where's Florin and Orrie?' Byren had to clear his throat before he could speak.

'She's gone back down to the farm to make sure Nan's all right and hear the news. We need more food. Orrie went with her.' Leif smiled and nudged a large pack with his foot. 'He left his sword in there. Will you teach me to use it?'

Byren sat up and grunted with pain as he leant forwards to drag the pack nearer. Orrade's sword, the one the Old Dove had carried into battle thirty years ago with King Rolen, was safe in its scabbard, which had been wrapped in an old blanket.

Byren drew the sword to see if it needed oiling. His arm muscles trembled with the effort of lifting it. Disgust filled him. He was useless.

Leif crept closer. 'Florin wants me to go stay with Nan but I want to go with you and win back Rolencia!'

'I couldn't ask for a better man at my back,' Byren said with a smile, 'in ten years time.'

'I wish I was ten years older now!' Leif muttered.

'And I wish I was well. If wishes were fishes we'd never go hungry!' Byren sheathed the sword. How was he going to defeat the overlord, when Palatyne held Rolenhold and his army rode across the valley terrorising the farmers?

He needed allies. He needed the support of warlords from the five spars. True, they had sworn fealty to his father only this midwinter just passed, but he couldn't appear before them weak from an injury and alone. They respected strength. It was his father's strength that had kept them in line.

He needed time to heal and gather loyal valley men. Then Overlord Palatyne would regret he had ever set foot in Rolencia.

THE SECOND TIME Fyn woke it was to the deep roll of the open sea and unremitting nausea. The hatch above him was open and he could see the silhouette of a small man against the cold blue light of the winter sky.

'He's moving. Lift him outta there, Jaku,' the man said in the trading dialect of Ostron Isle. A large arm reached in, caught Fyn by his tied hands, hauled him out and set him on his feet on the deck as if he weighed no more than a puppy.

Fyn's staggered a few steps before recovering his balance. His head spun. It was mid-morning and the sun was blindingly bright, sparkling off the sea. He stood between two masts. Great sails rose high above him, their horizontal ribs of fine, flexible wood creaking as the wind buffeted them petulantly.

He could invoke Halcyon's blessing and ask to be returned to port, but that would only work if this was a Rolencian ship, and he feared they were Ostronites. He squinted up at the mast, high above, to identify the ship.

It flew no flag and his skin went cold.

He studied the sailors. They wore a variety of clothes from the attire of a poor fisherman, through spar warrior, to Ostronite. He was out of luck. They were mercenary scum. Little better than the Utland raiders they resembled. Desperate, vicious men, they had committed crimes that had led to their banishment from the civilised lands of Rolencia, Merofynia and Ostron Isle. Calling the Utlands home, they roamed the sea flying false flags to get near their prey, honest merchant ships.

How had he ended up on this vessel? He remembered fighting that Power-worker and failing.

It made no sense.

Fyn searched the horizon. He could see the snow-capped peaks of a distant land, though whether it was one of the Utlands, the tip of a warlord's spar or the mainland of Rolencia, he could not tell.

The ship's timbers creaked as the vessel rode the troughs and peaks of the waves. The deck moved under his feet. Fyn failed to compensate. He fell to one knee, jarring his body and making his head ache.

'A fish outta water, Bantam.' The one who had manhandled him so easily grinned. He spoke the Ostronite trading dialect with the accent of a Merofynian.

'Empty your guts on the deck and you'll have to clean it up,' Bantam warned, then grabbed Fyn's bound hands and undid the knots with a practised flick of his strong, thin hands. Sailor's knots. 'You understand?' he asked in Ostronite, then switched to Rolencian. 'Or do I have to speak the tongue you sucked from your mother's tit?'

'I understand.' Fyn spoke Ostronite. His mother had made sure he was conversant in the languages of the three great powers. He rubbed his wrists. The ship slid into another trough. His stomach recoiled. With a groan, he staggered past Bantam to the side and leaned over to throw up.

The big one laughed, not unkindly.

Eyes watering, Fyn wiped his face and turned around to confront the older man. Now that he had a closer look, Bantam was not old, just worn by a sailor's hard life. A faded scar puckered the corner of his mouth, giving him a permanent half-grin, but his eyes were cool and calculating.

All the while, Bantam used the tip of a wicked little dagger to clean under the nails of his left hand. Despite his casual air, he watched Fyn closely. As he put the knife away his jerkin gaped open and Fyn saw a small tattoo amid the scars over his heart.

A butterfly... no, an abeille. Relief hit him, for this was the symbol of Ostron Isle. Part bird, part butterfly with beautiful double wings, this Affinity beast was as industrious as a bee, which was why the busy merchants of Ostron Isle had adopted it.

Fyn felt his knees tremble with relief. He might not be amongst friends but at least he was not amongst enemies. They were not lawless men at all, but daring sea-hounds. Sworn enemies of the Utland raiders, they hired themselves out to defend merchant convoys. And, on occasion, they formed fleets to hunt down the raiders. In this case, the booty they took remained their property. They had to be brilliant sailors, every bit as tough as the Utland raiders they hunted.

Unless... the tattoo dated from a time before this cocky little man was banished from Ostron Isle.

Fyn studied Bantam and took a gamble. 'If you're from Ostron Isle, what does the Merofynian Power-worker have to do with you?'

'I wouldn't know anything about a Power-worker. We're sea-hounds serving under Cap'n Nefysto, aboard the *Wyvern's Whelp*. Count yourself lucky, lad. You could have been press-ganged by the Merofynian navy and made to serve their king,' Bantam told him. 'Little Jakulos here ran off. Show the monk the way King Merofyn paid for your loyalty, Jaku.'

The giant slipped the shirt off his massive shoulders revealing a tattoo of a jakulos on his chest. These Affinity beasts were elegant, winged sea-snakes. Clearly, this was not the big man's real name, no more than Bantam was the other's. Although, the little man suited his assumed name better, reminding Fyn of a sprightly rooster as he strutted about the deck.

Jakulos turned. This time he revealed multiple scars, some older than others, crisscrossing the muscles of his broad back.

Fyn blinked. He knew life at sea was hard, but knowing it and seeing the evidence were two different things.

'As a Merofynian mariner you'd get a copper a week and a whipping for objecting. As a sea-hound you get a share of the booty and tipped overboard for objecting,' Bantam grinned, amused by his own wit. 'We lost some men after a disagreement with an Utland raider, so there's a place for you with us. What'll it be, monk?'

Fyn looked into Bantam's hard eyes and knew the man would have no compunction tipping him overboard.

It could be worse, at least he wasn't dead. It seemed Halcyon had been watching over him last night. The Power-worker must have dumped Fyn down by the wharfs, where he'd been picked up by the sea-hounds. Press-ganging unlucky men and boys to serve on ships was common practice. The only part Fyn did not understand was why the Power-worker had not turned him over to Palatyne, but he put that puzzle aside for now, grateful to be alive.

The ship dipped and Fyn's head swam. He gave a heart-felt groan.

'You'll get your sea legs in a day or so,' Jakulos told him, cheerfully, his deep voice rumbling. He gestured to a bucket of slops. 'Now, make yourself useful and be sure to throw downwind.' He laughed.

Despite his stomach's revolt and the thudding in his head, Fyn made no move to pick up the bucket. He had to return to Rolencia. Byren needed him. He had been a fool to go after the overlord alone.

Clearly he was not an assassin, but he could still help his brother. He might even risk using the Fate to find Byren, since it seemed the noble Power-worker, although not an ally, was not his enemy. 'I must return to Rolencia.'

'Is the little monk giving trouble, Bantam?' a newcomer asked, speaking Ostronian with a cultured accent.

'Nothing I can't handle, cap'n.'

Fyn turned. Captain Nefysto was not much older than Lence. Tall and spare, his skin was browned by the sun. Long black hair was pulled back and threaded with onyxes that winked in the sunlight. Three silver wyvern earrings dangled from his right ear. Sailors were notoriously superstitious, and it was said that silver wyverns, worn through the ear or around the neck, would protect one from attack.

A viridian, padded silk coat fringed with black lace stretched across Captain Nefysto's shoulders. Its hem brushed his knees, meeting knee-high boots. As he strode towards them the coat flapped open, revealing tight leggings. He might look like an Ostronite abeille but his hard thigh muscles told another story. Fyn would not make the mistake of underestimating him.

He guessed he was probably a younger son of one of the five princely merchant families of Ostron Isle, out to make his fortune. This gave Fyn hope.

He bowed to the captain, as befitted his rank. 'I am from Halcyon Abbey. As one man of learning to another, I ask that you return me to Port Marchand.'

Nefysto's lips twitched. His men gathered around to watch and a bad feeling settled in the pit of Fyn's stomach. While sea-hounds might be the sworn enemies of Utland raiders, they were not like his father's men-at-arms.

The captain stepped closer to inspect Fyn's scalp tattoos. 'What is a monk of Halcyon doing dressed as a fisherman? Spying on Overlord Palatyne?'

Since this was close to the truth Fyn could only shrug. His head throbbed every time he moved and his stomach heaved. He did not feel ready to confront this hard-eyed, young captain. He must not reveal who he really was, or that he could lead them to Byren. Nefysto's assumption would do. 'Overlord Palatyne lured the warriors of Halcyon Abbey into an ambush. He murdered the remaining boys and old men. I am sworn to avenge his treachery.'

'You might be, but the internal politics of kingdoms mean nothing to sea-hounds like us. We're kings in our own right, kings of the sea.' Nefysto gave Fyn a thoughtful look. 'You saw this attack happen?'

Fyn nodded.

'Get these lazy sea-snakes back to work, Jaku,' the captain said. He caught Fyn's eye. 'You may yet prove useful. Bring him to my cabin, Bantam.'

Fyn held his tongue as Captain Nefysto led him to the cabin under the high rear deck. A bank of windows ran across the bow of the ship, books sat behind glass-fronted shelves. Rolled maps were tucked into neat little niches. Everything was finished in polished wood, gleaming brass and glass.

From behind a screen came one bird song after another. Surely a dozen birds could not be caged in so small a space? Fyn identified a smell that reminded him of Piro's foenix and he made the connection. Could they be rare pica birds?

Ostron Isle was renowned for taming and breeding these Affinity beasts in captivity. Pica birds were natural mimics, and could be taught to mimic human speech in a sing-song way. They mated for life and the female could find her way back to the male no matter how far they were separated. Through judicious use of pica birds, the elector of Ostron Isle kept himself informed of developments across the known world.

It seemed Nefysto was more than just a sea-hound out to line his pockets. Fyn returned his attention to the captain, who dropped into the chair by the desk and propped his booted feet on the polished wooden top. He steepled his fingers, watching Fyn thoughtfully.

'How fresh is your news, little monk?'

'Seven – no, eight days, maybe nine. Overlord Palatyne has taken Rolenhold, though I don't know how he breached their defences.'

The door opened behind Fyn and he turned to see Bantam.

'What else can you tell me about Rolencia?' the captain asked. 'What is the fate of the royal family?'

'Rolencia is full of rumour.' Which was true enough. 'Merofynian soldiers roam the valley hunting for Byren Kingson. As for the rest of the royal family, people say they are dead.'

'Put him to work, Bantam.' Nefysto swung his boots off the desk. He grinned with gallows humour. 'We've had all kinds on the *Wyvern's Whelp*, but never a monk. We should be honoured.'

The captain dipped a quill in the ink and began writing. Fyn tilted his head, trying to catch the name the captain wrote with a flourish across the top of the page.

'It's code, boy.' Bantam clipped him over the ear. 'The captain writes in code. Back to work.'

Fyn hurried to obey, his ear still burning from the blow. He did not need to read the name to guess who the captain reported to. For all he knew, Nefysto was a younger son of the elector's own family. Hounding Utland raiders was considered an honourable, if dangerous, line of work, for someone from Ostron Isle. Rolencia and Merofynia encouraged the sea-hounds, because they helped keep the sea-lanes free of plunderers.

Once on deck, Bantam turned to Fyn. Despite being smaller than him, the little sea-hound exuded an air of menace. 'I'm quartermaster of this ship, which means my word is as good as the captain's. Now listen, lad, I'm not impressed by your fancy heathen tattoos. Behave yourself or you go overboard.'

Fyn shuddered. He could swim, but in the open sea, at this time of year, he would be dead of cold before the wyverns crunched his bones.

Bantam set him to work beside Jakulos, who was the ship's boatswain, in charge of the anchors, cordage and rigging. Jaku put him alongside a youth about his own age. Fyn did his best to keep up as they lowered the sails, now that the wind was rising. Fyn didn't understand why the captain wanted to slow their pace, but he'd learnt at the abbey to keep his head down and watch, so this was what he did.

The light wooden slats running horizontal across the sail had a concertina effect. Fyn was glad he had a good head for heights, if only the deck would stop swaying.

Hanging over the cross beam he saw a black and white bird fly up from the captain's cabin windows at the rear of the ship and disappear to the east. He guessed it was on its way to Ostron Isle.

What his father would have given for some pica Affinity beasts. But the electors of Ostron Isle kept the breeding and training of their messenger birds a closely guarded secret.

Fyn climbed down and returned to Jaku.

'Does the ruler of Ostron pay well for information?' Fyn asked Jakulos.

The big man laughed. 'The elector is dying. The nobles eat and drink and watch, waiting like vultures for him to drop so they can bicker over the electorship!'

Fyn frowned. If that was so, then who was Nefysto reporting to? There had to be a power behind the elector.

It did not concern Fyn. He would bide his time and obey Bantam on the *Wyvern's Whelp* until they put into Ostron Isle, where he would jump ship and barter a berth back to Port Marchand.

PIRO FOUND IT hard to say goodbye to Rolencia. She bit her bottom lip as she stood on the ship's deck, watching Port Marchand recede. True, they had yet to cross the bay and sail through the headlands, where Sylion Abbey perched high on the cliff, but it was symbolic, seeing the grand houses of Port Marchand fade in the distance.

High above her the sails, with their ribs of fine wood, caught the wind, creaking with the strain. If it hadn't meant leaving her homeland behind, she would have been excited. Her mother had told her so many stories about Merofynia, she felt as if she knew the palace already.

As it was, she couldn't help thrilling to the sight of their vessel sailing in formation with seven other fat-bellied merchant ships, all heavy with Rolencian booty, laden with warriors to fight off raiders. As well as this, four sea-hounds – fleet shallow-draught vessels, race-horses to the merchant plough-horses – kept pace with them, offering a further deterrent.

As long as she kept out of the overlord's way, she'd be safe. But that was hardly a plan. Until she could free her essence from the amber pendant, she dared not run away from Lord Dunstany. Frustration ate at her.

Dunstany's servant, Soterro, joined her at the rail. 'His lordship wants you.'

She took a step back. 'How long will it take to reach Port Mero?'

'Five days with a good wind, never if we meet up with pirates.'

He sounded so lugubrious, she laughed.

'Don't mock me. Our holds are crammed with Rolencian treasure, the perfect lure –'

'And hundreds of warriors, plus four shiploads of sea-hounds. That should be enough to keep us safe!'

BYREN SAT BY their smokeless fire that night, pleased to see Florin happy. Nan hadn't been harmed, but the Merofynians continued to scour the foothills, searching for the missing kingson. It made Byren suspect one of the brigands had escaped the ulfr pack and carried word of his near-capture back to the invaders.

'We can't go down into the valley to go back the way we came. We cannot risk walking into a band of Merofynian warriors, eager to win favour with their overlord.' Orrade looked grim. 'We'll have to trek across country, over the high foothills, and it will take days to pick our way through the ravines back to the camp.'

'I can guide you. Pa is a valley-man, but Ma was high-country bred. There are paths known only to hill-people,' Florin revealed. 'Hidden signs for those who know.'

Byren snorted. He had long suspected as much.

'Good. We leave in a couple of days,' Orrade announced.

'We leave tomorrow,' Byren corrected. 'I've had one day's rest and I can't bear to sit still any longer. As long as we go slow, I'll build up my strength. How long will it take?'

Florin shrugged. 'It would have been quicker to skate the canals. Through the ravines... five days, maybe more.'

Five days before he faced the survivors of Dovecote estate. Five days to make his plans and gather his strength. So much depended on him, the second son, the spare heir, now the only survivor of King Rolen's kin.

Sorrow and bitterness sat heavy in his belly like indigestible green fruit.

CHAPTER TWENTY-THREE

PIRO CLUTCHED THE rail, enjoying the rise and fall of the ship, and the feel of the wind in her face. Unlike Grysha, she did not suffer from sea-sickness. Today, for the first time, the boy was up and about, which was ironic, since they would make port tomorrow.

And they'd made it so far without incident. True, they'd sighted sails that kept pace with them at a distance, but the size of the convoy and the added threat of the sea-hounds must have convinced the Utland raiders the booty was not worth the risk. They'd be cursing themselves if only they knew how richly laden the ships were.

Grysha joined her at the rail. Physically he was a pale imitation of himself. The sea-sickness seemed to have distilled his essence, so that the nastiness, which had been hidden before under a boyish demeanour, was closer to the surface. 'The master wants you.'

She said nothing, heading downstairs to the first deck, midship. With two hundred fighting men aboard Palatyne's ship as well as the ship's crew, she was glad she travelled as Dunstany's page. Some of the men gave her strange looks as she passed by but no one dared to trouble her. She suspected it was not her disguise so much as fear of the Power-worker that protected her.

As she entered the corridor that led to the cabins, Dunstany opened the last door. 'Seelon, bring food fit for the overlord.'

She returned to the crowded midship, where the cook governed the galley with its huge iron stove. He piled savoury bread and tasty preserves on her tray. She thanked him, then picked her way over the legs of dozing sailors, past warriors playing the card-game version of Duelling Kingdoms along the narrow corridor to Lord Dunstany's cabin.

Palatyne had commandeered the captain's cabin up on the deck above, leaving the Power-workers and the captain to make the best of the below-deck cabins. In the cramped quarters the Utlander's hatred for the noble scholar was hard to miss.

Dunstany greeted Piro outside the door to his cabin, whispering, 'The overlord has requested an interview with me and he particularly asked after you, so keep your ears open and eyes down. Palatyne has grown daily more uneasy since we left Port Marchand. We land in Merofynia tomorrow and I think he plans something.'

Piro nodded her understanding, grateful for the warning. It was strange, since leaving Rolencia, she and the noble scholar had become conspirators, watching the Utlander and the overlord for signs of treachery.

When she backed into the room, Piro found Palatyne had taken the only seat. She had to step over his long legs to place the tray on the desk. Dunstany sat on his bunk, indicating Piro was to pour the wine from his private store.

'No Merofynian ruler has ever done what I've done,' Palatyne remarked in brash, spar-accented Merofynian, obviously pleased with himself. 'Now that I've conquered Rolencia, King Merofyn will not dare refuse me his daughter. By midsummer I will have Isolt for my wife. She's pretty enough and young enough to train so that she jumps at my word. Wedded to her, I'll be the king-in-waiting.'

Piro felt sorry for Isolt Kingsdaughter. But perhaps Palatyne was getting the worst of the bargain. Perhaps Isolt was just like her father, cunning and dangerous. Piro smiled grimly. Isolt Merofyn Kingsdaughter would have to get in line if she planned to kill Palatyne.

'Drink to the king-in-waiting!' Palatyne raised his wine. 'Come midsummer, I will no longer fear a toothless old man!'

'That toothless old man is still very clever,' Dunstany said. 'King Merofyn has ensured the loyalty of his nobles by taking their first born in his service. They dare not move against him.'

'I shall do the same when I am king.' Palatyne took a deep gulp of wine and wiped his mouth with the back of his hand. Today he did not wear the amfina surcoat, but an elaborate court gown of velvet and black satin, embroidered with stylised wyverns in royal azure. His clothes proclaimed the title he craved but his actions betrayed his barbarian origins. He drained his wine and wiped his mouth with the back of his hand again. 'Now I'm going to give you a chance to prove your loyalty, Dunstany. I know you are King Merofyn's spy, but I suspect you are also a man who can see where his best interests lie.'

The noble scholar spread his hands. 'My king is sick and old, but he could live another five years.'

'I don't want to wait that long. A king-in-waiting may never be king. My saddle girth could come loose and I could break my neck while hunting, just as King Sefon did. Then my betrothed would marry one of her father's favourites and I would never sit on the throne.' Palatyne leant forwards, dropping his voice. 'No. I want to ensure the old man is safely buried as soon as we are married. I need a poison which mimics a natural death and you are going to supply it.'

The overlord's meaning was clear. If the noble scholar did not supply the poison, Palatyne would have him killed.

Dunstany switched to Rolencian. 'More wine, Seelon.'

As she poured two more glasses, she had to admire his calm as he played the game of Duelling Kingdoms for real.

After she poured the wine, Palatyne caught Piro's wrist. 'I have been admiring your pretty slave since Port Marchand, Dunstany. Why dress her as a boy?'

'A boy is safer travelling with the army.'

'A man would have to be blind to think her a boy!' Palatyne frowned, studying Piro. 'I need a suitable proposal gift for the kingsdaughter.'

'There are many pretty girls,' Dunstany said quickly.

'But this one comes from Rolencia. She provides visible evidence of my triumph.' Palatyne smiled. 'I will have Seela for Isolt.'

Piro's gaze flew to Dunstany's face. For a fraction of a heartbeat, he looked startled, then annoyed. Had she betrayed herself? No, even though she was not meant to understand Merofynian, she would have recognised her assumed name. Rather, Dunstany was reluctant to part with her.

'Of course she's yours if you want her.' Dunstany spoke so smoothly that Piro thought she must have been mistaken. 'The girl has a sweet singing voice and she comes up well in clean clothes. Despite her crude language, she could learn to be a lady's maid. And she's not stupid –'

'Not too clever I hope?'

'No, thank the stars!'

They both laughed and Piro would have turned away to hide her burning cheeks but Palatyne pulled her closer. Taking the wine bottle from her, he spoke poor Rolencian. 'Let me look at you.' He took her chin in his hand, turning her face this way and that. 'Sing something.'

Hatred filled Piro's heart, threatening to choke her. But she could not afford to give in to her emotions. This was the man who had murdered her mother before her very eyes. He would not hesitate to slit her throat if he guessed who she was.

'Sing what, sor?' she asked.

'Anything.' Palatyne released her chin and she straightened, wondering what kind of songs a serving girl would know. It had been a shock to learn he meant to give her to Isolt, but living in the royal household as slave to the kingsdaughter would give her the perfect opportunity to kill the overlord.

Why, in the palace she could even kill King Merofyn!

Piro felt a smile curve her lips and hoped it did not look as wolfish as it felt. Tentatively, she sang the first few lines of a ditty she'd heard the washer women sing as they worked.

Both men laughed.

'Hardly suitable for a kingsdaughter to hear,' Palatyne remarked and she realised she had sung something ribald. There must have been double meanings in the words.

'Isolt has been reared as a kingsdaughter should, she won't understand a crude Rolencian song about a lonely widow,' Dunstany said.

'That's right.' Palatyne leered. 'I'll teach her all she needs to know!'

Face hot, Piro began to move away but Palatyne caught her, pulling her down onto his lap. She masked her revulsion by pretending to be shy.

'Would you like to serve a high-born lady?' the overlord asked. 'Do you like pretty clothes and fine things?'

'Oh, I do,' Piro replied, though the words stuck in her throat. 'I likes pretty things, sor.'

Dunstany's eyes narrowed and she wondered if she had overdone it, but Palatyne stood her up and slapped her bottom. 'She'll do.'

'Then she is yours, my overlord.'

Piro thought she caught the edge of anger in Dunstany's voice, but Palatyne was unaware of it. Strange, now that she knew she had only one more day in the noble scholar's company she felt lost. But she must not despair. Soon she would be part of the royal household and one step closer to avenging her family.

'There is still the matter of that other gift you promised me,' Palatyne remarked.

'Seelon, bring me the jewellery box from my travelling chest,' Dunstany instructed, before switching back to Merofynian. 'I have a most cunningly wrought assassin's ring for you, overlord.'

Piro brought the jewellery box across and held it open as Dunstany sifted through chains, both silver and gold, uncut stones and semi-precious stones, some loose, some set in brooches or pendants. Finally, he selected a ring. 'Put the rest away, Seelon.'

Palatyne's eyes gleamed.

Piro recognised the ring. It had been her mother's and, as Dunstany slid it onto his little finger, she recalled her old nurse showing her how to slip her thumb nail under the stone to flip it up and reveal a small hollow made for secreting poison.

'A pretty stone,' Palatyne remarked, glancing in Piro's direction. She pretended to be busy putting the jewellery box back in the chest.

'Aye. So it appears,' Dunstany said. 'Seelon, take the tray back to the cook.'

She knew that once she was gone the noble scholar would prepare the poison and hide it in the ring. And, sure enough, by the time she returned, their deadly business was finished. The overlord looked pleased, and the ring was on his little finger, a secret messenger of death.

King Merofyn's death.

Although Piro understood the forces that drove Dunstany to betray his king, she was still disappointed in him.

Palatyne raised his glass one more time. 'To King Merofyn. What a pity he will take sick and die on my wedding day!'

Dunstany raised his glass and sipped his wine, and Palatyne left them.

Piro cleared up the wine bottle and glasses.

'Leave that. Palatyne has an eye for a pretty face and I feared this might come to pass.' Dunstany sat down at the desk and beckoned. He indicated she was to sit on the bunk. 'I know your secret, girl.'

Piro froze. If Dunstany knew who she was, her life was forfeit. He'd sold out his king. He would not hesitate to hand her over to Palatyne.

'You are very clever, girl. I've suspected for a while, but today confirmed it.' He smiled gently. 'You speak Merofynian.'

Relief rushed her.

'Listen to me, Seela. Palatyne has a little Affinity. It is why he is so suspicious of everyone.' Dunstany grinned with black humour. 'He senses that no one likes him and they all wish him dead.'

'And he's right!'

Lord Dunstany laughed then grew serious. 'You are fated to walk a dangerous path, Seela. I want you to be my eyes and ears in the royal court. As Isolt's slave you will be able to go where I cannot.'

It was a dangerous task he asked of her but, her gaze went to the amber pendant hanging on his chest, it was a task she dared not refuse.

IN THE MIDDLE of the snowy clearing Byren settled himself with his back to a rock and prepared to rest. Late winter sun touched his face. Offering little warmth, it made the world beyond his closed lids glow red-gold. Opposite him, Leif uttered a soft snuffling sound and Byren cracked one eye open to discover the lad had fallen asleep sitting up. He grinned. Poor boy, he never complained, but they'd been pushed, going back over their trail several times to escape detection.

Florin was off attending to nature's call. She'd said they could reach the camp by midnight tonight or, if they rested overnight, tomorrow morning. They'd decided to take it easy, so they were in no rush and he was grateful for the chance to catch his breath. He must not appear before the loyalists weak and light-headed with weariness.

How could he inspire confidence if he couldn't string a sentence together?

The foothills were dangerous this time of year and they'd been lucky to get this far without trouble. But Orrade had spotted some ulfr spoor and he wanted to make sure the pack wasn't headed towards their people at the camp. Truth be told, Byren felt uneasy about confronting the pack, if it was his pack.

He snorted softly to himself. There he was again. Thinking crazy thoughts. But he could not deny he lived because the ulfr pack had saved him, twice. And so he was torn between needing to defend the loyalist camp, and letting the ulfrs go about their business in peace.

Normally he would only hunt them if they attacked farms.

A soft squeak of compacting snow reached him.

'Eh, Florin. Take a look at Leif.' Byren muttered, not bothering to open his eyes.

A huff of warm breath brushed his cheek. Was Florin about to kiss him? His lids lifted.

Not Florin...

Instead, the pack leader looked deep into his eyes. Byren inhaled and identified the ulfr scent. It was so familiar now it hadn't triggered any warning bells. He lifted one hand to caress the creature's thick neck ruff. 'You startled me.'

The creature whined.

'No. I don't need your help, but you'll need mine if you hang around here. Orrie will have a hunting party out after you in no time.' He gave the beast a shove and let his arm drop. 'You need to lead the pack up into the mountains now, it's almost spring cusp.'

The ulfr nudged his hand with its muzzle, much the way his hunting dogs back at the castle would when looking for food or a pat. 'No, we're nearly out of food. Nothing much to eat now, until we reach camp. And you –'

A ferocious yell made the ulfr spring around, light as a cat, while Byren scrambled to his feet.

Florin charged out of the trees, swinging a branch.

Instead of running like any sensible ulfr would, this one held its ground, between her and Byren. Leif gave a yelp of fright and scrambled away. The ulfr cast him one swift look, then went back to growling at Florin.

'Get away from it, Leif. Back off and come around behind me,' she ordered. Then she raised the makeshift club higher and gave another yell. 'Be off with ya, beastie.'

The ulfr didn't budge.

Byren let out a sigh and climbed to his feet. The ulfr was protecting him from Florin, while she tried to protect him from it. What had he done to deserve this?

'Put the stick down, Florin.'

She pulled Leif closer and thrust him behind her. Never dropping her gaze from the ulfr. 'No.'

It struck Byren that she would be like this with her children, protective and dangerous, and he had to admire her. But not right now. 'You're making yourself a target, Florin.'

'But –'

With another sigh, Byren walked past the ulfr, giving it his back, much to Florin's consternation. The Affinity beast did not attack. Nor did it lope off.

Byren came right up to Florin and took the branch from her grasp, though she did not give it up without some resistance.

'That thing was about to tear your throat out.'

'No, that's not what you saw.' Byren sent the makeshift club spinning off into the trees and turned to face the Affinity beast. 'It's over. Go on, be off!'

The ulfr hesitated, then trotted towards the tree line. At the edge of the clearing it paused, looking back this way. Several more of the beasts came out of hiding, edging closer to their leader. The ulfr gave a soft barking cough and the pack melted into the pines.

Byren sagged with relief. Without meeting Florin's eyes, he strode back to their camp and collected his travelling bundle. After a moment, Florin and Leif joined him. Neither spoke as they picked up their bundles. In their silence, he heard condemnation.

How was it possible to do the right thing by his people and by the Affinity beasts who had adopted him?

Byren grabbed Orrade's bundle and slung it over his shoulder. Then he lifted his head and gave the bird cry that would bring his friend back. He caught Florin's eye. 'Go to the other side of the clearing and wait.'

He heard Leif's soft question and Florin's brusque but unintelligible answers as they walked off. Byren glanced around. They hadn't seen another living soul for days. But they should hide their tracks. He looked up, studying the clouds. Snow tonight. That would be enough.

'Byren?' Orrade broke from the tree line, heading across the clearing to join him. 'I was headed back anyway. The forest is thick with ulfrs. Thank Halcyon, they haven't attacked. I –' He broke off as he spotted the tracks leading both in and out of the clearing. Frowning, he strode parallel to the ulfr tracks, pausing to study where Byren had sat, then joined him. Orrade was on the high side of the clearing and this made him as tall as Byren. 'Are you all right?'

'We had... I had a visitor.'

Orrade frowned, weighing up the evidence. 'Then that's why we haven't been troubled by Affinity beasts. The pack's been following us to protect you.'

It was the same conclusion Byren had come to, but to have Orrade confirm his suspicions finally made it real. 'Florin found the pack leader in the camp,' he said. 'She tried to scare it off but it tried to defend me from her.'

A grin tugged at Orrade's mouth and he nudged Byren. 'Bet she wasn't pleased about that. The way she fusses over you...'

Byren glanced to the young woman and her brother, who waited at the edge of the clearing, just out of hearing range of their soft conversation. 'They must see me as little better than an Affinity beast now.'

'Rubbish.'

'No. It's true. If my honour guard knew about this, they'd refuse to follow me.'

Orrade took a step closer. 'I'd never turn my back on you.'

His hand lifted. Byren brushed it aside, suddenly angry.

During this journey there had been a lot of touching. At first he'd been weak and needed help, then they'd slipped into an easy habit of physical closeness but it couldn't go on. With every touch, Orrade proclaimed his love. Now that they were almost back at camp it had to stop.

'Your things.' Byren handed his friend the bundle.

Orrade was silent for a moment, staring fixedly at the rolled-up blanket, then he took it and slung it across his shoulder as though nothing had happened. But they both knew Byren had rejected him. Again.

Orrade cleared his throat, face stiff. 'You're right. Your honour guard would not understand.'

Byren wanted to protest there was nothing to understand. He had not courted Affinity and he was not a lover of men. But facts had little to do with perception.

'Come on.' Byren headed off and Orrade fell into step at his side. 'We'll just have to make sure they don't find out. Florin and Leif are loyal,' he said, knowing that they could hear him now that he and Orrade approached. He met Florin's eyes. 'I want you to forget what you saw on this journey. Never mention it.'

The way she did not glance to Orrade told him she had already leapt to unwarranted conclusions.

She shrugged. 'Forget what?'

'The ulfr, silly,' Leif told her. His hand slipped into Byren's. 'Don't worry. I won't tell anyone. But I don't see why not. Do you think you could call a leogryf for me to ride? I'd love to fly.'

A laugh escaped Byren. Florin joined him. Orrade grinned, but his eyes were strained.

It hurt Byren to see how much he'd wounded his friend, but he could no more protect the ulfrs from hunters greedy for their pelts than he couldn't protect Orrade from the harsh judgement of others. This deliberate distancing was for the best.

FYN SAT CROSS-LEGGED on the deck next to Jakulos, who was teaching him to repair rope. With the light fading, his stomach rumbled in anticipation of the evening meal. He had gained his sea legs within a day and, since then, every day had dawned fine and crisp, the ship cutting through the sea like an arrow. If he hadn't been consumed with the need to get back to Rolencia, he would have enjoyed the voyage.

Jakulos was not the chatty type and Fyn's thoughts revolved around the things he had left undone back in Rolencia. Overlord Palatyne still lived. He would arrive in Merofynia victorious, having attacked a peaceful country and murdered most of King Rolen's kin. Fyn only hoped Byren remained hidden long enough to recover his strength.

Somehow, Fyn had to return to Rolencia to help cousin Cobalt find Byren. Together they could raise an army to drive out the Merofynians. Meanwhile, every day they sailed further from Rolencia, yet he would not let himself despair. If anything, the focus of his determination became purer for being contained.

Someone dug him in the ribs with a dirty, bare foot. Fyn had discovered the sailors didn't bother to wear shoes. Bare toes gave them a better grip when climbing the masts. He looked up to find the quartermaster standing over him.

'Cap'n Nefysto wants to see you, little monk.' Bantam grinned. Every time he used the word *monk* it was a calculated insult.

Fyn came to his feet, flexing muscles stiff from sitting so long. One of the Ostronite messenger birds had arrived a little while ago and, since then, Fyn had been mentally preparing himself for this interview.

As he stepped through the narrow cabin door, Captain Nefysto gestured to a quill and paper. 'Write down everything you can remember about the size of Palatyne's army, where they were deployed and anything you heard about Byren Kingsheir. My master is particularly interested in the state of the Rolencian army.'

'Why should I help you and your master?' Fyn countered. 'Maybe I want something in return. I'll strike a bargain –'

He gulped as Bantam grabbed him from behind. A scrawny but tough arm caught him under his jaw and a cold blade pressed to his throat. Fyn could have tried any one of the disarming techniques the weapons master had taught him, but the captain was also armed and there was nowhere to run.

Nefysto advanced on him, his face a cold mask, making him look older.

'I could order your death and no one would question it, monk. In fact they'd leap to obey me. Unlike you, my men have never known a privileged life,' Nefysto said. 'Do you understand?'

Fyn managed a small nod and, at the captain's signal, Bantam released him.

Nefysto gestured to the desk. 'If you make yourself useful, I may just let you live.'

Bantam shoved Fyn forwards. He staggered, ending up in the captain's seat.

'This is not Halcyon Abbey, lad. The rules are different here,' Nefysto told him. 'You'd do well to remember that. Now get to work.'

He went out on deck, leaving Fyn under Bantam's watchful eye.

Fyn wondered how much to reveal. He knew a lot more about the state of his father's army than a monk would. Nefysto's master might have other sources, so he kept as close to the truth as possible, while writing a brief outline of what he had observed.

As he did this, he was vaguely aware of cries on deck and a change in the ship's rhythm. At last he put the quill aside and massaged his cramped hand.

Captain Nefysto returned. 'Finished? That was good timing. Give him a weapon, Bantam.'

Fyn's heart lurched. Were they about to kill him for sport? If so, why give him a weapon?

He rose from the captain's seat, stretching his tense shoulders, playing for time. Bantam handed him a short curved sword. Fyn took the weapon, feeling the welcome but unfamiliar weight and balance.

Bantam regarded him keenly. 'I don't doubt you'd like to spill my guts on the deck, little monk. But before nightfall you'll be too busy saving your own miserable life!'

Fyn looked to the captain for an explanation.

'We've sighted a fat ship ripe for plucking. She's running before the wind, but her canvas is no match for ours. We should have her boarded by dusk and then we'll see if the fighting prowess of Halcyon's warrior monks is as great as rumour has it.'

Fyn's stomach knotted. A ship ripe for plucking? It sounded like a merchant ship. It seemed these sea-hounds did a little plundering on the side after all. And he was expected to kill at Captain Nefysto's command. Everything the abbey had instilled in him revolted. If he could not kill the man who had murdered Piro, how could he kill an innocent man?

But if he wanted to live long enough to jump ship, he'd have to win the captain's trust. Fyn decided he would turn the flat of his blade and when that failed, he would injure the merchant sailors, rather than kill.

Only to protect his own life would he take another's. He was not a killer and they could not turn him into one.

But perhaps he was wrong and the captain was about to live up to the sea-hounds' reputation by attacking Utlander raiders. Fyn went on deck, where he found the vessel they pursued had the distinctive outline of a fat-bellied merchant ship.

He was disappointed in Nefysto.

CHAPTER TWENTY-FOUR

PIRO HAD GROWN up on stories of Merofynia's wonders, but seeing Mulcibar's Gate was more astonishing than any of her mother's descriptions. A hush fell over the crowded deck. In the darkness, a stream of hot rock rolled slowly down the slope, gleaming like living fire. A dark outer casing covered it and, through the many small cracks, she could see the bright red, molten rock within. Waves crashed where it met the sea, sending steam high into the air as the two elements clashed.

Piro pulled her cloak more tightly about her shoulders, unable to look away from the battle between Cyena, goddess of the sea and winter, and Mulcibar, god of fire and war.

The headlands dwarfed their convoy. To her right on the eastern cliff was Cyena Abbey, where the abbess served the Merofynian goddess of the sea, ice and winter, much as Rolencia's abbess served Sylion.

But the eastern side of the bay's entrance belonged to Mulcibar, god of the earth, fire and summer. In many ways Merofynia was the reverse image of Rolencia. Mulcibar was not a warm nurturing deity like goddess Halcyon. Now, seeing Mulcibar's Gate, Piro understood why he was the patron god of war.

A particularly large wave crashed on the molten lava, sending steam high into the air.

'Mulcibar's breath, they call it,' Dunstany said. 'Now are you glad I made you get up early and come up on deck?'

'Is it dangerous?'

'It has been burning on and off like this for as long as the monks have been serving Mulcibar,' he said. 'Where the hot rock meets the sea it cools, forming new land. Mulcibar's monks have been taking measurements. They estimate, if it continues to form at this rate, Mulcibar's Gate will be closed in two hundred years. But I've calculated that it will miss Cyena's Headland, curving back into the bay.'

'What a pity you won't be alive to find out if you are right,' the Utlander remarked.

Piro stiffened. She had not heard him approach.

'Oh, I'm much harder to kill than you imagine,' Dunstany said.

The Utlander's eyes narrowed and he stalked past them, going over to Palatyne who stood at the wheel.

'I don't like that Utlander,' Piro whispered. 'And he doesn't like you.'

'Very observant.'

Piro studied Dunstany but, in the dim predawn light, could not make out if he was laughing at her.

He smiled, and she couldn't help smiling back. She was looking forward to seeing the place where her mother had been born and walking the corridors she had known as a girl.

Grief made her gut clench. Her mother was lost to her, and it had only been in those last few days, before the castle fell, that she had begun to know Queen Myrella. Piro felt cheated of a mother who might have grown to be a friend.

If only she had gone to the queen sooner with her fears. In a way Seela had kept them apart. Not that her old nurse meant to do harm. Seela was loyal to the bone. Piro was glad she'd sent their old nurse to Byren, that last morning in Rolenhold. As for Fyn, she only hoped he was safe. He had to be safer than her at least, after all she was being sent into the enemy's palace as a spy.

'...Seelon?'

'Sorry, Lord Dunstany, I was thinking.'

His black eyes fixed on her suddenly serious. 'Soon you go into a court fraught with intrigue, where few can be trusted. You will be my eyes and ears, report back everything you hear. I may do or say things that seem odd to you. But remember this, if you are ever in danger, you can trust me.'

She wanted to. But...

How could she trust him, when he held her soul captive in the amber pendant?

Somehow Piro avoided looking at the pendant and found a smile.

'Of course I trust you,' she lied, and she must have been getting better at lying, as the noble Power-worker looked satisfied.

DAWN FOUND FYN crouching behind barriers of stacked bales as arrows whistled through the air, striking any man foolish enough to peer over the makeshift shields. Their own archers clung to the ship's rigging. Agile as monkeys, they picked off targets on the merchant ship's deck, crowing each time they scored a hit.

Last night they had failed to catch the merchant ship. The Merofynian captain had tried evading them by weaving his ship through the islands, but the winds failed him. He'd tried to slip away during the night, but Captain Nefysto had second-guessed him, anticipating the direction he would take so that now, as the sun came up, they were closing in.

'Let her fly!' the captain ordered.

Flaming tar-dipped arrows streaked across the narrowing distance, some falling onto the deck where they were quickly stamped out, others hitting the canvas.

'That'll keep them busy,' Bantam muttered with satisfaction.

A flaming arrow flew over Fyn's barrier. He ducked instinctively and it landed harmlessly in the sea. Another struck the sail above them, spluttered and went out.

'Mage protection,' Bantam explained in answer to Fyn's unasked question.

Mages were the most formidable of Power-workers. According to abbey lore, all Affinity renegades aimed to become mages but ninety-nine out of a hundred fell by the way side. In fact, the only living mage was Tsulamyth, a native of Ostron Isle. An eccentric recluse, he was said to be more than two hundred years old.

Ten years of abbey teaching made Fyn shudder. To think their ship was tainted by the evil of a mage. Halcyon protect him, he had not even sensed it. 'Mage magic in the sails?'

Jakulos laughed and shook his head. 'Don't listen to Bantam. The canvas's been soaked in something that resists flame.'

Fyn wondered what the scholars at Halcyon Abbey would have made of this. Bantam stole a look over the barrier. 'Not long now.'

Fyn's hand clasped the sword hilt, his palm damp with sweat. Defending himself was one thing, attacking fleeing sailors was another. He had been filled with righteous indignation when he defended himself from the Merofynians in the abbey. Now he was filled with terror. He only hoped he did not disgrace himself.

He glanced around. Some of the sea-hounds were fingering lucky charms and religious icons, others whispered under their breath.

It surprised Fyn to discover they were all frightened, even Bantam. Hard as he seemed, there was a brittleness to the little sea-hound's voice.

Bantam risked another look, then cursed. 'Warriors. Just our luck to pick a ship transporting the army back to Merofynia!'

But Fyn was secretly relieved. He'd rather battle the enemy than sailors going about their living.

'Grapplers!' Captain Nefysto called.

Jakulos stepped from behind the barrier. He planted his feet and spun his grappling hook. Sea-hounds left the protection of their shields and scurried up the rigging, grabbing ropes as they prepared to swing across to the other deck. Fyn waited next to Bantam, a gangplank ready.

He risked a look. They were close enough to see the faces of the defenders. His heart pounded. Now he just wanted to get it over with.

'Steady... steady,' Captain Nefysto warned. 'Let them go!'

Grappling hooks flew across the gap, landing on the deck and in the rigging. There were too many for the defending soldiers to cut all the ropes. The two great ships' timbers groaned as they were drawn together.

Uttering shrill cries that mimicked the shrieks of attacking wyverns, the sea-hounds swung across the gap, landing on the deck, fighting even as they found their footing.

Bantam pressed the tip of his blade into Fyn's ribs. 'Remember, I'll be at your side, little monk. But I'll be watching my back, so don't think to plant your blade –'

'Merofynians murdered my family,' Fyn ground out. 'I owe them no loyalty.'

'Good.' Bantam turned to the others. 'Attack!'

They shoved the gangplank across the gap, which was less than a body length now and, light-footed as his namesake, Bantam ran across with Fyn at his heels.

When Fyn dropped onto the deck, someone collided with him. He spun to see Jakulos down on one knee. Of its own volition, Fyn's sword swung up to block a blow that would have severed the big man's neck. Fyn turned the Merofynian's blade aside, following through with a strike as he had been trained to do. But he used the flat of the blade at the last minute. Even so, the man fell to the deck, out cold.

Jakulos sprang up. 'Stay by me.'

He charged across the deck, expecting Fyn to protect his left side. Bantam was on Jakulos's right, fighting with a sword in one hand and a dagger in the other, as he battled to keep up. Fyn ran after them.

Block, strike, hack.

A man dropped with each step Fyn took. Merofynian warriors sprang forwards to attack him and his companions, but no one could stop them. Burning canvas fell. Men tumbled off the rigging screaming. The merchant sailors avoided confrontation where they could, letting the warriors do the fighting.

Jakulos made for the merchant captain on the bridge. A Merofynian warrior tried to prevent them climbing the ladder, but Jakulos hauled him off and charged up. Fyn was one step behind him. He could hear nothing but the roaring of men and flames.

Jakulos charged, driving the three warriors back. Fyn followed, hacking through these last defenders until only a middle-aged Merofynian noble confronted him. From the way the noble held his blade, he seemed a skilled swordsman. The Merofynian noble attacked Jakulos so fiercely the big man was hard-put to defend himself.

Fyn glanced around. They'd left Bantam behind. The upper rear deck was almost empty. Two men stood at the wheel. Fyn recognised the captain by his coat of office. Both men were watching Jakulos and the Merofynian noble.

Fyn darted around the flying swords to confront the merchant captain. As the man lifted his blade, Fyn could see he was not skilled. Fyn used Master

Oakstand's first disarming technique, catching the blade, turning his wrist and flicking. The merchant captain's sword was torn from his fingers and Fyn's blade pressed to his throat.

'Surrender the ship.'

'Well done, monk!' Captain Nefysto strode past Jakulos, who was cleaning his blade. The Merofynian noble was on his knees, wounded and disarmed. 'Not a wasted movement. Who was your teacher?'

'The abbey weapons master,' Fyn answered.

'Well, captain,' Nefysto confronted the merchant, 'your life or your ship? Either way, I'll have your ship.'

He grimaced. 'Helmsman, sound the surrender.'

Jakulos took the wheel and the helmsman went to the ship's bell. As it rang out the surrender, fighting ceased. Fyn cleaned his sword and sheathed it, noting it had suffered one or two nicks, confirming his suspicion that it was not a high-quality weapon. He felt strangely detached. He had tried to keep his promise, but in that mad rush across the deck he had struck and struck again, without thought to anything but preserving his own life.

'Wise decision, captain,' Nefysto told the merchant and strode to the rail, calling to Bantam. 'See that the flames are put out. Empty the hold.'

Fyn went to the rail, looking down at the mid-deck where two dozen disarmed Merofynian warriors stood in tattered azure and black, looking miserable.

Bantam cocked his head towards them. 'What of these men, cap'n?'

Nefysto joined Fyn at the rail. 'What a sorry lot!'

Fyn sensed movement behind them and spun. The wounded Merofynian noble had leapt to his feet and lunged, dagger aimed for Nefysto's back. Behind the wheel, Jakulos cried a warning.

Fyn's training took over. He stepped into the attack, avoided the blow, caught the hand with the dagger and twisted the wrist so that the blade flew from numbed fingers.

The noble gasped, then dropped to his knees, clutching his broken wrist.

As the man fell at Fyn's feet Captain Nefysto looked down, then up, meeting Fyn's eyes.

'That was very neatly done, little monk.' Nefysto straightened the ruffle of lace at his cuff. 'From that display, I gather you could have disarmed and killed Bantam at any time.'

'Halcyon's monks value life.'

Captain Nefysto studied Fyn, a slow smile spreading across his face. 'As long as it's *my* life you value!' Then he turned back to Bantam on the lower deck with a laugh. 'Send the warriors down into the hold. They can unload the Rolencian treasures for us.'

Fyn felt a rush of relief. He had been afraid Captain Nefysto would order the surviving warriors thrown overboard. Then he made sense of the last part of Nefysto's comment. This ship carried booty stolen from Rolencia. In that case, Fyn felt no remorse.

Knees suddenly weak, vision blurring, his stomach revolted and, even though Fyn hadn't eaten since last night, he ran to the side and threw up.

Bending double, he wiped tears from his eyes and tried to catch his breath.

'Come, little monk. A shot of Merofynian rum is what you need.' Jakulos dragged Fyn upright. Fyn tried to pull away, embarrassed, but Jakulos wouldn't let him go.

'It's what you do when it counts that matters,' he told Fyn.

Fyn blinked to clear his vision, surprised to hear such wisdom from a man he had thought a bluff, brainless oaf.

Jakulos led him over to the steps, where they sat to share a bottle of Merofynian rum while they watched the transfer of stolen treasures. Wiry little Bantam perched on the steps and Jakulos handed him the bottle without comment.

Bantam took a long gulp then wiped his mouth, eyeing Fyn with calculation that verged on suspicion. 'Cap'n's mighty pleased with you, little monk. He tells me you disarmed a man with your bare hands.'

Fyn shrugged. 'Abbey training.'

Bantam held his eyes for a moment, letting Fyn see that he was not so easily won over, and then nodded to the bundles of all shapes and sizes that were being carried across the gangplanks. 'And he's pleased with this plump cargo. The spoils of war from Rolencia will make us sea-hounds rich. Better in our pockets than King Merofyn's, eh?'

'As long as we fill the hold of the *Wyvern's Whelp* by the cusp of spring,' Jakulos muttered. 'I promised a girl on Ostron Isle I'd be back by then.'

'There's always a girl waiting for Jaku.' Bantam winked at Fyn, who felt an unexpected fellowship.

The weapons master would have said this was a normal reaction to escaping death. But by Halcyon, it felt good to be alive!

Jakulos nudged him. 'Don't hog the rum.'

Fyn passed it over. He would never have thought last midwinter – when he prepared for the race to win Halcyon's Fate – that he would end up a landless kingson, serving a sea-hound captain.

Now, why hadn't he seen this vision in the Fate? Isolt Merofyn Kingsdaughter had nothing to do with him.

Jakulos passed Bantam the bottle. He took a gulp.

'If the captain's pleased with me, will he take me back to Port Marchand?' Fyn asked.

Bantam shook his head. 'Our orders are to prevent as much of the spoils of war from reaching King Merofyn as possible.'

Fyn hid his surprise. It appeared either Captain Nefysto, or his mysterious benefactor, or both were Rolencia's allies. Even so, as soon as the *Wyvern's Whelp* returned to Ostron Isle Fyn would jump ship, and take passage back to Rolencia.

The ache of Piro's loss would never fade, but at least he could avenge her death. And to do this, he must help Cobalt find Byren.

BYREN STRODE INTO the loyalist camp as though he hadn't been near death only five days ago, hale and hearty. Word of their approach had been passed on ahead by scouts and everyone had downed tools and come out of the caves to watch. So many people.

So many old men and women, and small children.

This was not an army. It was a liability. Who was he kidding? He could not go to the spar warlords with these people in tow. It would make him look weak.

And they all depended on him to protect them and win back their homes. His heart sank.

Hiding his despair, Byren grinned and waved, calling to people he knew from his many visits to Dovecote estate. The cook was there, a little slimmer, but just as competent. Byren blew her a kiss, knowing she would like it.

'Da!' Leif took off at a run, going to his father.

Florin laughed and ran over to hug her father, then stood on the other side of him as Byren approached.

'I left Old Man Narrows in charge,' Orrade whispered, 'rather than the survivors of your honour guard. He was more experienced.'

Old Man Narrows was perhaps forty summers, with iron-grey hair, and stood half a head shorter than his daughter. So she didn't get her height from him.

He greeted Byren cheerfully, 'Well, you're a sight for sore eyes, my king.'

Byren flushed and shook his head. When he replied, his voice ground deep in his throat, tight with emotion. 'Don't call me that. Until I send the last Merofynian home with his tail between his legs, and stand in Rolenhold's great hall where my father stood, I won't be worthy of that title.'

A cheer broke from the men behind Old Man Narrows and Byren recognised four of his original honour guard. He acknowledged them with a smile, praying he would prove worthy of their devotion.

'So be it,' Old Man Narrows said. 'What d'you want us to call you?'

'Byren will do.'

Florin's father nodded and turned to Orrade. 'Well done, lad.'

'I'd never have found him without Florin's help.'

Leif made a sound of protest.

'Or gotten back without Leif's help,' Orrade added, with a grin.

Chandler, Winterfall and the other two honour guard claimed Byren. He welcomed them each with a hug while someone handed around tankards of ale. They'd saved the banner Garzik had designed and now they unrolled it.

It gleamed bright against the snow. A rearing leogryf attacking a foenix on a black background. The loyalists cheered. Reminded of Garzik's loss, Byren blinked tears from his eyes.

For now, everyone was happy, buoyed up by his return. But soon they would realise the immensity of what he had to achieve. Without trained men-at-arms it was impossible to convince the spar warlords to honour their oath of fealty to his father.

When Old Man Narrows drew Orrade aside to consult him about something, Byren was reminded that his friend had established the hidden camp, and kept everyone fed and protected from discovery. He always knew Orrade's keen mind would take him far.

To the execution block, if Byren failed and the Merofynians captured them.

Byren felt a fraud, but he managed to grin and trade friendly insults with his loyal honour guard.

When there was a lull in the conversation, Orrade returned to tap his arm. Byren barely restrained the impulse to shrug him off. The honour guard had chosen not to believe Cobalt's slurs about him and Orrade. But if Orrade revealed his true feeling by so much as a look, they would turn against Byren.

Steeling himself, Byren turned to his old friend.

'Old Man Narrows tells me someone arrived yesterday. They've been asking to see you,' Orrade revealed. 'Come on.'

'Can't it wait? I still have to work out how many able-bodied men we have, and how many mouths we need to feed.' Sylion's luck. How would he feed all these children?

'I can count heads for you. But this person is important.' Laugher lit Orrade's dark eyes.

A smile tugged at Byren's lips. He fell into step with Orrade, climbing up, around the track. Who could it be? All his family were dead. All of Orrade's family were dead. 'Who –'

'Come on,' Orrade insisted, not about to give him a chance to speak.

They'd gone several steps when Byren came to a stop. 'It's Garzik, isn't it? He found his way up here...'

But he broke off, seeing the sudden grief in Orrade's thin face. 'Orrie, I'm sorry. I thought for a moment he was safe.'

Orrade shook his head, unable to speak.

Aware that they were unobserved, Byren pulled his friend into his arms. 'I'm sorry, Orrie, truly I am. I'd give anything to bring him back.'

'I know.' Orrade pulled away, and brushed the tears from his face. 'Come.' He swept Byren uphill and into a cave.

Eyes blinded by the change from light to dark, Byren could barely make out the outline of a shrunken old woman.

He blinked. 'Seela?' Surely not. Their old nurse was a plump little thing, with twinkling eyes.

'Byren!' She beamed.

A thin, care-worn version of his old nurse embraced him. Tears stung Byren's eyes. Seeing Seela, who had so often stood beside his mother, admonishing Piro to behave, made him all the more aware of their loss. He hugged her tighter.

'Enough,' she complained. 'You'll crack a rib.' She pulled back to look up at him. Light bounced up from the snow outside, reflecting on the roof of the cave. 'Let me look at you, my beautiful boy.'

'They're dead, Seela,' Byren whispered. 'I tried to save Lence, but I couldn't. Elina, Garzik, I failed them all...' He could not go on, dropping to his knees.

As if he was still a little boy, she pressed him to her, whispering endearments. 'I know, love. Orrie told me. Elina –'

'I loved her. I was going to ask her to marry me.'

'Byren.' When she said it, his name held a world of sympathy. 'And little Garzik, lost too. Ah, he was a bright spark. But Byren,' She pushed him away from her, so that she could see his face. 'I bring good news. Piro lives!'

'What?'

Seela nodded, eyes brimming with happiness.

'Where?'

Seela's face fell. 'A noble Power-worker took her for his slave. I heard he's since sailed for Merofynia.'

This changed everything. He wasn't alone. Piro still lived. If so, maybe Fyn... 'And Fyn? Have you heard from him?'

Seela shook her head. 'No. But they haven't found his body.'

So there was hope. He had to hold on to that. And Piro was in Merofynia, enslaved.

'And Ma and Pa? I heard...' he couldn't bring himself to say it.

She let her breath out in a long sigh. 'Your father was killed under a flag of truce. Your mother tried to kill Cobalt. Took his arm off at the shoulder.'

Byren was amazed. He could not imagine his elegant, kind mother swinging a sword with lethal intent. But he was glad she had seen through Cobalt in the end. It meant she knew Byren had always been true. Again tears blurred his vision.

'Well.' It was too much. He had to clear his throat. 'Piro lives. And perhaps Fyn.' Although, now that he thought about it, his brother had never seemed the martial type, despite being trained as a warrior monk. Byren suspected he would have been happier as a scholar. He hoped Fyn had the ruthless streak he'd need to evade Palatyne and Cobalt. 'And Cobalt lives, you say?'

'He did when I left. Palatyne had appointed him his puppet ruler.'

'Not for long, if I have my way.' Byren allowed himself a moment of satisfaction as he imagined confronting Cobalt. But that would not happen unless... 'If only I had a couple of hundred trained men at my back, I could approach the spar warlords. I can't go to them, looking weak.'

'I can bring you those men.' Seela pulled up a stool and sat opposite him, eager as a young girl. 'I brought five likely lads with me when I arrived. I can travel from one end of Rolencia to the other, whispering word of Byren Kingsheir, living in hiding –'

'I can't let you do that. If they catch you...' He shuddered to think what they would do to his old nurse. Neither her gender nor her age would protect her. 'I can't –'

'Byren,' Orrade cut him off. He'd forgotten his friend was still there. Orrade came over and dropped to his haunches beside Byren. 'Seela's right. She knows our people. The Merofynians won't expect a harmless old woman to be preaching rebellion. She can go into Rolenhold, right under their noses, and lead warriors back to us. Back to the camp, the retreat.'

He glanced from his old nurse to his childhood friend. They were ready to risk their lives for him, for the dream of Rolencia free from the Merofynian yoke.

He could not fail them. 'Very well. But don't call this camp a retreat. That makes it sound like we're on the back foot, running away. Call it something more positive, like...'

'The Leogryf's Lair. Garzik would approve of that,' Orrade said. 'And all our people know you as Byren the leogryf slayer. Rolencians can speak of the Leogryf's Lair without arousing Merofynian suspicion.'

'Excellent!' Seela beamed at Orrade. 'I told Myrella you were the smartest of your generation.'

He blushed and Byren grinned, unworried by the comparison. He'd always known he was cleverer than Lence, but not as clever as Orrade.

His friend sprang to his feet. 'Think I'll go check our numbers, see who has arrived. We've already set up a smithy to mend and make weapons.'

When he had gone Seela patted Byren's arm. 'You're a good boy, Byren. Your mother would be proud.'

Unable to speak, he hugged her and went outside. Everyone had gone back to their tasks. Somewhere, not far away, he could hear the dull clunk of a smithy's hammer. They would have to cloak that noise somehow.

He inhaled deeply, smelling onions and pork cooking. His stomach rumbled. At least with Dovecote's cook they would eat well. If they could find enough food.

Byren knew there were no guarantees in life. He might fall on the battlefield and never avenge his father and mother, but today he felt much closer to winning back Rolencia.

One day he would sit in his father's great hall and send an ambassador to Merofynia, to barter for Piro's life. One day, if Halcyon had protected him, he would find Fyn and they would be together again, the last of King Rolen's kin.

ROWENA CORY DANIELLS

THE KING'S MAN

THE CHRONICLES OF KING ROLEN'S KIN

BONUS NOVELLA

CHAPTER ONE

ALL HIS LIFE, Garzik had followed Byren and Orrade around, trying to keep up with them, but his legs were never long enough. The five years' age difference meant they were seasoned warriors at nineteen, while he was still an untried boy. Not that his brother and the younger of the royal twins were cruel. They tolerated him with the absent-minded kindness of older brothers.

He hated being tolerated.

Tonight was his chance to prove himself and win a place in Byren's honour guard. Tonight Dovecote Estate had fallen to treacherous invaders, who'd murdered Garzik's father. This meant Orrie was the new Lord Dovecote – what a strange thought.

Garzik gave himself a mental shake. Right now his sister, Elina, and Byren's twin, Lence, were being held captive upstairs. Byren and Orrie were going to free Elina and the kingsheir, while Garzik lit the warning beacon.

They trusted him to alert Rolencia to the invasion. And he would do it.

Or die trying.

Garzik followed four of Byren's honour guard out of the cellars, trying to pretend he wasn't scared witless. Seven of them, dressed in servants' tabards to blend in, made their way up the steps through the kitchen and storerooms to the door of the stable yard.

No one asked what they were doing.

Thanks to the cook, the Merofynians were all drunk or getting that way. As for the invaders' servants, they'd been lured into a cold-cellar and the door bolted behind them.

If Garzik didn't light the beacon on the warning tower, King Rolen wouldn't know Rolencia had been invaded. Byren's father was busy planning for a wedding, not an invasion.

Treacherous Merofynians!

Garzik glanced to Winterfell. With his broken nose, the honour guard no longer looked like himself. He looked battered, but determined.

Conviction hardened Garzik's resolve. If he was honest, he was glad he wasn't leading the party to light the beacon.

Winterfell paused in the doorway to the rear courtyard. At almost seventeen, he had two years' experience on Garzik. Oldest of the honour guard, he had emerged as their leader. Three more honour guard stood between Winterfell and Garzik, so he couldn't see out the back door.

But he knew what lay beyond it. Across the courtyard was the original Dovecote stronghold, built back when their family and retainers' survival depended on stout walls.

This new house, with its gracious terrace, big windows and elegant chambers, was an affectation. A dangerous indulgence...

As the Merofynians had proven.

Anger and outrage churned in Garzik's stomach. His home had fallen, but Rolencia wouldn't fall to the invaders. Not if he could light the beacon.

He glanced over his shoulder to the two lads who brought up the rear. At thirteen, both looked up to him. Did they think it odd to see Lord Dovecote's youngest son in a servant's tabard?

Pale cheeked, eyes glittering, they watched his face. He hoped he didn't look as scared as them, but he suspected he did. This was not like hunting Affinity beasts with Captain Blackwing. Poor Blackwing. The captain had been amongst the first to fall, an honourable death in defence of Dovecote.

Not like his father, who had been disturbed at the dinner table... Garzik rode a wave of fury.

An old man who had already lost four sons to war and ambition before they could produce grandchildren, his father should have been enjoying his old age. Instead, he'd been attacked by invaders in his own great hall. Garzik hadn't been there to see it. He'd arrived after the estate had been overrun.

Discovering Lord Dovecote pinned to the front doors, a lance through his chest, had rocked the foundation of Garzik's world.

Even Orrade had staggered when they found their father's body. Respectfully silent, the eight honour guard had waited, while his older brother took him aside. 'Don't let anger or fear blind you, Garza. This was a calculated cruelty to cow the defenders.'

'I wish –'

'If we'd been here, we'd both be dead by now.' That was Orrade for you, always one step ahead.

Garzik was brought back to the present as Winterfell led them into the night. The nearest honour guard nudged Garzik and he followed, keeping close to the guard's heels. They ran in single file across the recently shovelled stable yard. Passing between mounds of knee-high snow, they reached the old keep where Garzik used to tag along after Lence, Byren and Orrade. In those days, he'd dreamed of being a great warrior and begged to be part of their king-of-the-castle games.

Now, he concentrated on not throwing up.

Inside the old stronghold's gate tunnel, they paused. Ahead of them was the courtyard. Light spilled from the open doors of the great hall and lanterns glowed in the tower's narrow windows. Garzik had heard singing from the tower earlier. He only hoped the cook had been generous enough with the wine.

Fierce whispering from behind made him turn. 'Quiet, you two.'

Three heads turned towards him. *Three?*

'Kiri?' Garzik blinked. What was he doing here? 'Kiri, go back.'

The skinny ten year-old shook his head, rabitty face resolute. He brandished a wicked little blade from the stables. 'They killed Regal. I'm going to cut their throats!'

'They killed Regal? Why?' Even as he asked, he knew why. The liver-coloured retriever, queen of his father's hunting dogs, would have sprung to the Old Dove's defence. Tears stung Garzik's eyes and his throat grew so tight he could hardly speak.

Even so...

'Kiri, you can't –' Garzik broke off as someone tugged on his arm. He turned to find the four honour guards darting across to the great hall. 'Go back to the stables and keep your head down. This is no place for you.'

With that, he turned and ran after the others. There were more important things to worry about than one stubborn stable-lad.

Inside the entrance to the great hall, they passed the open doors to the hall itself. A quick glance showed Merofynian men-at-arms everywhere. Some slept, snoring, while others drank and sang of bawdy women. Garzik felt nothing but contempt. The invaders thought themselves safe because no one knew King Merofyn had betrayed his word. What kind of king arranged a marriage to unite their kingdoms as a cover for an invasion?

In the entrance to a narrow passage, Winterfell turned to Chandler. 'Close the doors. Shut them in the hall.'

The other honour guard grinned and nodded to Wafin, youngest of Byren's honour guard. Winterfell kept going. The last honour guard and the two serving lads took off after him.

Garzik caught Kiri by the arm as he went to pass. The boy tried to shrug free. 'Go back. You'll –'

An ominous creak made Garzik let go and he looked over his shoulder. Chandler and Wafin struggled to move the doors, but couldn't budge them.

That's right, those hinges hadn't been used for a hundred years. Why hadn't he thought of that? Orrade would have.

Should he go back and help? What if the noise alerted...

'Here, what're you up to?' a man demanded in rough Merofynian.

Chandler ignored him and shoved his shoulder behind the door, wet boots slipping on the flagstones.

Garzik went to help, but little Kiri caught his arm. 'Come quick. Winterfell needs you.' Garzik hadn't even seen the lad go to the passage door.

The warning beacon was top priority. Even so, Garzik hesitated. Kiri tugged on his arm.

Leaving Chandler and Wafin to their fate, he ran ahead of the lad around the corner and down the narrow passage, over uneven flags laid nearly three hundred years ago in front of the oldest part of the stronghold, the base of the original tower.

He found Winterfell and the others standing over a dead man. From the opposite direction came voices and the sound of running boots.

Winterfell grabbed Garzik. 'You know the tower. Go light the beacon. We'll hold them here. Bolt the door behind you.'

And before he could speak up, he'd been shoved onto the first steps. Somehow, little Kiri was with him.

Garzik bolted the door while the boy danced with impatience. Then they were both running up the tower steps. Four floors, chambers filled with Merofynians, then the beacon. It was always prepared; his father had never forgotten the last Merofynian invasion thirty years ago.

His father... Garzik could not believe the fierce Old Dove was dead.

They passed the first floor door without mishap. A glance into the chamber revealed Merofynians dicing, too intent on their game to notice them. The second floor door was closed. Garzik began to hope – only two more floors, and he'd reach the beacon itself. Their boots made sharp scuffing sounds on the worn stone steps.

Shouting from below. Garzik cursed.

Kiri ran on past him.

'Wait,' Garzik whispered.

Kiri ignored him, following the curving stair towards the next balcony.

He stopped.

Garzik paused two steps below him.

The boy turned. There was something wrong with his face. For a moment it made no sense, then Garzik understood what he was seeing. A dagger hilt protruded from Kiri's eye.

The boy's knees gave way and he toppled forward, dropping his knife and hitting the wall with one shoulder before sliding down into Garzik's arms.

A Merofynian stepped into view above.

'He's only a boy,' Garzik protested. 'Just a boy.'

The man glanced beyond Garzik.

Who turned to find a fist coming towards his head. He tried to block but, encumbered by Kiri's body, couldn't raise his forearm in time. Knuckles struck his cheek, driving his head into the wall.

No. It couldn't end like this...

* * *

'WILL HE LIVE?' someone asked in a refined Merofynian accent.

Garzik tried to see who was speaking. One eye wouldn't open and the other wouldn't focus and, when he did get that eye open, light stabbed into his brain, making him wince.

Stabbed... Why did that word fill him with grief?

'Lord Travany doesn't want to go to the trouble of carting him halfway across Rolencia, and then ship him all the way back home, only to have him die before we get any work out of him.'

Garzik smelt smoke, charred wood smoke, like the winter three years ago when half of Doveton burned. How his father had cursed, blaming a clumsy baker.

Someone prodded his face, checked his mouth. 'Teeth are fine. Don't think he'll lose his eye. The cheek'll scar up. He's for field-work?' The gruff voice paused. 'Then his looks don't matter. He's a house servant, judging by that tabard, but even Rolencian indoor servants are tough. This one should pull through.'

'What about that lump on his head?' Lord Travany's servant countered. The tone of his voice told Garzik the servant wasn't going to accept responsibility if anything went wrong. 'An addle-pate's no use to his lordship. Check his skull.'

Fingers felt Garzik's head. How could he think with these hands prodding him? Why didn't they leave him alone?

He tried to tell them, but his tongue wasn't working properly and it felt like someone had wound a rag too rightly around his head. He lifted his hand to undo the binding, but his fingers encountered no cloth, only slippery, misshapen swollen flesh where his cheekbone and eye should have been.

'Here, don't touch.' Speaking poor Rolencian, the gruff servant pulled Garzik's hand away, then switched back to Merofynian. 'Can't say for sure if his brains are scrambled. Won't know until he talks, Master Cialon.'

'Should I throw 'im in the pit with the dead?' a third voice asked.

Garzik waited to learn his fate. He knew he should have been worried, but nothing made sense and it was too hard to concentrate.

'No, send him to port. If he dies at sea, we can throw him overboard and save on a burial. If he survives to reach Port Mero, he should live. Make a note.

One field-hand, aged thirteen.'

That wasn't right. He was fourteen, nearly fifteen.

'What should I put down for a name?' another voice asked, presumably the scribe.

'How should I know?' Master Cialon complained. 'Call him Wyvern. That'll do.'

Garzik wanted to protest, he was not some unwanted nobleman's bastard, named for the Merofynian royal symbol. He had a name, a perfectly good name.

If only he could remember what it was.

Again he tried to open his eyes. The light of the lantern made him moan.

'Slap some rosemary on that open wound and bind his head,' Master Cialon ordered and moved along, to discuss the next wounded man.

A different pair of hands took Garzik. Their touch was firm but gentle, reminding him of Willowbark, the family's healer. Why could he remember everyone else's name but not his own?

Why did he feel that if he did remember he'd be sorry?

After his head was bound, he could not open either eye. A flask was pressed to his mouth.

'Drink,' the healer urged in Rolencian.

Willowbark would have given him dreamless-sleep, that was what she'd done the time he'd broken his arm and they'd had to set it. This smelled like spirits. He opened his mouth to say no and the person tossed the liquid down his throat. That set him coughing so much he thought his head would burst.

Then he lay panting, with a warm glow in his belly. Voices moved on.

The smell of charred wood worried him. It held some significance, but he couldn't think what. He was still trying to figure it out when the spirits swamped his senses and he welcomed it.

CHAPTER TWO

EVERY TIME GARZIK surfaced, his head ached abominably. Along with the stench and the jolting, it made it easier to let the blackness take him.

There was a lot to be said for not waking up.

But eventually, his head cleared. He was shivering. Cold. His feet were cold. What happened to his boots? He opened his eyes. Someone must have removed the bandage – or had he imagined that part?

At any rate, he could open both eyes, but he couldn't seem to focus, one eye was worse than the other. Not that there was much to see. He appeared to be in a dark place that stank of miserable people packed too tightly. He could hear moaning. Inevitably, someone would tell them to shut up. Then came the blows and the whimpering and...

He must have blacked out again, because he woke as someone tried to dribble water in his mouth.

'Don't know why you bother. The brat's half dead. Save the water for yourself,' a voice advised. Although their tone was not helpful, they spoke Rolencian, which he took to be a good sign.

'We're seven-year-slaves, but that doesn't make us barbarians, like the Utlanders,' his helper said. His voice reminded Garzik of a tutor he'd once had. 'Not that I expect you to understand the distinction.'

'We're not in Rolenton now, Mitrovan. No one cares that you were a markiz's scribe.'

The scribe ignored his tormentor and adjusted Garzik's head so he could swallow more easily. 'That's it, drink up.'

'Why...' Garzik's voice cracked. He swallowed and sat up with difficulty.

There was a coarse wooden wall at his back. Splinters pricked his shoulders.
'Where –'

'We're in a ship's hold –'

'A shit hole, you mean!'

'Travelling to Port Marchand –'

'More's the pity. I had a sweet little widow lined up. I was about to marry her and spend the rest of my life bedding her and living off her pastry shop. Now I bet some Merofynian's lying in her bed, ploughing her furrow!'

Garzik's instinctive dislike hardened.

Mitrovan expelled his breath softly in disgust and ignored the interruption. 'From Port Marchand, we'll be shipped to Merofynia as part of Lord Travany's war booty.'

Garzik's stomach rumbled. 'Hungry.'

'You're not the only one,' the complainer muttered.

'They're not overly generous with our portions,' Mitrovan admitted. 'And I doubt they'll be feeding us again before we disembark –'

'Listen to him. Thinks himself a markiz.'

Garzik wished Byren was here. One good thump – that'd teach the lout to keep his mouth shut.

'You're not helping, Feo...' Mitrovan protested, but there was no conviction in his voice.

It made the scribe look weak and made Garzik appear cowardly by association. The men Garzik had grown up with would've had no patience with someone like Feo. His father despised...

He had a flash of the Old Dove hanging off their front door, pinned by a lance. Bile rose in Garzik's throat. His father was dead, cruelly murdered. He could not imagine life without the iron-willed old man.

But... he'd better get used to it.

If he was a Merofynian captive, that meant Byren had not retaken Dovecote.

Had Byren saved his sister? What of Orrie? One thing was certain – his brother would never let Byren be taken, not while he lived. Orrade was honourable to the bone.

Another flash of memory. Kiri on the stairs, a knife through his eye. Silly, brave Kiri, trying to avenge the hound's death.

Freezing Sylion! He'd failed to light the beacon. He'd failed Byren.
Garzik gasped in horror.

'Don't move about. Give your head time to settle,' Mitrovan advised, mistaking his gasp for one of pain. 'What's your name, boy?'

Shame silenced him.

'Don't worry.' The scribe squeezed Garzik's shoulder. 'It'll come back to you. With a head blow like that, it's not unusual to –'

'So you're a healer now?' Feo sneered.

Anger bubbled up in Garzik. Merofynians had killed his father, ransacked their home, raped his sister, captured the kingsheir and, for all he knew, Byren and Orrade were dead – yet all this lout could think about was scoring points off the scribe. It was too much. 'If you haven't got anything useful to say, I'll thank you to keep your tongue between your teeth.'

It was his father talking, and the moment the words left his mouth, he knew they were a mistake.

In the stunned silence that followed his outburst, he tried to think of a way to mend things, but came up blank.

With a curse, Feo lunged for him. Hands closed on Garzik's throat. Feo shook him. Weak as a day-old kitten, he couldn't fight back.

Head thumping into the wall, Garzik fought to breathe; managed a gulp of air, as a stream of vile obscenities hit him, carried on putrid breath.

Mitrovan tried to pry Feo's hands off him. 'Leave him be. He's just a lad, a foolish lad.'

As they fought over him, Garzik's head hit the wall for the fourth time. It was too much. He threw up all over them. Not that there was a lot in his stomach. They both released him. The smell made Garzik gag and bile burned his throat again.

'You little bastard!' A calloused palm slammed into his head, stinging his ear and toppling him sideways.

He must have blacked out, because the next time things made sense Mitrovan was wiping his face with a scrap of damp cloth.

With consciousness came the horror of his failure. Freezing Sylion, may the god of heartless winter take him, he'd failed Byren. How could he ever go home?

He had no home. The invaders had claimed it.

'You've made an enemy of Feo. He'll take pleasure in causing trouble for us now.' The scribe spoke in a desperate whisper, voice breathy with fear. 'You'll get us both killed. You mustn't talk back, lad. Do you understand?'

Garzik nodded because Mitrovan needed him to, and sat up gingerly. As long as he didn't move his head too quickly, he could fight the nausea and dizziness. As for pain, a slap or a beating was nothing new to him. But in the past, he'd always earned the rebuke. Captain Blackwing used to despair of teaching him sense. He'd been too busy dreaming of becoming a great warrior like Byren to listen.

But Captain Blackwing would never have struck an injured man or a woman. He was a warrior, not a bully. You knew where you stood with a man like Blackwing. Dismay settled in the pit of Garzik's stomach. He was out of his depth. The rules he'd grown up with did not apply in the hold of a sled-ship.

Soft whispers and moans came from the other men in the hold. Either it was getting lighter, or his sight was improving, because he could see Mitrovan's dirty face now. The scribe's slightly protuberant eyes studied him. Under all that dust, Mitrovan's hair was black; he was not old, just fussy and frightened.

'Someone took my boots –'

Feo laughed.

'Forget your boots,' the scribe said. 'Keep your head down and we'll be all right.'

Garzik wanted to tell him there was no 'we.' He was not a coward who gave in to bullies. He was Lord Dovecote's younger son, a warrior in training. He held his honour high.

But Byren had asked him to do one important thing and he'd failed.

Did Byren still live? May it please Goddess Halcyon, bringer of bountiful summer, let Byren live. Let him have rescued Lence and escaped with Orrie and Elina. Let them all be safe up in the foot-hills of the mountains.

Garzik searched his memory of the overheard conversation between Master Cialon and Lord Travany's other servants, but the details were hazy and he could not recall any mention of Byren's name. Surely, if the king's son been captured or lay dead, the Merofynians would have been crowing?

'What news of Byren?' he asked the scribe. 'Does Byren Kingson still live?'

'I've no idea. He wasn't at the castle when the Merofynians attacked. There was hardly any warning.' Mitrovan looked beyond Garzik, into the past. 'Before my master escaped with his family, he entrusted me to oversee the loading of his prized possessions on a ship bound for Ostron Isle. I should have joined him there, but the ship never left the dock. When the castle fell, it –'

'The castle fell? Rolenhold has never fallen. It's –'

'Keep your voice down. Feo's just waiting for a chance to take out his temper on someone,' the scribe hissed. He glanced over his shoulder and then leaned closer. 'I'm no fool and you're no servant. Only a nobleman's son would have taken that tone with Feo. There's no need for you to stay here with us. Why don't you identify yourself? Lord Travany can contact your father to arrange a ransom.'

Garzik shook his head. Anger and shame made it impossible to speak, even if he'd wanted to.

'I don't see why anyone would become a seven-year-slave, if they could avoid it. I don't understand...' Mitrovan broke off with a little gasp, eyes widening. 'You're a spy, sent to report on the Merofynian nobles. The markiz was always telling me to beware Ostronite spies trying to get the inside information on his deals. But this... this is spying in the service of Rolencia.'

Garzik looked down, wishing his reason for being here was so noble. 'I'm not... I don't –'

'Of course,' Mitrovan agreed, voice low and full of repressed excitement. 'You can rely on my discretion. But if you want your disguise to work, you need to take a more servile tone. Your tabard is good quality and your accent is refined, so you'd best present yourself as an indoor servant. Is that what you're pretending to be, a scribe like me? Because a lord's personal scribe knows when to keep his mouth shut.'

Garzik looked up. 'I'm not a spy. I'm...' He could not bring himself to reveal his failure.

The scribe shook his head. 'That's no good. You need a strong story, one that holds water. You're lucky you met up with me. I can teach you how to be a nobleman's scribe. You'll want to win a place in Lord Travany's household, win his trust and become privy to his secrets. I know just the way to go about it.' He nodded to himself as he squeezed Garzik's shoulder. 'Don't worry. I'll help you.'

And because this illusion was far better than the bitter truth, Garzik let it slide. 'The castle fell, you say?'

'In just one day. I heard a rumour they were betrayed from within. King Rolen died even before the castle fell, murdered under a flag of truce –'

'What?' Garzik shuddered. The king had been like a second father to him. Kind, in his bluff way. Anger choked Garzik. 'Those cowardly Merofynians... But what can you expect of a king who offers his daughter's hand to cement an alliance, when he's really planning an invasion?'

Garzik's mind ran on. Queen Myrella would be heartbroken. As for Piro... The thought of how she'd bristle at finding herself a prisoner made him smile.

A year younger than him, she'd plagued him all his life, wanting to join in with what the big boys were doing. Only last summer, after he'd won a coveted place on the fishing boat with Lence, Byren and Orrade, she'd talked her way in. He would have willingly pushed her into the lake that day.

But since the time she'd dressed as a goat-herder to help Byren restore the Warlord of Unistag Spar... well, he'd been thinking about her a lot lately. 'I suppose the queen and her daughter are prisoners?'

The scribe blinked. 'You don't know –'

'Queen Myrella's dead?' Garzik felt sick. His own mother was long dead; Byren's mother had been the closest thing he had to a mother.

Mitrovan shook his head. 'Yes, both of them were killed.'

Not Piro. He could not believe it. Would not. 'But Piro's only thirteen and a kingsdaughter. She'd be a valuable prisoner. Why kill her? You must have it wrong –'

'They burned the bodies,' Mitrovan whispered. 'The day the castle fell, they burned their bodies to make sure no one could take trophies.'

He said it with such finality.

Turning away from Mitrovan, Garzik curled up, covered his head with his arms and willed the world to go away.

And it did. For a while.

When next he woke, the sled-ship's movement had changed and he was even hungrier. He sat up. 'I think we're approaching Port Marchand.'

Mitrovan shifted and sat up next to him. He listened for a moment. 'I think you're right.'

'They'll have to transport us from the lakeside-wharves across port to the bay.' Garzik had been here last spring with his family. Happier times... If Piro and Queen Myrella were dead, dare he hold out hope for Elina? Despair made him curl up again. He'd never realised heartache could cause physical pain.

'We'll be up on deck soon, in the fresh air,' Mitrovan told him.

He was right. Not long after that they were herded out of the hold up onto the deck, where they blinked in the weak sun, under the brilliant icy-blue of the Rolencian winter sky.

Garzik shivered, his bare feet freezing on the cold wood of the deck. He could really have done with his boots.

Now that they were in the light, he counted his companions. There were fifteen of them, all young, all with injuries that would heal. Master Cialon had made sure Lord Travany would get his seven years' service out of them.

Garzik's head spun and he had trouble staying upright. He hated being so weak, hated having to rely on the scribe who, now that he got a good look, was probably not much older than Byren. Mitrovan adjusted his weight to better support Garzik. The movement made the tall, skinny scribe grimace with pain.

'What happened to you?' Garzik gestured to the where he favoured his right side. 'Did a Merofynian –'

'Nothing like that.' The scribe looked rueful. 'I slipped on the ice and cracked a rib.'

Garzik grinned.

A familiar voice made him turn and look. In the light of day, with his arm in a sling, Feo did not appear too threatening. Garzik frowned. Wait a moment; hadn't Feo attacked him with both hands? 'What's wrong with Feo's arm?'

'Nothing.' Mitrovan kept his voice low. 'He made a sling from a torn up shirt and fell in with us, because he thought he'd be able to escape from the injured group, but they watched us too closely. He was right about one thing though, we did have an easier time of it than the healthy seven-year-slaves. The Merofynians made them load the war booty, while we all sat and watched. You won't remember that: you were out cold.'

Garzik had never come across someone like Feo before, a man who took pride in shirking his duty. He was thin, with a misleadingly handsome face; it was only when you looked into his eyes that you knew something was missing.

Feo caught Garzik staring and gave a nasty smile.

Garzik turned away. The sudden movement of his head made his balance go and the scribe had to steady him. Around them, the others shuffled and looked hopefully towards the wharf. The smell of beans and onions carried from the nearest tavern. Garzik's stomach rumbled loud enough to hear.

'Hopefully, when we get to the Merofynian ship, they'll feed us,' Mitrovan said.

But an argument developed between Master Cialon and someone on the dock. Apparently, there were no cage-carts for hire due to the large number of slaves being sent to Merofynia. Transport would be available tomorrow at the earliest.

Master Cialon turned around, frustration in every line of his body. He was a little man with a big opinion of himself. Garzik had come across his type before.

'We could march them across,' one of his burly servants suggested.

'March this lot?' Cialon rolled his eyes. 'Why did I get stuck with fools for helpers? March them across the port with only the three of us to guard them? Do you want them to escape?' He shook his head in disgust. 'Drive them back into the hold.'

Some of the boldest protested. The two burly servants clipped them over the ears. 'Get below.'

'What's this?' The ship's captain came out of the cabin. 'Why aren't you disembarking?'

'No cage-carts.' Master Cialon let his disgust colour the words. 'None available until tomorrow.'

The captain was already shaking his head. 'I'm not housing your cargo one more night. Not when there's cargo waiting to be picked up in Rolenton. You'll have to find somewhere else for them to sleep tonight.'

'What do you suggest I do? Put them up in a tavern?' Master Cialon countered.

The ship's captain shrugged and folded his arms.

Garzik noticed movement in the corner of his eye as Feo tried to climb over the side. It was about two body-lengths to the ice and freedom.

But Cialon was too quick. 'Grufyd, stop him.'

One of the burly servants caught Feo by the scruff of his neck and dragged him back onto the deck, delivering a blow to the side of his head that left him lying stunned on the deck.

Garzik felt only the slightest satisfaction. It was as if everything happened at a great distance and none of it mattered.

So it didn't worry him when Lord Travany's servant negotiated to hire the ship for one more day and they were sent back to the hold.

CHAPTER THREE

ANOTHER NIGHT IN the hold meant nothing to Garzik, just as the indignity of being caged up like chickens going to market and paraded through Port Marchand meant nothing.

The good folk of Marchand turned their heads and went about their work. Down every street the cart passed, business boomed as the invaders travelled through the port, sending their war booty back home.

Surely the invasion was not over?

Even if the castle fell, there were still King Rolen's twin sons. Lence and Byren, with Orrie's help, would unite the people, call on the warlords beyond the Dividing Mountains to honour their allegiance to King Rolen and strike back.

But all that would take time.

And it was impossible if Lence, Byren and Orrade were dead.

Garzik refused to accept this.

At the seaside-wharves, so many ships had been coming and going, they'd kept the harbour free of ice. Amongst the many fat-bellied merchant ships flying the Merofynian flag, Garzik spotted the sleek lines of sea-hound vessels. Race horses to the merchant plough horses, they were designed to hunt down Utland raiders. And those Utlanders would be waiting along the trade routes to attack unwary captains.

Garzik shuddered. Lence had been going to lead a reprisal raid on the Utlanders this spring. Everyone had been up in arms because a shipload of Utlanders had slipped into the bay and raided Cobalt Estate, killing Cobalt's father and bride.

Only now that he knew Cobalt, Garzik was not so certain of his facts.

Master Cilaon's three carts – two loaded with wine, the third with the injured seven-year-slaves – came to rest. Garzik felt the other captives let out a sigh of relief. They were packed so tightly they could barely move. Unable to stand or stretch their legs, other than hanging them through the rails, their only consolation was the way the press of their bodies kept them warm.

They waited.

No one came to let them out.

'What's going on?' someone asked from the far end.

'Shall I ask Master Cialon where our cabin is and order a hot breakfast?' Feo demanded.

After that no one spoke.

An argument arose up near the first cart. From what Garzik could overhear it seemed, despite their delayed arrival, Lord Travany's ship was still anchored, waiting its turn to load at the wharves.

Master Cialon marched towards them, meeting up with his two servants at the middle cart. 'I'm going to sort this out. Grufyd, stay here and watch over our cargo.' He beckoned the other burly servant. 'You come with me.'

He went to stride off.

'Here, wait up,' the oldest carter protested. 'While me carts are sittin' here, I'm losin' coin. There's loads aplenty on the lakeside-wharves.'

After some negotiation, Master Cialon paid for the hire of the carts until midday. As he stalked off in a foul mood, Garzik pitied the harbour master. But the wharves were packed with Merofynian lords and their self-important servants loading spoils of war. Master Cialon would just be one more disgruntled Merofynian.

The moment he was out of sight, the carters retreated to the closest tavern, leaving Grufyd to watch the three carts. With a curse, Grufyd settled himself on the seat outside the tavern and demanded a pot of ale.

This meant he was about three body lengths away, directly facing the second of the three carts.

'Try the catch,' someone urged, not far from Garzik.

Of course! The busy wharf was a perfect opportunity to run. Garzik's heart raced, and the captives went very quiet. He heard rattling, then a curse.

'Can't budge it. Freezing Sylion!'

'Here, let me try. I'm a cabinet-maker.' Someone on the far side of the cart shuffled through.

Silence followed as they waited for the cabinet-maker to force the gate. 'No luck. If I had my tools –'

'Well you don't, so shut up about it,' Feo snapped.

After that no one spoke.

Garzik was hungrier than he had ever been. None of them had been fed last night or this morning.

Mitrovan shifted, bumping a youth behind him. 'Sorry.'

The other gave a glum nod.

'I'm a scribe,' Mitrovan offered. 'What did you do before –'

'Baker's boy. Final year of my apprenticeship. I specialised in fancy pastries for the merchant markizes.'

'You'll end up in Travany's kitchen,' Mitrovan predicted.

Garzik thought the youth looked like he'd been sampling too many of his wares. At least he had some padding. Garzik had always been small and thin. He'd been hoping he would have a growth spurt soon, but if he didn't get enough to eat...

Whispered conversations began amongst the captives. No one spoke to Feo.

'Why did that pie seller have to set up her stall right across from us?' Mitrovan whispered, shifting his weight on the bare boards. The scent of hot pies was torture.

Garzik had been trying to ignore the mouth-watering smells. Apart from hunger, he felt better than he had since he'd first woken. His head was clear and he could think straight.

A cart laden with carpets and chests trundled past. Every pier was busy, every berth in use. Cartloads of seven-year-slaves arrived and were loaded aboard ships, along with famed Rolencian red wine and luxurious furs from across the spars, beyond the Dividing Mountains,

'I swear they're stripping Rolencia bare,' the scribe whispered. 'It'll take a generation for the merchants to recover. Between storms and Utland raiders... they'll need capital to risk a voyage. They'll have to borrow from one of Ostron Isle's five families. Master won't like having to pay a percentage of his profits to the Ostronites.'

But Garzik wasn't interested in the problems of merchants. 'Look at all those grain sacks. They must've emptied every storehouse between here and Rolenton. What'll our people eat while they wait for this year's crops to ripen?'

'What will *we* eat,' Mitrovan corrected in an under-voice. 'Only a lord would say what "will our people eat."'

Feo pushed his way through the others to their side of the cart. No one dared object. 'Sod me, those pies smell good. And that pie girl looks as tasty as her pies. Reckon I could get her to spread her thighs, if I wasn't...' He gave the bars a shake.

Garzik ignored him.

Meanwhile, the pie seller did a great trade, serving hungry Merofynian men-at-arms, lords and their servants.

'Pretty pie girl,' Feo called out. 'Yes, you with the saucy smile. Spare a pie for a hungry man?'

She laughed and shook her head, but she did cast her eye over the cage.

'A crust then? Spare a crust for poor Rolencian men-at-arms,' he wheedled. 'Take pity on us, this being our last day in our homeland. Some of us might never see Rolencia again.'

The girl shook her head, but Garzik could see she was moved.

Their cart seemed forgotten. The day stretched. Still no food. Master Cialon's other servant came back, spoke with Grufyd and went into the tavern.

'What's happening?' someone asked from the rear of the packed cart.

'Grufyd's ordered a meal,' Mitrovan supplied.

'May Sylion freeze his balls!' Feo muttered.

For once, Garzik agreed with him.

It was the utter helplessness of it. He was faint with hunger, and he was bored to boot.

Mid afternoon, the pie girl passed them with her empty cart.

'Going home for the day, pretty puss?' Feo asked. 'Can you take a look and see if there's a crust or two for us, for the fighting men of Rolencia?'

She shook her head and glanced significantly over her shoulder. That was when Garzik noticed a bald, barrel-chested man with a cudgel tucked under one arm. He followed about a body length behind the pie cart.

With the king dead, the rule of law had broken down. Every man was out for himself and even a pie girl needed protection.

A little later she returned, her cart freshly stocked, and trade was brisk once more, so the war was not all bad for everyone.

Resentment coalesced in Garzik's empty belly.

Late in the day, as night closed in, the pie seller closed up her cart. Garzik was no longer hungry; now he felt chilled and lethargic. As the sun set, painting the distant headlands a brilliant pink, the cold closed in.

'They can't mean to leave us here overnight?' Mitrovan muttered. 'We'll catch our death.'

The pie girl approached with her cart. She paused at the tavern door. 'Grab a tankard, Ozig. I won't tell.'

He ducked his head and darted inside. At that moment, Grufyd happened to be leaning through the open window, chatting to those inside.

Or maybe it was not a coincidence, maybe she'd picked her time, for the moment both men were distracted the girl opened her cart, swept broken pie crusts into her apron and came over to them.

'Halcyon's blessings on you!' Feo told her. 'May you find a strong husband to give you a dozen children and may they never go hungry!'

'Fat chance of that, with the Merofynians stealing everything that isn't tied down,' she said. 'The pie shop used to belong to me Ma, now there's a Merofynian waiting at home to count the coppers we earn!'

Hands thrust past Garzik, demanding their share. Feo ignored them, but Garzik and Mitrovan passed crust backwards to those behind. The girl filled her apron again.

This time Garzik could not hold back. Stomach cramping with pain, he stuffed broken crusts into his mouth, stuffed them in without thought as to whether the fillings were sweet or savoury. Pie crusts had never tasted so good.

Chewing the last mouthful, he leant up against the cage bars. Meanwhile, the girl dusted off her hands, looking pleased, and turned to go.

'Wait,' Garzik pleaded thickly. He swallowed. 'Do you have any news? I know the castle fell, but surely one of the king's sons is rallying the people?'

She glanced over her shoulder to the tavern door and Grufyd, who was still distracted. 'I heard the Merofynian say that Lence Kingsheir is dead. But there's a reward for the king's other two sons, so we still have hope, even if Halcyon Abbey has fallen.'

'They desecrated the abbey?' he repeated, but he shouldn't be surprised. The Merofynian king had proven he was without honour. Lence dead... He expected to feel grief, yet felt only relief, which was odd. But if the Merofynians were searching for two king's sons it meant both Fyn and Byren lived. If Byren lived, then he could hold out hope for Orrade and Elina.

If Byren was free, he could hold out hope for Rolencia.

'Here.' Feo leant up against the bars. 'Give us a kiss before we sail. Give us a kiss and I'll die happy.'

The girl flushed, but caught his face through the bars and kissed his bruised cheek.

Garzik shook his head. He'd never behave so brazenly.

Which was why he'd never been kissed. Now he probably never would, for what girl wanted a seven-year-slave?

But he wasn't going to remain a slave. He'd escape.

Byren lived!

Garzik's mind raced. Somehow, he had to make his way to Byren and make up for failing him. Orrade would be with Byren. Only death would stop him. Orrie was smart. He'd lead Byren into the foothills of the Dividing Mountains. Amongst those steep ridges, caves and forests you could hide a thousand warriors. All Garzik had to do was escape.

Just then the pie girl's protector returned.

'Here, get away from them,' he yelled.

She hurried over to where the goat waited patiently in the cart's shafts. Not satisfied with her ready compliance, the man clipped her over the ear with his open hand. She staggered, but didn't fall. Without a word of protest, she took the goat's halter and led him off. Back to the pie shop, her mother and the Merofynian who had installed himself in their home.

Garzik bristled, but there was nothing he could do.

'This looks hopeful,' Feo muttered.

Garzik followed the direction he indicated. Master Cialon's other servant had joined Grufyd, and now the carters came out of the tavern. Garzik's heart raced. This was it. Soon they'd open the cart and lead them to the ship. Soon he'd get his chance to escape. If he could walk.

His body was cramped from being packed into the crowded cart.

'What's happening, Grufyd?' Feo called as the burly servant came towards them.

'We're going home, that's what happening,' Grufyd said. 'An' about time. Even the ale tastes wrong here.'

In the few moments it took for the carters to climb onto their seats and gather up the traces, Garzik rubbed his feet and hands, to encourage circulation. Curse the thief who took his boots.

As they trundled along the curve of the wharf, he watched the side streets, recognised one and retraced the memory of his brief visit to Port Marchand the previous spring, when they'd visited a merchant markiz. He thought he remembered how to get to the markiz's house.

Even though the lamplighters were taking their ladders from pole to pole, plenty of people were still coming and going. With no sign of the loading slowing down for the night, he could blend in when he got away.

At the far end of the wharf they came to the last pier, presumably where Lord Travany's ship waited. The cart travelled along the pier until it was opposite the ship.

Stores stood stacked, waiting to be loaded. Lanterns hung on posts, casting haloes of light in the cold air. It was harder to get away here, with the ship's captain and sailors, and Master Cialon and his servants.

Garzik watched the gathering mist, willing it to grow thicker. It didn't oblige. While they waited, around fifty captured Rolencian men-at-arms were herded onto the ship and down the hatch. More unlucky seven-year-slaves.

When they were all safely belowdecks, Grufyd opened the cart's door and they clambered out, stumbling and moaning as circulation returned to numb legs and aching backs. By lantern light, breath misting in the cold,

Grufyd drove them across the pier, up the gang plank, onto deck and down the hatch to a cabin below.

It was all over so quickly, Garzik had no chance to slip out of line, no chance to go over the ship's side.

Mind you, with the cold, he'd be risking death in that sea.

Garzik cursed himself, furious. He should have taken the chance afforded on the sled-ship, when Grufyd belted Feo. They'd all been watching the by-play. It would have been easy to slip over the side and make his way off the ice.

Why hadn't he used his wits? Orrade would have been on alert. Orrade would never have gotten himself in this position. His brother had never failed Byren.

Feeling sick, Garzik blinked as they were herded into the cabin. No chance to escape here. No windows. One narrow bunk, a fold-up table and a fold-up chair hanging from a hook. The fifteen injured captives shuffled in, filling the narrow space. A sailor threw some blankets and a bucket after them and shut the door, leaving them in the dark. Being last in line, Garzik heard the bolt shoot home.

As good as blind, the others scrambled for blankets.

'What, no dinner?' the baker's apprentice muttered.

'Be thankful we're not spending the night in the cart,' the cabinet-maker answered.

'I heard what you said to the pie girl,' Mitrovan whispered to Garzik. 'Is she a spy, too?'

For a heartbeat, Garzik was tempted to say yes. Mitrovan had gotten it into his head the pair of them were part of a big adventure, spying for Rolencia, and Garzik wished it was true. 'No. But King Rolen's youngest two sons still live, so –'

'Who's talking of King Rolen?' the cabinet-maker asked.

Garzik said nothing and Mitrovan took his cue from this.

'Goddess bless King Rolen.' The cabinet-maker was undeterred. 'They were Halcyon's days under his reign. Thirty years of good harvests and peace.'

'May Goddess Halcyon bless King Rolen,' several others echoed.

'My old gaffer said we won't see the like again,' the baker's apprentice offered.

'You wouldn't be so quick to praise King Rolen if you saw your family's farm confiscated because your father had Affinity,' Feo snapped. 'I bet you never saw your mam forced onto the streets to feed you and your brother, never saw your little brother take the Goddess Halcyon's service because it was that or banishment?'

Silence greeted this outburst.

'Don't talk to me of good King Rolen.' Feo made a disgusted sound.

'King Rolen only issued the Affinity decrees to protect us. Those touched by Affinity must serve the church or risk becoming channels for evil,' the cabinet-maker stated.

'Affinity is a tool, like fire,' Feo said. 'Evil lies in the hand that wields it and the heart and mind that directs the hand.'

An uncomfortable silence greeted this sacrilege.

'If your father and brother had Affinity, perhaps you also have it?' a new dry voice suggested. 'Maybe you'll be right at home, amongst the ungodly Merofynians.'

Feo surprised them by laughing bitterly at this insult. 'D'you think if I had one skerrick of power of my own, I'd be here locked up with you lot of sorry-faced gimps?'

No one answered.

'Fools,' Feo spat.

There was silence for a bit.

'I've never been on a ship. Never left Rolenton,' the baker's apprentice muttered. 'You hear tell of storms and Utland raiders and wyvern attacks and –'

'It's a quick voyage to Merofynia,' Mitrovan spoke up. 'Usually between five and eight days, depending on the winds. My master's ships used to make the trip all the time.'

'And how many of those ships foundered on spar rocks?' Feo asked.

That was the problem. Thanks to Queen Myrella's tutelage, Garzik could visualise the rival kingdoms of Rolencia and Merofynia. He could still hear her voice describing the two as horse-shoe islands. Rolencia faced north and Merofynia south. From the mountains that formed the outer curve of the horse shoes, long fingers of land stretched out like the spokes of a wheel, the spars.

'A captain must make a choice,' Mitrovan said. 'Either he makes his way through the broken tips of the spars and risks the rocks, or he plots his course wide –'

'And risks Utland raiders,' Feo finished for him. 'Either way our goose is cooked.'

'We sail in convoy with sea-hounds to protect us.'

'Great. So we'll reach Merofynia safely to serve out our seven years of slavery!' Feo made a disgusted noise. 'Wish I'd made it over the side back in Port Marchand.'

'We all wish that,' the dry voice muttered.

There were some surprised chuckles.

'Everyone wants to go home,' Mitrovan said quickly before Feo could retaliate.

The captives grumbled some more, but Garzik ignored them.

Leaning his head against the cabin wall, he weighed up his chances. If Grufyd let them out while the ship was still in port, he would slip over the side into the sea and make a swim for it, cold or not. But that was a big 'if.'

Eventually, the others settled down.

A sliver of light came under the door. As his eyes adjusted, Garzik saw that three of the injured now shared the single bunk, while the rest stretched out across the floor. They were packed like fish in a net, for the cabin was only as wide as Garzik was tall.

Through the cabin walls, he heard shouts, creaks and thumps as the Lord Travany's stolen riches were loaded aboard. His stomach cramped. Instead of filling him, the pie crusts seem to have made him hungrier.

Despite his discomfort, he must have slept, because some time later the door opened, throwing a shaft of light into the crowded cabin. He winced, protecting his eyes.

Someone shoved a pot of hot soup in, along with a basket of bread stubs.

Garzik squinted to see a lad of about his age in the doorway. With Grufyd behind him there was no chance of slipping past. He turned back to find the others all crouched around the pot. Garzik's stomach knotted with hunger, but...

'Where's our bowls?' he asked the lad.

The lad and Grufyd looked at him, then at each other. As one they burst out laughing.

Mitrovan shoved a heel of bread in Garzik's hand. 'Scoop out the soup with this. And be quick about it, or you'll miss out.'

By the time he'd come to his knees and pushed through to the pot only the oily scum was left on the bottom. But he scraped his bread across it anyway and sucked the soup from the bread. It tasted so good: beef and onion.

Tears stung his eyes. Who thought food could make you cry?

The others settled back to gnaw on their bread. Garzik tried one more scrape of the pot but it was empty.

'Push the pot and empty basket out here,' Grufyd ordered.

He did as he was told, and the cabin door was shut in his face.

Garzik leant against the wall and chewed his way through the bread, savouring every mouthful. With food in his belly and the combined warmth of the cabin he felt a glow move through his body and sleep creep upon him.

He should stay awake in case a chance presented itself to escape.

He woke when the ship's motion changed. It felt like a lot of time had passed; he had to pee. From the muffled shouts they were sailing with the tide. He'd missed his chance.

Now he'd end up in Merofynia serving Lord Travany, just as the scribe said. In fact... he'd be in an ideal position to spy. Between them, he and Mitrovan could find out something useful to help Byren.

Now, he was glad he'd let Mitrovan believe he was a spy.

CHAPTER FOUR

BY MIDDAY, EVERYONE was seasick. At first they complained and whined. In the end, they endured.

The one bucket acquired a queue. Not everyone made it to the bucket. There was nowhere to empty it, and soon they were all soiled. The soup, so good going down, soon covered the floor. The stench, combined with the lack of light, convinced Garzik he had never been more miserable.

In all his days, fishing on the lake, he'd never been seasick; but back then he'd been in the open air.

When the cook's lad turned up that evening with another tub of thin soup, he took one look inside the cabin and backed off.

'Bring another bucket,' Mitrovan called.

'Bring a dozen,' some wit yelled.

A few moments later an old sailor opened the cabin door for Master Cialon, who took one breath and backed up, sleeve over his mouth and nose. The door was shut and locked.

Garzik waited, hopeful for hot water to wash in, some sailor's remedy to settle their stomachs and a change of clothes – at the very least, some time on deck in the fresh air.

They were left in their own filth.

Garzik no longer felt sick. He no longer felt anything.

It might have been mid-morning the next day when the door finally opened. Grufyd stood there, watching over the cook's lad, who carried buckets and mops.

As the lad handed these over, Grufyd told them, 'clean up and you'll be allowed out to wash.'

Garzik had never cleaned his own clothes or scrubbed a floor in his life, but if it meant getting out of that cabin, he'd do it.

Three of the captives were too sick to move. The others pitched in, some mopped up and the others shuffled out of the way, while Garzik and Mitrovan scrubbed.

Once the cabin was clean and the filthy bedding rolled up, Grufyd let them out. They carried the three weakest up to the middeck, where they all stripped off and were doused with icy-cold sea water.

Meanwhile, the sailors and Merofynian men-at-arms mocked them. A lad of no more than nine or ten scampered about. Egged on by the jeers and cheers of the audience, he darted in to pinch cold buttocks.

'Make them squeal, Yorwyth!'

Garzik was sorely tempted to trip the lad, but it would have only brought the ire of the men-at-arms down on them, so he ignored Yorwyth and took advantage of the saltwater soap to wash; it stung his abraded skin.

By the time the bathing was done, Garzik was blue with cold, teeth chattering so badly he couldn't speak. Feo kept up a constant stream of complaints, but never loud enough for their captors to work out who was speaking.

Given dry blankets, they rubbed their chilled skin to get some feeling back. The ship's surgeon inspected their injuries, repacked the wounds of the weakest three and announced they would have to be moved to the sickbay.

Their clothes and blankets had gone into a tub of seawater and now had to be washed. Naturally, when there was work, Feo was nowhere to be seen. Fed up with him, Garzik wrapped the blanket around his hips and plunged his hands into the cold water.

After a moment, Mitrovan joined him.

'This is not right for your disguise,' the skinny scribe whispered. 'This is women's work. No man, let alone an educated scribe, willingly does women's work.'

'Then why are you helping me?'

'To cover for you.'

'What about scrubbing the cabin?'

'That...' Mitrovan shuddered. 'That was self-preservation.'

Garzik grinned.

He didn't mind washing. Moving kept him warm and work took his mind off the seasickness. Although, now that he was out in the fresh air, he felt better. Almost hungry.

It was so good to be out of that foul cabin.

While the others huddled in their blankets in a corner of the deck, out of the wind, he and Mitrovan wrung the clothes and hung them on the rigging.

A man-at-arm grabbed his crotch. 'I got something here needs wringing out. How 'bout you come over an' fix it.'

Garzik pretended he didn't understand him. With the wet washing flapping around them, Mitrovan pursed his lips in disapproval.

'You speak Merofynian?' Garzik whispered, although the man's gesture had been enough to convey his meaning.

'As do you.' Mitrovan cast him an assessing look. 'I read and write it, too, Ostronite as well. You?'

Garzik nodded. He was beginning to think the skinny scribe was as smart as Orrade.

'That makes you very well educated for a lord's son,' Mitrovan said.

He was right. Most lords had basic reading and writing skills and left the rest up to their scribes. Garzik neither agreed nor disagreed because, although Mitrovan claimed he was discrete, the scribe was always fishing for clues as to Garzik's true identity. To distract him, Garzik said, 'I visited a markiz in Port Marchand. His scribes could figure numbers in their heads, but when it came to writing, they knew only Rolencian.'

'That's because they were counting-scribes.'

'So you can't do numbers?' Garzik teased gently.

'Of course I can do numbers, I...' Mitrovan broke off and gave a sheepish grin. 'I can do everything the average scribe can, and more besides.'

They were alone. This was his chance. Garzik lowered his voice. 'You're right. I am a spy and I need your help.'

'I knew it!' Mitrovan crowed, then glanced around and dropped his voice. 'What do you need me to do?'

'Keep your eyes open. If you see anything that might help Byren reclaim Rolencia, pass the information along to me.'

'You can rely on me, Garzik Dovecoteson.'

Garzik blinked.

Mitrovan's eyes gleamed. 'You're wearing the Dovecote crest on your indoor servant's uniform and you say Byren Kingson's name like he's your friend.' The scribe grew serious. 'You really must be more careful.'

Garzik nodded. 'I'm Wyvern, the scribe who can't remember his name.'

Hands red from the cold and rough soap, Garzik hung the last wet blanket on the rigging then hitched his own blanket over his shoulders, tucking his hands under his armpits. 'Feel like I'll never get warm again. My hands are so numb I can hardly make a fist.'

Mitrovan adjusted his blanket and they turned to join the others. 'As long as we get fed, I –'

A high pitched scream from above cut him off. Someone crashed down through the rigging and fell in front of them, hitting the deck hard with a solid thump that cut off his cry.

They both jumped back.

The boy who'd teased them mercilessly lay sprawled on the deck, one leg bent at an impossible angle. His terrified eyes stared up at them as his mouth opened and closed like a landed fish.

Mitrovan darted forward.

'Don't move him.' Garzik warned. He knelt to study the boy.

Yorwyth's breath came in rapid, terrified gasps.

Dimly, Garzik heard sailors shouting and feet running. He was aware of someone kneeling opposite as he placed one hand on the lad's shoulder and looked into his eyes.

'Trust you to fall off the rigging, Yorwyth. Always showing off.' It was the kind of thing Captain Blackwing would have said, and it worked.

The terror ebbed from the boy's eyes as he tried to sit up.

'Wait a moment,' Garzik advised. 'Let the ship's surgeon run his hands over you. He has to earn his keep.'

'That leg...' Mitrovan whispered.

'What's wrong with my leg?' Yorwyth shrilled.

'You've gone and broken it,' Garzik told him, keeping his tone matter-of-fact. 'Nothing a splint and rest can't fix.'

The surgeon arrived and they were sent off to join the rest of the captives.

'Is he going to be all right?' the baker's apprentice asked.

'Serve the brat right if he broke his neck,' Feo muttered.

'Leg's broken,' Garzik said, watching as the sailors lifted the lad between them and carried him into the cabin under the rear deck, with the ship's surgeon following like an anxious mother hen. It seemed a lot of fuss for a cabin boy.

After that nothing of interest happened. Several of the captives still suffered from seasickness but all they could do was dry retch. No one had anything in their stomachs.

A little while later, they heard a short scream and then silence.

'Poor little bugger,' the cabinet-maker muttered. 'No fun getting the bone back in alignment.'

The baker's apprentice made a strangled sound in his throat and ran to the side.

Despite this, Garzik's stomach growled. He thought he'd been hungry before. But now...

The wind blew strong. Not a cloud marred the winter-blue sky as the convoy of Merofynian ships laden with war booty wove their way through the broken tips of the spars. They passed steep-sided islands with small patches of fertile land, home to stunted bushes and wild birds.

Now that the swelling had gone done enough for Garzik to open his bad eye, he was grateful to discover he could see clearly.

No one came near them. But enough of Lord Travany's men-at-arms wandered the deck to deter any thought of jumping overboard. And besides, that would only lead to death, for even if they were lucky enough to be swept onto an island before the cold killed them, most of the far-flung spar islands were little more than rocky outcroppings and those that were suitable for habitation were settled by stoic spar warriors and their families.

Little better than Utlanders, not only did these spar inhabitants bear no love for Rolencians or Merofynians, there was no food to spare in their cottages at any rate.

The smell of lunch cooking wafted up from the galley. Chicken, oregano, onions and beans never smelled so good. It got Garzik's stomach going. At this rate he'd gnaw off his own leg.

Soon the majority of men-at-arms went below. Garzik watched them go, stomach clenching and unclenching with hunger pains. The captives remained seated, huddled together for warmth, dressed only in blankets, while their clothing dried.

'Say, Feo,' the cabinet-maker prodded. 'Reckon you could charm some scraps from the cook?'

'Not a chance. I don't suck cock. Why don't you try it?'

The cabinet-maker threw off his blanket and came into a crouch. 'Watch your mouth, braggart.'

'Look!' Mitrovan pointed desperately. 'They're bringing us food.'

Animosity forgotten, they turned to see the kitchen lad carry a pot towards them. From the smell, it contained the same dish. Grufyd followed with a basket of bread scraps.

More than half the injured captives surged towards the food. This time Garzik knew what to do and was on his knees with a heel of bread ready to get his share when a voice said. 'You.' He looked up. 'Yes, you.'

As much as he wanted to ignore the command, Garzik came to his feet, hiding the bread under his blanket.

'Come here.' It was the sailor who'd knelt beside Yorwyth and another one, older, grizzled. From the way the sailors had jumped when the older one spoke, Garzik guessed he was the first mate.

Garzik took a step closer, aware that Mitrovan had also come to his feet. The scribe was half a head taller than him but so skinny he looked like a puff of wind would knock him over. All the same, Garzik appreciated his support.

'That's him? You sure?' the first-mate asked, looking Garzik up and down with some misgivings. 'With a face like that, he'd scare small children.'

'He handled Yorwyth well,' the other insisted. They spoke Merofynian, unaware that both Garzik and Mitrovan understood.

'I hope you're right. With a drunken sot for a doctor...' The first-mate switched to rough Rolencian. 'What's your name, lad?'

Garzik opened his mouth. Nothing came out.

'He can't remember,' Mitrovan said. 'The blow to his head –'

'But his wits are all there,' the sailor assured the first-mate. 'According to Master Cialon, he's an indoor servant. They've named him Wyvern, so he gets Wynn for short. He'll clean up all right and, when his face heals –'

'He'll still have a scar.'

'He's a scribe,' Mitrovan offered, as though he didn't understand what was being said. 'So am I. We could be useful.'

'And why would you offer your services to a Merofynian?' the first-mate asked.

Mitrovan shrugged. 'Anything to get out of that cabin. I don't want to be covered in puke again.'

Both sailors laughed.

'Let's hope you're right, Sionor.' The first mate beckoned Garzik. 'Come this way.'

Garzik hesitated.

Mitrovan leant close. 'This is your chance to impress Master Cialon and put in a good word for me.'

Garzik nodded and adjusted his blanket as he followed the first mate, who had not waited to see if he would obey. While Garzik jogged to catch up, he gnawed at the bread. It was hard crust, but he didn't care.

Instead of taking him below to Master Cialon, the first mate led him into the captain's cabin under the high rear deck. The captain stood over the ship's surgeon, who knelt beside a bed roll where the boy lay. His leg had been splinted, and he looked pale but asleep. Garzik assumed they'd given him dreamless-sleep.

'This is the one,' the first mate said. 'Sionor says he has a way with the lad.'

The three men turned to look at Garzik. Who swallowed a mouthful of bread and tried to look respectable. But he was only too aware of his swollen face and naked body under the blanket.

'You're sure?' the captain asked. 'He's not well favoured.'

'It's the bruising. He'll heal up in a week or two,' the surgeon said, speaking Merofynian with the unmistakable accent of an educated man. His clothing had been fine once, but now it was as creased as his thin face. Fixing bleary eyes on Garzik, he switched to Rolencian. 'Do you know how to care for a broken leg?'

Garzik nodded. 'I broke my arm two summers ago. The healer gave me willowbark for the pain and told me to rest while the bone knitted.' He lifted the arm in question. 'Works fine now.'

The men exchanged looks.

'He's well spoken for a scribe,' the captain muttered in Merofynian. 'Sounds like a noble. Should make you feel right at home, Rishardt.'

The surgeon ignored him, beckoning Garzik, who knelt beside him.

'It'll be your task to care for this lad. I've given him something for the pain, but he'll wake by dusk and he'll be complaining. You're to give him five drops of this tincture in wine. No more, even if he begs. Understood?'

Garzik nodded. 'For how long?' The surgeon blinked. 'How long before it wears off and he needs more to dull the pain?' Garzik asked, noting the wine on the surgeon's breath. 'Can he have it around midnight?'

'Yes.' Rishardt gave him a thoughtful look. 'And more again at dawn.' He went to stand then stopped. 'Mind you do a good job with him. He's Lord Yorale's youngest son.'

The name meant nothing to Garzik, but he nodded and stayed by the boy as the surgeon and captain spoke above his head.

'Rishardt, I'm confiscating your wine until he's safely delivered to his father,' the captain said. 'That man's –'

'A prick, I know.'

The captain's chuckle covered Garzik's stifled gasp.

'Worse, he's a noble prick,' the captain agreed. 'Bad enough his son fell and broke his leg while serving our lord, but if his leg festers and we have to take it –'

'This seven-year-slave's smart. Really smart. He'll do a good job.'

'He will if he knows what's good for him.'

Garzik dismissed the surgeon's words. Rishardt only thought he was smart because they'd never met Orrade.

'Fail me in this, Rishardt, and I'll sail to the nearest wyvern eyrie and feed you to them!'

The surgeon shrugged. 'I'll do what I can. But there are things beyond any surgeon's control.'

To Garzik, the captain's threat seemed like the kind of exaggerated joke Byren would make, but Rishardt's reply had been serious.

Out of his depth, Garzik was not sure how to take these men. He knew enough of Merofynia to know it was customary for the younger sons of lords to be fostered out to noble families, where they served as squires to learn their warrior-craft, or cabin boys to learn their sea-craft. This created bonds of obligation and alliances between the lords that were almost as strong as marriages of alliance. Clearly, Lord Yorale was not the kind of man Lord Travany wanted as an enemy.

Head down, Garzik smiled to himself. Mitrovan was right. He was in an ideal position to spy for Rolencia. Once he worked his way into Travany's trust, he could find out what the Merofynians were planning and...

And what? How was he going to get a message back to Rolencia, let alone Byren?

If only he really was spying for Byren. It would all be so simple. Orrade would have organised a system for relaying messages.

Frustration churned in him. Here he was, right under the Merofynians' noses, with no way of getting word back to Byren. But it was too good an opportunity to miss. Somehow, he had to figure out a way to get messages back to Rolencia, to someone who was in sympathy with Byren, and then they could make sure the message reached the kingson.

What was he thinking? If both the kingsheir and the king were dead... Byren was the uncrowned king. Garzik sat back on his heels stunned.

Then he noticed the surgeon had left. A sailor announced that Master Cialon wanted to see the captain but, to Garzik's surprise, the captain sat down at his desk and deliberately kept Cialon waiting. He did this for no reason that Garzik could see other than because he could.

By the time the captain bade him enter, Master Cialon radiated fury.

'What's this I hear? You've no right to commandeer my cargo.' He gestured to Garzik.

'He's not your cargo. He's Lord Travany's, and you can bet his lordship will thank me for using him to take care of Yorale's brat.'

Garzik hid a smile. It seemed the captain didn't like Yorwyth either.

Just then, Sionor returned with a change of clothes for Garzik. Not the torn tabard he'd been captured in, but a sea-man's serviceable breeches, knitted under-shirt and sealskin vest. No shoes. But then the sailors didn't wear shoes. They needed a good grip when they climbed the ropes to adjust the sails.

Garzik turned his back, dropped his blanket and dressed, grateful for the warmth that radiated from the brazier beside the captain's desk.

'Another thing.' Master Cialon changed tack. 'You can't have Grufyd or his brother, I need them.'

'Not as much as I do. There's fifty healthy seven-year-slaves in the hold and a dozen injured in the cabin below us. Who's going to clean up after them, if not Grufyd and Grudor?' The captain made a dismissive gesture. 'I told you not to feed them before we left port, but would you listen?'

'The injured hadn't been fed for a day and a night, and the healthy ones had been languishing in a storehouse for two days without food. His lordship's seven-year-slaves are no good to him if they're dropping dead from starvation.'

'Which is why I need Grufyd and Grudor to keep them in line,' the captain said. 'I can't send the kitchen lad down to feed your healthy seven-year-slaves, not after what they tried the first time.'

'Use the men-at-arms.'

'They're warriors, not nurse-maids. They won't play servant to slaves.'

'If you take Grufyd and Grudor, who's going to serve me?'

'There's the other scribe,' Sionor said.

Both men turned to him.

'Beggin' yer pardon, cap'n.' He bobbed his head, then gestured to Garzik. 'This one's friend was also a scribe.'

'I don't want a filthy Rolencian in my service, let alone my cabin,' Master Cialon protested. 'I'd have to watch everything I own. I wouldn't sleep safe.'

'Beggin' yer pardon, Master Cialon, but he seemed more interested in getting a cushy post than which master he served.'

'A turncoat, just what I need!' Master Cialon threw up his hands and strode out.

Garzik watched him go, sorry he hadn't been able to put in a good word for Mitrovan, but he wasn't even supposed to understand what was being said.

When the captain was alone, he turned to Garzik, switched to Rolencian, and gestured to the injured lad. 'I'll thank you to keep him quiet. If his leg festers and we have to take it, I'll take yours.'

Garzik gasped, biting back a protest. Captain Blackwing would never have laid such an unfair charge on one of his men. But Garzik was no longer among honourable men.

CHAPTER FIVE

THE NEXT THREE days passed in a blur, with long passages of boredom, interrupted by passages of intense worry as Yorwyth became feverish and thrashed about, causing himself pain.

Garzik did not leave his side. Surgeon Rishardt came each time the captain called him. By the end of the first day, his hands were shaking and he stank of wine. Despite this, he examined the lad with care and left instructions with Garzik.

Now that he was warm and well fed, Garzik had time to think. With no method of sending messages back to Rolencia, there was no point remaining a slave and spying. Just as soon as he had useful information, he would escape, return to Byren and deliver the news himself.

Maybe then Byren could forgive him for failing to light the warning beacon.

Who was he kidding?

He'd frozen on the tower stairs, and because of it, King Rolen had had no warning and Rolencia had fallen. How could he go back?

Orrade would never have let Byren down like that.

But if he returned with important information, surely he could win back Byren's respect?

In the dark of night, when he knelt by Yorwyth's bedroll, spongeing the lad's hot skin to bring down his fever, the arguments went round and round in Garzik's head, until he was heartily sick of them and himself.

At least one thing worked in his favour.

Thanks to Byren's mother, he spoke Merofynian with the accent of a noble. All he needed was the chance to snatch some decent clothing and a coin purse. Then he could impersonate a noble's son, off to make his fortune in the conquered country and book passage on a ship returning to Rolencia.

On the morning of the third day after the fall, Yorwyth opened his eyes, clear headed. He frowned at Rishardt, who was checking his leg, and tried to sit up.

'Lie still for the surgeon,' Garzik advised, taking care not to slip into Merofynian.

Yorwyth's eyes narrowed. 'I know you.'

Since he'd spoken Merofynian, Garzik pretended not to understand and offered him water.

'Your leg is healing well, young lord,' Rishardt reported. He looked worse today, his skin grey.

There had been a man with a drinking problem back home. If Garzik's father had known, The Old Dove would have banished him from the estate. Instead, Captain Blackwing had taken the man into the forest, dug a pit, dropped him in and left him there for a week. Ignoring his cries for help, Blackwing provided him with food and water, nothing more. The man's ravings were terrible to hear. Blackwing had said it was an important lesson to Garzik and Orrade, never to let wine rule them. After a week, they'd thrown down a rope, washed the man in the lake and taken him back to the hall. He'd never touched alcohol again.

'Careful, you fool!' Yorwyth grimaced. 'I'm hungry.'

'That's a good sign.' Rishardt ignored the insult and gestured to Garzik, switching to Rolencian. 'Go fetch him some broth from the galley.'

Garzik ducked his head and left the cabin.

It was the first time he'd been out on deck since he'd been assigned to serve the lad, and it was good to stretch his legs. The air was fresh and sharp, and the sails billowed in the wind.

Down in the galley, he waited while the cook served up a meal. When Mitrovan arrived with an empty tray, Garzik hid his surprise.

They exchanged looks and the scribe nodded to the passage. A few moments later Garzik left with Yorwyth's food and found the scribe waiting for him.

Garzik gestured down the hall to the cabin they'd shared with the injured. 'They let you out?'

'Haven't you heard?' Mitrovan whispered. 'I serve Master Cialon now. Thanks for putting in a good word for me.'

'I didn't get a chance. One of the sailors suggested you,' Garzik answered, then frowned. 'But Cialon was set against having a Rolencian servant. How –'

'Oh, he's much like my old master, petty and self-important. The more he despises me, the better he feels about himself. I plan to make myself indispensable. To hear Cialon speak, he's Lord Travany's right-hand man. Travany's not the wealthiest or the most powerful of nobles, but he is part of Lord Yorale's circle. And Yorale is close to the king. So we're sure to hear something useful.'

'You learnt all that in three days?' Garzik was impressed and felt he'd wasted his time. 'I've done nothing but nurse-maid Lord Yorale's brat.'

'Perhaps you should try to get on the lad's good side. His father...'

But Garzik was already shaking his head. 'I swear if I had to serve him, I'd end up strangling him.' He glanced up and down the passage. 'Keep your ears open. When we learn something useful, we'll escape and take the news back to Byren. I'll travel as a Merofynian noble and you can be my scribe.'

'Let's hear your Merofynian.'

Instead of taking offence, Garzik obliged him.

Mitrovan nodded. 'You make a more convincing Merofynian noble than you do a Rolencian scribe.' Just then, Mitrovan glanced over his shoulder and spotted the kitchen lad coming down the passage with an empty pot. His tone changed immediately. 'So I don't mind how often he beats me, as long as I get three square meals a day.'

Garzik went to ask who beat Mitrovan, then noticed the bruise on the kitchen lad's cheek.

'There you are, Mitrofan.' The lad used the Merofynian form of his name. 'Master Cialon's looking for you.'

'Thanks, Arolt,' the scribe said. As he turned back to Garzik, he sent him a significant look and hurried off.

Taking a leaf from Mitrovan's book, Garzik nodded to the kitchen lad. 'Better get this food up to his little lordship, before it goes cold. You should hear him complain, nothing's ever done to his satisfaction.'

The lad grinned. 'Pity he didn't fall and break both legs.'

Pleased with himself, Garzik continued along the lower deck to the ladder, and climbed one-handed, balancing the tray. Yorwyth would surely complain if the broth was spilled.

But up on deck he found Grufyd supporting Yorwyth at the ship's side as both of them stared towards the headland.

'Mulcibar's Gate,' Yorwyth was saying when Garzik came up behind them. 'Now I know I'm home.'

Mulcibar's Gate? The sight stole Garzik's breath. Of course, he'd heard stories about the river of slow moving hot rock that met the waves in foam and steam, but seeing it was an entirely different thing. Each time a wave dashed itself on the rocks, the water hissed and great gouts of steam shot up.

'Breakfast at last.' Yorwyth spotted him. 'I'll eat out here.'

In no time at all a table and two chairs had been brought out so the lad could sit with his broken leg elevated, eat his meal and watch the convoy enter Port Mero.

Now that they were safe, Yorwyth complained the sea-hounds had not earned their money. He seemed disappointed the fleet had not run into Utlanders after all. He complained because he had to go home with a broken leg and would have to spend the spring and summer recuperating. From what Garzik could gather, his older brother was serving as a warrior's squire; he'd been in the thick of the fighting during the Rolencian invasion and would return home a hero.

Then Yorwyth complained because he'd talked so long the broth had gone cold, which meant Garzik had to go below to reheat it.

When he returned, the big bay stretched out around them. Nestled in its many inlets were little fishing villages, just like back home. Lord Travany's ship made for the wharves on the far side, below Mont Mero.

If Yorwyth had been anyone else, it would have been a pleasant morning. But, just as he'd delighted in teasing the captives, he delighted in teasing Garzik. When he sent him to fetch a book, it was the wrong book and the fault was Garzik's. Before long, Garzik would have happily thrown the boy overboard.

'What's the hold up?' Yorwyth demanded of a passing sailor. 'Why are we dropping anchor instead of berthing?'

'Too many ships trying to unload. We have to wait our turn, young lord,' Sionor said. As he hurried off, he sent Garzik a sympathetic look.

'I'm sick of being cooped up on board,' Yorwyth announced.

He was not the only one annoyed by the delay. Master Cialon confronted the captain. They were up on the rear deck, so Garzik could only catch snippets of conversation, but it seemed for once they were in agreement. Master Cialon had to deliver the Rolencian war booty to Lord Travany and the captain was eager to get back to Port Marchand where there was cargo in waiting to be collected.

A moment later, sailors lowered a boat and Master Cialon climbed overboard, with two sailors to handle the oars.

'I bet he's going to speak to the harbour-master,' Yorwyth told Garzik smugly. 'My father won't be pleased when he hears how we were kept waiting.'

Perhaps this was true, because the rowboat returned presently without Master Cialon and the ship was ushered past other vessels to a berth. By this time it was mid-afternoon and Mitrovan had joined Garzik. In Master Cialon's absence, the scribe had the run of the ship and no one to answer to.

Garzik noticed the surgeon sitting on a bale at the other end of the deck. He had his nose buried in a book. 'I don't understand what a man like him is doing on this ship.'

'Escaping disgrace.' Mitrovan leant close. 'Apparently, he fought a duel over a woman. Killed a powerful man. Had to leave Merofynia to save his family's honour.' The scribe snorted softly. 'Nobles and their honour.' Then he glanced to Garzik, his expression far too knowing.

Garzik felt the injustice of his unspoken accusation. 'I failed to light the warning beacon. I failed Byren.' Tears burned his eyes and he fought to hold them back. 'Because of me, Rolencia fell.'

'How do you know it wouldn't have fallen anyway? From what I heard there was a traitor in the castle.'

Garzik shook his head. The scribe was only trying to make him feel better. Shame seared his cheeks, and his throat grew so tight he could hardly speak. 'I failed Byren, that's why I have to make up for it with important information.'

'What are you two whispering about?' Yorwyth demanded fretfully.

'We're looking forward to dinner,' Mitrovan answered.

Yorwyth wasn't interested. 'Fetch me a blanket, Grufyd. I'm cold. And fetch a cushion. This seat's too hard. Wait.' He sat up straighter in the chair. 'Come back here and lift me up. I swear...'

When Grufyd lifted him, he smiled, pointing to the pier as the ship drew closer. 'Look, my father's carriage and my old tutor!'

He waved.

The tutor spotted Yorwyth and turned to speak with two large servants. The moment the gangplank was fixed, they all came aboard. The two burly servants picked Yorwyth up between them and carried him down to the carriage, accompanied by fretful admonishments to mind his bad leg. Meanwhile, the tutor went into the captain's cabin.

Sailors threw hatches open and made ready to unload the cargo.

'I wonder where Master Cialon is,' Mitrovan whispered.

'I'm just glad to see the last of the brat,' Garzik admitted. His stomach rumbled. 'Today I've had to sit and watch him wolf down more food than I've had in a week. And none of it was good enough for him!'

Mitrovan glanced over his shoulder. 'No-one's watching. Even Grufyd's disappeared. Let's go below and see if we can get something from the galley.'

But they only got as far as the hatch before Grufyd spotted them. 'Go pack the master's things and get your bundle.'

Feeling light-hearted and much closer to his goal, Garzik followed Mitrovan below. Together they packed Master Cialon's belongings. No sooner were they done than Grufyd and his brother collected the chests.

There was just time for Garzik and Mitrovan to grab some bread and cheese from the galley, before going up on deck.

In the short time they'd been below, lanterns had been lit, bringing an early twilight. Just like back in Port Marchand, the sailors kept working by lamplight. The remaining injured seven-year-slaves stood lined up, ready to disembark. Each carried a blanket. When Feo saw Garzik and Mitrovan arrive, he said something derogatory to the cabinet-maker and spat over the side.

'We'll have to watch out for him,' Mitrovan warned. 'If he learns we're spies, he's just as likely to sell us out to the Merofynians to win his freedom.'

Master Cialon turned to see them. 'There you are, Mitrofan. Where are my lists?'

The scribe had to dig them out of a chest.

When he tried to hand them to Cialon, the man gestured for him to hold them. 'Tick this lot off. Fourteen injured seven-year-slaves, none lost at sea.'

The scribe hesitated. 'Don't you mean fifteen, master?'

'Did I say fifteen?' Cialon snapped. 'I meant what I said.'

Mitrovan glanced to Garzik.

'He stays.' Cialon waved a dismissive hand. 'The captain requested him.'

Garzik opened his mouth to speak, but Master Cialon directed Grufyd and his brother to escort the injured seven-year-slaves down the gang plank.

Mitrovan barely had time to clasp Garzik in a quick hug.

'Don't worry. I won't let you down,' he whispered. 'And I'll find some way to get the information back to Rolencia.'

Then he hurried after Master Cialon. Feeling utterly lost, Garzik watched the scribe go. All his plans were suddenly in disarray, and now that Mitrovan was gone, Garzik realised the scribe had been his one friend in all of this, and he felt the loss keenly.

A hand tapped Garzik's shoulder.

'You're wanted below,' Sionor said. 'The ship's surgeon asked for you.'

So Garzik found himself entering the surgeon's little cabin.

'There you are,' Rishardt greeted him. He sat at his bench, a wine bottle open. His eyes had that bleary look again, which meant he'd been imbibing already. But the alcohol did not seem to impair his speech or movements as he gestured to the rack of vials and jars. 'Inventory. We need to restock before returning to Rolencia. I'll call the name, you tell me if we've almost run out. Come now, there's no time to waste. The captain wants to put to sea with the dawn tide.'

Garzik ran his eyes over the rack. The names were Merofynian, but he could guess the Rolencian translation. Back home their family healer had a whole wall of herbals. But then Rishardt wasn't a healer. His job was to sew up injured men and set bones.

Just then, the healthy seven-year slaves headed up the passage, towards the ladder to the middeck. Hearing the Rolencian language, Garzik froze and watched them shuffle past the cabin door.

'Count yourself lucky,' the surgeon told him. 'They'll be working in the fields, the mines or the ship-yards, up to the necks in freezing cold water. Half of them'll die of the flux or the lung rot.' He shut the door and took another drink. 'If you keep your wits about you, lad, you'll be a surgeon by the time your service is up.'

The thought of spending seven years at sea, serving Merofynians, horrified Garzik.

Seeing his expression, Rishardt smiled grimly. 'I saved your life. Show a little gratitude.'

'Why did you start drinking again?' Garzik blurted, then flinched, expecting a blow.

But the surgeon glanced to the wine bottle, seemed to forget the question and poured himself another drink.

'There was a man back home with a drinking problem,' Garzik said. 'We put him in a pit and left him there until he'd gone a week without drink. When we hauled him out, he never drank again.'

'For how long?'

'What?'

'For how long did he stop drinking? One season, one year?'

Garzik thought back. They'd put him in the pit summer two years ago and Garzik knew the man had been killed in the Merofynian attack. 'Until the day he died.'

'Which was?'

'Less than two years later,' Garzik admitted.

'So you've remembered your past. I take it that includes your name?'

Garzik flushed and closed his mouth.

'Then Wyvern it is. Wynn for short,' Rishardt told him. 'Now that you're my apprentice, I'll have to teach you Merofynian.'

Garzik nodded and turned away, but the surgeon caught his arm. 'I might be a drunkard, but I'm no fool and you're no scribe.'

It was almost word for word what Mitrovan had said. Was he such a bad actor?

Garzik looked down at the hand on his arm.

'Don't worry. I'm the last person to ask what you're running from.'

Rishardt gave Garzik a shove in the right direction. 'Back to work.'

As the surgeon fired off words, Garzik repeated them, pretending to commit them to memory. But all the time he grappled with the sudden change in his fortune. Their ship was going back to Rolencia.

As much as he wanted to go home, how could he return to Byren empty handed?

While they checked the stores, sailors unloaded Lord Travany's war booty and the rest of the seven-year-slaves. By midnight, the depleted ship's stores had been replaced and the vessel pulled away from the dock so another could take her place.

When the kitchen lad delivered a tray of beans and bread, the ship's surgeon pushed a plate in Garzik's direction. Continuing to tutor Garzik in the Merofynian language, he poured himself another drink. A second wine bottle was almost empty. Despite this, he was no drunker.

Garzik could not reveal his deception, so he deliberately stumbled over the supposedly foreign words.

Rhishardt chuckled. 'You're asleep on your feet. Don't worry, we've got seven years to teach you. Eat up, Wynn. You can bunk down under the bench.'

Grateful as he was for the food, Garzik hardly tasted it. Tired and stunned by the turn of events, he finished his meal and lay down to sleep under the surgeon's table. Straps hung off the table legs.

He didn't want to think what they were used for, but of course his mind presented him with the image of an injured sailor, restrained while the surgeon operated on him. Garzik shuddered. He wasn't brave enough to be a ship's surgeon. And he wasn't as good a spy as Mitrovan. Somehow he must work out what to do next.

But he fell asleep before he could.

It seemed like only a moment later that Garzik woke, with sunlight coming through the cabin's small window and the sensation of the ship cutting through the waves.

He woke with a dream conversation running through his head. He'd been on the battlements at Rolenhold, earnestly telling Byren how he'd sent

Mitrovan to infiltrate the king's inner circle. He'd been trying to convince Byren and Orrade to send him back to Merofynia so he could collect the scribe's messages for Byren. It all made perfect sense in the dream.

And, once he was awake, it still made sense.

A weight lifted from his shoulders. This was how he could redeem himself. As the go-between for Mitrovan, who would do the actual spying, since he was so much better at it.

Now all that remained was to escape the ship when they returned to Port Marchand.

For the rest of the voyage, he made himself useful. The surgeon was not a demanding master and he never drank so much that he passed out. But Garzik had to watch himself. Despite the wine, Rishardt was observant. If the surgeon realised Garzik spoke Merofynian, he'd be quick to anger.

And, to his surprise, Garzik discovered he didn't want to disappoint the surgeon.

Six days later, Garzik stood on the middeck watching the Rolencian headlands slide past, his heart racing with excitement. Soon he would be back home. Then he'd hunt up a certain pie shop girl and see if she had news of Byren. Even if she didn't, he knew how Orrade thought. His brother would have taken Byren into the foot-hills of the Dividing Range, those same foot-hills where Captain Blackwing had taught them both to hunt.

A smile tugged at his mouth as he imagined Byren and Orrade's surprise when he walked into camp. Even better, how their eyes would widen when he told them about Mitrovan. The hard part would be convincing Byren to let him travel back to Merofynia as the scribe's contact, but he had all his arguments marshalled.

Relief filled his chest and his throat grew tight with emotion. To be home, to be amongst friends, but best of all, the chance to redeem himself in Byren's eyes.

A noise made him turn to find the kitchen boy behind him.

'You're wanted,' Arolt told him.

Garzik followed the lad below. Arolt led him past the surgeon's cabin to another door.

Garzik peered in. It was dark and smelled of onions. 'Surgeon Rishardt's in here?'

The words had barely left his lips, when the lad shoved him between the shoulders and slammed the door. Garzik collapsed on his knees amidst bags of stores. The door swung shut, leaving him in darkness, and he heard the bolt slide home.

Fool, he should have seen this coming. Of course they'd expect him to try and escape, and they'd take measure to prevent it. Orrade would never have fallen for such a simple trick. Fury burned him.

Shins stinging, he spun around and pressed his face to the tiny sliver of light and fresh air coming through a crack in the door.

'Arolt, let me out,' he pleaded. 'Arolt?'

'What, and get a beating?'

'Tell them you couldn't find me. I'll hide and slip overboard, swim for it.' It would be icy cold, but he was a strong swimmer and Captain Blackwing had taught him what to do if he fell through the ice on a lake. 'I don't belong here. Please, Arolt?'

'You think I wanted to be the cook's bum-boy?' the lad demanded, emotion making his voice vibrate. 'I was a cabinet-maker's apprentice when they grabbed me. This is where the cook shuts me up when we return to Port Mero.'

'Tell you what.' Garzik pressed his face to the gap. 'Let me out and I'll take you with me. Your Rolencian is good. You can finish your apprenticeship.'

Nothing.

'Arolt? It's busy on the wharf. Easy to disappear.'

Nothing.

'Arolt?'

He knelt listening. With the creak and pitch of the ship it was hard to tell if anyone was on the other side of the door.

'Arolt?'

'He's gone, Wynn,' the surgeon said. 'I knew first chance you got, you'd try to escape. You're angry with me now, but if you were free, you'd slip over the side, join the Rolencian resistance and get yourself killed. One day you'll thank me for this.'

Fury bubbled up inside Garzik. 'I'm not like you. I'm not going to hide in a bottle. Whatever it takes, I'm going to redeem myself!'

Silence.

'You hear me?'

No answer.

Garzik retreated to sit on a sack that, by the feel of it, contained potatoes. He cursed his bad luck.

Then he cursed his too-ready tongue. He should never have accused the surgeon of hiding in a bottle. He couldn't afford to make an enemy of Rishardt.

He should have anticipated this trick.

Now how would he serve Byren?

Frustration churned in his gut.

CHAPTER SIX

GARZIK HAD NO idea how long it took, but eventually the thin stream of light intensified as someone came up the passage with a lantern. Desperately hungry, he'd just eaten a raw potato, and now he regretted it. The unpleasant feel of the dirty skin remained on his lips. Grit still crunched between his teeth.

From the pitch and roll of the ship, they were well out to sea and any chance of escape was long gone.

Some warrior he'd turned out to be.

The door swung open, lantern light speared into his eyes, making made him flinch.

A thick-fingered hand reached in and dragged him to his feet. 'Bring beans, an' onions. Come.'

He'd been expecting the kitchen lad or the ship's surgeon; certainly not the cook. The man was big, beefy and impatient. His Rolencian was minimal and Garzik knew from the bruises on Arolt's face that the cook let his hands do the talking.

Since there was no point arguing, Garzik found a sack of beans and onions and followed the man along to the galley, where a meal bubbled away.

Immediately, his stomach knotted with hunger.

The cook slit the bag's stitching and upended the beans into a pot, then he gestured to the chopping board. 'Onions.' He imitated dicing.

'Isn't that Arolt's job?' Garzik dared to ask.

An open hand caught the side of his head, knocking him into a bench and bruising his ribs. Ear burning, head ringing, he picked up the knife. For a heartbeat he imagined driving it through the cook's chest.

The man grinned and beckoned him.

Garzik turned away to the chopping board. Soon onion-induced tears streamed from his eyes. Trapped in the galley, he could not escape the cooking smells and his stomach contracted painfully.

He kept expecting Arolt to return from running an errand, but there was no sign of the lad. The longer it went on, the more worried he became. But with the reminder of his stinging ear and sore ribs every time he breathed, he wasn't about to ask after Arolt. He'd prepared enough meals while hunting with Captain Blackwing not to disgrace himself in the galley. Once the onions were done, he handed the chopping board to the cook, who tipped the contents into the pot.

Garzik licked his lips. 'Uh, I really have to pee.'

The cook used the knife to gesture for him to go. 'Back quick, or...' He mimed what he'd do and Garzik instinctively covered himself.

Not sure why he had been demoted to kitchen lad, Garzik went along the passage to relieve himself. On his way back, he spotted the surgeon, who must have been watching for him.

Rishardt beckoned from the doorway of his cabin and Garzik hurried over to join him. They both ducked inside.

'What happened to Arolt? Did the cook hurt –'

'Arolt jumped ship in Rolencia,' the surgeon told him. 'You're the kitchen lad until we can find another one. Whatever you do, don't anger the cook. He killed the lad before Arolt with one blow, just lashed out and cracked his skull.'

Garzik shuddered.

'Don't worry. He knows he'll have to deal with me, if he hurts you.'

'Why...' Garzik began, recalling how rude he'd been to the surgeon last time they spoke. 'Why –'

'Help a seven-year-slave?' Rishardt shrugged. 'I might be a drunken sot living amongst men who act like beasts, but that doesn't mean I have to sink to their level.'

In that moment the surgeon reminded Garzik of Captain Blackwing. A surge of fellow feeling surprised him. Neither of them could ever go home. Garzik's home no longer existed. As for Rishardt, a powerful noble would ruin his family if he returned. No wonder he drank. One rash act had changed his life. Talk about being led around by your prick. Still...

'I'm sorry. I shouldn't have said what I did.'

The surgeon blinked in surprise.

Loud, raucous laughter reached them from the lower middeck where the men-at-arms slept and ate. They both stiffened, responding to the underlying threat.

'That's Lord Neirn's honour guard. Watch out for them,' Rishardt warned. 'They're full of hubris and contemptuous of anyone who isn't a warrior. In that, they're like their lord. Travany wants him for an ally. He wants this so much Trafyn serves as Neirn's squire.' He saw Garzik did not understand. 'Trafyn is his youngest son, he –'

'Boy!' the cook bellowed.

'Go. And keep your head down.'

Garzik went.

Preparing food for the whole crew, a lord and his squires and his men-at-arms in a tiny galley required organisation and timing. The cook kept Garzik on his toes.

By the time the first pot was ready to serve, Garzik was no longer hungry. He'd gone past hunger. Instead, he felt faint; and sounds echoed strangely in his head.

No seven-year-slaves this trip. The ship carried Rolencian treasures and a dozen elite men-at-arms, lord Neirn's honour guard. A lowly kitchen boy was beneath their notice, as Garzik discovered when he served up their meal. Several of the honour guard were seasick, but the rest devoured their dinner. Then there was the crew to feed.

Eventually, the cook sent Garzik to deliver a more elaborate meal to the captain's cabin, where a youth no older than himself took the tray at the door.

While the squire looked the food over with a frown, Garzik glanced past him to the table where Lord Neirn sat opposite the captain. He was in the prime of life, with only a touch of silver at his temples. And there was another squire, a little older than the first. Either of them could have been Lord Travany's youngest son.

'Tell cook he'll have to do better,' the squire told Garzik. 'And bring wine. A crisp Merofynian white. Neirn hates crude Rolencian reds.'

Since he'd spoken Merofynian, Garzik summoned a confused look and used the one Merofynian word, he'd 'learned' so far. 'What?'

The youth cursed in Merofynian, then switched to Rolencian, repeating himself. '...and don't say there's no white wine. This is my father's ship. I know he keeps a good wine cellar.'

'Trafyn, what's the delay?' the second squire came over. Taller than both of them and well dressed, he didn't even bother to acknowledge Garzik.

'Just a stupid seven-year-slave, Isfyl,' Trafyn told him, then switched to Rolencian. 'Don't stand about. Bring the wine and the rest of the food.'

This meant several more trips, as the spicy beans were not to Lord Neirn's liking. After Garzik had delivered an alternative dish, whipped up by the cursing cook, he had to stand in the doorway while the two squires served Lord Neirn and the captain. He knew the ship's captain well enough now to realise this was another lord the captain considered a prick, and a dangerous one at that.

Neirn twice returned wine bottles, demanding a better vintage. It worried Garzik; he suspected the uncorked bottles would find their way to the surgeon's cabin. All the while Neirn boasted of his prowess on the battlefield and his cunning as a commander. According to him, Rolencia had been an easy conquest.

'...and the women. Such beauties. Worth every scratch. In fact, the more they fought the better!' He reached down to cup himself. 'I swear I had a different one every night and sowed a bastard in every last one of them. It was a feast of Rolencian cunny.' He grinned and gestured to Isfyl. 'This one managed three in a row. Even Traf dipped his wick and came up smiling!'

Fury washed through Garzik. His sister had been at home when the Merofynians captured the family estate. Elina would have fought, but she was fine-boned. No matter how fierce her will, she was no match for a man's strength. Had she been left with a Merofynian bastard in her belly? His father would turn her out.

Lucky for her, Orrade was the new lord.

But even that thought could not make him smile. If he'd had a knife and the opportunity, he would have gelded Neirn and his squires.

Poor Elina. Did she still live? He found himself wishing selfishly that she did. Even if it meant she bore a bastard. At least Piro hadn't suffered before she died. He hoped.

'The spoils of war,' the captain agreed. 'What of the king's missing sons? Any news?'

Garzik looked up swiftly, forgetting that he wasn't supposed to understand Merofynian. No one noticed. They were all watching Neirn.

'Not yet.' He waved his fork dismissively. 'But their days are numbered. We've offered a reward that would make a farmer rich as a merchant markiz. Someone will reveal their hiding place.'

He's wrong. Rolencia would never betray Byren, Garzik thought. Then he remembered Feo. A man like him might betray Byren for a fortune. It all depended on whether he hated Merofynians more than he loved luxury.

When the conversation moved on to the voyage and the problem of Utland raiders, who were particularly bad this year, Garzik stopped listening. Instead, he watched the food disappear, stomach cramping with hunger.

What Neirn did not eat was taken from the table and devoured by his two squires. Isfyl had first pick, leaving Trafyn with the leftovers.

Finally, when they were all done, Garzik was told to clear the table and take the scraps away. He kept his eyes lowered, piled the first tray high and backed out. As soon as he was alone on deck, he sank to his knees and grabbed the nearest chunk of half-eaten bread, stuffing it in his mouth. Soggy with onion gravy, it tasted wonderful, but even as he swallowed, self-contempt seared him.

He had become a savage, grateful for scraps.

The same instant he thought this, he heard Orrade's dry voice in his head, correcting him. Instead of hating himself, he should reserve his contempt for the men who had driven him to this.

It was true. But logic did not fill his belly.

Ignoring any sailors who passed by, he ate everything he could, because he didn't know when he'd get to eat again.

'Best get below,' a familiar voice advised. He looked up to see Sionor, leaning over him. 'We're in for a bit of a blow.'

Garzik finally noticed the stiff breeze and activity as the sails were reduced. Nodding his thanks, he grabbed the tray and headed down to the galley. It took three trips to clear the captain's cabin, and by then, the pitch of the deck made scrubbing the pots and plates a challenge.

While Garzik worked, the cook secured the galley, putting everything away and banking down the brazier.

With the last pot scrubbed and secured, Garzik turned to find the cook watching him, and he did not like the glint in the man's eye.

'Surgeon Rishardt said he needs me,' Garzik lied.

'Be back before dawn.'

Garzik ducked past him, heading straight for the surgeon's cabin. He didn't feel safe until he'd closed the door and bolted it. The cabin was dark except for the glow of the brazier. By its light he spotted Rishardt fast asleep in his bunk, fully dressed with a bottle of wine in his arms.

Taking the bottle by the neck he tried to slip it free.

The surgeon woke instantly.

Garzik gestured to the bottle. 'I thought you might drop it.'

Rishardt released the wine.

After putting the bottle away, Garzik made sure everything was secure. The surgeon watched him.

Gesturing to the surgeon's chest, Garzik asked, 'do you want your nightshirt?'

Rishardt shook his head. 'If I'm going to drown, I don't want to drown in my nightshirt.'

Garzik blinked, not sure if the surgeon was joking.

'Go to sleep, Wynn. The ship's survived hundreds of storms.'

Yet the surgeon remained fully dressed.

Garzik curled up under the bench with a blanket. Although he was grateful for his bed, he did not look forward to spending the whole voyage at the cook's beck and call.

By dawn, the seas were so high the cook could not prepare a hot meal. Garzik was sent around with a basket of smoked meat, bread and cheese.

By midday, he, like everyone else, was holding on for dear life.

* * *

TWO DAYS OF being thrown around, sleeping wedged under the surgeon's bench, eating smoked meat and stale bread until that ran out. Two days of the men-at-arms and even sailors being sick. The smell was enough to turn Garzik's stomach, but he wasn't sick again, which was just as well because the surgeon found the wine and drank steadily. Then he threw up everything in his stomach until he was a trembling wreck.

In the middle of the second night someone banged on the surgeon's door. Garzik stumbled to his feet, lit the lamp and opened the door. Two sailors helped a third inside. They were all sopping wet, even with their seal-skin vests securely fastened. The middle one held his cap in place as blood poured down his face.

'A wave knocked Lleu off his feet,' a sailor explained. 'Gashed his head open.'

'Almost swept him overboard,' the other confirmed.

'I'm fine. Just fine,' Lleu insisted, when clearly he wasn't.

Rishardt ignored this. 'Strap him to the table.'

'No need for straps,' Lleu insisted. 'I won't flinch. I'll sit still.'

'No one can sit still in this,' the surgeon told him. 'You'll be strapped in or I'm not touching you.' The surgeon caught Garzik's hand, putting it on the sailor's head. 'Keep pressure on the wound.'

As they followed instructions, Rishardt gathered what he needed. This done, he sent the others off.

Garzik had to hold onto the bench and brace his legs against the pitch of the deck, but he kept the pressure on.

Meanwhile, the surgeon brought the lantern closer, hanging it from a hook. He propped a tray on the injured man's chest. 'Hold this.'

Garzik noticed it contained a needle and thread, much like the ones used on the sails, only smaller.

'I'm fine,' Lleu said, yet again.

The surgeon ignored him. He nodded to Garzik. 'Pull the cap off.'

As soon as he removed the sodden wool cap, dark blood welled from a wound that revealed the white of bone. The sight of the sailor's skull both fascinated and repelled Garzik.

Rishardt pressed a clean, folded cloth to the wound, once, twice. Each time he removed it the blood welled up again, but it was now clear that the wound was long and ragged, down to the bone, which had not cracked.

'Lucky for you, you have a hard skull,' he told Lleu. 'You'll need stitching. Another scar to impress the girls.'

The sailor nodded, or tried to. He faced away from them, securely strapped. The surgeon washed the wound with watered wine, then told Garzik to keep up the pressure, while he threaded needle.

But with the pitching and the way his hands shook, the surgeon couldn't manage it.

Without a word, Garzik pressed the pad to the injured man's head with his elbow then took the needle and thread from Rishardt.

He threaded the needle and offered it to the surgeon.

Rishardt went to take it, but his hands trembled.

They both glanced to the man's head. The pad that Garzik pressed to the wound had steadily darkened.

Rishardt swallowed and grimaced. He took the needle, but it was clear he'd do more harm than good with it. The surgeon glanced to the cupboard where he kept his wine.

Anger drove Garzik to take the needle.

For a heartbeat, he thought the surgeon would protest, then he nodded.

Garzik gulped. Although he'd watched their family healer sew up wounds, he didn't feel ready.

'You have to learn some time, Wynn. Might as well start now.'

So he found himself stitching the sailor's scalp. As long as he thought of it as a job, like a tailor or cobbler stitching cloth or leather, he could manage. Once the stitching was done, he bound the wound then called for the sailor's companions to help him to his bunk.

Garzik turned around to face Rishardt, who had sunk onto his bunk, head in his hands.

Now Garzik trembled.

Rishardt lifted his head. 'You did well.'

'What if it had been a broken bone?'

They both glanced to the cupboard where Rishardt kept his wine.

Almost of its own volition, the surgeon's hand moved to open the cupboard.

Garzik made a disgusted sound.

Rishardt flinched. Then he grimaced. 'If it offends you, get out. I'm sure the cook would welcome you.'

Disappointed, Garzik turned away, grabbed his blanket and left.

He felt his way down the passage to the store room and curled up amidst the sacks. Fine for tonight, but could he avoid the cook for the rest of the voyage?

THE NEXT DAY dawned fine, although the sea was still high. The cook fired up the stove and began to prepare a huge pot of beans. It seemed to be his speciality. He kept Garzik on the run, delivering food to the men-at-arms and then the captain's cabin.

After delivering the last tray, he had a few moments to himself. Once, he would have sought out the surgeon. Now he took this chance to stretch his legs on deck. A pale winter sun hung in a sky swept clean of clouds. After the danger of the storm, it was good to be alive.

But something felt odd. He shaded his eyes, searching the sea. 'Where's –'

'We've lost the fleet,' Sionor said. 'Blown off course.'

Nothing but sea in all directions.

Garzik searched the horizon. No sign of the other merchant ships or the sea-hounds that had protected them. 'How –'

'The storm tore the fleet apart. Captain's had the look-out searching for sails since dawn.'

Recalling tales of Utland raiders, Garzik gulped. 'Will we be safe?'

Sionor shrugged. 'She's a big sea and we're just one little ship.'

When Garzik returned below, he wanted to seek out Rishardt, but pride stopped him. Instead he went straight to the galley and began to scrub the pots. 'We've lost the fleet.'

The cook grunted.

'Sionor says we'll be all right, but the Utlanders –'

Thunk! The cook slammed the cleaver into the chopping board. 'Utlanders!' *Thunk. Thunk.*

Garzik grinned and the cook returned his smile, revealing three missing teeth.

They both turned at the sound of running feet, which came down the passage past them to report to the honour guard.

'Utlanders,' a voice announced. 'Lookout's spotted a sail.'

Shouts and thumps as the elite men-at-arms reached for their weapons. Garzik froze, listening.

'Keep scrubbing,' the cook snapped. 'Utlanders far off. See sails on...' He searched for the word, then gave up and pointed to the horizon.

'So they won't catch us?' Garzik asked, then frowned. 'I thought their ships were race horses compared to merchant plough horses?'

'Horses?'

'Faster.'

The cook nodded his understanding. 'Faster no help if can't see us.'

'So, as long as we can keep ahead of them until dusk, we can slip away in the dark?'

The cook nodded. 'That, or...' He picked up a heavy skillet and mimed hitting someone. They'd fight.

That evening, after he'd finished in the galley, Garzik went up on deck. It seemed everyone was there, watching the sea and cursing the clear sky. No clouds meant starlight bright enough to cast shadows, starlight that clearly revealed the ship to their pursuer, even though they'd doused all the lanterns.

Garzik wandered through the groups, listening to sailors and the honour guard. The sailors were fearful, the honour guard boastful and ready to prove their mettle.

'Sometimes they kill the whole crew, right down to the last man,' Sionor said.

'Sailors!' One of Neirn's honour guard spat his contempt.

Sionor stiffened. 'It's true.'

'If they kill the whole crew, how do you know this?' the elite man-at-arms demanded.

'Everyone knows it,' Sionor said and his companions nodded. 'Captured Utlanders boast of it even as we throw them overboard.'

Garzik flinched. If only they hadn't been separated from the sea-hounds. He searched the horizon, spotting the silhouetted sails against the frosting of stars.

'Surely they know the ship will be filled with returning men-at-arms?' Garzik muttered to himself.

'They know all right,' the surgeon said.

Garzik moved over for him. In the face of the Utland menace everything else seemed petty.

'But they also know the ship's hold will be filled with Rolencian treasure.'

'So they'll catch us?' Garzik asked.

'Maybe. Maybe not.' Rishardt grinned. There was no wine on his breath tonight. 'The night could cloud over. A fog could roll in.' He shrugged. 'If you believe in the gods, tonight's a good night to pray.'

'I don't know what I believe,' Garzik admitted.

'Only fools are certain.' The surgeon laughed grimly. 'Of that I'm certain.'

And Garzik laughed. Orrade would have liked the surgeon.

CHAPTER SEVEN

No FOG, NO clouds. The gods had abandoned them. All night they fled, but not fast enough to elude the sleek Utland vessel. Around midnight, the men began to sharpen weapons.

Despite the grinding of the whetstone, Garzik dozed, tucked under the surgeon's bench. But the soft sound of the surgeon's return woke him instantly.

Rishardt had pulled out a leather apron. He turned as he strapped it on and spotted Garzik watching him. 'It's time, Wynn. We need to prepare for the injured.'

Garzik rolled to his feet, telling himself it could not end this way for him. He had to get home, find Byren and become the courier for Mitrovan's messages.

He could not die here.

But the fact was – he just might.

Heart racing, he lit the lantern and hung it on its hook, while Rishardt laid out his tools: the saw, the scalpel, the needle and pads to sop up the blood. Tonight his hands trembled, but no more than Garzik's. He also removed a sword from his chest, a noble's sword, plus a dagger. Evidence of his past.

'How did you learn the surgeon's trade?'

'On the job, like you,' he admitted. 'There's not much to it. The greatest skill a surgeon can have is speed. Dreamless-sleep only dulls the pain. But most of the time, we can't get it. The Rolencian monks guard the secret of its production.'

A shout and running feet on the deck above made them both look up.

'Not long now, Wynn.' Rishardt clenched and unclenched his hands, but a fine tremor remained.

'Do you need a drink?' Garzik asked.

'Yes.' Rishardt gave a short, bitter laugh. 'But if I'm to die tonight, I'll die sober.'

Rhythmic chanting, interspersed with low drumming.

'The Utlanders.'

It was a hungry, impatient sound that made Garzik's stomach cramp. He wondered if he had time to run to the jakes. He didn't want to disgrace himself.

'It'll be easier once it starts,' the surgeon told him.

'Why?'

'No time to think.'

A roar. Raggedly defiant shouting. Several separate distinct thumps.

'Utlanders swinging across to land on our deck.' Rishardt had to raise his voice over the shouting and the clatter of metal on metal.

'How many times have you survived an –'

'Twice.'

'Third time lucky?'

'Let's hope.'

They shared a look. The surgeon's eyes were particularly alert tonight. But then every detail seemed sharp to Garzik, from the smell of the surgeon's few herbals, to the way the lamplight glinted on the expensive sword and dagger.

Shouting, screams, thumps and the constant scrape of metal on metal.

'They'll be bringing the worst of the injured down soon,' Rishardt said.

Garzik prepared himself for blood, lots of it, as they both looked up at the ceiling.

'Was she worth it?' the question just slipped out.

Rhisardt glanced to him.

'The one you fought the duel –'

'I know who you mean.' A particularly despairing scream made them both glance up. The fighting continued. 'Yes, she was worth it. He beat her. With his death, I set her free. She never married again. I don't care what it cost me. What about you?'

Garzik hesitated.

Running feet down the passage. Shouts. More running feet. Cries. The clank of metal.

'They've broken through.' Rishardt grabbed his sword. 'Take the dagger.' Garzik moved behind him to grab it.

The door swung open. Over Rishardt's shoulder he saw a wild man. Blood covered his chest, matted his beard and poured from his head where his ear was missing. Despite the cold the Utlander was almost naked. All this Garzik saw in a flash.

The surgeon leapt forward, driving the blade past the Utlander's hasty block. Somehow, the one-eared man side-stepped, avoiding the strike. Rishardt's sword tip buried itself in the wood of the door jamb.

As he struggled to pull the blade free, Garzik heard the roar of the cook and a man's screams.

The Utlander pulled back his arm to drive his sword into the surgeon's back. Garzik dove in, dagger lifted to spear up under the Utlander's ribs.

At the same instant Rishardt freed the sword and spun, blade lifted. Again the Utlander seemed to anticipate him, darting away. Everything slowed. Garzik had time to realise Rishardt's sword arc was aimed right for his head.

The surgeon's eyes widened in surprise. He tried to pull the strike. At the same instant, the Utlander struck, his blade sliding between the surgeon's ribs like a hot knife through butter.

Rhisardt lost his grip on his sword, but it continued its arc. The Utlander's hand shot out, shoving Garzik off his feet. The sword missed the top of his head.

Garzik flew sideways, struck the bench and had the air knocked out of him. He slid to the floor.

Rhisardt lay nearby in an ever widening pool of blood, gasping, pink bubbles on his lips.

Garzik dragged a breath into his aching chest and raised his hands only to discover he'd lost the dagger. The one-eared Utlander stepped over the surgeon to crouch in front of Garzik, who scuttled back until he was wedged between the bunk and the wall.

The Utlander kept coming, watching his face, bloodied sword ready to skewer him.

'Why?' Garzik whispered. 'Why save me, when you mean to kill me?'

The Utlander pressed the blade to Garzik' neck, tilting his face, watching him wince as the tip dug in to the place where his neck met his jaw and ear.

Very deliberately, the Utlander reached out, took Garzik's ear in his hand and moved so fast...

Garzik didn't understand what had happened until the Utlander held his bleeding ear between them. With a cry, Garzik covered the open wound, pressing hard, as Rishardt had taught him. Now it stung like fire.

The Utlander mimed eating his ear.

Garzik lurched forward to empty his stomach. His tormentor side-stepped the vomit.

As he retched, Garzik heard a sharp voice from the doorway. He was aware of the one-eared Utlander rising, his answer slow and mocking.

Wiping tears from his eyes, Garzik spotted a big Utlander who had to be as tall as Byren. He gestured to One-ear to get out. The Utlander collected Rishardt's sword and dagger as his prizes then left. As he went through the door, the big Utlander delivered a thump for good measure.

Garzik had seen Captain Blackwing do the same thing with his men. Sometimes they needed a thump to keep them in line.

The big Utlander met Garzik's eyes, then swung the door shut, leaving him there on the floor in a pool of vomit and blood.

For five heartbeats he did not move as he tried to make sense of what had just happened. Then he gave up and crawled over to Rishardt, but the surgeon was already dead. Judging by the wound, nothing could have saved him.

His burning ear drove Garzik to stand. He didn't know why he still lived, but he needed to bind his head. Methodically, he washed the wound, wincing when the watered wine stung, then placed a pad over where his ear had been and wound a bandage around it.

He could still hear out of the other ear. From above he heard the occasional shout, striding feet and dragging sounds. But now the shouts didn't hold threat, they sounded like men going about their job. He even heard laughter.

Footsteps came along the passage. Garzik straightened. The door swung inward and Trafyn stumbled in. He tripped over the surgeon's body, falling on his hands and knees in the vomit and blood with a cry of distaste.

An Utlander followed him, carrying someone over his shoulder. He tipped the body onto the bench. Isfyl groaned but did not wake. Garzik could see no wound on him. Must be a head blow. He knew how that felt.

Even as he thought this, the Utlander grabbed Rishardt's legs and began to drag him out the door.

'What're you doing with him?' Garzik asked. His voice sounded funny, everything sounded strange.

The Utlander said something derogatory by the tone, but the words were in the strange Utland tongue. The Utlander swung Rishardt's body over his shoulder and closed the door.

For a moment Garzik considered checking the door to see if it was locked, but the Utlanders obviously had the run of the ship, so escaping the cabin made no difference.

'Disgusting.' Trafyn muttered in Merofynian, as he came to his feet and tried to wipe his hands and knees clean of blood and vomit. Noticing Garzik, he switched to Rolencian, gesturing to the floor. 'You, clean this up.'

Garzik ignored him. Going over to where Isfyl lay on the bench, he straightened his limbs, then strapped him in so he wouldn't roll off. This done, he checked him for injuries. There was a swelling on the back of his head, but the skin hadn't broken.

Trafyn watched dubiously.

Isfyl rolled his head away from Garzik's hands with a groan. His eyes fluttered open. 'Who're you?'

Garzik almost answered, then remembered he wasn't supposed to understand Merofynian, then wondered if there was any point keeping up the pretence.

Trafyn pushed past him. 'He's the cook's seven-year-slave.'

Again Garzik was tempted to correct him, but it might still be to his advantage to hide his proficiency with the Merofynian language, so he held his tongue.

Isfyl ignored Garzik. 'What happened?' He tried to sit up and discovered he was strapped down. 'Why... what?'

'Set him free,' Trafyn ordered in Rolencian. He could just as easily have done it himself.

Nevertheless, Garzik went around the bench, undoing the buckles while the two squires spoke.

'The last I remember is the honour guard breaking,' Isfyl said.

Trafyn nodded. 'When they broke, the Utlanders swept past. Four of them tackled Lord Neirn. He fought like a cornered leogryf, but there were too many of them. He went down roaring defiance. I didn't see when you were knocked out. They brought us down here.'

Garzik noted he wasn't wounded. Since it was hard to avoid walking through the pool of blood and vomit in the small cabin, he mopped it up, but he couldn't empty the bucket.

A scream, cut off by a splash made him look up. He realised he'd been hearing splashes for a while now.

'They're throwing the crew overboard, the living as well as the dead,' Isfyl said in Merofynian. 'Even if they can swim, the cold will kill them quickly.'

Trafyn shuddered as another scream was abruptly cut off. Garzik was glad Rishardt hadn't been alive when they threw him over.

Tears stung his eyes. He blinked them away.

Odd... When he found his father dead, if someone had told him he would mourn a Merofynian's death, he wouldn't have believed them.

'Why are we still alive?' Trafyn whispered.

Isfyl gestured to Garzik. 'Utlanders need slaves, too. We're young and healthy.'

'We're to be slaves?' Trafyn repeated, dismayed.

Both squires glanced to Garzik, who pretended he didn't understand.

'Don't worry. We won't stay slaves. We're noble born. The Utlanders can ransom us.'

As footsteps approached down the passage they all turned to the door. An Utlander opened it and barked a command at them, accompanying it with an exaggerated beckoning gesture.

Trafyn looked to Isfyl, who swung his legs to the floor. He hesitated as if dizzy. Remembering how he'd felt when he came around, Garzik was tempted to help him.

Impatient, the Utlander gestured for Trafyn to help Isfyl to his feet. They negotiated the door, with Garzik following them. He told himself Isfyl was right. They would be kept for slaves. There was no point throwing them overboard, not after they'd deliberately preserved their lives. An Utlander stepped in behind them with a lantern.

Up on deck they found no sign of the old crew, but the middeck was lit up like festival night and crowded with Utlanders. How did they fit so many men on their ship?

A steady stream of Utlanders carried Rolencian war booty across the deck and tossed it down onto their ship. Rather than being told to climb down to the other ship, Garzik and the two squires were driven to one side and made to understand they were to sit.

A quick glance told Garzik the second ship had been lashed to the first. She was lower and smaller, built narrow and lean.

As two Utlanders rolled a barrel of wine across the deck and sent it to the Utland ship, Garzik searched for the one-eared Utlander, but didn't spot him. It was hard to tell them apart, with their beards, long wild hair and the witchy Utlander eyes. Garzik had only heard this spoken of, but now he saw it in face after face. All the Utlanders had it to some degree, a pale circle around the pupil of the eye. They all wore breeches and had bare feet. Many went bare chested. All bristled with weapons. Only one wore a cloak made of wyvern hide, the scales glinting in the lamp light.

'What's going on?' Trafyn whispered, indicating the high rear deck where half a dozen Utlanders stood in a way that suggested something formal. The one who wore the wyvern cloak was obviously in charge. Threaded through his plaited beard were wicked-looking wyvern teeth.

'Rewarding a brave man-at-arms?' Isfyl suggested. Both squires spoke Merofynian and made no attempt to include Garzik in their conversation.

The big one who'd told One-ear to leave Garzik alone stood next to an Utlander of average size. The one wearing the wyvern cloak embraced the strong-arm's friend and made an announcement. Everyone on the middeck cheered.

Then the crew separated, with about a third choosing to remain on the captured Merofynian ship.

The rest returned to the Utland vessel, trouping past Garzik and the two squires. Last to go was the captain, who said something to the newly-made captain, shared a laugh and went to leave.

He noticed Garzik and the others, ran his eye over them then pointed to Isfyl and beckoned.

Trafyn reached for the older squire. Isfyl squeezed his arm. 'Don't worry. We'll be ransomed.'

He came to his feet, staggering a little, still dizzy from the head wound. After Isfyl climbed over the side, Trafyn wiped his face surreptitiously. Garzik pretended not to notice.

With shouted comments and jests, the Utlanders released the ropes and the two ships separated, but did not part. They matched sails and course.

Meanwhile, the new captain said something. His crew cheered, slapping their swords on their shields in a rapid tattoo. This had been the drumming Garzik heard before the attack.

With much laughter and jesting, the Utlanders opened wine bottles and passed them around. The new captain came down from the rear deck. He was followed by the big one, Strong-arm, who opened several chests. The captain pulled out a silk shirt and stripped off his own bloodstained vest.

'That's Lord Neirn's chest,' Trafyn muttered indignantly, as the new captain draped himself in Neirn's finest velvets and strutted about. Recalling who he spoke to, Trafyn repeated himself in Rolencian.

The Utlanders broke open the food stores, passing around smoked meat, last year's apples, preserved peaches, dried fruit and nuts. Garzik's stomach rumbled. The Utlanders drank, ate, sang and cheered while Captain Strutter distributed golden necklaces, jewelled pendants, rings, hair combs and more. This done Strutter pulled out some pipes and played a tune that got everyone singing.

'They should feed us,' Trafyn complained, then brightened. 'Here comes someone now.'

It was One-ear, and he carried wine, not food. Garzik frowned.

One-ear assessed them swiftly. Garzik looked away. But One-ear's gaze settled on Trafyn. He grabbed the lad by the shoulder, pulled him to his feet and offered him wine.

Trafyn took a mouthful, then returned it. 'I'm hungry. I want –'

One-ear caught him, tilted his head back and poured wine down his throat.

Garzik fought the instinct to protest. After all, what could he do for Trafyn? Rising to his knees, he peered over the side of the ship. The Utland vessel was less than a bowshot away. On its lower deck, he spotted Isfyl being forced to drink wine.

Since when did they give slaves wine to share in a celebration?

Shrinking down, he edged back between the bales, but he'd been seen. One of the Utlanders hauled him out and thrust a wine bottle into his hand.

'Drink, I know.' To save himself the indignity of being force-fed, he took a big mouthful. It wasn't enough to satisfy the Utlander, who urged him on. By the time Garzik had downed half the bottle, his head spun and he staggered. Pleased, the Utlander took the bottle from him and dragged him over to his friends. He heard Trafyn's protest. The squire's words cut out on a gasp.

When the Utlander deposited him on the deck, Garzik staggered. Hands steadied him. The next thing he knew hands tugged at his breeches. He tried to stop them. Tried to protest, but when he opened his mouth, they poured more wine down his throat.

Coughing and spluttering, he found himself on his knees. Tears of fury stung his eyes.

Why couldn't Neirn have lived? It would serve him right. Serve Isfyl and Trafyn right. But him...

He'd never even kissed a girl. His head spun and he blacked out.

He surfaced several more times, only to find he was being passed around. When they thrust the wine in his hands, he gulped it down. Eventually, he sank into oblivion.

CHAPTER EIGHT

GARZIK WOKE TO a pounding behind his temples, a fierce need to urinate and a throbbing on one side of his head. The world sounded strange and it took him a moment to remember his missing ear, now covered by a bandage. His legs were warm, but his shoulders cold. Why was he naked? Why were hairy thighs pressed against his legs?

He sat up, wincing as he took weight on his buttocks. It all came back to him.

His gorge rose. No time to look for his breeches.

He made for the side at a run and emptied his stomach. Just up from him, Trafyn was doing the same, only he sounded like he was never going to stop.

Garzik felt a pang of sympathy for the squire as Trafyn hung over the side, wearing only his thigh-length undershirt.

Which reminded him, he must find his own breeches.

Garzik relieved himself down-wind, then turned around. The deck was covered in Utlanders sprawled in various states of undress, some wrapped in sleeping furs, some stark naked despite the cold. They ranged from lads his age to men like Captain Blackwing, forty perhaps. No white-haired old men. He suspected you didn't grow old on the Utland Isles. Man and boy alike, they'd drunk themselves into a stupor. That triggered a memory of the Utland lads being used last night, same as him and Trafyn. What had he landed himself in?

If only a sea-hound ship could find them now.

For a heartbeat he indulged himself, imagining how the sea-hounds would cut a swathe through the naked, vulnerable Utlanders and retake the ship.

He searched the horizon. This was a merchant ship, not a sleek Utland vessel. It would never be able to escape a sea-hound ship. The new captain was taking a risk commandeering this vessel.

Unfortunately, there was no sign of the fleet and its sea-hound protectors. The only sail in sight was the original Utland vessel, which had drawn closer during the night until there was only a gap of about four body lengths between them.

A shouted command made him turn to see Strong-arm going about the deck, kicking a man here, grabbing a man there. All the while, he repeated a string of words over and over – the Utland equivalent of *Get up you lazy, bastards*, Garzik guessed.

With only a vague idea where he'd started out, Garzik began to sift through discarded clothes for his breeches. As he did, flashes of last night came back to him and his gorge rose again. How could he go home after this? The shame...

He should just end it all. Throw himself overboard. Isfyl had said death would be quick in the cold, cold sea.

But he couldn't. Only he knew about Mitrovan and the scribe's information might be crucial to Byren. Conviction filled Garzik. No matter what, he had to endure.

Tears burned his eyes but he knew he'd made the right... the *only* decision. Turning away from the deck, he blinked fiercely to clear his vision.

On the deck of the lower Utland vessel he saw Isfyl stagger to his feet. From the look of him, he no longer felt so cocky about raping three Rolencian maids in one night.

Serve him right.

Like Garzik a moment before, Isfyl staggered to the rail and vomited. When he was done he looked up and across the gap.

Their eyes met.

Garzik raised a hand. He expected a response – after all, they were in this together – but Isfyl did not acknowledge him. The older squire tilted his head up to the midmorning sky and closed his eyes. Was he praying?

When he lowered his chin, his face was curiously calm.

Garzik envied Isfyl his composure. Despite his own decision to live to serve

Byren, he flipped back and forth between shamed outrage and numb misery.

Trafyn waved to Isfyl, drawing Garzik's gaze to the younger squire. Garzik glanced back to Isfyl, but the older squire didn't acknowledge Trafyn, either.

Instead, Isfyl climbed up on the rail, holding onto the rigging.

Trafyn ran along to join Garzik. 'What's he doing?'

'Ending his shame,' Garzik guessed. He'd only just rejected the same idea. Now that he was close to Trafyn, he registered the bruises on his neck and arms, and down his thighs.

So far, no-one on the other ship had noticed Isfyl. But as Garzik turned back, there was a shout and an Utlander made for the squire.

Too late. Isfyl stepped out and down, dropping into the sea with a splash. The ship sailed on, ploughing through the waves.

Garzik leant over and looked back, searching for Isfyl, expecting him to surface.

But there was no sign of the older squire. His head didn't bob in the waves in their spreading wake.

'He couldn't swim,' Garzik whispered.

With a moan Trafyn turned around and sank down, his back pressed to the gunwales. He hugged his knees, staring dully at his feet. 'I'm a coward. I'm a coward...' He repeated over and over. 'I'm without honour.'

Garzik felt his misery.

'Dying is easy,' Garzik told him. 'But there's more honour in surviving to serve your king.'

Trafyn blinked up at him, tear tracks on his dirty cheeks. For a heartbeat he did not react, then anger sharpened his features. 'You speak Merofynian!'

Garzik blinked.

'You filthy...' Trafyn sprang to his feet, leaping for him. The collision drove them both backwards. Garzik tripped over a sleeper's legs, falling to the deck with Trafyn on top him. The impact drove the air from his chest in a painful gasp.

While sitting across Garzik's chest, Trafyn grabbed two handfuls of his hair and used them to thump Garzik's head on the deck over and over. 'Filthy Rolencian. Filthy...'

Utlander laughter rang in Garzik's ears as his head pounded with each impact and he fought to force air into his chest, fought against Trafyn's weight. Pin pricks of light spun in his vision.

Then as suddenly as it started, it stopped and he could breathe.

Strong-arm stood over him, holding Trafyn by his shirt. The Utlander was so big he held the squire off the ground like a kitten.

Strong-arm said something; the gathered Utlanders laughed.

The big Utlander gave Trafyn another shake for emphasis, then tossed the squire aside.

Garzik scuttled back, got his feet under him and sprang upright, half expecting Trafyn to attack him again.

Why couldn't the squire see they had to work together?

Strong-arm seemed to be saying something to that effect as he gestured to each of them and spoke a stream of Utlander.

Garzik had no idea what he'd said, and Trafyn looked just as lost. Meanwhile, Garzik's missing ear was throbbing worse than ever and he felt the bandage. His fingers came away smeared with blood. Great, he was bleeding again, thanks to Trafyn.

Strong-arm gestured to another Utlander who led them off, and pointed them in the direction of a bucket and scrubbing brushes. The middeck still bore evidence of the attack and subsequent celebration. Clearly they were supposed to clean the deck.

Garzik repeated the phrase Strong-arm had used just to be sure and got a clip over his good ear for his trouble. He didn't care. He'd found it useful to understand his Merofynian captors. Now that he was an Utlander captive, he had to learn their language.

'My breeches!' Trafyn darted over to collect his pants and pulled them on.

Garzik looked for his breeches, spotted them and did likewise. Then they both got down to work. Garzik's skin had grown mottled with cold, but the scrubbing soon warmed him. He concentrated on the action of scrubbing to distance himself from the pain of his missing ear.

'You spoke Merofynian all the time. What were you doing?' Trafyn demanded under his breath. 'Spying for Rolencia?'

'Many Rolencians speak Merofynian.'

'Like a noble?'

Garzik shrugged.

'You were sent to spy –'

'I saw my father killed before they knocked me out. For the first couple of days I didn't know who I was. No-one sent me.' It was a self-appointed task.

'I don't believe you. When we get out of this, I'm going to tell my father. You'll be executed!'

'Who says we'll get out of this?' Garzik countered, even though he had every intention of making it back to Rolencia. Baiting Trafyn helped distract him from the throbbing pain.

'My father's Lord Travany. He'll gladly pay my ransom. Just as soon as I can make myself understood, I'll –'

He grunted in pain as a passing Utlander kicked him in the ribs and said something that might have been *Less talking, more working*.

Garzik thought he recognised a couple of the words. He definitely recognised the voice, as the ache where his ear had been became more intense. One-ear leered down at them. Garzik looked away quickly

Unlike Trafyn, who sat on his heels to rub his ribs and complain. 'I shouldn't be scrubbing decks. I'm the son of a lord. I –'

'Shut up,' Garzik hissed and tossed the second scrubbing brush into his lap. Trafyn caught it automatically. 'Don't talk back. That one's crazy. He cut off my ear and threatened to eat it.'

Trafyn looked up in horror.

One-ear grinned and licked his lips. Without another word, the squire went back to work.

Garzik glanced to the surgeon's sword and dagger. A man like One-ear shouldn't have them. The Utlander saw the direction of his gaze and caressed the sword's hilt.

'Jost,' Strong-arm called him away.

It was only as one-eared Jost walked off that Garzik realised the Utlander had understood enough Merofynian to get the gist of what he'd said.

Or had he gestured to his missing ear? He couldn't remember now.

At least the work had warmed him. But even after his run-in with One-ear, he was hungry. He suspected the Utlanders would not treat their slaves well. According to Captain Blackwing, life was brutal on the scattered Utland Isles.

He felt a pang of loss. In some ways, that quiet, firm man-at-arms had been more of a father to him than his own father, who had been over sixty when he was born.

To think, he'd gone from lord's son, to captive of war, to Merofynian seven-year-slave, to this... an Utland slave. Surely, he could sink no lower.

As Trafyn bemoaned their bad luck, Garzik asked himself what Orrade would do. His brother would not sink into self-pity. No, he'd be watching, learning his enemy's strengths and weaknesses, learning their language. Orrade would be ready to seize any opportunity to escape.

So that's what Garzik would do.

MIDMORNING, TWO DAYS later they spotted a patch of jagged rocks, skirted by foaming sea. Several dark specks circled high above the rocks.

'A wyvern eyrie,' Garzik guessed, even though he had only ever heard of them.

No sane sailor went near a wyvern eyrie, especially in spring. They were past midwinter, but not into breeding season yet. This time of year the saltwater wyverns would be sluggish, conserving their strength. Blessed, or cursed, with an affinity for power, these beasts were smarter than ordinary animals, hence the circling lookouts.

Garzik studied the direction of travel. 'Why would the captain take his ship into danger?'

'What?' Trafyn had been staring dully at his toes, as he huddled out of the wind.

'See.' Garzik pointed. 'A wyvern eyrie.'

Trafyn sprang to his feet and sighted along his arm. He took a step back. 'The captain's mad. We'll all be killed.'

Garzik ignored him; the Utlanders had lowered the merchant vessel's sails and strapped the wheel. Now the ship wallowed in the wave troughs.

With some shouted words that sounded like encouragement, the original Utland ship changed course. It pulled away, but kept Garzik's ship in sight.

A rough voice called to Garzik and Trafyn. Garzik turned, but not fast enough as Jost clipped him over his head and grabbed him along with Trafyn. Eyes stinging with pain, Garzik blinked to clear his vision. The one-eared Utlander led them over to Strong-arm, who stood next to the main mast holding a rope.

Trafyn tried to hang back.

Jost thrust him forward into Strong-arm's chest. The big Utlander shoved Trafyn up against the far side of the mast.

'What are you doing?' Garzik asked, rising voice betraying his fear.

No-one answered him. Instead, Jost shoved him until his back was pressed to this side of the mast and, between them, Jost and Strong-arm quickly bound them to the mast.

Once that was done, Jost left and Strong-arm tugged at the binding over Garzik's missing ear, removing it with a flourish. It stung something awful as the padding peeled away. Had it started bleeding again?

Blinking back tears of pain, Garzik discovered that almost all the Utlanders had left the deck. He spotted them watching through the windows of the captain's cabin. Out of that cabin came Captain Strutter. Barefoot and bare-chested, wearing nothing but his breeches, he was armed only with a dagger and sword.

Squawking made Garzik strain to peer around the mast in the other direction. Jost had brought two chickens up from the store. With a practiced flick, he chopped off their heads, swinging them by their legs so that their blood sprayed across the deck.

'What is he doing?' Trafyn's voice was high and breathy with panic.

Garzik didn't answer. Looking up, he spotted a wyvern circling far above. They had excellent eyesight and sense of smell.

Leaving the chicken carcasses, Jost retreated to the cabin.

Strong-arm looked up, said something to the new captain.

Strutter grinned, slapped him on the back and sent him off.

'Tell me he's not going to try to kill a wyvern on his own?' Trafyn muttered.

'Didn't you notice the captain of the other ship wore a wyvern cloak and there were wyvern teeth woven into his beard?' Garzik asked. 'I'm guessing it's a rite of passage, and we're bait.'

At this Trafyn shouted, pleading to be set free. He tugged and strained on the ropes, making the bindings constrict around Garzik.

Meanwhile, Captain Strutter, armed only with his dagger and sword, retreated to crouch under the steep steps to the rear deck.

'Shut up, you'll attract a wyvern,' Garzik warned. 'Shut up, I tell you.'

But Trafyn was beyond reason.

Garzik glanced to the Utlanders in the cabin. They nudged each other, much entertained by Trafyn's antics.

Garzik wanted to thump the squire.

Where was that Wyvern? He looked up. No sign of it. Perhaps...

A downbeat of air, then a thump as something heavy hit the deck. Trafyn went utterly silent, except for his ragged breathing.

Garzik tried to peer around the mast to the other side of the deck. A long scaled tail came into view. It curled delicately, reminding him of a cat investigating something. He heard snuffling and a low growl. He smelled... serpent.

Looking the other way, he saw the Utlanders watching through the windows, utterly transfixed. Captain Strutter came out from under the steps, moving silently on bare feet.

How was he going to tackle the wyvern? Their scales deflected blades. Their weak spots were the throat, under the jaw and in the joints where the limbs met the body.

A whimper came from Trafyn.

Garzik did not blame the squire. Even on the other side of the mast, he was terrified.

Straining against the ropes, he tried to peer around the far side of the mast and was in time to see the tail disappear and the tip of a half-open wing appear, growing closer. The wyvern had noticed Trafyn.

No sound but for the wind whistling through the ropes.

Garzik strained to hear.

Trafyn screamed once, sharply.

Garzik tried to see around the mast. He could hear Trafyn whispering over and over. 'Kill it, kill it.'

The beast howled.

The tail whipped past Garzik's face, caught him a blow across the chest, scales tearing through his shirt and drawing blood. He was already pressed back as far as he could go against the mast.

The wyvern came rolling past, writhing as it tried to dislodge Strutter from its back. When this ploy failed, the wyvern sprang to its feet with agility of a cat, rather than the lizard it resembled.

Despite this, Strutter clung one-handed to the beast's back. How...

He clung to his dagger, which was buried hilt-deep where the wyvern's shoulder met its neck, but it wasn't enough to kill it.

Wings flexing and contracting, tail lashing, the wyvern threw back its head and screamed in frustration. This was exactly what Strutter was waiting for. He swung the sword around, driving it through the wyvern's thick neck from one side to the other, then pulled the blade forward, taking out the beast's throat.

Hot blood sprayed the deck, sprayed Garzik, hitting his eyes, landing in his open, gasping mouth. He shuddered and spat, trying to rid himself of the Affinity that the beast's blood carried.

As for the wyvern, its cry ended in a gargle of bubbling blood. Strutter held on, riding the beast as it bled out, then stepping off its back like he was dismounting from a horse.

His cocky expression astounded Garzik. It had been a planned attack. Sure there had been danger, but the Utland captain knew what he was doing.

Strutter's crew poured out of the cabin, cheering and shouting his name. *Rusan, Rusan, Rusan!*

Strong-arm clapped Captain Rusan on the back and they hugged, laughing. Seeing them together, reminded Garzik of Byren and Orrade, warrior brothers, one big and the other thin and wiry. Only their positions were reversed, with the smaller one being the leader.

Amongst the Utlanders, who valued strength, Captain Rusan had to have more than brute strength to keep them in line, and now he'd proven it by killing the wyvern.

The Utlanders broke open the wine, laughing and congratulating Rusan. Meanwhile, Garzik and Trafyn were untied and directed to help in the butchering. Trafyn shook so badly, he was useless.

Garzik had butchered enough beasts, Affinity or otherwise, to know what needed to be done, and he assisted the four Utlanders. Soon they were elbow deep in gore.

All the while, he kept waiting for someone to settle the beast's Affinity, but no one came forward to do this.

Back home, if Affinity beasts came down from the mountains and terrorised his father's people, they were hunted and killed. When this happened, one of the family's priests said the words to return the beasts' innate power to the earth.

Here, the Utlanders skinned the wyvern, plucked its teeth from its jaws, cut prime chunks from its body and set about sawing the horns from its skull. It was an adult male with broad horns set on a bony brow ridge, so this was no easy task.

As he worked, Garzik kept his face turned away and tried not to inhale, but he knew he had to be absorbing Affinity through his skin, even if he couldn't feel it.

He'd been tested as a child and had proven blind to Affinity. Just as well, if he'd had innate Affinity he would have been sent to serve the abbey. According to King Rolen, a kinship for power left the bearer open to evil.

Garzik wasn't sure if exposure to power could trigger Affinity. Maybe you had to be susceptible. He had heard stories of people developing Affinity later in life, and having to leave their families, but didn't know what triggered it.

Now that he thought about it, there was a lot he didn't know.

But he did know this much – unadulterated Affinity affected people, even if they were blind to it. The Utlanders had all gone a little crazed as they whooped and shouted, dancing about the deck. Even he felt light headed and excited for no reason.

Well, not for no reason. He had survived the wyvern attack. The thought made him laugh and he stopped himself immediately. Cheeks hot, he glanced around, but no one was looking at him. In fact, everyone behaved the same way, laughing and carrying on as if they were drunk.

At some point, the second ship had returned and Strong-arm went to the side to toss prized cuts of wyvern across to the other deck.

By evening, the meat was cooked and the Utlanders passed seared, bloody chunks around. They tore into it, grease dripping down their chins, and Garzik's stomach grumbled fiercely.

One Utlander appeared to be retelling the story of Captain Rusan's triumph, complete with actions, while another accompanied him with music.

'They're eating meat tainted with Affinity,' Trafyn muttered. 'Don't they know any better?'

Garzik recalled something Byren's old nurse had said, something about people who ate unclean Affinity meat and how it showed in their faces. Maybe the Utlanders weren't really a different type of people. Maybe they only looked different because their food was tainted with Affinity and that was what gave them the witchy look around the eyes.

Strong-arm sauntered over, said something that was half jest, half mocking, and tossed them a bone with enough meat on it to make a decent meal.

'Bet you he's thanking us for being bait,' Garzik muttered.

Trafyn snorted and folded his arms as he turned his face away.

Garzik kicked the meat far from them before he could be tempted.

Strong-arm shook his head, shrugged and returned to his place by Strutter's side.

The meat remained on the deck. Garzik was so hungry. That meat smelled better than anything he'd ever eaten. But neither he nor Trafyn moved to touch it.

'Eh, Olbin?' one of the Utlanders called.

Strong-arm turned.

The Utlander said something, gesturing to the meat then to Garzik and Trafyn

The big Utlander, Olbin, said something.

They all laughed uproariously. Garzik's face burned.

'If they think I'm going to eat unclean Affinity meat...' Trafyn muttered. 'We could never go home.'

'I don't think one meal would make a difference,' Garzik said. 'I think it has to be eaten repeatedly to cause the changes you see in the Utlanders.'

Trafyn glanced to him.

He met the squire's eyes.

Trafyn crawled over and retrieved the bone. He returned to Garzik's side, teeth tearing into the meat.

This close the smell made Garzik's stomach knot with hunger. Before he could weaken, two Utlanders came towards them bringing wine.

Garzik swore softly under his breath. They'd been left alone the last couple of nights, sleeping together for warmth because the crazy Utlanders slept on deck, under their furs when there were perfectly good cabins with braziers.

Trafyn made a panicky sound under his breath.

'Drink lots of wine,' Garzik advised, planning to take his own advice. 'Pass out.'

One thing could be said for the Utlanders, they were generous with the wine. This time he kept his wits about him. It wasn't just him and Trafyn who were used this way. And it wasn't everyone who joined in. And, when one of the other lads had had enough, they left him alone.

For the Utlanders, it was just part of ship life.

CHAPTER NINE

FOR DAYS, THE two ships searched the trade routes, on the lookout for lone merchant ships journeying between the twin isles of Rolencia and Merofynia or their more distant neighbour, Ostron Isle.

Several times they spotted sails. Each time Captain Rusan studied their prey through the farseer. Each time the two ships slipped away, hiding below the horizon, accompanied by grumbling from the Utland sailors.

'Why don't they attack?' Trafyn complained. 'Maybe we could escape.'

'They're not going to attack a convoy protected by sea-hounds. They're not going to attack unless they have a good chance of success. Captain Rusan's no fool.'

Trafyn narrowed his eyes. 'You almost sound like you admire him!'

Garzik shook his head, but if he was honest, he did admire Rusan and Olbin. They made a good team. Like Byren and Orrade. That didn't mean he liked them.

Dusk, three days later, the lookout spotted a lone Merofynian merchant ship unlucky enough, or foolish enough, to be caught without an escort. To disguise the Utland vessel's distinctive sail profile the raiders approached at dusk from the direction of the setting sun and manoeuvred their original vessel behind the captured Merofynian vessel.

The Merofynian ship made no attempt to escape and no preparation for battle. If anything they were pleased to see another of their countrymen on the dangerous sea. Safety in numbers.

'Filthy Utland savages,' Trafyn muttered. He glanced about wildly. 'How can I warn them?'

'You won't have to. Every ship carries a farseer. Captain Rusan's trusting to the twilight to hide his crew, but soon the other captain will recognise his sailors for Utlanders,' Garzik said. 'It's only a matter of time.'

And it was, but by the time the other ship realised the merchant vessel was not manned by Merofynians, the two Utland ships were too close to avoid. Even as their prey hoisted more sail and tried to escape, the Utlanders cheered and jeered, and their sleek hunting vessel gave pursuit.

Without warning, Jost grabbed Garzik and Trafyn, dragged them to the main mast and tied them up. Jost laughed at Trafyn's expression. As the two Utland ships closed in, the Utland chanting and thud of weapons on shields made Garzik's stomach knot with fear.

The Merofynian ship did not stand a chance.

With cries and jeers, the Utlanders made fast to the merchant vessel. Garzik developed a kink in his neck from trying to peer over his shoulder to watch the attack unfold. Jost had tied them up so that Trafyn was on the mast side facing the attack. Trapped between two ships, the Merofynian crew were quickly overcome.

Just as before, the dead and injured were thrown overboard, and the spoils divided. At this point, Garzik stopped watching.

If the other ship carried a cabin boy or kitchen boy, Garzik did not see him. Presumably, he was sent to the original Utland ship to replace Isfyl.

Then the Utlanders set the merchant vessel adrift and aflame. As the ship fell away behind them, the two Utlander vessels divided the spoils.

Trafyn cursed under his breath.

'What is it?'

'The one-eared Utlander's coming to untie us. And he's bringing wine.'

Garzik gulped down a surge of panic and put what he'd learnt last time to the test. While Trafyn sucked back the wine at every opportunity, he didn't. When the celebrating got to the next stage, Trafyn was in no state to refuse.

There were plenty who were willing to oblige, which made it easy for Garzik to avoid the clumsy reaching hands. No one seemed to care when he drifted over to where Rusan played his pipes. Half a dozen Utlanders sang along with him.

Garzik crouched just outside their circle, wrapped a fur around him and listened.

*   *   *

THE NEXT MORNING the two ships returned to their search pattern. Days passed. Garzik realised he should have been keeping a tally. The Utland captains successfully attacked two more ships. Each time, Garzik avoided the celebrations. He tried to convince Trafyn he could avoid it too, but the squire seemed to prefer to get drunk.

And then, one morning, they turned north and kept on that heading. By dusk of the second day Garzik was sure.

'The Utlanders are headed home,' he told Trafyn.

'How do you know?' The squire frowned. 'And why are you so pleased? They're taking us further away from our home.'

'True, but once they've unloaded we'll head south again. Maybe the ship will be taken by sea-hounds, who'll set us free.' And, although he wasn't about to admit it to Trafyn, he was curious about the Utlanders' home. Since the day he'd seen Captain Rusan take down an adult male wyvern on his own, he'd discovered a growing admiration for the Utlanders.

With their fierce independence and strong warrior code, the Utlanders reminded Garzik of Captain Blackwing. He'd thought his father's men-at-arms tough, but these Utlanders endured their injuries without resorting to dreamless-sleep and without complaint.

'I wish I could make myself understood,' Trafyn muttered. He sat huddled at Garzik's feet, staring at his dirty toes. 'There's no need for them to plunder ships, not when my father'll pay a small fortune for my return.'

Garzik ignored this old refrain. He stood, leaning against the ship's side, enjoying the feel of the wind in his face.

When Olbin yelled an order at him he recognised the phrase; the big Utlander wanted him to lower the sails. He scrambled up the nearest mast. From up there he could see the horizon and the last sliver of the setting sun. Clear sky meant a cold night. But the breeze was strong so they'd make good time.

Every day he learnt more about the running of the ship. He knew the sailor's knots and he was learning to read the sea and the weather.

He was... not happy exactly, but no longer frightened.

This came as a surprise to him as he hung there, clinging to the mast.
And it made him feel guilty. He had a duty to return to Byren and restore
his honour. He wasn't about to forget.

CHAPTER TEN

WITHIN THREE DAYS they spotted islands, great craggy rocks that rose sheer out of the sea. The soaring cliffs stole Garzik's breath. Far above him, birds wheeled high on the air, their cries piercing and clear. He'd always imagined the Utland Isles as small, but some were huge.

It was early spring, and there were still floating chunks of ice. He got used to the Utlander words *beware iceberg* being called at all times of the day and night.

Four days later they approached an island that seemed larger than most. Although it appeared just as bleak as the others, it seemed to be the Utlanders' home. They laughed more freely, and spoke with anticipation of what they'd do. Not that he understood all of what they said, but some of it was unmistakable as they cupped themselves suggestively.

Clearly, for all that they'd used the lads on the ship, they had wives and girlfriends at home.

The cliffs seemed impenetrable, until a long narrow inlet opened before them. Once through the headlands, it became a steep-sided valley, shrouded in snow. At first Garzik thought there were no houses, but he spotted spirals of thin smoke and realised the buildings were built into the hillside like the highland cottages back home in the Dividing Range.

As the two ships rowed across the still waters of the narrow bay, he spotted the jetty. It was substantial, with room for at least two ships, and there were bollards along the shore where ships could be tied up. How many ships did the settlement have?

Three, or four at least.

One thing struck him as curious. There was no ice blocking the inlet's narrow bay. Before he knew he meant to do it, he'd turned to Olbin and asked, 'why no icebergs?'

Olbin looked surprised and Garzik realised he'd spoken the Utland tongue. The big Utlander grinned and replied. 'No icebergs here because...' And rattled off a string of the new words. Seeing his confusion, Olbin laughed. 'No icebergs. Safe, hot-lander!'

Hot-lander... it was what they called everyone else, and it was an insult. From what Garzik could gather, it carried the connotation of being lazy and weak in both body and mind.

As Olbin strode off calling to the Utlanders to make ready to secure the ship to the bollards, Trafyn came up behind Garzik. 'Why did you do that? Now they know you understand them.'

Garzik shrugged. It had been an accident. 'I hear the Utland tongue all day long. The question just slipped out.'

Trafyn shook his head. 'Don't know how you do it. My tutor had to drum my language lessons into me with a cane. And I swear he enjoyed it, the bastard.'

Garzik studied the steep-sided valley with the eye of an estate holder. Patches of colour drew his gaze to places where early blooming flowers had pushed their way through the snow. Brilliant pinks and purples. Very pretty. But there was not much arable land other than a narrow lip around the shoreline. Behind this, the valley rose sharply and soon grew too steep even for snow, except in the cervices where hardy spruces clung to the rock. 'How do they farm?'

Trafyn shrugged, clearly uninterested.

'I suppose they could build terraces like on Ostron Isle.' Garzik frowned. The snow was too deep to tell if the valley was terraced, which made him wonder again. 'What's stopping the sea ice from forming?'

'Why do you care?'

Garzik shrugged again. 'The more I know about my enemy, the better.'

'So you are a spy!'

'No, I'm a survivor.'

'I wish they understood Merofynian,' Trafyn whined. 'I wouldn't have to be here if they –' He broke off, fixing on Garzik. 'You can translate for me!'

'I don't know...' Garzik thought about it. 'I understand more than I can say, but I don't know the word for *ransom*, or *father*.'

'You'll learn them,' Trafyn insisted. 'And when you do, they'll treat me properly.'

Garzik was tempted to refuse, just to spite Trafyn, but Queen Myrella had reared him to be a better man than that. He pointed. 'Look, here come their families.'

People poured out of cottages, running down to the wharf, calling happy greetings. Women, children and youths, they all dressed alike: breeches, fur-lined boots and thigh-length smocks. These were tied off around their thighs with colourful braid. The same braid trimmed around their necks and cuffs. Children turned cartwheels in the snow and danced with excitement.

Then the work began.

The raiders pulled on boots to plough through the snow up to the settlement. Trafyn was all right – he still had his boots – but Garzik's toes were numb with cold. He went over to Olbin, pointed to the nearest raider who was pulling on his boots, then pointed to his feet.

Olbin said something too quickly for him to catch. The next thing he knew, he was carrying a bundle, plodding through the snow up the slope after the big Utlander.

When they came to a patch of clear ground, they stacked the bundles. Women were going through them, sorting things, sending different things to different store rooms.

'Here.' Olbin thrust something at him.

He turned to find a pair of peasant's shoes – simple leather soles, straps and grass stuffing to insulate them. Better than nothing. He sat down and pulled them on, lacing them up around his ankles.

'Come on.' Olbin urged.

Unloading the cargo from both ships took the better part of the day. Everyone pitched in, including the three dozen or so youths, beardless boys whose voices hadn't broken. For all that they weren't as strong as the men, they worked alongside them, putting their backs into the unloading.

Of course, Trafyn tried to do as little work as possible, moving slowly, resting as often as he could. The Utlanders weren't fooled. Passing men and women, even children of nine or ten, would clip him over the ear and tell him to get moving.

They didn't have to do that to Garzik. He figured the sooner the ships were unloaded, the sooner they would be restocked and return to sea.

The sooner he could escape and return to Rolencia.

'Rusan, Olbin!' A big woman with iron-grey hair swept the captain and his first mate into her embrace.

They pulled back, laughing, as she congratulated them on winning the ship. Her resemblance to Olbin convinced Garzik she was his mother, but she seemed equally fond of Rusan. She appeared to be in charge of where everything was being sent, and all the Utlander raiders deferred to her judgement.

At one point, Garzik and Trafyn were called over and displayed. He didn't catch what was said as she looked them over with sharp, assessing eyes. Then they were sent back to work.

He got the impression she was in charge of the settlement.

Other than a couple of very old white-haired men, he'd spotted no adult males besides the returned raiders. There were quite a few beardless youths and – now that he came to think of it – there weren't many women. Here, it looked like the men spent their time out raiding, while the women ran the settlement and reared the children. But that still didn't explain why there were so few women.

Another thing puzzled him. How did they decide which youths remained behind to guard the settlement and which went raiding?

With another word to the two captains, the iron-haired woman headed back up to the settlement. When she spotted Trafyn sitting on a bale resting, she berated him, calling him something that sounded like *lazy-legs*.

He muttered sullenly, then got up so slowly Garzik knew he courted trouble. Iron-hair grabbed him by the ear and dragged him off, followed by taunting children.

Rusan and Olbin hooted with laughter. Garzik glanced to them.

'Belongs-to-no-one will work in kitchen.' Olbin answered Garzik's unspoken question. 'No lazing there!' He grinned proudly. 'The women whip him into shape. Women tough.'

Belongs-to-no-one was an insult, meaning there was no-one to avenge the person's death. Garzik thought it might mean slave as well, because it also seemed to mean belongs-to-everyone – as in the person must work for everyone.

The days had been getting longer, but they had only just finished the unloading when children of eleven and twelve returned with long-haired goats and shaggy, horned cows. If the goats and cows had been foraging there must be pockets where grass had pushed its way through the snow.

When summer finally came, it would come quickly. At least, that's what it was like back home. A hot, intense summer of steaming days and nights when plants and animals threw off their winter stupor to grow and procreate madly. By evening, Garzik was ravenous.

All this hard work meant he needed to fill his belly. Right now, he could smell food cooking and his stomach growled in anticipation, but Olbin sent him down to the shoreline to bring back the children. He could hear them shouting and laughing behind a row of snow-shrouded spruce trees.

Trudging down there, he was thinking only of returning to find some food but, behind the trees, he found a dozen naked children laughing and frolicking in a pool of steaming hot water. It was formed by diverting water from the stream into what appeared to be a man-made rock pool. As the children jumped and laughed, water lapped over the far end and flowed into the bay. He tested the water in the stream and found it to be lukewarm, but the water in the pool was steaming; something under the ground must be heating it.

Ingenious, and it explained why the bay wasn't iced up.

Watching the children laugh and leap about, boys and girls all in together too young to care, he felt a smile tug at this lips. He glanced over his shoulder. No sign of the grown-ups. In a moment he was naked and in the water as well. It was hot, almost too hot, and fresh enough to drink. The children were wary of him at first, but soon started splashing him. Their high laughter carried, echoing off the valley's steep walls.

For the first time since he'd been captured, he scrubbed himself and felt clean, really clean.

He swam to the top end and discovered the water was cooler up this end.

So he swam along until he felt the water warm up. Then he dived under the surface to see if he could spot where the heat was coming from, but he couldn't see any source for it. Maybe the rock itself was hot?

When he came up for air again he found several beardless youths waiting for their turn, with more arriving all the time. Most of the children had already clambered out quickly and Garzik followed suit.

Not quickly enough for one of the youths who'd lost an eye to a claw – a leogryf attack, by the looks of it. Claw-face slapped him on the buttocks and shoved him in the direction of his clothes. The other youths laughed and mocked him as they waited for him to dress and leave, before beginning to strip.

Garzik would have preferred a fresh set of breeches and vest, but he wasn't a lord's son now. So he hastily pulled on his sailor breeches and vest, then trudged up the slope.

The Utlander's settlement was not large and most of the buildings were built into the steep hillsides. Other than the long-hall, there were only half a dozen chimney pots poking out of the snowy roofs. The path led to a patch of relatively flat ground in front of the long-hall where the children headed. A free-standing building stood off to one side, connected by a passage. Probably the kitchen. Free-standing cook-houses were a common precaution in case of fire.

The hot swim, coming after a day of hard work, had exhausted him and he was asleep on his feet by the time he stumbled into the long-hall after the last youngster. He spotted the pelt of a leogryf, complete with maned head, on the wall. The wingspan was twice the height of a tall man. A beautiful sun-on-sea Wyvern skin glistened in the lamplight. Over the fireplace, he spotted manticore chitin, fashioned into shields, carved with the same stylised symbol of the leogryf figurehead from the Utlander's original ship.

The long-hall had been dug into the stone and ran along the valley wall. There were dark storage rooms at the back that might originally have been caves. A steeply pitched roof allowed room for a mezzanine floor, which he guessed held bedchambers.

The women had been feeding the small children and infants and they now took them up the stairs to bed. By this time, the beardless youths had returned and they were fed. They'd only just received their meal when the Utland raiders returned, wet-haired and laughing. The raiders took pride of place at the top of long table, and there they were joined by the women, among them several older women like Iron-hair, who they treated with deference.

Food trays were delivered by children of around ten and eleven, and some adults. He wasn't sure if the adults were slaves; they had the same witchy look around the eyes as the Utlanders. He was having trouble working out the hierarchy.

Since there was no-one telling him what to do, Garzik went in search of a meal. He followed the slaves and serving children down the passage to the kitchen.

Here it was all a bustle as food was served up. Here, he found Trafyn up to his elbows scrubbing pots.

As soon as the squire noticed Garzik, he left his post. 'You have to get me out of here. I'm a lord's son.' He gestured disgustedly to the busy kitchen. 'This is beneath me.'

An old woman spotted him, clipped him over the ear and dragged him back to work. When he looked like he was about to argue, she slapped his face. Furious, he raised his hand.

One of the beardless youths caught his wrist before he could strike the old woman. Claw-face swung Trafyn around and smacked him so forcefully the squire fell to his knees.

A string of fast, nearly unintelligible Utland speech left Claw-face's lips. It might have been impossible to understand the words, but the meaning was clear.

Something else was also clear. Claw-face was not a beardless youth. Claw-face was a woman. And suddenly the mystery of the missing women was explained. They dressed and acted like men.

But why?

As Claw-face turned away, she noticed Garzik staring. 'What?'

'You're...' he didn't have the right word.

'A beardless,' she said, as if it meant *great warrior*.

'But...' He opened his mouth then realised even if he could phrase his question it was impossibly rude to ask why she took the role of a man. So he ducked his head to show respect and retreated.

Back in the long-hall, he found a warm spot near the fire not far from the long table and sat hugging his knees. Now the interactions at the table took on more complexity, for Claw-face and the other beardless flirted with the young women as much as the raiders did.

If he hadn't been feeling faint with hunger, he would have been happy just to sit and watch and try to figure out what was going on. But he was starving.

What the Utlanders didn't eat, they threw to the dogs. He was just about to try fighting off the dogs for a bone, when a girl of about eleven came by with a bowl for him.

He wondered if it contained tainted Affinity meat and hesitated.

The girl wrinkled her short nose, as she mimed eating. 'Is good.'

He took a mouthful. So good: rich and tasty. He gulped down another mouthful. Right now, the chance of Affinity contagion didn't matter. It was more important to keep up his strength.

He'd been afraid the Utlanders would starve their slaves, but here they seemed generous. The soup filled his belly.

'Rusan, Rusan!' the Utlanders called on Captain Rusan to tell the story of how he'd killed the wyvern to confirm his captaincy.

The story unfolded with much laughter as Rusan strutted about and acted out his part while Olbin took the part of the wyvern. Two children were roped in to play the parts of himself and Trafyn. They pretended to be tied to a mast and cried for help. He flushed. He hadn't panicked, Trafyn had.

The story finished and the other captain stepped forward to act out his adventures.

Tired as he was, Garzik couldn't sleep. It was all too new and interesting. But he did doze, slipping into a half-sleep where the singing and laughter of the Utlanders mingled with memories of King Rolen's great hall... Byren returning with the manticore chitin and gifting it to his father to make a fabulous coat of armour. Piro pretending to be a goat-herd and driving him crazy with worry for her. Piro telling him she was going to be a beardless warrior like an Utlander because she had Affinity after all and she couldn't bear to live her life locked away in Sylion Abbey. Piro laughing, taunting him as she ran up the tower steps ahead of him. He just knew if he caught her and kissed her, he could convince her to give up this mad idea.

But when he reached the top of the tower he found himself in the Utlander's long-hall and remembered Piro was dead. A wave of sadness swamped him.

Someone walked past, an old woman leading two children. They looked to be about ten years old and seemed to be playing some kind of game, for they had their arms linked so they could walk back-to-back in perfect unison. As they passed him to stand directly in front of the fireplace, he saw the second child's face.

It was identical to the first. Twins, then. Everyone waited breathlessly, watching the identical twins and the old woman.

Iron-hair welcomed the three with great courtesy.

The old woman removed the twins' cloak to reveal their nakedness. They were girls, joined at the base of the lower back. Fused.

Was he dreaming, after all? Garzik sat up, rubbing his face.

Seeing them reminded him of something. When he was little, he used to creep over to the men-at-arms' table to listen to their tales. Now a story came back to him, one that had made no sense at the time. They'd called the Utlanders in-bred, claimed that brothers took sisters to their beds and their union produced monsters.

Later, he'd asked Byren and Orrade about it. They'd dismissed it as the kind of stories men told about their enemies to make them seem less than human.

Now...

With eerie coordination, the fused-twins walked the length of the long table, escorted by the old woman. Every now and then they would swap, one taking the lead instead of the other. The switchover was smooth and effortless.

When this happened, the one in the lead one would indicate a particular person then whisper to the old woman, who would make an announcement. Her voice was surprisingly young for someone with pure white hair.

Most of what she said made no sense to Garzik. He could follow instructions at sea but there were many new words on land and, besides, everything the old woman said rhymed and the words seemed to be chosen for their pleasing sound patterns.

Some of the things the fused-twins said through her made everyone laugh. Some things were greeted with hushed silence, then awed whispers. The fused-twins stopped in front of one-eared Jost. He sat up, looking hopeful. His two friends leaned forward.

But neither of the fused-twins whispered to the old woman. They moved on until they came to Olbin. One of them said something which was greeted by silence, then Captain Rusan clapped his friend on the back and congratulated him.

Oracles.

The fused-twins were oracles. Affinity-blessed oracles. If this was Rolencia they would have been given to Sylion Abbey at birth.

That or exposed on a hillside.

Garzik couldn't take his eyes off them. The fusion of their naked bodies exercised a terrible fascination. He couldn't help wondering how much of their bodies were joined. Did they share one back passage? It was hard to tell.

Their task done, the fused-twins returned to the fireside. The old woman picked up the cloak. As she helped them dress, he realised it was really a robe with two head holes and four holes for their arms.

After settling the garment in place, the old woman went to escort them out, but one of the fused-twins turned very slowly towards Garzik. This meant the other one had to turn away. She looked over her shoulder with curious detachment.

As the first girl studied Garzik her lids lowered and her eyes rolled back in her head, and he knew she must be tapping into Affinity.

She whispered something to the old woman, who leant closer to Garzik.

For the first time he looked at her, really looked at her.

She had the smooth skin of a young woman; her hair wasn't white due to age. She was also Affinity touched. Her odd pink eyes fringed by white lashes held him transfixed.

He was so surprised her words made no sense, although he did catch something about striking a light.

He pulled back, stunned. Her words had rhymed like a children's word-game and he replayed the words over and over in his head as he tried to fathom them.

'Good news or bad?'

He looked up to find Olbin crouched opposite him. The white-haired woman and the fused-twins had gone.

'What did she say, hot-lander?' Olbin asked. 'What did the Yesterday, Today and Tomorrow say?'

'Yesterday, Today and Tomorrow?'

Olbin nodded. He touched his own black hair. 'White-hair is Today, mother of Yesterday and Tomorrow. What did they say?'

Garzik repeated the rhyme. 'But I don't understand it. Something about lighting a lamp?'

'Not lamp. To make fire.' Olbin gestured to the fireplace and mimed striking flint to tinder. Then he added a string of words, saw that Garzik did not understand and tried again. 'You light the fire tomorrow and tomorrow.'

'I thought they were Yesterday, Today and Tomorrow?'

Olbin laughed and Garzik got the impression he was being thick; that, or Affinity oracles were known for being cryptic.

Someone called for a song. A girl of about fifteen came forward, her clear, high voice carrying in the long-hall. Rusan produced his pipes, Claw-face a stringed instrument and someone else a drum, and they accompanied her.

Rusan had eyes only for the singer. She would have been pretty, if it wasn't for the witchy look around her eyes. She entranced Olbin, who did not look away.

Garzik caught one word in five of her song. Like the oracles' speech, the lyrics seemed crafted for the pleasing balance of their sounds as much as their meaning.

When the singer reached the end of a verse, everyone joined in, their voices blending. The effect was beautiful, but sad.

For some reason, it made Garzik think of his home, of things lost, people passed, Piro...

Tears stung his eyes.

The girl resumed her solo part and, to his amazement, Olbin wept openly.

Garzik looked around. All of them wept, unashamedly – women and warriors alike.

When the songstress finished, Olbin wiped his eyes.

'Good song.' He thumped his chest, over his heart and said something else that Garzik didn't understand but took to mean the song was good because it made him feel strongly.

Rusan put his pipes aside and set out to charm the songstress. She perched on the table, swinging her legs, listening intently.

Olbin joined them. He tried to cajole the singer into sitting on his lap. Songstress laughed and refused, but she obviously enjoyed the attention. The only one not happy was Jost. He cast both Rusan and Olbin dark looks and muttered to his two companions.

Iron-hair called for another song, something about lost raiders returning home. Soon the whole settlement was singing along with the chorus as the adventures of the lost raiders unfolded.

Children climbed into the laps of fierce warriors and drifted off in their arms. It was odd seeing men who had thrown injured sailors overboard without a qualm rocking children to sleep.

So many marvels... Garzik drifted off, carried on a wave of sound and half-grasped imagery.

THE NEXT DAY the returned raiders and beardless tackled the task of repairing the ships, while some of the raiders helped with the heavier jobs around the settlement. Garzik kept his eyes opened, listened and mostly followed what was being said.

At one point he saw Rusan and Olbin head up the valley carrying a selection of foods and treasures from their ship. They went to a lonely cottage tucked into the hillside, where a thin stream of blue smoke rose on the still air.

The door opened and they handed over the gifts. Even from this distance, Garzik could see it was the white-haired woman. It made sense that she and her daughters would be valued by the settlement.

Living as they did, out here on the edge of the habitable islands, Utlanders would need people who had an affinity with the gods to intervene on their behalf.

While the men and beardless worked, young children helped by running and fetching. Back home, Garzik had been in training to become a warrior. He could hunt, plan a battle, read and write, but he was no carpenter. He couldn't make a mortise and tenon joint, so they sent him to chop firewood. There was a large wood heap waiting to be cut down. Like cooking, it was a never-ending task.

Yet it was satisfying.

After a while, he paused to wipe his forehead and noticed Songstress coming down the path with a tray of honey cakes and cheese. The eleven year-old girl trotted along behind, carrying a jug of ale and cups with great concentration. Now that he looked, Songstress had the same short nose and full lips as the girl.

Sisters, no doubt about it.

When Songstress reached Rusan's ship, the captain called a halt and came down the gangplank to see her. Olbin was only one step behind him. Watching them, Garzik couldn't tell which one she preferred. It amused him, but it didn't amuse Jost and his friends.

Apparently, it didn't amuse the little sister either, because she mimicked her big sister and rolled her eyes as if flirting was a chore. She already carried herself like one of the beardless. Garzik grinned. Cheeky-puss reminded him of Piro.

And that reminded him of all he'd lost.

He felt like someone had punched him in the gut. Needing time to think, he left the axe on the wood block and went to the out-house. It was after he'd doused his head and shoulders in cold water and was headed back that he heard someone calling his name. He turned to find Trafyn beckoning from behind a snow-shrouded spruce.

What now?

With a quick glance to make sure no one was watching, he darted over to join Trafyn.

'I'm running away. Are you with me?' Trafyn demanded. One eye was swollen shut and he held a bundle to his chest.

Garzik gestured to his face. 'What happened?'

'One of those Utland bitches punched me. I nearly lost my eye.'

'She punched you? What did you do?'

'Nothing. I just objected to doing women's work,' Trafyn said, aggrieved. 'I've had it. I'm not putting up with this any longer. How dare they treat me like a slave?'

'You are a slave.' Garzik felt like laughing, but he controlled the urge and searched for words. 'We're Utland captives. That makes us their slaves. If you pull your weight, they'll treat you well.' While the food lasted. Captain Blackwing had told him the slaves were the first to starve on Utland islands. 'You just have to work hard.'

'Why should I work for them? I'm Lord Trafyn's son. Servants work for me.'

Garzik didn't know what to say in the face of Trafyn's wilful blindness. 'You coming?'

'Where?' Garzik gestured to the valley, the sheer sides reflected in the mirror-like bay. 'The only way out of here is by ship.'

Trafyn glanced up to the peaks.

'Inland?' Garzik shook his head. 'Into the wild highlands.' He'd heard the perils of the highlands described in songs last night. 'Didn't you notice the Affinity beast trophies in the long-hall? There's nothing in the highlands but dangerous beasts, snow and ice. You wouldn't last a day on your own.'

'So you're happy to be a slave?'

'Of course not. But I'm not stupid either. When the ships are repaired, Rusan and the other captain will be going back to the hot-lands and I'll be going with them. That's when we can escape.'

'I wouldn't need to escape if you'd talk to them and explain who I am.'

'I will, when I know what to say. For now, come back to the long-hall. Keep your head down. Bide your time,' Garzik advised. He didn't know why he bothered. 'We'll be sailing south soon.'

CHAPTER ELEVEN

BUT THREE DAYS later, only one of the ships left the valley. Rusan's stolen Merofynian vessel remained. The captain had decided to lighten the ship. Beds, cabinets and anything vaguely worth using were dismantled and carried off the ship, then distributed.

Garzik gathered that the lightening of the ship meant less of the vessel below the sea's surface, which meant less drag, resulting in a faster ship. And since the Utlanders slept on deck, belowdeck could be used for storage.

It was another six days before the ship was fitted out to Rusan's liking. During this time Trafyn managed to keep out of trouble, although Garzik suspected the squire did as little work as possible.

As for Garzik, he kept his mouth shut and listened. The more he listened, the more he understood, and the better he became with the Utland language.

He didn't mind the work. There was something satisfying about getting things done. In a settlement this size one person's efforts made a difference. The busy days flew by and, in the evenings, he watched Rusan and Olbin competing for the pretty singer's favours. It was as good as watching a mummers' play back home in King Rolen's court.

Garzik was inclined to think Rusan's ability to play the pipes gave him an edge with the songstress over Olbin. It meant they shared a love of music. Certainly Jost was out of the running. Even his captured nobleman's sword and dagger failed to impress her.

That evening, Garzik took his customary place, sitting with his back against the wall, knees drawn up, to observe the long table. Knowing the raiders sailed with the dawn tide, Garzik watched Rusan and Olbin to see if either of them would succeed with the girl tonight. Both seemed equally determined to woo her but, strangely enough, this didn't cause friction between them.

When Cheeky-puss passed Garzik, he pointed to Rusan and Olbin. 'Which one will win her?'

The girl blinked at him like he'd missed something.

Recalling Iron-hair and her air of authority, it came to him that Utland women were not prizes, they were partners. He rephrased the question. 'Which one will your sister choose?'

The girl laughed.

He flushed, certain he was still missing something.

Cheeky-puss's sharp witchy eyes held amusement leavened with intelligence. 'You think like a hot-lander. Lazy hot-landers have an easy life. We Utlanders live a hard life.'

She waited as if he should be able to work out what she meant.

He lifted his hands in confusion.

'In the Utlands children go hungry, children die. One man can't feed half a dozen children, so brothers make a pact.' She gestured to Rusan and Olbin. 'Same mother, different fathers. No need for Sarijana to choose between them.'

They would share her? No wonder his father's men-at-arms used to tell those stories. Garzik felt heat stain his cheeks and looked away.

'Hot-landers!' Cheeky-puss snorted. 'You think our way is wrong?' She tilted her head watching him. 'In the hot-lands what happens to a woman and her children if her man dies?'

Sometimes one of the man's brothers married the woman and raised the children, but if he didn't and there wasn't any family to take her in, the woman was turned out. She had to sell herself on the street to feed her children. Garzik struggled to find the right Utland words.

'Life is hard.' Cheeky-puss was nodding before he finished. 'But Utland life is harder. Men die in battle. They die on raids and fighting Affinity beasts. But they die knowing their family will be looked after.' She held his eyes. 'How can you say your way is right and our way is wrong?'

That stopped him in his tracks. Then he thought of something. 'There'd be enough girls to go around if half of them didn't become beardless.'

'Not enough girls is not the problem.' She rolled her eyes like he was stupid. 'Who do you think defends our home when the raiders are away? Beardless are brave and fearless. We sing songs about them. I'm going to be –'

'But...' What a waste. She was smart and he found her more interesting than her sister, who liked to flirt. One day, when she grew up, Cheeky-puss would set men's hearts hammering. 'I'd marry you.'

'You?' She threw back her head and laughed. 'You can't even feed yourself. You have no sword and no brothers.'

It was true. Shame stung his cheeks. As she walked off, he ducked his head, wrapping his arms around his bent knees. A little later, he saw Cheeky-puss talking with Sarijana. The singer looked his way and laughed.

Angry, he jumped to his feet and stalked out. In the cool night air the narrow valley was illuminated by a froth of stars, which silvered the sea and the remaining patches of snow.

His cheeks cooled, but his heart didn't. Here he was a slave who didn't even have place at the table. Back home he was the son of a Rolencian lord. He'd modelled himself on Byren and Orrade, both honourable men.

And not that different from Rusan and Olbin, he had to admit. But they weren't his people. He didn't owe them any allegiance.

Tomorrow, he would sail south.

Head home to serve Byren.

First however, he had to escape the Utland raiders, then find Byren, then convince him Mitrovan would make a good spy.

And, if he did all that, he still had to hope Mitrovan discovered something useful, because if he didn't, Garzik didn't know how he was going to look Byren in the eye and ask for his forgiveness.

So much to accomplish before he could become the king's man.

He'd worry about it tomorrow. Right now he was tired. Turning around, he went back into the long-hall, heading for his spot against the wall.

Iron-hair met him halfway. He'd thought she just happened to be passing by him and wasn't prepared when she stopped to speak to him. 'You might understand our language, but that doesn't mean you understand us, belongs-to-no-one. You still have a lot to learn. That you ask questions is a good thing.' She gave him a nod of approval, then gestured to where Rusan and his raiders sat. 'Prove yourself and you may yet win a place at the table.'

Then she moved on.

Her approval warmed him, and he was surprised to discover he did want to win a place at the table.

But his loyalty was to Byren. Always would be.

Mind made up, Garzik stretched out and put his back to the long-hall.

He fell asleep, expecting to be up with the sun.

Instead, he woke to shrill, inhuman screams. The raiders rolled to their feet, shouting instructions. Someone lit a lantern, then torches. The beardless came running, even as they threw on boots and buckled weapons. Barefoot women came running with whatever weapons came to hand. Even children of ten and eleven came running, ready to fight.

At first Garzik thought the settlement was under attack, but when he darted outside there were no extra ships in the star-silvered bay.

The sounds came from up the valley, from one of the cow byres. Every able-bodied child and adult ran towards it, torch flames flickering.

By the time they got there, they found that the wall of the cow byre had been torn down, some animals had been dragged off and the remaining animals had run off in a panic.

People shouted, trying to recapture the startled animals. The small, shaggy cows had covered a surprising distance. They were not as docile as cows back home and they tried to kick and bite the youngsters sent after them. The goats were even more cantankerous.

As the Utlanders speculated as to what had attacked the cow byre, Garzik went looking for signs. He took his torch and went around the far side of the hill, where he found a patch of snow with drag marks, alongside manticore prints.

The sight took him back to Narrowneck, when he had been with Piro and they were being stalked by a manticore pride. Clever and cooperative, the manticores had had them cornered and they'd only escaped because Byren and Orrade kept their heads, and Piro killed a manticore. The Utlanders would have admired her.

'What is it?' Rusan asked.

'Manticore.' Then, in case the Rolencian word was unfamiliar, he mimed the shape of the great feline body and the way the chitinous tail curled over the creature's back, ready to stab and poison.

Olbin and Rusan nodded their understanding.

'You know manticores?' Rusan asked, using an Utland word for the beasts.

Garzik nodded. 'Last winter a pride stalked me and my friends. We set a trap and killed them all. Took the chitin to make armour.'

Rusan and Olbin exchanged looks and he wondered if they thought he was boasting.

Rusan gestured towards the peaks and the highlands beyond. 'Winter lingers on up there. They'll have cubs to feed.'

'No point chasing them tonight.' Olbin nodded. 'Too dangerous –'

'We can't let them get away with this,' Jost protested, stalking over with his friends. 'They'll be back. They'll cause no end of trouble.'

'We'll go after them tomorrow,' Rusan said.

'Tomorrow?' Iron-hair joined them. 'Tomorrow we need the cow byre repaired and reinforced. Two goats and a calf have been taken. We can't afford to lose more. What do you think, Danja?'

Claw-face – Danja – and a companion came back from further up the valley, arriving in a pool of torchlight. 'This is a big pride. We found seven separate tracks, but there could be more. At least three were hungry juveniles. If we don't cull the pride, it won't be safe to use the high pastures this summer. We'll have to go into the highlands tomorrow.'

More beardless and raiders had joined them, and they were quick to volunteer.

'The manticores have a large territory. Last time I was up there I saw two dens, one cave at each end of their territory. They'll return to one of the dens to hide their kill and feast. We'll need two groups. I'll lead one.' Danja gestured to her companion, a quiet beardless who usually sat back and watched. She reminded Garzik of Orrade and how Queen Myrella had once said of him, *still waters run deep*. 'Polonika will lead the other.'

The quiet one nodded.

And just like that, Danja was in charge. It didn't seem to matter to the raiders that she was female. She was beardless, that was enough.

*　　*　　*

NEXT MORNING THE hunters set off. About a dozen beardless remained behind to repair the cow byre. Because Rusan and Olbin had put in a good word for him, Garzik went with the hunters, but not Trafyn. The squire would be happy to be overlooked.

As for himself, he had a healthy respect for manticores, for all Affinity beasts. He still bore the scars of the amfina attack.

Affinity beasts tended to be smarter than ordinary animals, and consequently more deadly. But he felt reasonably confident after watching the raiders and beardless prepare for the hunt. There were just over fifty of them, enough so that, after the groups separated, they would still have the numbers to tackle the manticore pride.

They packed dried food to supplement what they could forage along the way. They wore warm clothes. Garzik was loaned a fur to cover his too-small sailor's vest and breeches.

They carried hunting bows. The arrow heads were notched so they would sink into flesh and not dislodge. If the arrow didn't kill outright, which took a perfect shot, the hunters could track the wounded beast, wait until it faltered, weak from blood loss, then finish it.

The climb out of the valley took the better part of the first day. The higher they went, the more magnificent the view, and the smaller the settlement seemed. Most of the snow had melted around the shore. A deep green blush covered the valley. From up here Garzik could see the women and children planting out the few decent fields.

Once they were through the pass into the highlands, the countryside changed. For one thing, an icy wind blew, sending flurries of fine snow. Ahead of him, fold upon fold of jagged, snow-covered valleys stretched into the north, illuminated by the setting sun. The valley floors were densely wooded and would prove difficult to traverse.

Despite their harshness, the Utland highlands reminded him of the Dividing Ranges and going hunting with Captain Blackwing.

Danja and Polonika checked the trails, then reported back. Garzik was used to being next to whoever was in command, either Byren and Orrade or

Captain Blackwing, and he gravitated to the discussion. He wanted to know what was going on, to learn everything he could.

Danja gestured back to the track. 'Just as we feared. The wind's wiped out any sign of the manticores' tracks. Tomorrow, we'll separate. I'll lead a party north-west. Polonika, you take your party north east.'

'We'll go with her,' Jost insisted, nodding to his friends.

Danja did not look happy about this.

'Looks like we're with you, Danja,' Rusan said, slinging an arm around her shoulders. 'Just like when we were kids.'

She rolled her eyes. 'This time do what I say and you won't break your leg.'

'She's got you there.' Olbin laughed.

As they settled in for the night, the icy wind whistled across the highlands and Garzik was glad of the borrowed furs. Manticores weren't the only threat.

The next morning the two groups separated and Garzik was not sorry to see the last of Jost. As he watched Polonika and Jost's party disappear into the western valley, he wondered if they would be the ones to find the right den. One part of him would be happy never to have to face another Affinity beast again.

'Don't worry, hot-lander, we'll find the manticores,' Olbin assured him, mistaking his expression for disappointment. 'It'll be glory for us. I have it on good authority.'

It took them five days' steady marching to approach the den and before they reached it they knew it was no longer home to the manticore pride.

'Leogryfs and manticores are mortal enemies.' Danja looked up from the leogryf droppings. 'Since last summer a leogryf pair must've taken over this end of the manticores' territory.'

Garzik glanced up, instinctively looking for leogryfs circling far above them, not that there was much chance of them attacking a party this size, not unless they were defending their young. It was spring, so...

'Explains why the manticores came over the pass to raid our cow byre.' Rusan nodded. 'Half the area to hunt and they have cubs to feed.'

Danja agreed. 'No glory for us –'

'We should head home,' Olbin announced, rising and brushing his hands off on his thighs. 'The oracles said I would defend the settlement. I thought they meant from manticores, but they must've meant from something else.'

Danja glanced to Rusan who nodded.

'Did they say when?' she asked Olbin. For a heartbeat, Garzik thought she was kidding, then he realised they were all serious.

'No idea when.' Olbin shook his head. 'But we should go back.'

Even though it was late afternoon and they'd been travelling all day, no one complained when they turned around and set off right away.

Although they were retracing their steps, they'd set off late in the evening and Olbin pushed them, so that they came to the pass late on the fourth day, rather the fifth.

CHAPTER TWELVE

A QUICK SCOUT around revealed their old camp was undisturbed. No sign of the other group having returned this way.

Garzik noticed Danja searching the ridges to the north-west, obviously thinking of Polonika. She caught Olbin's eye. 'Maybe we should go help Polonika. Maybe you are meant to kill the manticores, after all. Did the oracles give you any clues?'

Olbin opened his mouth, then shut it.

'Oracles...' Rusan made a disgusted sound. 'Why can't they just tell us 'do this' or 'do that'? Why leave us guessing?'

Danja shrugged. 'Who knows the ways of oracles? We'll camp here and go home tomorrow.'

Everyone settled down for the night. It was Garzik's job to tend the fire and cook their meal. When the food was almost cooked, he noticed Olbin and Rusan. Olbin was waving his hands around, trying to convince Rusan of something. Finally, Rusan nodded and they both slipped away.

At a guess, they were going through the pass to check on the settlement. Clearly, the Utlanders took the warnings of their oracles seriously.

Garzik hesitated. As a slave he owed the Utlanders nothing. But his instinct was to go after them, just in case they needed help.

He told himself Captain Rusan's ship was the only way he had to get home, which was true. But, if he was honest, he was worried about Cheeky-puss and others back at the settlement.

He called everyone to come get their dinner, then set off for the pass. It was a narrow defile between sheer stone walls. Hardy spring ferns had already sprouted in the crevices. Garzik suspected it would soon be completely full of ferns and hard to find. Already, he'd lost track of Rusan and Olbin and had to run to catch up.

Coming out the far side, he still hadn't caught up. There was no sign of the two Utlanders. But there were two more ships sitting down below on the still water of the narrow bay. They'd moved Rusan's ship and taken both places at the jetty.

The sun had dipped behind the valley walls. Long, rippling clouds stretched across the sky, reminding him of sand left by the retreating tide. The clouds caught the setting sun's fiery rays, reflecting in the bay so that the silhouetted ships seemed to ride the clouds.

Were these new arrivals settlement raiders returned with more booty stolen from the Merofynians, who'd stolen it from Rolencia?

At this distance he could not make out the carvings on the ship's prows. From what he gathered, there were at least another two shiploads of settlement raiders. He could see a stream of tiny figures carrying bundles from the store-houses to the jetty, not the other way around. Traders, then.

But something made Garzik uneasy. He frowned.

The smoke... it wasn't the blue-white of carefully tended cooking fires, but the black smoke of destruction, and there was too much of it coming from one of the cottages. Even as he realised this, he saw one of the men cuff a child struggling under a heavy bundle. The man shoved the child in the back, sending him towards the ships.

One thing about the Utlanders had impressed Garzik. They might beat a slave, but even the roughest of men were patient with the children, never raising a hand against them.

'Down.' Danja grabbed him, surprising an undignified yelp from him. She pulled Garzik along after her as she sought shelter further down the path.

Here they found both Rusan and Olbin watching the settlement from behind a rock shelf.

'Olbin was right, Danja,' Rusan whispered. 'Two ships, anywhere between sixty to eighty renegades.'

Danja cursed under her breath. 'We can't wait for Polonika's return, but there's only twenty-six of us.'

'They won't set sail this late,' Rusan said. 'They think they're safe; we'll have surprise on our side.'

Olbin cursed fluently and eloquently. 'If they lay a hand on Sarijana. I swear –'

'Who are they?' Danja asked. 'Can you tell?'

Rusan shook his head. 'Too far to see.'

'But the women down at the settlement would know who they are and which island they come from,' Garzik said. 'Wouldn't that bring down a retaliatory raid on their settlement? Why risk their families by attacking yours?'

Olbin shook his head. 'Always asking question, this one.'

'They're renegades. No families, no home.' Rusan spat in disgust. 'Killed the wrong man or woman. Too wild to raise children.'

'Why do you think we beardless take the vow to defend our sisters' children?' Danja asked. 'Sometimes renegades steal from fellow Utlanders, rather than take the honourable path.'

Capturing hot-land ships was honourable? Garzik supposed it was – from an Utlander's point of view.

'We should go.' Olbin went to rise.

'Wait for us.' Danja caught his arm. 'I'll go back and get the others.'

She darted away.

Garzik waited, stomach churning. If he felt this bad, he didn't know how Rusan and Olbin could sit still.

Rusan checked the cloudy sky. 'Getting dark. Be a cloudy, starless night. If we don't leave now we'll have to light torches. Might as well go knock on the door.'

Olbin and Rusan exchanged looks and came to their feet.

'She said to wait,' Garzik called after their retreating backs.

They didn't bother to answer.

He cast one look over his shoulder and ran after them.

There was still enough light to see by, but only just. Rusan was right; soon that light would fade and the night would be utterly black. Danya and the others would have to risk lighting torches.

Outnumbered as they were...

Rusan and Olbin ran single file down the path, with Garzik on their heels. It was all downhill and they made good time. He looked back twice, but couldn't spot the others following. Either they weren't through the pass yet, or they were hidden by the folds in the rock. After that, he concentrated on running.

Garzik had grown since winter. He still wasn't as tall as Rusan, but his legs ate up the distance and he kept up with both of them. His heart hammered, then settled into an easy rhythm as he fell into a distance-eating run.

The after-glow of the setting sun gradually faded. Even with his eyes wide open and adjusted to the dark, it was getting hard to see. He followed Olbin and Rusan more by sound and instinct than anything else.

They passed the remains of a burned-out cottage, where coals still blinked in the ashes, and he almost ran into them. Olbin steadied him. Garzik smelled yesterday's dinner and furs on the air – a cottage. But there was also blood. Death. No light burned in the cottage, no glow came through chinks in the shutters.

'Cow byre's empty, too,' Rusan said softly. 'Come on.'

A whimper made them stop.

They turned towards the dark opening that was the cottage door. The whimpering cut off abruptly. Whoever was inside could see them, probably silhouetted against patches of snow on the far side of the valley.

Rusan approached, calling softly.

Someone ran out the side door. Garzik tackled them on instinct and heard a Merofynian curse. 'Trafyn?'

'Lazy belongs-to-no-one!' Olbin was there in an instant, hauling Trafyn to his feet, shaking him. 'What happened?'

The squire whimpered. 'Don't hurt me, don't –'

'They won't hurt you,' Garzik told him and translated Olbin's question. 'What happened?'

'Ships came around midday. They seemed friendly at first. That bitch didn't want to trade...' As Trafyn spoke, Garzik translated, editing what he said. 'The traders wouldn't take no. They –'

'They never meant to trade,' Rusan muttered. 'Who was it?'

'What figure-head?' Garzik asked. 'On the ships. What was the figure-head?'

'I didn't notice,' Trafyn confessed.

'How many of them? Where is everyone?' Rusan asked.

'I don't know. I don't... They killed anyone who picked up a weapon against them. Knocked children senseless.' Trafyn whimpered. 'I ran away. It wasn't my fight.'

Garzik didn't translate that last part.

'Useless!' Olbin shook the squire, which made Garzik suspect he understood some Merofynian.

'Bring him,' Rusan ordered.

Olbin dragged Trafyn with them, but not before warning him. 'Make one sound to betray us and I'll wring your neck like a chicken!'

As they neared the settlement, it became clear only the long-hall and the cook-house were inhabited. The sound of the evening meal being prepared came through the cook-house open window. But there was no laughter, no chatter.

The two Utlanders stopped in a hollow about a stone's throw from the cook-house's open window. There was just enough light to make out each other's features.

'They think they're safe. Most of them will be in the long-hall,' Rusan said.

'It'll be a while before Danja and the others get down here.' Olbin made a frustrated gesture.

'If we attack, they'll use our families as hostages,' Rusan warned. 'We need to lure them out of the hall.'

They fell silent. Unable to follow the conversation, Trafyn huddled down, obviously wishing himself elsewhere.

'When I think of them sitting at our table, eating our food, forcing our women and children to serve them,' Olbin growled. Garzik knew how he felt. He'd been in a similar position when the Merofynians took his father's hall. 'When I think of Sarijana in their hands –'

'Set fire to their ships,' Garzik suggested. 'That'll draw them out.'

Olbin brightened. 'That's –'

'One ship,' Rusan cut in. 'Two ships would be suspicious. One ship could be an accident. We mustn't alert them to our presence. Not until we're ready to attack. If one ship caught fire that would be enough to draw them down to the jetty.'

'Good,' Olbin said. I'll –'

'Not you,' Rusan told him. 'Belongs-to-no-one should do it, him and the lazy one.'

Garzik felt like saying *I have a name*. They'd never asked. They were his captors, even Cheeky-puss who had thought so little of him that she laughed in his face.

'I'll fetch oil and coals from the cook-house,' Rusan said and took off.

Olbin watched him go, then turned to Garzik and Trafyn. 'You two creep aboard one of the ships, set it alight. When they come running out, we'll slip into the hall, kill any who stayed behind and get our families out. Hopefully the rest'll be too distracted to realise what's happening.' He turned Garzik around so that the dim light from the cook-house fell directly on his face. 'You understand?'

'It was my idea.'

Olbin grinned. He ruffled Garzik's hair. 'You're all right for a hot-lander.'

Then he turned back to watch Rusan who peered in the cook-house's window before leaning inside to speak with someone.

Trafyn leant closer to Garzik. 'What's going on?'

Garzik explained.

Even before he finished, Trafyn was protesting. 'Are you crazy? If they catch us torching their ship they'll kill us. They're barbarians. Worse even than this lot!'

Olbin cuffed him over the head. 'Keep your voice down.'

Trafyn didn't need to understand the Utland tongue. He lowered his voice, but he was still furious. 'Why are you even doing this? You're their slave. Why risk your life?'

It was a fair question. Garzik could have said they needed the raiders to sail home. It was the kind of logic Trafyn would understand. He could have said he was worried about the defenceless women and children in the long-hall.

He said nothing because Trafyn should not have had to ask.

The squire went to protest further, but Rusan returned with a small pot of coals, a jar of fish oil and some rags. He gave these to Garzik. 'You know what to do. Don't fail to light the fire.'

And it came to him – this was what the oracles had meant. He could still light the fire.

He hadn't been able to save Rolencia but he could save the Utlanders.

The irony of it stung.

CHAPTER THIRTEEN

IT WAS JUST as well he knew the settlement, knew the path down to the shore and knew the jetty.

What he didn't know was the layout of the Utland vessels. He'd spent his time on a captured Merofynian vessel. Only one of the renegade's ships seemed to be occupied. A glow came from the hold. Perhaps they were still stowing the stores they'd stolen. On the other ship the renegades had either doused the lantern and gone to sleep, or they'd left it unattended.

Garzik carried a small cooking pot of live coals, a jar of fish oil and a handful of rags. Trafyn carried nothing.

Other than the glow from the hold of one ship, there was no light. Mindful of the importance of his task, Garzik crept down the path to the jetty, picking his way with care.

Trafyn went as far as the beginning of the jetty then stopped. 'That's it. No further. I'm not dying for filthy savages.'

'Stay here, then.' Garzik kept his voice low. 'I don't need your help.'

He felt the planks of the jetty under his shoes. They made hardly any sound on the weathered wood of the jetty.

Ignoring the ship on his right, where he could hear voices coming from the hold, he made for the ship on the left. The tide was low and there was a drop of almost a body length from the jetty to the deck.

He put the pot and oil down on the jetty, tucked the rags into his vest, then lowered himself. A wave of relief swept him as his feet found solid deck.

It was so dark he might as well close his eyes. Keeping them open only produced colourful swirls that his over-active imagination turned into all manner of threats.

Lifting his arms above his head, he felt along the jetty for the jar and the coal pot and nearly burnt his fingers in the process. A pox on Trafyn; he should have been helping.

Last time, when he went to light the warning beacon, he'd had plenty of help. Everyone had been ready to die to make sure he succeeded. Silly little Kiri.

Concentrate.

Garzik closed his eyes and breathed slowly, listening. There was the gentle lap of the sea. The slight rock of the deck. The softest of snores. Someone slept on deck.

Feeling for the side of the ship, he edged along, making his way to the rear of the ship. There were bales stacked in places and more piled up at the rear. He knelt to place a rag in the gap between two bales and poured a little oil on it. Taking the end of the oily rag, he dipped it in the coal pot and blew softly. The hot coals glowed red. Once, twice... on the third time a flame ran up the rag.

It fascinated him, so dainty and fragile now, but so deadly once it took hold.

He backed off and turned away.

A glow came from behind him and he recognised rolls of carpet, bales of flax and wine bottles. Those should burn well.

No time to hesitate.

As he headed towards the prow of the ship, he could just make out the deck now and he saw someone sleeping near the open hold.

Which gave him the idea of dropping a burning oil rag into the darkness below.

A crackling came from behind him. The flames had taken. Giving up on secrecy, he ran lightly across the deck.

The sleeper snored on. A boy younger than himself. Garzik caught the scent of alcohol now that he was close and winced. He tried not to think how the boy had been used.

In a rush now, he knelt, poured oil over the remaining rags, dipped them in the coal pot and blew on it.

'Here. What're you doing?' a high voice demanded.

He dropped the oily rags into the hold and tipped the rest of the coals after them for good measure. Saw the rags fall away, bringing illumination to a half-packed hold.

'Stop that.'

Garzik spun around.

The boy held a knife, the blade glinting in the flickering light of the flames. If the lad gave the alarm and told the renegades the ship had been deliberately set alight, they'd be on alert for Rusan and Olbin.

The boy titled his head, surprised. 'You're no Utlander.'

In that moment of distraction, Garzik lunged forward and smacked the coal pot down on the boy's knife arm. He heard a crack and kept swinging the coal pot to hit him in the side of the face.

The boy went down like a dropped sack, all loose limbs.

Garzik heard a cry from the other ship. They'd come up on deck and noticed the flames.

He couldn't leave the boy to burn.

Bending his knees, he hefted the boy across his shoulders and ran for the side of the ship.

By now the fire was a roaring dragon, intent on devouring everything. Garzik swung one leg over the side, then the other and let his momentum take them both. The splash he made as he hit was drowned out by the fire.

Cold. So cold...

He surfaced, gasping for breath, struggling with the weight of the boy. The fact the lad was unconscious worked in his favour. Garzik was able to turn the lad around, hold his head above water and swim for shore.

Tufts of tall grass provided excellent cover as he dragged the boy out and left him there. Keeping low, he peered over the grass.

The Utlanders' ship was well alight now. Several wine bottles exploded, and flames shot into the air. There was no sign of Trafyn on the jetty. Half a dozen men darted about, calling for buckets, calling for help, cursing. All this he guessed from their gestures because the roar of the fire drowned out their voices.

Scrambling onto his hands and knees, he crawled up the bank and into a small field of newly planted rye. He felt vulnerable as he darted across, but no one pointed him out, or gave pursuit.

Ahead of him, he could see the long-hall, its door standing open as men raced down to the jetty. Some carried buckets or blankets, some swords.

Keeping to the shadows, he ran up slope. Where were Rusan and Olbin? They'd been going to lead the women and children to safety. He saw one of the old kitchen women, making off into the dark with several children.

Shouts and screams came from the long-hall. He abandoned stealth and ran towards the open door.

Inside it was chaos.

Women had taken up kitchen knives, chairs, anything they could use as weapons. They tackled the remaining renegades.

He spotted Rusan and Olbin battling a dozen renegades, who were half-dressed, but none the less deadly. Picking up a fallen chair, Garzik brought it down on a naked back. The man staggered and turned in surprise. When he saw Garzik was unarmed, he lifted his sword. Cheeky-puss darted out from under a table and stabbed him in the groin.

Before Garzik could react, she disappeared again.

The man toppled, bleeding out.

Garzik grabbed the fallen sword, a nasty nicked blade, and laid into the renegades nearest him. Hack, block, duck. Kill without being killed. No time for finesse. Captain Blackwing would not be impressed.

Olbin spotted him and beckoned with a grin.

Screaming from outside.

Garzik ran to the window. Danja and the others had arrived and were tackling the renegades down by the jetty.

A hunting horn sounded.

No, it was the call to retreat. The renegades inside the hall turned and ran, intent on getting out before their ship sailed.

Now it was a race to chase them down to the departing vessel. By the light of the burning ship, Garzik could see they'd raised the sail of the remaining ship and were hastily preparing their oars.

Several renegades leaped off the jetty onto the deck. Others missed and had to swim for it. Still others ran along the shore as their ship gathered speed. They leaped into the bay to swim out as it passed. But many others never made it. They were hacked down without mercy.

When there were no more running renegades, the Utlanders followed the ship along the shore, jeering, mocking and waving weapons.

Hardly able to believe it was over, Garzik watched the sails fade into the night.

The children and beardless who had followed the ship along the shore jeered for a bit longer, then returned. Most of them were uninjured, but many of those who'd remained at the jetty limped or staggered.

The burning ship had reached the waterline, and the last flames were extinguished as it sank. Everyone cheered.

Those who were whole and hearty helped support the injured as everyone made for the hall. Garzik offered an arm to one of the beardless. She accepted his help, wincing with each step. When they reached the long-hall, she headed over to the fireplace, where the injured were being treated.

'More lamps. I need more light!' Iron-hair called as she tried to hold a bleeding wound closed. Sarijana ran to help her.

'Here's one!' Children dragged an injured renegade out from under a pile of bodies. 'Over here!'

Rusan cut his throat without hesitation. No mercy.

'Do that outside, Rus,' Iron-hair snapped. 'There's enough mess on the floor.'

'Sorry, Ma.' Rusan sounded twelve.

Garzik blinked, suddenly very tired.

Several of the older children, Cheeky-puss amongst them, were dragging dead renegades outside, while others gravitated to the fireplace to help with the injured. Old women gathered the wailing infants and small children, and took them upstairs to sing them to sleep.

'Here, help me get rid of this.' Olbin indicated a renegade's body. He left the dead man with Garzik and collected another body.

Garzik caught the first renegade's legs and dragged him outside, only to be directed down to the field near the jetty, where they were building a pyre to burn the bodies.

It seemed vaguely obscene to drag the man's body over the rutted ground.

Garzik tried not to look at his face.

'Leave that one for the fire.' Olbin gestured to the heap, where he had already thrown the body he'd carried.

No ceremony for the enemy.

Garzik straightened up. Everything ached.

'Well, who would have thought?' Olbin muttered.

Garzik turned to see what he meant. Trafyn was coming up from the shore dragging a body.

'I killed him!' the squire crowed. 'Tell them. Tell them I killed him!'

Garzik felt a growing sense of dread as Trafyn pulled the small body closer. Strong-arm picked up the lad and threw him onto the pile.

No mistake. It was the boy Garzik had saved. The boy's throat had been cut. Probably while he was unconscious.

'Put up a fight, did he?' Garzik asked, voice thick with fury.

'Something fierce,' Trafyn boasted.

Garzik punched him, smashing the squire's nose.

Trafyn went down, holding his face.

As blood seeped between his fingers, Garzik advanced on him.

'Hold up.' Olbin grabbed his arm. 'What's going on?'

'He punched me!' Trafyn protested thickly in Merofynian. 'Did you see that? He punched me!'

Olbin turned Garzik around. 'What was that for?'

Tears of fury glazed his vision. Coward, sneak, braggart... words he didn't know in the Utland tongue choked him.

'Well?'

'Why don't you ask him?' Garzik countered.

Olbin glanced past him to Trafyn.

Who hastily backed up, scrambling to his feet. 'Whatever he says, I didn't do it. He's just mad because I didn't help set the ship alight.'

It was on the tip of Garzik's tongue to reveal how the boy had died, but then he realised the Utlanders would probably have cut the lad's throat anyway.

These weren't his people. Not the Utlanders and certainly not Trafyn. He'd never felt more alone.

Garzik flung off Olbin's restraining hand.

The big Utlander searched his face.

Garzik shook his head.

Olbin shrugged. 'Go back, clean the hall of bodies.' He gestured to Trafyn. 'You too.'

Garzik stalked off, ignoring Trafyn, who wisely avoided him. He'd never trust the squire to protect his back.

Back in the long-hall he found everyone organised. The fury drained from him, leaving him even more exhausted than ever.

Somehow he kept going.

Garzik carried yet another body down to the funeral pyre and he was there beside Olbin when an eerie wailing made him jump.

'They're mourning the dead.' The big Utlander turned slowly to face the rise to the long-hall.

Everyone looked up towards the hall as if they dreaded going up there. Of course they would. In a settlement this size, everyone knew everyone else. No one would be untouched by death.

'Might as well face it,' Olbin muttered and strode up the hill. 'Come on.'

Garzik followed.

The bodies of the settlement's dead were being laid out in a neat row in front of the long-hall. Of the beardless who'd been left behind to mend the cow byre, not one survived. Three women were dead. Two children.

So senseless.

It was the children that got to Garzik. He wanted to cry, but he felt nothing.

Just a horrible emptiness.

More and more people came out to see who had died. The wailing grew louder and louder as others added their voices to the ululating cries.

The combined grief of the settlement was a terrible thing. Out of respect, Garzik backed away to let them mourn their dead in peace.

Inside the hall, he found the injured all bandaged up by the fireplace. From the look of some, there could be more dead tomorrow. Danja was pale and tense and her breath came in shallow gasps.

He went over and knelt next to her. 'Is there anything I can get you?'

Her one eye flickered open. For a heartbeat she didn't recognise him, so deep had she sunk into the pain. Then she shook her head.

He backed off, feeling useless. He had only the most basic of healing training.

He noticed Rusan and Olbin deep in conversation with Iron-hair. Out of habit, he wandered over to listen in.

'...Vultar. Heard he'd taken up the holdings on the Isle of Dead,' Iron-hair was saying.

Since Garzik had heard this place mentioned in song, he'd thought it was an allegorical name for the afterlife.

'I didn't believe it,' Iron-hair admitted. 'But he boasted of it. Nothing is sacred to him.'

'Sarijana... was she...?' Olbin began and could not go on.

'Her. All of them. Even me.' She touched her mouth where her lip had been split open. 'Just as well you didn't go after the others and the manticores. Vultar planned to set to sail tomorrow with all our young women.'

'It was Yesterday, Today and Tomorrow who made me come back early,' Olbin admitted. Garzik noticed Rusan go very still at the mention of the oracles. 'They said I was meant to save our people and –'

'Has anyone checked on them?' Rusan interrupted. 'Did Vultar ask after the oracles?

'No. Not a word,' Iron-hair said.

'He should have.' Rusan looked worried. 'The twins and their mother are known throughout the Utlands. Everyone wishes they had oracles like ours.'

Olbin turned. 'You think –'

'Go check on them,' Iron-hair urged. 'Go quickly.'

Garzik grabbed a lantern.

As Rusan and Olbin went to leave, Iron-hair beckoned them back. 'Don't mention this to anyone. They have enough to worry about.'

They nodded then turned to find Garzik waiting with a lantern. They acknowledged him with a nod.

The three of them left the long-hall in grim silence. Outside, Rusan fitted the lantern to a pole so Garzik could hold it high to light their way.

No one spoke as they retraced their steps. This was where they'd hid to plan the burning of the ship. This was where they'd found Trafyn hiding.

Where had he got to? Doing as little work as possible, no doubt.

This was where they'd passed the empty cow byre.

Rusan cursed as the oracles' cottage became visible in the circle of lantern light. The door swung off the hinge.

'They might still...' Olbin began then broke off as, with another step, something pale appeared just inside the cottage.

Rusan ran a few steps ahead and darted inside, stepping over the body of the twins' mother. The back of her head had been stove in. Most of her white hair was dark with blood. Those odd pink eyes remained open. Glazed.

Both Rusan and Olbin fell to their knees next to her.

Garzik raised the lantern to check the one-room cottage. It had been stripped of all valuables, and there was no sign of the fused-twins. 'They're gone.'

'Of course. They were the real prize.' Rusan nodded to himself. 'Now Vultar has the greatest oracles in all of the Utland Isles, he'll –' Rusan broke off suddenly, horrified. 'Were they on the ship you burned?'

Garzik took a step back, heart racing with horror. 'I don't know. I –'

'Think. Did you see –'

'I didn't see them.' The hold had been half full. He'd chosen that ship because... 'There were men on the other ship, in the hold with a lantern. I guess they were guarding the oracles.'

'If only we'd known!' Olbin sprang to his feet and slammed his fist into the wall, leaving a bloody graze on the lime-washed stone. He prowled like a caged beast.

'I should've thought of it.' Rusan sank his head into his hands. 'I should've –'

'You can't think of everything,' Garzik told him. 'You did all you could with the information you had. You chased off Vultar and –'

'But I lost the oracles. I've failed my people.'

'No, Vultar has to answer for this.' Garzik stepped in front of Rusan and held his eyes. 'There were factors beyond your control. You did the best you could with what you had at your disposal –'

He broke off as sudden conviction filled him.

A wave of relief rolled through him and he closed his eyes as he realised he'd done the best he could, when Byren sent him to light the warning beacon. Despite this, he'd failed. Who knows if it would have made a difference? Someone had betrayed Rolenhold castle from within. Mitrovan had tried to tell him, but he'd refused to hear it. He'd been too consumed with grief and self doubt. Now...

Garzik opened his eyes to discover both Rusan and Olbin watching him.

'What is it...' Rusan said. 'What's your name?'

Garzik hesitated. He wanted to tell them his real name, but he was going to escape first chance he had. 'It's Wynn, short for Wyvern.'

'Wynn. Smart, quick on your feet like a wyvern.' Olbin grinned. 'Suits you.'

Garzik looked down, torn. He didn't want to lie to them.

'What's wrong?' Rusan asked.

Garzik recollected his point. 'Don't waste time and energy blaming yourself.' And he said this to himself as much as to them. 'Think about what must be done next.'

'Next?' Rusan rocked back onto his heels and sprang to his feet. 'Next we take her back to our people to mourn.'

Rusan took the head, Olbin the legs. Garzik held the lantern. They travelled slowly, solemnly in a pool of lantern light.

Even before they reached the long-hall, children came running. Their cries of horror brought the adults, and soon they were surrounded by a crowd of worried Utlanders. They whispered and looked on anxiously.

Rusan and Olbin laid her reverently with the rest of the dead, then stepped back. As the others closed in on the dead mother of the oracles, Iron-hair beckoned Rusan and Olbin. Garzik followed them in.

Iron-hair led them over to the head of the long-table. Someone went past with a big pot of potato and onion soup. Garzik's stomach contracted painfully. How could he be hungry?

Bowls, day-old bread, hot soup. He made for the table. Stepped over the nearest long stool and sat down. When the old woman with the soup ladle came along, he held out a bowl.

She objected. 'Belongs-to-no-one has no place at our table.' Raising the ladle, she went to clip him over the head.

Olbin was already on his feet. In two strides he caught her hand before she could complete the strike. 'Here, none of that.'

'Serve him.' Rusan raised his voice, not moving from his place beside Iron-hair. 'The belongs-to-no-one earned a place at the table tonight. He set fire to Vultar's ship. More than that, he suggested the diversion.'

Rusan met Garzik's eyes and held them, and Garzik recalled Captain Blackwing saying a true leader didn't feel threatened by initiative in others. All those at the table turned to look at him.

'No longer is he a belongs-to-no-one,' Rusan stated, as if this was a ritual. 'I say he belongs-to-us on my ship.' And he looked to Iron-hair expectantly.

She studied Garzik, a smile in her eyes. It warmed him. 'I say he belongs-to-us on our island.'

And just like that he was no longer a slave. He was an Utlander.

Olbin pulled him to his feet and hugged him so hard he saw stars and almost stumbled when he was released.

'Wine for the ceremony,' Olbin said. 'Wine for Wynn.'

'No ceremony tonight,' Iron-hair said. 'Not when our people lie dead outside. Later.'

'Later,' Olbin told him and clamped one large hand on his shoulder. He pushed Garzik down into the chair and gestured to the old woman. 'Serve him.'

As she ladled out some soup the conversation resumed. They spoke of what they'd lost, how many warriors they could muster, Vultar's numbers, the Isle of Dead and the danger of going there.

Rusan shook his head. 'It's been empty for generations –'

'Vultar lives there now,' Olbin countered. 'How –'

'Because he's a renegade,' Iron-hair insisted. 'He's lost all honour.'

'I still think we should follow him,' Olbin said. 'Attack. Wipe them out. We'd be doing all the Utland Isles a favour. There's only one shipload of them now –'

'Vultar boasted he had four other ships. Claimed the renegades of the sea are flocking to serve him. He could be lying, but...' Iron-hair shook her head. 'We don't make a move against him until all the captains come back.'

That made sense and Garzik finished his soup.

With food in his stomach there was no denying sleep. He curled up near the wall. His usual place was taken by the injured. Even so, Cheeky-puss found him.

She offered him one of last year's apples.

He looked up at her and slowly accepted it. She sat down next to him, and bit into her own apple.

The apple was floury and old, but he appreciated the sentiment. 'The beardless paid the highest price tonight. Still going to join them?'

'How can you ask?' She waited, but he didn't have a reply, so she took another bite, chewed and swallowed.

His head buzzed with exhaustion.

'They took turns raping the women. I hid in the wood heap.'

'Very wise.'

'But not very brave.' Tears spilled over her cheeks. 'Ilonja is not brave.'

He lifted one arm and pulled her close. As she sobbed on his chest, the heat of her damp tears seeping through the material, he wished he could have held Piro at the end.

'Sometimes it is wiser to run away,' he whispered. 'Ilonja?'

But she'd fallen asleep, so he settled her on the floor next to him in the pile of furs.

He took the apple from her hand, finished both and curled up beside her. Dimly he was aware of the Utlanders organising things. Then he was aware of nothing.

Then the dreams started. The fire, running, fighting for his life. He woke several times. From the moans around him, others were also troubled by nightmares.

CHAPTER FOURTEEN

THREE DAYS LATER Jost returned with his depleted party and the chitin of three manticores. He returned without Polonika, but Danja wasn't there to mourn for her. She had died the second night after the attack.

Jost strode into the settlement expecting to be hailed a hero. Instead, he found everyone in mourning. They'd lost cows, goats, many provisions, the precious lives of defenders, mothers and children and, what's worse, they'd lost their oracles.

When Jost heard the full story, he and his group were all for going after Vultar, sailing to the Isle of the Dead and attacking.

As far as Garzik could tell, Iron-hair ran the settlement, but each captain ran his ship. Jost had no ship. It took half a night of argument but finally, the one-eared Utlander accepted Rusan's decision with poor grace.

They would go raiding for now. Their people needed more supplies. The settlement's other four ships' captains would return. Then they would mount an attack on Vultar.

Garzik hardly listened.

He wouldn't be here. He was going to escape when they sailed south.

He would find Byren, tell him about the spy, Mitrovan, and become a courier, but he no longer felt he had to make up for failing Byren.

In battle you could make a plan but, once the battle started, plans were just scribbles on paper. The trick was to survive. He was a survivor. He wished he'd realised this back in Rolencia.

* * *

THE NEXT MORNING, Rusan ordered his ship stocked. By evening, they were ready to sail with the dawn tide.

That evening, Iron-hair consulted with Rusan and Olbin, deciding who would remain behind to defend the settlement. They'd lost nearly half their beardless. A couple of the older raiders volunteered to stay, not that they thought Vultar would return. He'd gotten what he wanted, but there were still the Affinity beasts.

All this went on while Garzik sat at the table, being served like one of Rusan's crew.

'Wynn, over here,' Olbin called.

As he came to his feet and turned around, he saw Iron-hair and Rusan standing in front of the fireplace. Rusan held a sword, Iron-hair held a bundle of furs and skins.

By the time he'd crossed the paving, everyone was silent.

Garzik glanced over his shoulder to Olbin, not sure what he should do. The big Utlander grinned and gestured him on.

Rusan stepped forward, lifted the short sword and cut the Merofynian sailor's vest and breeches from him. They were too small now anyway. While he did this, Rusan said, 'Wynn earned his place at the table during Vultar's raid.' He picked up the threadbare breeches and vest and tossed them onto the fire. 'I say he belongs-to-us on my ship.'

His crew cheered, thumping the table.

A rush of shame made Garzik's face burn. He was going to betray them and desert Captain Rusan's ship first chance he got.

As Rusan stepped back, Iron-hair stepped forward. 'This one works hard. He will be an asset to our island. I say he belongs-to-us on our island.'

As she handed him the bundle, the women and beardless cheered then fell silent.

He ducked his head, speechless.

'Well, get dressed. Stop flashing your arse at us,' Olbin told him.

There was general laughter as he pulled on the leather breeches and laced them up. The fur-lined boots were soft and roomy. When he unrolled a raider's bad-weather sealskin, an Utlander smock fell out. It was red, made of goat's wool and decorated with elaborate braid around the neck and the hem. He'd seen the women and men sitting around the fire, working this beautiful braid, and he felt a fraud.

Still, he pulled it on and brushed hair from his eyes.

Rusan handed him a belt with a sheath and raider's short sword. Laughing at his expression, Rusan buckled the belt up and pushed him down to his knees.

'Now you give your oath of allegiance to me. Repeat after me.' And he told Garzik the right words.

As he swore to protect his brother raiders and die for them, the words tasted bitter on his lips. As far as he was concerned, he'd already sworn to serve Byren back when the kingson was accepting his honour guard. This made him foresworn.

Rusan helped him to his feet and turned him around to face the hall.

They cheered.

Garzik noticed Trafyn. His nose was swollen and both eyes were black, but there was no mistaking his expression. His mouth twisted with contempt.

Rusan slung an arm around Garzik's shoulder. 'Wynn sails with us tomorrow.'

'You can take him, too.' The old woman who was in charge of the kitchen dragged Trafyn forward by his ear. 'This belongs-to-no-one's more trouble than he's worth.' She shoved the squire so that he almost fell at Rusan and Garzik's feet.

'Out of the way, belongs-to-no-one,' Rusan aimed a kick at Trafyn's thigh and the squire scrambled to one side, joining the dogs as they gnawed on bones.

The raiders mocked Trafyn, even as Olbin welcomed Garzik back to the bench by the table. But the ceremonies weren't over yet; everyone fell silent.

'What now?' Garzik whispered.

'Swearing in the new beardless,' Olbin said. 'They'll be trained up so our raiders can return to sea.'

One by one the girls of twelve and thirteen stepped forward. Rusan had moved away to give Iron-hair pride of place before the fireplace, and she took their vows as the girls swore to take the beardless path.

No men and babies for them. They'd fight to the death to protect their island home.

Garzik was not surprised to see the last one was Ilonja. She spoke up, her voice strong and clear; no doubts now.

Ilonja turned and grinned at him, before going to join the beardless at the table. He felt it was a waste, but he understood.

Conversation resumed.

'Wait.' It was the singer, Sarijana, who stepped forward. 'I want to give my vow.'

Olbin gasped and looked to Rusan, who'd clearly had no idea this was going to happen. Face stony, Rusan watched as Sarijana took the solemn oath. Garzik could feel the tension in Olbin's massive body.

When she'd finished and joined the beardless on their bench, Olbin left the table and went over to join Rusan by the door. Both of them stepped outside. Garzik wasn't going to follow them, but he noticed Jost and his two friends leave the table, then drift out.

Garzik stepped over the bench. As he darted across the hall, he felt Trafyn's eyes on him. Ignoring the squire, he slipped out the door.

Where he found Jost and his friends confronting Rusan and Olbin. They'd taken off their weapons and tossed them aside. Garzik spotted the surgeon's beautifully worked sword and dagger.

'Now no-one will have her, and you know what?' Jost leered. 'I'm glad they raped her. If I can't have her, I don't –'

Rusan struck him. Then it was on. A flurry of blows, two against three, with Garzik ready to jump in if it looked like Rusan and Olbin needed help.

It was all about solid thumps, grunts. The whoosh of air being driven from the chest. At one point the door opened and Iron-hair looked out. She took in the fighting, glanced to Garzik, then went back inside.

By the time Garzik looked back, Rusan and Olbin were occupied with Jost's two friends, while the one-eared Utlander reached for his sword.

Garzik rapped him over the head with the flat of his own sword. Furious, Jost would have gone for him, but a glance over his shoulder revealed his two companions were out cold and Rusan was pulling Olbin to his feet.

Jost went to help his friends, while Rusan and Olbin retrieved their weapons and Garzik sheathed his sword. The look Jost sent Garzik told him his interference would not be forgotten.

There was no laughter and slapping of backs, no invitation inside for a drink.

'This isn't over,' Jost told Rusan, when they were all on their feet. The captain lifted his hands as if to say, *come on*.

But Jost and his two friends turned and strode inside. As they passed Garzik, Jost gave him a filthy look.

Rusan and Olbin came up to Garzik. Both were flushed, bleeding and dishevelled.

'Watching our backs, Wynn?' Rusan asked.

He nodded.

But it didn't make any difference. He was escaping, first chance got. He had to break his oath to Rusan. Byren needed him.